The Sapphire Goddess: The Fantasies of Nictzin Dyalhis

Introduction by D.M. Ritzlin

Cover art by Margret Brundage

The Sapphire Goddess: The Fantasies of Nictzin Dyalhis copyright © D.M. Ritzlin 2018

ISBN 978-0-9909900-5-5

All rights reserved

"When the Green Star Waned" originally appeared in the April 1925 issue of *Weird Tales*.

"The Eternal Conflict" originally appeared in the October 1925 issue of *Weird Tales*.

"He Refused to Stay Dead" originally appeared in the May 1927 issue of *Ghost Stories*.

"The Dark Lore" originally appeared in the October 1927 issue of *Weird Tales*.

"The Oath of Hul Jok" originally appeared in the September 1928 issue of *Weird Tales*.

"The Red Witch" originally appeared in the April 1932 issue of *Weird Tales*.

"The Sapphire Goddess" originally appeared in the February 1934 issue of *Weird Tales*.

"The Sea-Witch" originally appeared in the December 1937 issue of *Weird Tales*.

"Heart of Atlantan" originally appeared in the September 1940 issue of *Weird Tales*.

Special thanks to Doug Ellis and Eva Flora.

DMR Books

www.DMRBooks.com

DMRBooks.storenvy.com

www.facebook.com/DMRBooks

CONTENTS

Introduction by D.M. Ritzlin
- 5 -

When the Green Star Waned
- 8 -

The Eternal Conflict
- 38 -

He Refused to Stay Dead
- 83 -

The Dark Lore
- 103 -

The Oath of Hul Jok
- 141 -

The Red Witch
- 189 -

The Sapphire Goddess
- 223 -

The Sea-Witch
- 260 -

Heart of Atlantan
- 299 -

ALSO AVAILABLE

The Thief of Forthe and Other Stories by Clifford Ball – After the death of Robert E. Howard, Clifford Ball was the first writer to follow in his footsteps and pen sword and sorcery stories for *Weird Tales*. For the first time ever, all of Ball's stories are collected into one volume. A must-have for pulp historians and fans of fantasy, horror, and weird fiction!

Lands of the Earthquake by Henry Kuttner/Under a Dim Blue Sun by Howie K. Bentley – The first split release from DMR Books in the tradition of the Ace Double series! *Lands of the Earthquake* is a classic science-fantasy adventure from the pulp era that has never been published in book form before. On the flip side you'll find a brand new sword-and-planet tale. A US soldier hijacks a Nazi spaceship and lands on a planet threatened by snake-men! This title is available exclusively from DMRBooks.com.

Swords of Steel Volume I – The first groundbreaking anthology of fantasy and horror stories written by heavy metal musicians. Features E.C. Hellwell's previously unpublished "The Riddle Master," which was the basis for the Manilla Road song of the same name. Also includes stories by Byron Roberts (Bal-Sagoth), Howie Bentley (Cauldron Born) and more.

Swords of Steel Volume III – The latest installment of the wildest and most unrestrained anthology series on the market! Features the conclusion of Byron Roberts' saga of Captain Blackthorne and a story by Mike Browning based on Nocturnus' classic science fiction death metal album *The Key*!

Introduction

Nictzin Dyalhis wrote thirteen stories for pulp magazines between the years 1922 and 1940. Eight of those appeared in *Weird Tales,* which were very popular among that magazine's readership. But—who the Hell was this guy? I mean, that has to be a fake name, right?

Even back then some assumed Nictzin Dyalhis was a pseudonym. In a 1932 letter to Donald Wandrei, *Weird Tales* editor Farnsworth Wright wrote: "I think this chap Low, who claims that he wrote WHEN THE GREEN STAR WANED, under the pen name of Nictzin Dyalhis, is all wet. Nictzin Dyalhis is a real person and that is his real name." Wright went on to say that all of Dyalhis' checks were made out to that name.

Even though Nictzin Dyalhis was the eccentric author's legal name at that time, it's highly unlikely that he was named that way at birth. He claimed that "Nictzin" was a Toltec Indian name and "Dyalhis" was an old English (or, alternately, Welsh) surname. Neither of these claims is true. Many speculate that his real name was Nicholas Douglas or Nicholas Dallas or something similar, which he modified into something more exotic.

Dyalhis gave conflicting statements regarding his date and place of birth as well. On his draft registration card of 1918, his birthdate is listed as June 4, 1873. (It also listed his occupation as "box nailer" and noted "One eye gone. Other one good.") The 1930 census shows his age as 50 (which, if true, would mean he was born in 1880). He sometimes claimed to have been born in Massachusetts and at others in Pima, Arizona. When he began his career as a writer, he lived in Sugar Grove, Pennsylvania.

Sometime around 1930 Dyalhis separated from his first wife, Harriet, after she was committed to the Warren State Hospital, an insane asylum. He remarried a woman whose name appeared on various documents as Netulyani Del Torres Dyalhis and others as the less-exciting Mary G. Sheddy. They had one daughter, Mary Agnes, born 1932. Dyalhis died May 8, 1942, in Salisbury, Maryland.

It's only fitting that a man so adept at fictionalizing the details of his life would become a pulp writer. His first story, "Who Keep the Desert Law," appeared in the October 20, 1922 issue of *Adventure*. Dyalhis was a good friend of Arthur Sullivant Hoffman, the magazine's editor at the time. Possibly it was Hoffman who encouraged Dyahlis to start writing in the first place. In a short biographical piece to accompany the story in that issue, Dyalhis said he was nearly fifty years old. He had formerly been a prospector and was currently employed as a chemist (quite a step up from being a box nailer four years earlier!). A month later, *Adventure* published "For Wounding—Retaliation," which was a Western, like the previous story.

It would be three years before another story by Dyalhis would appear. He made his *Weird Tales* debut in the April 1925 issue with the science fiction/space opera tale, "When the Green Star Waned." It was a massive hit with the readers, who voted it the best story of the year. It is notable for coining the term "blaster" for a hand-held laser/disintegrator pistol (although Dyalhis spelled it "blastor"). A sequel, "The Oath of Hul Jok," appeared in 1928.

Although Dyalhis would only write eight stories for *Weird Tales* over a fifteen year period, he proved to be as popular as he was unprolific. Half of his stories were voted the most popular story of the issue in which they appeared, and he earned the cover five times. Dyalhis only wrote three stories for other magazines during this time, one for *Ghost Stories* and two for gangster/crime magazines.

Some common themes reoccur throughout Dyahlis' work. "The Eternal Conflict" and "The Dark Lore" both involve interdimensional travel to Hell. The concept of reincarnation is the basis for "He Refused to Stay Dead," "The Red Witch" and

"The Sea-Witch."

Amazingly enough, despite Dyalhis' popularity during his time and his incredible talent, a collection of his stories has never before been printed. I first encountered his work in the anthology *Worlds of Weird* (1965), which reprinted "The Sapphire Goddess." It was the highlight of an excellent collection, and I wanted more. But I couldn't find any more. Eventually I acquired scans of the old magazines. Reading tales like "The Sea-Witch" for the first time was just as exciting as when I first discovered Clark Ashton Smith. With the release of this collection, no longer will you need to go to such lengths to find the stories of such an undeservingly obscure author. I'm sure you will appreciate and enjoy these tales as much as I do.

D.M. Ritzlin

When the Green Star Waned

Ron Ti is our greatest scientist. Which is to say that he is the greatest in our known universe, for we of the planet Venhez lead all the others in every attainment and accomplishment, our civilization being the oldest and most advanced.

He had called a meeting of seven of us in his "workshop," as he termed his experimental laboratory. There came Hul Jok, the gigantic Commander of the Forces of Planetary Defense; Mor Ag, who knew all there was to know about the types, languages and customs of the dwellers on every one of the major planets; Vir Dax, who could well-nigh bring the dead to life with his strange remedies; Toj Qul, the soft-spoken, keen of brain—the one Venhezian who could "talk a bird off a bough," as the saying goes—our Chief Diplomat of Interplanetary Affairs; and Lan Apo, whose gift was peculiar, in that he could unerringly tell, when listening to anyone, be that one Venhezian, Markhurian, or from far Ooranos—planet of the unexpected—Lan Apo could, I repeat, tell whether that one spoke pure truth or plain falsehood. Nay, he could even read the truth held back, while seemingly listening attentively to the lie put forward! A valuable man—but uncomfortable to have about, at times!

Lastly, there was myself, whose sole distinction, and a very poor one, is that I am a maker of records, a writer of the deeds of others. Yet even such as I have names, and I am called Hak Iri.

Ron was excited. That was plain to be seen in the indifferent, casual manner he displayed. He is like that. The rest of us were frankly curious, all but that confounded Lan Apo. He wore a faintly superior smile, as who should say: "No mystery here, to me!" I love that boy like a brother, but there are times when I ardently desire to bite him!

Ron stood before a huge dial. Now this is not a record of his invention, but a statement of the strange adventure in which we seven figured because of the events called to our attention by means of that wonderful device, so I shall not attempt its full description, merely saying that it was dial-formed, with the symbols of the major planets graven on its rim at regular intervals, and from its center there swung a long pointer, just then resting at a blank space.

"Listen," commanded Ron, and swung the pointer to the symbol of our own world.

Instantly there broke forth in that quiet room all the sounds of diversified life with which we Venhezians are familiar. All six of us who listened nodded comprehension. Already our science knew the principle, for we had long had dials that surpassed this one, apparently; for ours, while but attuned to our planet alone, could, and did, record every event, sight, or sound thereon, at any distance, regardless of solid obstacles intervening. But this dial—it bore the symbols of all the inhabited worlds. Could it—?

Ron swung the indicator to the symbol of Markhuri, and the high-pitched uproar that immediately assailed our ears was characteristic of that world of excitable, volatile-natured, yet kindly people.

Planet after planet, near and far, we contacted thus, regardless of space, until Ron swung the pointer to the symbol of Aerth.

And silence was the result!

Ron's look spoke volumes. We looked into each other's faces, and read reflected therein the same anxiety, the same apprehension which we each experienced.

That something was radically wrong with our neighbor, everybody already knew, for many years before the green light of Aerth had become perceptibly dimmer. Little attention, however, had been paid at first, for, by interplanetary law, each planet's dwellers remained at home, unless their presence was requested elsewhere. A wise idea, if one stops to consider. And no call had come to us nor to any other world from Aerth; so we had put it down to some purely natural cause with which, doubtless, the Aerthons were perfectly capable of coping without outside help or interference.

But year by year the green light waned in the night skies until finally it vanished utterly.

That might have been due to atmospheric changes, perhaps. Life, even, might have become extinct upon Aerth, so that no one lived to hold communication with anyone on any of the other inhabited worlds of the Planetary Chain, but it was hardly likely, unless the catastrophe were instantaneous; and in that case it would needs be violent. Anything so stupendous as that would have been registered at once by instruments all over the universe.

But now—this invention of Ron Ti's placed a remarkably serious aspect upon the question. For, if Aerth still occupied its own place—and we knew beyond doubt that it did—then what lay behind this double veil of silence and invisibility?

What terrible menace threatened the universe? For whatever had happened on one planet might well occur on another. And if Aerth should perchance be wrecked, the delicate balance of the universe would be seriously shaken, might even be thrown out completely, and Markhuri, so near the sun, go tumbling into blazing ruin. Then horror upon horror, until chaos and old night once more held sway, and the unguessed purposes of the Great Mind would be—

Oh, but such thoughts led to madness! What to do? That course alone held fast to sanity.

"Well?" demanded Hul Jok, the practical. "What are you going to do about it, Ron?"

That was Hul Jok all over! He was Ron's best friend and ardent admirer. He knew Ron's scientific ability, and firmly believed, should Venhez crack open, that inside of an hour Ron Ti would have the crevice closed tight and re-welded until inspection would fail to find any traces of the fracture! But at that, all Venhez thought the same way about Ron Ti's abilities, so Hul Jok was, after all, no better than the rest.

"It is matter for the Supreme Council," replied Ron gravely. "I propose that we seven obtain permission to visit Aerth in one of the great Aethir-Torps, bearing credentials from the council explaining why we have trespassed, and, if it be possible, try to ascertain if this be a thing warranting interference or no."

Why record the obvious? When such as Ron Ti and Hul Jok make request to the Supreme Council, it is from necessity, not for amusement.

The council saw it in that aspect, and granted them free hand. We started as promptly as might be.

The great Aethir-Torp hurtled through space in smooth, even flight, Hul Jok in command. And who better fitted? Was he not our war prince, familiar with every device known for the purposes of offense and defense? Surely he whose skilled brain could direct whole fleets and armies was the logical one to handle our single craft, guide her, steer her, and, if need arose, fight her!

With this in mind I asked him casually yet curiously:

"Hul Jok, if the Aerthons resent our inquiry, and bid us begone, what will you do?"

"Run!" grinned the giant, good-humoredly.

"You will not fight, should we be attacked?"

"Hum!" he grunted. "That will be different! No race on any planet may boast that they have attacked an Aethir-Torp of Venhez with impunity. At least," he added, decisively, "not while Hul Jok bears the emblem of the Looped Cross on his breast!"

"And if it be pestilence?" I persisted.

"Vir Dax would know more about that than I," he returned,

shortly.

"And if—" I recommenced; but the giant released one hand from the controls, and clamped his great thick fingers on my shoulder, nearly crushing it.

"If," he growled, "you do not cease chattering when I am on duty, I shall most assuredly pitch you out through the opening of this conning-tower into space, and there you may start on an orbit of your own as a cunning little planet! Are you answered?"

I was. But I grinned at him, for I knew our giant; and he returned the grin. But he was quite right. After all, speculations are the attempts of fools to forestall the future. Better to wait, and see reality.

And as for surmises, no one could possibly have dreamed any such nightmare state of affairs as we found upon our arrival.

A faint, dull, but lurid reddish glow first apprised us that we were drawing near our destination. It was Aerth's atmosphere, truly enough, but thick, murky, almost viscous, like a damp, soggy smoke.

So dense it was, in fact, that it became necessary to slow down the speed of our Aethir-Torp, lest the intense friction set up by our passage should melt the well-nigh infusible plates of Berulion metal of which our Aethir-Torp was built. And the closer we drew to Aerth's surface, the slower were we obliged to proceed from the same cause.

But finally we were gliding along slowly, close to the actual surface; and, oh, the picture of desolation which met our eyes! It happened that we had our first view where once had stood a great city. Had stood, I say, for now it was but tumbled heaps of ruins, save that here and there still loomed the shape of a huge building; but these, even, were in the last stages of dilapidation, ready to fall apart at any moment.

In fact, one such did collapse with a dull, crashing roar,

merely from the vibrations set up by the passing of our Aethir-Torp—and we were a good half-mile distant when it fell!

In vain we sounded our discordant *houtar*; no sign of life could we discern, and we all were straining our eyes in hopes. It was but a dead city. Was all Aerth thus?

Leaving behind this relic of a great past, we came to open country. And here the same deadly desolation prevailed. Nowhere was sign of habitation, nowhere was trace of animate life, neither bird, nor animal, nor man. Nor anywhere could we discern evidence of cultivation, and even of vegetation of wild sorts was but little to be seen. Nothing but dull, gray-brown ground, and sad-colored rocks, with here and there a dingy, grayish-green shrub, stunted, distorted, isolate.

We came eventually to a low range of mountains, rocky, gloomy, and depressing to behold. It was while flying low over these that we for the first time saw water since we arrived on Aerth. In a rather wide valley we observed a narrow ribbon of sluggish, leaden-hued fluid meandering slowly along.

Ron Ti, who was then at the controls, brought our craft to a successful landing. This valley, especially near the stream banks, was the most fertile place we had thus far seen. There grew some fairly tall trees, and in places, clumps and thickets of pallidly green bushes as high as Hul Jok's head, or even higher. But tree-trunks and bushes alike were covered with dull red and livid purple and garish yellow fungi, which Vir Dax, after one look, pronounced poisonous to touch as well as to taste.

And here we found life, such as it was. *I* found it, and a wondrous start the ugly thing gave me! It was in semblance but a huge pulpy *blob* of a loathly blue color, in diameter over twice Hul Jok's height, with a gaping, triangular-shaped orifice for mouth, in which were set scarlet fangs; and that maw was in the center of the bloated body. At each corner of this mouth there glared malignant an oval, opaque, silvery eye.

Well it was for me that, in obedience to Hul Jok's imperative command, I was holding my Blastor pointing ahead of me; for as I blundered full upon the monstrosity it upheaved its ugly bulk—how, I do not know, for I saw no legs nor did it have wings—to one edge and would have flopped down upon me, but instinctively I slid forward the catch on the tiny Blastor, and the foul thing vanished—save for a few fragments of its edges—smitten into nothingness by the vibrations hurled forth from that powerful little disintegrator.

It was the first time I had ever used one of the terrific instruments, and I was appalled at the instantaneous thoroughness of its workings.

The Blastor made no noise—it never does, nor do the big Ak-Blastors which are the fighting weapons used on the Aethir-Torps, when they are discharging annihilation—but that nauseous ugliness I had removed gave vent to a sort of bubbling hiss as it returned to its original atoms; and the others of the party hastened to where I stood shaking from excitement—Hul Jok was wrong when he said it was fear!—and they questioned me as to what I had encountered.

Shortly afterward, Hul Jok found another one and called us all to see it, threw a rock the size of his head at it, hit it fairly in the center of its mouth; and the rock vanished inside and was apparently appreciated, for the nightmare quivered slightly, rippled a bit, and lay still. Hul Jok tried it with another rock, but had the mischance to hit his little pet in the eye—and seven Blastors sent that livid horror to whatever limbo had first spawned it! And it was above our heads in the air, hurling downward upon us when we blew it apart! Lightning scarcely moves swifter! Even Hul Jok was satisfied thereafter, when encountering one, to confine his caresses to pointing his Blastor and pressing the release stud, instead of trying to play games with it.

But that was, after all, the sole type of life we found in that valley, although what the things fed upon we could not then ascertain, unless they devoured their own species.

We found others like them in another place—blob-things that could not be destroyed by our Blastors; and we saw, too, what they were fed with. But that in its proper place!

We spent some time here in this valley, but then finding nothing new, we again took to our craft and passed over the encircling mountains, only to find other mountains beyond. Also, other valleys.

At length we came to a larger valley than any we had before seen. This was, rather, a plain between two ranges, or, to speak more accurately, a flat where the range divided and formed a huge oval, to re-unite and continue as an unbroken chain farther on.

And here we again landed where a grove of trees gave concealment for our Aethir-Torp in case of—we did not know—anything! But upon us all there lay a heavy certitude that we were in a country inimical to our very continuance of existence.

Why? We could not tell that, yet each of us felt it, knew it, and, to some extent, feared it—for the bravest may well fear the unknown.

It was Mor Ag who had spoken the words which guided our actions for some time past.

"Were Aerth inhabited as we understand the word," he had said, sententiously, "the great city we saw would be no ruin, but teeming with life and activity, as was the custom of the Aerthons before the light of the Green Star waned. So, if any be still alive, it is in the wilderness we must seek them. Wherefore, one place is as another, until we learn differently."

How utterly right he was, speedily became manifest.

The pit-black murk of the night slowly gave place to the pallid, wan daylight wherein no actual sunlight ever shone, and as we gathered up our Blastors and other impediments, preparatory to setting forth, Toj Qul raised a hand in warning.

There was no need for speech. We all heard what he did. I think the dead must hear that infernal, discordant din every time it is sounded. Describe it? I cannot. There are no words adequate!

When our ears had somewhat recovered from the shock, Vir Dax shook his head.

"O-o-o-f-f-f!" he exclaimed. "To hear *that* very often would produce madness! It is agony!"

"Perhaps," growled Hul Jok. "But I have already gone mad because of it—gone mad with curiosity! Come along!"

He was commander. We went, leaving our Aethir-Torp to care for itself. But never again were we thus foolish.

We proceeded warily, spread out in a line, each keeping within sight of the next. The noise had come from the north side of the flat, and thither we directed our steps. Well for us that we were hidden by the trees and bushes!

As one we came to a sudden halt, drew together in a group, staring amazed, incredulous, horrified.

We were at the very edge of the high-bush, and before us was open space clear to the foot of the towering cliff-walls, which rose sheer to some ten times the height of a tall male.

Half-way up this there stuck out a broad shelf of rock, extending completely across the face of the cliff from the western end to the eastern, and at regular intervals we could perceive large, rectangular openings, covered, or closed, by doors of some dully glinting, leaden-hued metal.

And all the space between the edge of bush-growth and the foot of the cliff was occupied by the same sort of loathly monstrosities as we had previously encountered! There they lay, expectant, apparently, for their attentions were seemingly concentrated upon the shelf of rock high in air above them.

A door close to the western end opened and a procession emerged therefrom. At last we had found—

"Great Power of Life!" ejaculated Mor Ag profanely. "Those

beings are no Aerthons!"

And he was right. Aerth never had produced any such type as we then beheld!

They had faces, and they had not faces! They had forms and they were formless! How may I describe that which baffles description? We are accustomed to concrete, cohesive, permanent types of form and faces, and these were inchoate! Never in any two moments were their aspects the same. They elongated, contracted, widened, expanded. At one moment the lower parts of one of these beings would apparently vanish while the upper parts remained visible, and again, conditions were reversed. Or a front aspect faded instantaneously, leaving but the rear section visible, only to promptly reverse the phenomenon. Or a left side disappeared, leaving the right side perceptible; then—but picture it for yourself! I have said enough!

It made me dizzy; it provoked Mor Ag because he could not name them; it enraged Hul Jok, inflamed him with desire to attack the whole throng, shatter them—he could not have told why, but looking at them made him feel that way.

Ron Ti was mildly curious; Vir Dax frantic with ambition to study such beings. Our Lady of Bliss deliver me from the curiosity of Vir Dax, his methods of study!

Only Toj Qul and Lan Apo remained unperturbed; Toj Qul because he is a diplomat, therefore in nowise startled or amazed at, or by, anything. And Lan Apo was contemptuous; for as he looked at them, any race thus shifting as to bodily aspect must inevitably be shifty as to minds, and he had naught but despisal for a liar of any sort. Strange argument, strange stimulus to courage, yet perhaps as good as any!

Only one permanency had these beings—and even that fluctuated. They were of a silvery color and they were black, of that blackness which is blacker than black. Later, we learned what manner of beings these were, and whence they came to afflict Aerth with their presences.

They formed in a row well back from the shelf-edge, and then, from out the same door from which they had emerged, came another procession, or rather, a rout or rabble. These were, as Mor Ag at once asserted, unmistakably Aerthons. But how had that once wise and mighty race fallen! For these men were little better than brutes. Naked, round-shouldered, bowed of heads, cringing, shambling of gait, matted as to hair, and bearded—the males, at least—and utterly crushed, broken, dispirited!

It had long been a proverb on all the inhabited planets, "As beautiful as the Aerthon women;" but the females we were then beholding were, if anything, more abject, more deteriorate, than the males.

Many things became apparent to us who stared at these poor unfortunates. Very evidently, some *things*, from some *where*, had enslaved, debased that once mighty race who were, or had been, second to none in all the universe—and this, *this*, was the result!

Hul Jok shifted his feet, stirred uneasily, growling venomously deep in his throat. Despite our giant's ferocious appearance, his heart was as a little child's, or like that of a girl, gentle, tender, and sympathetic where wrong or oppression dared rear their ugly heads. And here, it was all too apparent, both those pit-born demons had been busily at work.

The rabble of Aerthons halted at the very edge of the shelf, grouped together, about equidistant from each end of the long line of the Things we could not name. And as the Aerthons stood there, the animate abhorrences on the ground fixed their malignant eyes upon the wretched creatures, the triangular mouths gaped wide, and from all that multitude of loathly *blobs* came beating against our shrinking, quivering, tormented ear-drums that same brain-maddening discordance we had previously heard, even before we left the Aethir-Torp.

Of a sudden the Things standing behind the Aerthons ceased

flickering, became fixed as to forms, although the change was anything but improvement. For, although they became in shape like other living, sentient, intelligent beings, their faces bore all evil writ largely upon them.

Acquaint yourself with all the depravity, debauchery, foul indecency ever known throughout the universe since the most ancient, forgotten times, multiply it even to Nth powers, limitless, and then you have not approximated their expressions!

Personally, even beholding such aspects made me feel as if, for eons uncountable, I had wallowed in vilest filth! And it affected the others the same way, and we knew, by our own experience, what had befallen the Aerthons.

Had such foul things once gained foothold on the great central sun, even the radiant purities of that abode of the perfected would have become tainted, polluted by a single glance at such unthinkable corruptiveness!

They, the Things, slowly raised each an arm, pointed at one Aerthon in the group. He, back to them as he was, quivered, shook, writhed; then, despite himself, he slowly rose in the air, moved out into space, hung above the *blobs* that waited, avid-mouthed. The Aerthon turned over in the air, head down, still upheld by the concentrated wills of the things that pointed...

Breathless, my eyes well-nigh starting from my head at sheer horror of what must in another moment befall. I stared, waiting the withdrawal of the force upholding the wretched Aerthon.

Half consciously, I saw Hul Jok's Blastor swing into line with the poor shrieking victim, and, just as he commenced dropping toward those triangular, gaping, hideous orifices which waited, slavering, saw him vanish—and silently blessed Hul Jok for his clemency and promptitude.

Then, momentarily, we all went mad! Our Blastors aimed, we pressed the releases, and swept that line of Things. And, to our aghast horror, nothing happened. Again and again we swept their line—and they were unconscious that aught was assailing them! The deadly Blastors were impotent!

Ron Ti first grasped the situation.

"These Things are not 'beings' — they are but evil intelligences, of low order, crafty, vile, rather than wise! They are of too attenuate density — the vibrations of disintegration cannot shatter, put pass unfelt through their atomic structures! We can do naught save in mercy slay those poor Aerthons, and destroy those foul corruptions which wait to be fed."

We did it! It was truest kindliness to the Aerthons. Yet, despite the seeming callousness of our deed, we knew it for the best. And one thing it proved to us — low as the Aerthons had sunk, they had not fallen so far from their divine estate but that in each the silver spark that distinguishes the soul-bearers from the soulless was still present. For as each body resolved back to the primordial Aethir from whence it was formed, the silver spark, liberate at last, floated into the air until in distance it disappeared. Then we turned our attention to the blob-things.

But even as we smote the filthy Things, we noted that the strange beings on the rock-shelf had grasped the fact that a new phase of circumstance had entered into Aerth's affairs. They stood amazed, startled, bewildered for a space of perhaps a minute, then passed into activity with a promptitude well-nigh admirable.

Several of them calmly stepped from the rock-shelf into air and came hurtling toward us. In some way they had sensed our direction. In no time, they hovered above us, descended, and confronted us.

One, evidently of importance among his fellows, made articulate sounds, but we could not understand. Nor did we wish to! For with such as those there can be but one common ground — unrelenting war!

And so, again and again we tried the effect of the Blastors, and, as previously, found them impotent. I caught Hul Jok's eye. He was fairly frothing at the mouth with wrath.

The Things, close by, seemed to emanate a vibration that was abhorrent, stultifying. Little by little I felt a silent but urgent command to start toward the foot of the rocky cliff. Unthinkingly, I took a step forward, and Hul Jok's mighty arm slammed me back.

"I can feel it, too," he snarled at all six of us. "But," he thundered sternly, "I command you by the Looped Cross itself, that you stand fast. 'Tis but their *wills!* Are we babes, that we should obey?"

Suddenly — I laughed! Obey the wills of such as these? It was ridiculous! Answering laughter came from the rest of our party. Hul Jok nodded approvingly at me.

"Well done, Hak Iri!" he commended. "The Looped Cross thanks you — the Supreme Council shall give you right to wear it, for high courage, for service rendered!"

And he had promised me our planet's supremest gift, highest honor for — laughter! Yet, though I myself say it, perhaps the service was not so trivial after all. For there is, in final analysis, no weapon so thoroughly potent against evil as is laughter, ridicule! To take evil seriously is to magnify its importance; but ridicule renders its venom impotent, futile. Try it, you who doubt — try it in your hour of utmost need!

The Things became all black, no silvery tints remaining. One attempted to seize me, thrust me in the desired direction. Something — I had not known that it lay dormant within me — flamed into wrath. My hand closed, became a hard knot, my arm swung upward from my side with no volition on my part, and my fist drove full into the face of the Thing — left a horrible, blank orifice which slowly filled into semblance of a face again. The Thing emitted a strange, gasping squawk of pain.

"Aho!" shouted Hul Jok, gleefully. "They may not be shattered nor slain, but — they can be hurt!" And he swung his Blastor up as a truncheon and brought it down full on the head of the nearest. The stroke passed through the Thing as through soft filth, yet that Thing, evidently having enough, rose hurriedly into air and sped to safety, followed by the rest.

"Back to the Aethir-Torp!" commanded Hul Jok, and we retreated as swiftly as legs would take us. At that, we did not arrive there first.

To our dismay, we found it in possession of a horde of those Things. They were all over it, even inside; and worse still, all about it on the ground were Aerthons, a great crowd of them formed in solid masses, all facing outward, bearing in their hands long, shimmering blades of brightly glinting metal, sharp as to points, with keen cutting edges.

"Swords," gasped Mor Ag. "I had thought such weapons obsolete on Aerth ten thousand years ago! Ware point and edge!"

"*Hue-hoh!*" shouted Hul Jok. "The Blastors, quick!"

Oh, the pity of it! I know that tears streamed from my eyes before it was finished. Ron Ti was equally affected. Hul Jok himself was swearing strange oaths, and, had it not been for Lan Apo, I doubt if we had had the necessary fortitude to go through with the ghastly affair. But as the silver sparks floated upward, a smile, almost beatific, came upon his set, white face.

"But they are rejoicing!" he cried out to us who grieved even while we smote. "I can feel their gratitude flowing to us who give them release from a life which is worse than death. They are glad to depart thus painlessly!"

And thereafter we sorrowed no more.

The Aerthons were almost all disposed of when Mor Ag shouted:

"Catch one or more of those slaves—alive! I would question—"

Hul Jok leapt forward, caught one by the wrist, wrenched his blade from his hand, slammed him against the hull of the Aethir-Torp, knocking him limp, threw him to us; and dealt likewise with another.

Meanwhile, our Blastors played unrelentingly, and presently

there were no more of the unfortunate Aerthons to be seen. Yet, the Things who, through sheer will-force alone, had compelled the Aerthons to face annihilation—for they could not fight; the Blastors slew from far beyond reach of sword-blade or hurled rock—those Things still held our Aethir-Torp. Surely, Our Lady of Venhez kept them from guessing that they had but to slide the stud atop one of the great Ak-Blastors from the white space to the black one, and we—ugh! Well for us that there was no Lan Apo among them to catch our thoughts!

A long while afterward, we found out that they were acquainted with the principle of the Ak-Blastors—and I can only account for their not using those on us by the supposition that they wished to capture us alive in order to gratify their fiendish propensities, so refrained from slaying us, willing to go to any lengths rather than do so, for the dead can nowise be made to suffer!

We drew back, shaking from excitement and from the strain induced by their evil minds, or wills, beating upon us; for, though they could not make us obey, still that force they directed was almost solid in its impact. Our craft was still in their possession, and we were standing on open ground, and sorely perplexed as to how we were to regain possession of our Aethir-Torp.

Hul Jok, war prince, solved our dilemma. He grasped a young tree, thick as his wrist, tore it from the ground, broke it across his knee—

"Club!" he grunted. "Our million-year-ago ancestors used such on Venhez. There are records of such in the Central War Castle!"

Hurriedly he prepared one for each of us, talking as he wrought.

"They can *feel*," he growled, "for all that they may not be slain. Very well! We will beat them from the Aethir-Torp!"

And this is precisely what occurred. On Venhez I had, at

times, worked with my hands, for sheer delight of muscle-movement. But never had I dreamed what actual hard work was until that hour, during which, club in hand, we stormed our own craft, until at last we stood watching the last of the Things as they rapidly passed through the air toward their cliff-abode—all but one, which we had finally cornered alone in a compartment into which it had strayed from the rest. We hemmed it about, beat it with our clubs until it cringed from the pain. Then Ron Ti thrust his face close to its face...

We caught Ron's idea, added our wills to his, overbore that of our captive. It became confused, bewildered, shifted from silver to black, to silver again; the black became dull, smoky; the silver paled to leaden hue; the Thing crouched, palpitant with fear-waves, manifest in dim coloration.

"We have learned enough," declared Ron Ti solemnly. "Back to Venhez! This is matter for the Supreme Council, as I feared even before we started. Here we cannot cope with conditions; we seven are too small a force. Back to Venhez!"

"Nay," Hul Jok demurred. "Let us remain and clean Aerth of this spawn!" And he indicated the captive Thing with a contemptuous gesture of his foot.

But Vir Dax added his voice to that of Ron Ti; and I—I was eager to go—to stay—I knew not which. The others felt as I did. Both courses had their attractions—also their drawbacks. For myself, I fear me very greatly that I, Hak Iri, who ever held myself aloof from all emotions of violence, desiring clear mind that I might better chronicle the deeds of others—I fear, I say, that in me still lives something of that old Hak Iri, my remote ancestor who, once in the Days of Wilderness of which our minstrels still sing, made for himself a name of terror on all Venhez for his love of strife.

But Mor Ag really settled the argument.

"We have this—Thing," he declared. "It must be examined, if we would learn aught of its nature, and that must be done if we hope ever to cope with such as it has proved to be in structure"—here an unholy light shone transient in the keen, cold eyes of Vir Dax—"and we can, while on the return to Venhez, learn what has actually happened to Aerth from the two Aerthons—"

"One Aerthon!" interrupted Vir Dax. "The other died. Hul Jok knows not his own strength!"

He bent over, examined the living Aerthon and promptly brought him back to consciousness. Mor Ag spoke to him. The Aerthon brightened a trifle as he became assured we meant him no harm. He brightened still more when he observed that we held captive one of his former masters.

Then the Thing caught the Aerthon's eye, and Lan Apo hastily turned to Hul Jok.

"It were well to confine this—where the Aerthon may not win to it," he warned emphatically. "Otherwise the will of the Thing will compel the enslaved fool to assist it to escape or work us harm in some manner."

We left the captive Thing in the little room, fastened the sole door, and Hul Jok retained the ward-strip which alone could unlock it again. The Aerthon said something to Mor Ag, who smiled and patted him on the shoulder, reassuringly.

"He thanked us for putting it beyond his power to obey—"

He broke off to ask the Aerthon another question, then gasped.

"Dear Mother of Life!" he ejaculated. "The Things are from the dark side of the Moun, Aerth's satellite!"

The Aerthon nodded.

"*Avitchi!*" he exclaimed, and added another word: "Hell!"

We knew not his language—that is, none save Mor Ag—but we all caught his meaning. He referred to the abode of evil, as it was understood on Aerth.

We would have questioned the Aerthon further through the medium of Mor Ag, for we all were intensely curious, but just then that occurred which put an end to questioning, and served likewise to hasten our departure from this sorely afflicted planet.

A crackling, sizzling hiss of lightning and a terrific crash of thunder—the world, so far as we were immediately concerned, all one blinding glare of violet-tinted light—and the great Aethir-Torp rocked under the impact.

"Aha!" shouted Hul Jok. "What now?" And he dashed to one of the lookout openings just as another levin-bolt struck.

We joined him, and one glance was enough. All about us and above us were swarming great iridescent globes, and it was from these that there now came incessant streaks and flashes of lightning—powerful electric currents.

Our commander leapt into the conning-tower, and the others of us sprang each to his station at one of the Ak-Blastors, of which our craft mounted six, and we promptly left the ground.

We had little to fear, for the metal Berulion, of which Aethir-Torps are built, could in nowise be harmed by lightning, nor could we who were inside be shocked thereby. But some part of the controlling mechanism might have been seriously disarranged by the jarring concussions, and, besides, it was not part of our natures to submit tamely to attacks from any source.

With a *swoosh* we shot into the air and Hul Jok headed the sharp-pointed nose of our great fighting cylinder straight into the thick of the shining globes that swooped and floated and swirled about and above us. Their thin walls gave them no protection against our impact, and we shattered them as easily as breaking the shells of eggs.

With the Ak-Blastors we could and did shatter some of the globes which we failed to ram, but the vibrations of disintegration from those had no more effect upon the occupants of the globes than had the little hand Blastors previously—and Hul Jok fairly stamped in rage.

"Ron Ti," he exclaimed wrathfully, "your science is but a

fraudulent thing! We mount your improved model Blastors, purported to slay aught living, disintegrate anyone, and now—"

His anger well-nigh choked him.

"Content you," soothed Ron. "If we come again to Aerth—"

"If we come again to Aerth," Hul Jok asserted grimly, "Aerth will be *cleaned*, or I return no more to Venhez! But," he went on, imperatively, "you must find that which will destroy these Lunarions. We shattered and rammed their foolish globes, from which they play with the powers of thunder and lightning, but them we might not harm. They did but float, insolent, safely down to Aerth!"

"We have one Lunarion upon whom to experiment," suggested Vir Dax meaningly.

"Ay," snapped Hul Jok. "And I look to you and Ron Ti to produce results! See to it that you fail not!"

I have known the giant commander since we were children together, but never had I seen him in such a mood. He seemed beside himself with what, in a lesser man, I should have classed as humiliation, but I realized, as did the others, that it was merely that in him the dignity of the Looped Cross had been proffered insult, amounting well-nigh to defeat, and that to him the Looped Cross, emblem of our planet, was a sacred symbol, his sole object of adoration; and his high, fierce spirit was sore, smarting grievously, and could nowise be appeased until, as he himself had phrased it, "Aerth was clean!"

We had formally made report to the Supreme Council and had handed over to them, for disposal, both the Aerthon and the Lunarion we had brought back with us. And the Supreme Council, in their wisdom, had commanded Mor Ag and Vir Dax to examine and question the Lunarion, with me to make records of aught he might say—but he would say naught, seemingly taking fiendish delight in baffling us.

The Aerthon, whose name was Jon, had told Mor Ag, while we were on our homeward flight, all that was to be known as to the conditions on Aerth. Here is no space to record it all, but briefly it was as follows:

Centuries ago, the Aerthons, divided into nations, warred. A mighty empire, hoping to dominate the planet, attacked a little country as commencement. Another and larger nation hastened to the rescue of its tiny neighbor. A great island kingdom was drawn into the fray. A powerful republic overseas took hand in the matter; so, ended the strife.

But rather than ending warfare, it did but give fresh incentive to inventions of deadly devices. Somebody found that the element—metal—gold, had strange qualities, previously unguessed. Another discovered that gold could be produced by artificial means, synthetically, to use Aerthly terminology. But the producing was by drawing it from out the storehouse of the universe, the primordial Aethir, wherein, dormant, are all things objective and subjective. And the drain on the Aethir opened strange doors in space, which heretofore, by fiat of the Great Wisdom, had been fast sealed.

Scientists of a great race, Mongulions, made too free use of the Aethir, hoping in their turn to subjugate the races of the West. Because of the vibrations set up in their labors, they made easy passage from Aerth to Moun. And on the dark side of the Moun dwelt a race of fiends, soulless, beyond the pale of the Infinite Mercy, who moved about to keep the Moun's bulk always between them and the hated light of the Sun. These had ever hated Aerth and its dwellers, for once they had inhabited that fair planet, until they became too wicked, and they, and the Moun, broken from its parent Aerth by Almighty wrath, had been set apart in the sea of space. The Moun, although circling ever about its parent planet, revolved never on an axis, so had one side turned ever toward Aerth; and these lords of the Dark Face, in their eon-old hate, saw chance, at long last, to regain their lost world, upon which they looked with envy when the lunar phases brought them during the dark of the Moun to the side facing Aerth. In their Selenion globes they invaded Aerth, availing themselves of the openings the Mongulions had unwittingly established.

Aided by these unholy powers of evil, the Mongulions had dominated, even as they had planned, all other races, reduced them to conditions of abject servitude, and were, in turn, subjugated by the Lords of the Dark Face, through sheer will-energy alone.

So, reduced to conditions wherein they were less than beasts, the Aerthons had remained, prey to their fiendish conquerors, subjected to such treatments as even now, while I write, sicken my soul within me to think of, and are unfit to describe—for why afflict clean minds with unnecessary corruptions?

Only those who have heard that Aerthon's story can conceive of what had, for ages, taken place in the ghastly orgies of the Lunarions—and we who did hear will never again be quite the same as we were before our ears were thus polluted.

So utterly abhorrent were conditions on Aerth that our Supreme Council decreed that such must be abolished at any cost. Not the planet, but the state of affairs prevailing. For they feared that the very Aethir would become putrescent, and moral degeneracy reach eventually to every planet of the Universal Chain!

But that, again, involved every planet in the matter. So they, the council, sent out invitation to all other planets for conference. Then came delegates from them all. They talked, discussed, debated, consulted—and that was all.

Hul Jok, the practical, violated interplanetary etiquette, finally.

"Talk!" he shouted, rising from where he sat with the other Venhezians. "What does talk do? We be no nearer than when we started. Since none can offer helpful suggestions, hear me! I am War Prince of Venhez, not a sage, but I say that Ron Ti, if allowed sufficient time, can find that which will slay these Lunarions—all of their evil brood, and this is what is needed. Leave this matter to us of Venhez!"

A gravely genial delegate from Jopitar rose in his place.

"Oh, you of Venhez," he said in his stately, courtly speech, "your War Prince has spoken well. Since Ron Ti is acknowledged greatest of inventors on any world, he has but to demand, and if we of Jopitar can place aught at his disposal to further his investigations, he has but to communicate with us, and what we have is at his disposal."

One by one, delegates from all the planets confirmed the Jopitarian's proffer, repeating it for those whom they represented. And one delegate, a huge, red-hued, blue-eyed being, went even farther, for, springing to his feet, thundered:

"But if there is to be actual affray, we of Mharz demand that we participate!"

Hul Jok strode forward and slapped the Mharzion on the shoulder.

"Aho!" he laughed. "One after my own heart! Brother, it is in my mind that crafts and fighters from all the planets will be needed before this matter is ended!"

It seems cruel, I know, but what else was there to do? From then on, that captive Lunarion was subjected to strange, some of them frightful, tests. Poisons and acids Vir Dax found had no effect upon him. Cutting instruments hurt, but failed to injure him permanently. Already we knew that the Blastors—deadliest weapons known to any planet—were ineffective.

Ron Ti was at his wits' end! Two of our Venhezian years passed, and all to no progress. Then a girl solved for him the one problem he was beginning to despair of ever solving for himself.

He had a love—who of all Venhez has not?—and she, entering fully into his ideals and ambitions with that sweetly sympathetic understanding none but a maid of Venhez can bestow, had free access at all times to his workshop, wherein he toiled and studied for planetary benefit.

And she one day seeing his distress at bafflement in his researches, saying naught, withdrew, returning shortly bearing in her arms her chiefest treasure, an instrument of many strings from which she proceeded to draw sweet strains of music, hoping thus to soothe his perturbed mind.

There came a wondrously sweet strain recurring in her melody, and the first time it sounded, the Lunarion winced. Repetition of that strain made him howl! And realization came to Ron Ti in one blinding flash of lightlike clarity.

"Harmony!" he shouted, rejoicing. "The blob-thing is discordant in its essential nature!"

Never a maid of Venhez was so proud just then as that love-girl of Ron Ti's. She had, at least, produced some sort of impression on the fiend, made it suffer grievously. So over and over she played that selfsame strain, and, ere many minutes had passed, the Lunarion fell prone, writhing in anguish, howling like a thing demented.

"Enough, Alu Rai," Ron bade her after watching the captive's misery for a space. "You have rendered the universe a service! Now depart, for I would think. Herein lies the worst of the weapon which will purge an afflicted world of its wo!"

It was a mighty fleet which started for Aerth on that never-to-be-forgotten expedition of rescue and reprisal. Practically speaking, all the craft were of similar appearance, for the Aethir-Torps had long been conceded to be the most efficient type for inter-spatial voyaging. Even the Aerthons had used them before they were subjugated, and Jon the Aerthon stated that the Lunarions themselves had a large fleet of them housed away in readiness against the day when they might desire to win to other worlds. But, he likewise told us, until the Lunarions had exhausted Aerth's resources, they would remain there, and for Aerthly voyaging in the air their Selenion globes were more satisfactory to them, moved by will-force as they were, than the great Aethir-Torps which were managed by purely mechanical methods.

Naturally, the Aethir-Torps from the different planets varied slightly, as, for example, those of Venhez had the conning-towers cylindrical in shape, and placed midway from nose to stern; the noses sharply pointed, sterns tapering to half the size of the greatest diameter—that of the waist of the craft; our Ak-Blastors were long, slender, copper-plated. The Aethir-Torps from Mharz were lurid red in color; blunt of nose; rounded as to sterns; with short, thick Ak-Blastors; and their conning-towers were well forward of the middle; octagonal in shape. But why amplify? Surely the Aethir-Torps of each planet are familiar to the dwellers of all the other planets.

And, of course, each craft bore the symbol of its home-world. The Mharzions bore the Looped Dart in gold, even as we of Venhez painted upon the nose of ours the Looped Cross—but the symbols of the worlds are too well known to require description.

Ron Ti and Hul Jok had full authority over the entire squadron, although the war-commanders from all the worlds fully understood the carefully laid plans of aggression. And all the Aethir-Torps, in addition to the Ak-Blastors, now mounted before their conning-towers a new device consisting of a large tube, much like an enormous *houtar*, terminating at the snout-end in five smaller tubes.

It was black night when Aerth was reached. And it was not until the sickly, wan daylight broke that actual operations commenced.

Spreading out, we quartered the air until the great oval flat showed plain. It was our good luck that it was our own craft which was the first to come above it, and, as we identified it,

Hul Jok's eyes glowed in wrathful joy — if such emotion may be thus contradictorily described. He caught Ron Ti's eye and nodded.

Ron Ti, obeying, threw over a lever. A most dreadful and terrific din shook the air with its uproar. From afar to the northward came a similar bellowing howl. Then from the eastward the same sound reached our ears, being replied to, a moment later, by the signal from the distant west. And from the southward came the answering racket, and we knew that all Aerth's surface was under surveillance of one or more of the Aethir-Torps comprising the Expeditionary Fleet.

Slowly, deliberately, we began circling above that infernal ovoid valley. But after that one hideous, bellowing howl, the tubelike arrangements before the conning-towers changed their tones, and from them came the same wondrously sweet, heart-thrilling, soul-shaking strain of melody as that which Alu Rai, the love-maid of Ron Ti, had produced to the exquisite torment of our captive Lunarion.

Over and over the strains were played, and still nothing happened. The idea was Ron Ti's, and I began to wonder if in some manner he had miscalculated. Suppose it did not affect all the Lunarions alike? In that case not only would the expedition be doomed to failure, but the name of Ron Ti would become the subject for many a jest on many a world. And we of Venhez must, perforce, walk with bowed heads.

But Ron Ti was smiling, and Hul Jok's fierce face bore an expression of confident, savage expectancy, and I — I waited, curious, hopeful still.

So swiftly that we could barely see it, an iridescent globe spun through the air, rising diagonally from the cliff-base, shooting straight at our Aethir-Torp. A touch of Ron's hand, and the strain of music sounded even louder, clearer, sweeter.

The globe, when within a quarter of a mile, shot straight upward, discharged a terrific, blinding flash of chain-lightning against our craft, followed it by a second and even more intense discharge—and still the sweet strain of harmony was all our reply.

The globe swooped until it nearly touched us—and I slid forward the stud on the Ak-Blastor behind which I stood.

The Lunarion bubble was not more than a hundred feet away at that instant, and, like a bubble, it vanished incontinently. As ever, for all that we could shatter their Selenion Globes, those demoniacal Lunarions themselves we could not disintegrate, or so we deemed then, and I know that I said wrathful profanities in my impotent disappointment.

But Hul Jok grinned, and Ron Ti nodded reassuringly to me, saying consolingly: "Wait!"

Well, I waited. What else could I do? But by this time the same game was going on all over the Aerth. Wherever the Lunarions had abode, the strains of melody were driving them into a frenzy of madness, and they came swarming forth in their globes, hurling lightning-flashes at our Aethir-Torps, which might not thus be destroyed.

Yet, in a way, honors were even, for if they could not damage our Aethir-Torps, neither could we do aught but blow their globes into nothingness, while they themselves did but flee though the air back to their abodes, unharmed by the vibrations from the Ak-Blastors.

And in this manner, for three days and nights the futile warfare continued, and by morning of the fourth day I doubt if there was left to the Lunarions a single Selenion Globe. At least, for two days and nights, we continued playing that music over and over until all Aerth vibrated from the repetitional soundwaves.

But on the next morning following, we had clear proof that the Lunarions had had all that they could endure of suffering. An Aethir-Torp, of a far different model from any we were acquainted with, shot into air with incredible speed, and catching a craft of Satorn unawares, rammed it in midair, completely wrecking it—only to be shattered into dust in its turn by the Ak-Blastors of a Markhurian Aethir-Torp. The crew of the ill-fated craft we could not save, but they were amply avenged ere long.

It happened that we witnessed this ramming, and Mor Ag shouted his surprize.

"But that Aethir-Torp, despite its speed, is of an age-old model," he affirmed excitedly, and Hul Jok nodded agreement.

"Our Lady of Love grant that their Ak-Blastors be of equally antiquated model," he chortled. "If they are, their vibrations are of too long and too slow wave-lengths to affect the modern Berulion metal of which we now build our fighting craft!"

And so it later proved to be.

We could very easily have shattered their old-model crafts, taking our own good time therefor, but to what avail? It would leave us the same old problem. The Lunarions, with their levitational powers, would descend safely to the ground and would still inhabit Aerth, overrunning it like the evil vermin that they were.

But the far-thinking brains of Ron Ti and Hul Jok had laid out a carefully evolved plan, and aside from continuing to drive the Lunarions mad with the hated music and evading further collisions with their Aethir-Torps (no light task, either, considering their speed) we of the expedition refrained from using our Ak-Blastors until the Lunarions must have come to the very conclusion our master-strategists desired them to reach eventually—that in some manner we had exhausted our vibratory charges.

At last, one morning we were made the objects of a concerted attack. From all points came hurtling those old-style Aethir-Torps, and we—we fled from before them! Finding that their old-model Ak-Blastors had little or no effect upon us, protected as we were by the Berulion plates, they fell back on their levin-bolts, and these they hurled incessantly, until they, as well as we, were well out of Aerth's atmosphere, and into the great Ocean of Aethireal Space.

But ever we played that same maddening music, and it acted as powerful incentive to hold them to the pursuit, for they had lost all caution in their rage. And ever, as we fled from before them, we laughed.

And at last, some five million miles from Aerth's surface, we turned upon them!

Stretched out in a long, curved line, we awaited their coming, and as they came within our range, every Aethir-Torp commenced whirling about as if on a transverse axis, presenting one moment the nose, next a side, then the stern, and again the other side, and once more the stern or prow, in this manner giving play to all six Ak-Blastors—the forward one, the two on each side, and the one pointing to rearward.

And the Lunarions, although heretofore we might not injure them, were soon without protection, their Aethir-Torps shattered, left exposed to the deadly chill of outer space, and their forms, loose though they were in structure, subjected to the awful pressure of the inelastic Aethir!

It compressed their bodies as if they had been density itself. And, having no defense, they instinctively drew close to each other—and Aethiric pressure did all that was necessary.

They were jammed into a single mass, and *then* we played upon that with the Ak-Blastors until that mass, too, became as nothing!

Only from that blank space where the fiends, the Lords of the Dark Face, had been, floated in all directions a shower or swarm of dull red sparks, which, even as we watched, slowly flickered and burned out in depths of Abysmal Night!

Ron Ti bowed his head in reverence to that great Power which had permitted us to be the instruments of its vengeance, signing in the air before him the Looped Cross, symbol of Life.

"As I suspected," he said, gravely, "they were soulless. They had naught but form and vitality, mind and will—life of the lower order, non-enduring. The red sparks proved that—and even those have burned out, resolved back into the Sea of Undifferentiated Energy. Our work is ended. Let Aerth work out its own rehabilitation. That wondrous race of Aerthons will soon rear the foundations of an even greater civilization than their world has ever before known."

The Eternal Conflict

APOLOGY

I am a member of a great and secret Occult Order, despite the fact that I am—or was—a businessman dwelling in New York City, and living in the midst of this practical Twentieth Century.

We hold, as do many, that the universe is ruled by a Supreme Power whose name no man knows, and whose attributes can be but dimly surmised.

We hold that the Presence is served by many beings throughout the universe—Archangels; Angels; Planetary Rulers; a Celestial Host.

We hold that, among these, and not the least, is One, feminine rather than masculine in appearance and attributes, whom we consider to be the goddess of Love, Beauty, Light, and Truth.

To her is our Temple dedicated; and to her we give reverence. We are not idolators in any sense of that word, for we know that she is but one of those who serve the Presence.

After all, is the idea so *outré?*

This universe is a "going concern", as we would say of a huge industrial plant. Such a plant has its general manager; assistant managers; superintendents; foremen, etc. Why not the universe, which is the greatest plant of all?

We hold that our Order is but incorporated into her department—that is all. So, if in the following narration of the stupendous events and adventures through which I have just recently passed (and which would never have been written without her permission) I refer to her as a *goddess,* it is not that I seek to impose my views upon anyone. I do but ask from others that privilege I myself am overjoyed to extend—tolerance of viewpoint and respect for divergent opinions.

One statement more I would like to add. It is useless for anyone to search for our address in any directory. We publish no periodical. We seek no converts nor members. I say this lest anyone should think this story is put forth as a new and subtle form of propaganda—for it is not so intended.

Likewise, where I have spoken plainly of the powers and forces of nature; the vibrations of the ether; the transmuting of latent energy into active dynamism; and of the multiplicity of the realms, regions, and planes of greater space; believe as much, or as little, as you please. It matters not.

Yet bear this in mind: The mystery of today is the common experience of tomorrow—as the mystery of yesterday is the common knowledge of today. Science advances by degrees, nor is there any limit placed upon its progress.

So, to my tale.

I entered the outer hall of the Temple, went direct to one of the little dressing rooms, undressed, bathed, and donned the robes of my rank. Thence I went on into the great room of the Temple proper; and made my way direct to the Black Shrine. So long as I was outside its walls, there were faint, dim lights shining all about; sufficient at least to see my way.

But once inside the Shrine, not even a cat could have seen—anything; for the place was so arranged as to exclude all reflected and latent light. Also, it was constructed entirely of black marble, unpolished, so that no reflections could by any possibility occur.

But I know the mystic chants, for I am a high initiate—so, raising my arms, in a whisper I intoned the mighty words.

Slowly the blackness lessened, and I ceased. I knew what was coming, and waited, There grew a faint, dim, all-pervading luminosity too vague to be styled "light"; but this gradually strengthened until it became clearly perceptible, although it was more of a glow than genuine light.

Suddenly as though ripped apart, it divided, brightened, formed into four columns in the four quarters of the Shrine — to north, east, south and west. That to the north assumed a white hue; the eastern one turned as blue as the noonday skies; that to the south glowed ruby red; and that to the west became a soft, warm yellow.

Yet in the center of the Shrine was still only blackness absolute. But it was a blackness wherein one could see — although all that could be seen was the square, black stone altar; bare of everything, not ornamented or carven in any manner.

The altar was nine feet high, and before it at foot of the eastern face stood the "couch of dreams", which was a stone slab seven feet long and a fraction over three feet in width. This was raised above the floor about two feet by small, square blocks of black stone placed under the four corners.

Crouched on the floor before the altar was one of the "Doves" of the Temple — a girl of surpassing loveliness. She had fallen asleep, and, as I stood above her, looking down, the intensity of my gaze penetrated to her dormant mind.

Her eyes opened. Hastily yet gracefully she rose to her feet, her perfect form reflecting shimmeringly through her sheer draperies the lights of the Shrine. Crossing her hands on her breast, she bent her head in acknowledgement of my rank and status; then raised her eyes to mine, half timid and half bold.

"Fortunate me!" she murmured. "It is but seldom that *you* come alone to the empty shrine. Never before has it been my lot to be here on such an occasion. I have seen you when the full chapter was convened—"

"Nor did I come here now to be with you," I reproved quietly. "Keep your allurements for those of lesser status. You know your task — perform that!"

I stretched myself full length on the stone slab, lying on my back with my hands crossed on my breast in the position of a corpse. The "Dove", rebuked, flitted about her task; lighted the burners of incense, and commenced singing softly the "Dream Chant". And I knew, although my eyes, fixed upon the ceiling above me, could not see her, that she was weaving about me with twinkling, gliding feet and waving hands, the Dance of Sleep.

I do not mean the ordinary sleep of the material world—but the mystic Temple-sleep wherein the bodily faculties are all in abeyance and the self is free—free to go, but, perchance, never to return—free to reach to whatever plane it merits, be that plane one of the many hells of the universe, or—to the very Presence itself.

Softly, sweetly, the voice of the singer came to my ears, and, highly attuned as I was, I could sense in every nerve-fiber the vibrations which were fast filling the place; due to the mystic geometrical patterns and figures formed in the ether by her words, her tones, and her motions.

To me came the sensations one would experience were that one reclining full length in a boat on a gently heaving sea. It was a slow, easy, inexpressibly soothing lift and sway and rise and fall. I was drifting, half-conscious. The light of the shrine, even through my closed lids, became softer than moonshine yet surpassing vivid sunlight... an even greater rise and fall... a *lift*, with no after-feeling of sinking back—and I was free!

If an arrow from a powerful bow has sensation, it must feel as I felt in that moment. I was shooting through space—at first the ordinary atmosphere of this gray old earth which the ancients very truly styled *Myalba,* the "Abode of Trouble."

Thence I passed out into interplanetary space; through the blue-blackness of night wherein stars, planets and suns shone as bright spots of different colored lights, yet gave forth no illumination.

On and on I sped until a vague fear assailed me and several very definite questions took form within my consciousness— for I had not counted on any such extended trip as this!

"Whither was I bound? What lay before me? Should I ever return to earth, my home-planet? Or had the merit I had acquired during life been of such evil nature that I was to be expelled out of the known universe into some unknown and probably very dreadful realm outside all finite concept?"

I tried to check my progress, but to no avail. I tried to slow down my speed at least. Utterly futile! In fact, the effort seemed to accelerate it.

I noted, as I shot past it, a constellation to my left very near, and my astronomical knowledge informed me that it was one of the remotest in our solar system. And at that, the fear became anything but vague; for I became certain that ahead of me lay the Unknown — and what effect would *that* have upon me?

I thought of the Temple; of my brethren in the Occult Order; I thought of the couch whereon lay my earth-body. I thought of the Black Shrine; of the cubical stone altar; and finally I bethought me of that awful, beautiful and terrible, supernal goddess to whom that shrine was dedicated, to whom that altar had been raised, and who — if the whispered word spake truth — sometimes descended and rested thereon for a few moments; manifest as a tongue of flame of dazzling silvery brilliancy.

Would she let one of her followers come to grief — to an eternal wo? True, I knew that great though she was, she still was subordinate to the Presence Itself — although she was one of Its ministers — and might not be able to aid, despite her known powers.

I knew that to utter her secret name unworthily meant death on earth and punishment thereafter. But it seemed to me that never again could my need be so desperate — and I pronounced (not vocally, for my body was lacking, but shall I say "telepathically"?) her awful word.

Nothing happened! Yet, everything happened. I still continued that awful flight through space; but all fear left me. I was serenely conscious that all was well, that for all she had in nowise made herself manifest, I was under her direct protection. I felt certain that in some way as yet uncomprehended, my entire recent actions had been inspired by her will.

And once that certitude became fixed in my consciousness, I surrendered myself completely to that now delightful sensation of terrific momentum.

Eventually, far ahead of me I saw a faint, nebulous glow. Somehow I became convinced that it was my destination. And even as before I had experienced a vague, unnamable fear; so now I felt a very definite desire to reach that slowly increasing brightness. For I was fully convinced that there I should find and know the hitherto unknowable.

Brighter and yet more bright it shone, and I realized that it was neither planet, star nor sun; and for a little space I was lost in speculation as to what it could actually be.

The color changed, as I drew nearer, changed from an indeterminate tinge to a wondrous ruby red — inexpressibly *soul-comforting,* if I may use such a word. But, as I drew still closer, it shifted to a tender azure blue. No! It was clear topaz! Why, it was emerald — violet — orange — cerise — it had no color — it was of all colors — it was *color!* Color well-nigh celestial; and over me crept a strange reverence and awe.

I was in the luminescence itself. It did not burn, nor even warm, but oh, how it did invigorate! There was something spiritually magnetic about it, and I reveled in the radiance.

That wondrous effulgence streamed and scintillated from tower and temple and buildings. It sparkled and shimmered in the very "air" itself. It shone and gleamed from the streets and the ground.

Oh! I know that I am using the phraseology of Earth. Yet, if I do not, how may I make my meaning plain to dwellers of Earth? So if I say "air," "ground," and other familiar words; find for me in your minds pardon and allowance, and eke out with your imaginations my poor descriptive attempts.

But to return to my narration. I was in a city of some sort. That was certain. But where? And why? How, I already knew.

Constantly I am confronted by the impossible, for how shall I describe the beings I saw? They were formed even as we of earth are shaped; but far more radiant, brilliant, seeming to glow with an internal light which shone through what looked to be translucent flesh that was not flesh. Yet of raiment, they wore none. But their chiefest glory lay not in beauty of forms and color; although no two shone with quite the same tints of light. Rather, their beauty lay in their faces and their eyes.

Had I reached to the great Central Heaven? I wondered. But even as I thought it, I received from all those shining beings a reply in a very definite yet calm negative.

As I say, it was a city, but not on any planet. Of that I felt assured. There was nothing to give the impression of planetary solidity—no gravitational pull, for example.

And these bright beings, although appearing to walk the streets, in truth, did but touch the surfaces of the walks and ways, nor did they move their feet as do we of earth, but rather glided along.

I noted that I, shooting high above their heads in contact with nothing, appeared conspicuous; so I deliberately willed myself to descend and progress as did they—and found to my delight that I could do so. Yet, here and there, as I passed, I caught the thought flashing from one to another: "An earth-mortal whom She has summoned!"

I found myself before a vast building which shone with the combined light of all the lights, colored by the blending, or rather, the intermingling, of all the colors. And I knew that here was my actual destination.

I entered, and those whom I met, one and all, gave me salutation. It was but a gravely courteous bend of the head; yet it conveyed in some subtle manner a greater cordiality than any welcome I had ever known on earth.

Direct as if I had been long accustomed to tread that way, I went straight to a central sheen of light and passed within its effulgence.

"Welcome, my servitor from Earth!"

The voice was that of all music. For one brief second I stared—and oh! here again, description baffles me!

It was a throne of ebony blackness, and seated thereon was that goddess to whom our Order upon Earth gives reverence. Had she stood, she had towered some thirty feet or more in height. Her form (for she like all others in that abode of light) was devoid of apparel, was of transcendent splendor. Yet there was about her majesty no suggestion of the nude—not even in the sense in which we speak of it in art and sculpture.

She was seated, and I came scarcely to her knee; yet I had already noted that my stature was half again that which it appears while inhabiting the house of clay.

But it was not her beauty of form or of face that stamped her with that awful yet gentle majesty. For she seemed formed of translucent silver light, rather than glowing super-flesh; and it was spirit, and spirit alone, that invested her with that supernal grandeur.

In deepest awe I knelt there on that night-black dais, before that shining silver foot above which I dared not raise my eyes.

"Nay," murmured that thrilling strain of music that, for want of a better word, I must call her "voice." "Kneel not, but rise and give attention. I have called you to my throne, for I have need of you!"

Did I hear aright? Could such as She, one of the Celestials, one of that shining host who serve the Presence, have need of *me,* an Earthman? It seemed absolute madness to think it. Yet she herself had just said it. In sincere humility I waited; rising and gazing straight into that glorious countenance, so calm, serene, so awe-inspiring.

"Will it please thee to make thy meaning clear?" I asked boldly. "My wits are but those of the dull Earth—I do not understand."

She smiled, and all the countless throng of those who stood to either side and back of the throne smiled likewise, much as drops of dew, sparkling, give back the sunrays which touch them.

"I mean just this," she replied. "I have an enemy whom I may not reach; with whom as yet I cannot cope! Always has the balance of power between us been equal; although between us twain has always been war. Yet it has been—thou knowest what I am?" she broke off to query.

"Thou art Love itself—its Prototype," I responded as directly as she had asked. She nodded, well pleased, but amplified for my benefit the statement I had just made.

"Aye," she answered, "I am Love. But not alone am I that as it is understood upon thy world. For I am Love's Self. I am the love a man holds for a maid; the love the maid gives to the man of her heart's choice; yet I am the love the mother bears for her babe; the tigress for its young; the serpent for its little snakes. I am even the love the miser knows for his treasure; that the warrior holds for strife; that the worshipper feels for his divinity—I am, as thou hast said, 'Love's Prototype'. Yet as abstract love touches each nature, that nature transmutes it into terms of its own desires—now hast thou begun to comprehend?"

"Very dimly," I replied, for my thought was racing, amplifying even beyond her revealing words, and I was amazed at the extent and ramifications of what I comprehended. For *that* love, carried to its extreme scope, includes desire for wisdom, and all that distinguishes man from beast—angel from demon!

"So," she approved; "I believe thou hast in truth grasped some faint idea as to my Self—ah, well! let that pass for the present. Yet, on every planet, on each world, in all the illimitable regions of space; wheresoever in all the universe the conscious egos have abode, there am I to be found in one ideal or another.

"So, too, this enemy of whom but now I spoke! He is Lord of Hate, even as I am Lady of Love. And even to him my power penetrates; for—strange words to go together!—*he loves to hate!* For it is in this wise that his nature transmutes! And so too, it is with me—for I, despite my nature, am touched by that power flowing from him; and my nature transmutes it all to hate of *Hate's* source.

"Learn, then, that these be natural laws! Nor can mere 'will', not even that of us Celestials, alter these, no matter how greatly we may desire to do so.

"And so, throughout all the universe the balance swings; the old, old patient contest of Love against Hate—the frenzied, virulent enmity of Hate against Love. But thus far, knowing what we know, there has been no overt strife. It has been rather a quiet, silent struggle ever working in the conscious coils of the egos inhabiting the various planes.

"But now I have sure tidings that he meditates actual aggression—his hate having overruled his judgment! Not here, against my city of love alone, does he plot, but everywhere that my influence reaches! And oh! but he is served by such fiends, such demons, such *things* of absolute, concrete malignancy, that I sicken at thought of what must befall the universe if he actually takes the field of war!

"And that he so intends, I know for sure, but what his plans may be, I know not; for I am not omniscient. *That* is the attribute of the Presence Itself, and not that of us who do but serve.

"So, I have picked thee out and drawn thee to me. I need a spy! None of these who serve me can approach him; for if they did, terrible indeed would be their sufferings. For they carry about them always the vibrations of love; and even in the realms of hate, still would their presences be recognized.

"But thou art of Earth—as capable of hate as of love; and he, the Terrible, is served and followed and even adored by egos from all the worlds. An Earthman more or less would scarce be noted among his subject throngs. Now, dost thou realize my need of thee?"

I understood! And knew, as only the Self can know, the wild, thrilling allure of anticipated adventure! Say as they will; Mars may or may not be the planet of war; Jupiter may or may not preside over the plane of judicial intellect; and Mercury may or may not rule the selves of mechanics and inventors and those of excitable, volatile natures—but this is certain: Earth, that gray old planet that shines with the strange green radiance in the night skies, is unquestionably the abode of the true adventurers.

No other planet in the universe is inhabited by so bold, daring, and hardy a race of egos. To them, space is merely a little-understood ocean; to be charted, mapped, traveled if possible in safety, but traveled anyway. Why, that courageous creature, "Man," has even the temerity to attempt to measure the measureless; to find, if possible, the limits of the illimitable!

Nay, let him but once dream its possibility, and he will devise methods of transportation and storm the walls of the Highest Heaven! And this he will do in no spirit of blasphemy, but simply from the sheer love of achieving the hitherto unaccomplished—the joy of the adventure itself! For thus is "Man" constituted!

And because he is thus, he has the right to style himself the "Apex of Creation." It is not arrogance, but simple truth. On all the other planets, in all the other realms of space, the dwellers are either content to obey the "Law" or to exist in sulky rebellion against it. But Man, the investigator, confronted with "laws", rests never content until he has explored their workings, fully comprehended them and reordered his observations for the benefit of others to be born in the years to come. And then, if in any way it may be achieved, he harnesses their energies and bends them to his will, and makes them do his work!

Knowing this, and proud of my heritage, I raised my head and smiled full into those glowing pools of light — her eyes.

"Great honor is mine," I replied; "that to me, of all Earthmen, has been given this mission. Let me go, O Shining One! I may fail or I may succeed — but this I promise: you shall have no shame from your messenger, nor regret because of your choice."

"There spake the true Earthman," she smiled. "Proud, confident, arrogant! Yet I would not have thee otherwise. I am well pleased with my choice. *Go!*"

I had no time in which to ask questions, receive directions, or even think. *I was gone!* To all intents and purposes, the glowing city of light, the shining inhabitants, the goddess herself, might as well never have existed! For I was once again hurtling through space at a hundred times my previous rate of speed.

I may have passed some few swarms of planets of suns or asteroids. But if I did I never knew it. True, several times I was aware of a flicker of light, but so transitory that each time it might mean anything or nothing.

Once more the blackness lessened, glowing faintly with a lurid, angry, deep crimson light shot through by streaks of sullen black and jagged lines of glaring, venomous scarlet. I had touched the borders of the regions of Hate! I knew it, felt it; through every atom of my disembodied body I could sense that terrific emotional vibration.

It may be a matter of wonderment to some, that I had found my way so accurately through the uncharted and unknown voids of space; but a moment's reflection will clear this up.

A freed ego, released into space, is inevitably attracted by the "Law of Affinity" to whatsoever plane it is in greatest sympathy with. So it will be noted, that I, by the time the Silver One had made clear to me her requirements and fears, so thoroughly hated the cause of her apprehensions that there remained to me in all space no other destination possible.

Too abruptly for immediate realization, I found myself standing on what felt like solid ground. And, furthermore, I felt myself re-embodied. For a long minute my shocked mind refused to grasp the stupendous fact. But then, applying all my long scientific training to the solution of the problem, I came to a full realization of what had happened to me.

Hate is one of the lowest of the emotions. And the lower phases are invariably denser than are the higher ones. So where hate has surcharged the ether, density is a natural outcome.

And the ego, let it find itself wheresoever it may be borne — by fate or otherwise — throughout all the universe, by the "Law of Attraction" promptly is covered by an envelope commensurate to its needs and requirements for functioning in that environment.

And so I was once again an embodied ego, and I must say that I was in nowise proud of my appearance.

For after all, the Silver One was right, I am an Earthling; and as such I am as capable of hate as I am capable of love. Nay, within me are forever the two natures; as they are in all others. But in the shining city of light, I towered half as tall again as upon earth and shone with a clear brightness — while now I found myself, where the hate nature predominated, dwarfish, stunted, distorted, ugly in face and form and hue!

That I was strong in spirit goes without saying, and is no vanity on my part, because no spiritual weakling can ever hope to reach to the high status I held in our earthly Order. Our drastic tests and ordeals have sent many more aspirants to madhouses than have ever attained to the inner mysteries.

And so that strength of spirit was like to prove my undoing; for I sensed within me all the potentialities of a most malignant fiend! Worse, it was only by most strenuous efforts that I could remember clearly that Silver One and her mission upon which I had been sent.

And then I realized that I dared not *think* too strongly of her. No, the thought came to me to hate her; but was rather a comfort and a sort of stay whereto I might hold fast—but I feared that if I let my thoughts be too deeply tinged with her image, the fact would betray me to some of the inhabitants of this plane. And then the least that could ensue would be failure, and my ambitious spirit aspired to succeed.

It seemed a great, barred, rocky plain whereon I found myself. It was inexpressibly dreary and devoid of anything resembling towns or villages or even single habitations, so far as eye could reach. And of beings, either bipedal or quadrupedal, I could perceive none.

"When in doubt—take the initiative!"

That is an old maxim upon earth. Likewise it is sound philosophy. I did not know what to do nor where to go, so—I raised my voice in a shout! Rather, it was a most dismal *howl*—such a miserable, croaking bellow as I had never before thought I could emit!

But it did its work. Did it altogether too well! So well, in fact, that I came near to ending right there and then, before I had got fairly started.

But from a gaping hole beneath a huge drab-colored boulder nearby burst a monster. It was part lizard, part toad, part serpent; yet none of these words describes the repulsive outrage to the eyes! The *thing* was not so large in girth when it emerged—not much bigger round than a vat or large hogshead. But once it drew all its loathly length free, it developed an amazing power of expansion. It swelled, bloating until it was big enough to make a bulk equal to that of four or five elephants.

Straight at me it charged so swiftly that I could not hope to avoid it. Wallowing, squirming, hopping, writhing, tumbling and rolling—its gait was a queer medley of all these compounded.

Swiftly I stopped, caught up a rock and noted that the rock grew hot even as I took it into my grasp, but at that moment I failed to get the significance of this. I dashed the stone fairly into the nightmare horror that must for want of better words be called the creature's "face".

Undoubtedly that hot rock must have hurt; for the thing made a mumbling, hissing, whistling outcry of pain and rage. But the puny missile only served to arouse its anger, and it accelerated its speed toward me. The awful, ghastly head darted suddenly and — in one gulp I was swallowed!

Urgh! Such sensations! Those blubber lips had no sooner closed over me than I went sick all through. It was in no wise "fear", only repugnance, disgust. The thing's mouth was filled with sharp corrugations much like the teeth of a rasp of a file. Its breath was a loathsome, putrescent exhalation. And as with a single contractile movement of its throat muscles it shot me downward, I felt a viscous slime besmearing me from head to foot, sticky, clinging, clammy, repulsive as rubber cement!

Plup! I landed, fortunately, on my feet in its nearly empty stomach. It nearly strangled me to breathe, but I had to breathe, or choke — and either way, there was little to choose — merely the way of choking!

Well, I tried breathing! It was not pleasant, but I did it, some way. But my sole emotion was wrath. There was no fear about it. I was just plain *mad!* Mad all through! Frenzied with hate! To think that this confounded *thing* had dared — actually *dared*, swallow *me!*

I never even thought of the probable physical consequences to myself once the digestive processes within the beast commenced. My sole reaction was a demoniacal desire to wreak vengeance. I wanted to rend, tear, wrench, and utterly destroy by torments unbelievable, this ugly monstrosity!

Apparently hate is a creative force, in its own plane. At least sufficiently so to enable the hater to supply himself with the means of destruction.

For no sooner had I formulated the wish than I found myself holding a fearful and wonderful weapon firmly grasped in both hands.

It had a short, thick, metal handle immensely strong; and at one end were half a dozen hooks, razor-sharp on the inner edges. Actually, the thing looked exactly like a metal hand and arm with sickle-shaped blades in place of fingers—and the intensity of my wrath turned the metal instrument and claws red-hot! Even in my extremity, I recall grinning with malevolent satisfaction as I contemplated the devilish contraption!

Whirling the thing above my head like a miner with a many-pointed pickax, I set to work. I have said enough! There are some things too repulsive to write down for human eyes to read. Suffice it to say that long before actual harm had occurred to myself, I was once more free. And the *thing*, with a great, gaping, ragged hole torn in its side, was tumbling about seeking me, to wreak vengeance in its turn. But I had disappeared from its sight, having fled into a thicket of bushes nearby. They looked a safe hiding place enough!

Oh, yes! they looked innocuous, but every leaf and twig and branch and stalk and trunk were covered with an impalpable powder which rose in faint clouds about me and then settled again—mostly on me!

We've a little plant growing on Earth. It's called the "Nettle." We've another called "Ivy"—"poison ivy" some name it. Take a good-sized wisp of each and thrash your bare flesh with them until the tingling blood suffuses the surface skin. Let the effects *take* well—and you will have some dim idea as to what that dust did to me.

I burst from that thicket like a partridge from a covert! Not far from where I came out in such a hurry, I perceived a pool of water. I was too frenzied by that time to think ahead or exercise any caution, so I made straight for the pool and plunged in. I wanted to soothe my flesh from the agony of that burning dust as well as to cleanse it from the pollution of that beast-thing's interior, some of whose secretions still besmeared me in streaks and spots.

But I plunged out of that hole of water much more expeditiously than I had plunged into it! Had I stayed another instant, I had been *cooked;* for the fluid was scalding hot!

In agony I rushed from there as rapidly as my leg muscles could betake me, knowing that if I moved fast enough the passage of my body through air would equal a breeze blowing against me were I standing still. The idea was good, and I really derived a slight benefit from it. But it got me, after all, into fresh trouble.

For I had not run far when behind me I heard the soft *pad-pad-pad* of pursuing feet, and, glancing back over my shoulder, I perceived to my horror that a horde of creatures like earth-wolves, only twice as large, were chasing me!

I had laid my claw-club weapon on the brink of the scalding pool when I jumped in—and had not waited to pick it up and take it with me when I jumped out again, being in too great haste to depart; so I had nothing wherewith to fight.

I thought longingly of the guns of earth. But that failed to work like my desire while I was in the beast-thing's inwards. For this time, I was afraid! And fear is seldom positively destructive. But, run as I would, the brutes were fast overtaking me!

I tripped, fell forward, and became the center of a worrying, snapping, snarling pack of four-legged demons; and every one of them had the rabies, to judge from the foam-froth flying and slavering from their mouths!

In one brief, lightninglike flash, I saw a vision of myself lying there—a badly torn, lacerated, mangled thing; writhing in all the anguish of hydrophobia, yet unable to die. The goddess? How could she aid, let alone rescue me, here on this plane, where, she herself had stated it, she dared not let her servitors come? At the least, I had failed her—and as a failure, I knew that I deserved anything that might happen to me.

Suddenly, cutting through my terror and despair, I heard a volcanic eruption of crashing, searing oaths, spoken in good plain English! And accompanying the tirade of blasphemy, I heard the *thud* and the unmistakable *chuck* of edged weapons chopping into flesh and bone. I caught the snarls and yelps of fear and pain; the howls of rage and the dying whines and whimpers of the wolves that had harried me—

Powerful hands seized me and yanked me to my feet. I was in agony, bitten all over, yet still able to stand, albeit shakily. Dazedly I stared, and well I might!

Before me stood a man clad in the armor of the period of the First Crusade! He was tall, broad-shouldered, huge of body and thick of arms and thighs; and repugnantly brutal in features, although he was grinning at me from out the opening of his helmet. Yet that grin was not all goodfellowship. Partly it was malicious.

"Why!" he roared in a bull's voice. "Art an Earthling, man; e'en as I be myself?"

I nodded assent, noting as I strove to control my trembling limbs that the beasts were either all sorely wounded or fled; and that his followers were crowding about, staring at me quite as curiously as I was gazing at them.

Evidently they were from all planets and of all periods and races. None of them was at all prepossessing to look upon. Every countenance bore either ferocity or malignancy or both writ largely. I admit that as I looked at them I experienced greater fear than I had so far felt—their horrific weapons were enough to frighten anyone—swords, barbed spears, war-axes, clubs and things I cannot name, not knowing the arms of the different planets.

But I strove to brazen the matter out. Turning to the huge leader, I held out my hand in the age-old gesture of our race, intending to clasp hands with him; the while I began expressing my thanks, my gratitude for this timely rescue.

"Well for me that you came when you did," I began, and got no farther. He stared down at my hand outstretched in amity; then with a snarl he caught my wrist, turned my hand palm upward, and deliberately, insultingly, spat into it; while a look of utter venom disfigured his bestial countenance still farther than nature had done.

"Well for thee?" he roared mockingly. "Little we cared for thee, thou oaf, thou fool! 'Twas but the hate we bear for the beasts! It did please us to cheat them of their sport!"

Utterly taken aback, I knew not what to say. Before I could formulate anything my arms were pinned from behind and bound thus; a noosed cord was thrown about my neck, the other end being held fast by the most bestial-faced, apelike, lumpish-looking lout it has ever been my bad luck to behold—and we started for where I knew not.

What ghastly tortures did they intend inflicting? I wondered. The mail-clad leader caught my thought, read it accurately, and sneered in my face.

"Fear not," he jibed. "The dainty Earthling shall come to no harm at the hands of my sweet babes" — by which he meant his villainous crew of followers, I supposed — "not but that we would enjoy dalliance with thee," he went on vindictively; "but all who come to this realm must be brought before our lord intact!" I shuddered at the sinister implication of that last word, and noting it, he burst into a hoarse, braying laughter.

But in truth they did me no actual harm; although they did heap upon me every insult, contumely and indignity their depraved intelligences could devise. So that it was in anything but a spirit of pleasurable anticipation that I wended along with that crew, my pace accelerated every so often by a vicious yank from the ugly specimen holding the other end of the noosed cord about my neck.

Very evidently, when I volunteered for the service I was now engaged in carrying out, I had let myself in for something. And just as obviously, I was getting it, full measure and running over!

The sole gain that I could see lay in the fact that I was being taken directly to the presence of the one personage I most greatly desired to meet—albeit that promised to prove as detrimental as anything that could possibly happen. For there was little doubt as to the reception I might expect. Something unpleasant, unquestionably. No chance of its being otherwise. So, as I have said, my mood was the reverse of happy.

Eventually I found myself standing surrounded by the ugly-natured crew just outside the lofty walls of a great city. The mail-clad leader was holding parley with the guards who apparently kept watch and ward at a small, narrow, arched doorway.

What passed of countersign and password between them I know not, but in another moment we were admitted. I had braced myself in anticipation of a renewal of petty annoyances from the inhabitants once we were within the city, but nothing of the sort happened.

Obviously, they were too accustomed to seeing captive arrivals from the various planets to pay attention to such, except to glower, malignant, as we passed. But by that time I had been fully impregnated with the all-pervading aura, so returned glare for glare; hate for hate; nor felt shame that I should feel so.

It was a mighty city, I must say that. It seemed, in a way, much as the cities of the Middle Ages in Europe appeared; and that type anyone can imagine for himself, so I shall not bother to describe farther.

Finally after marching through dismal streets we entered a lofty, gloomy building, which, I judged aright, was the palace of the Archfiend. And a few minutes later, I was standing in his very presence. I had prepared myself to confront a demon—and I found myself facing a gentleman, a prince!

He wore a darkly vivid red robe; and about his head, in place of crown of other insignia of his rank, there played a faint but clearly perceptible nimbus of scintillant flame of lurid crimson, garish purple, and somber sinister blue.

He was seated on a wondrously hideous yet highly ornamented throne of bronze which glimmered and gleamed with all the tints and shades of all the metalline oxides. His finely shaped head rested negligently on his hand, his elbow propped on the broad arm of his throne-seat; and his deep, lustrous eyes swept me from head to foot in one all-inclusive, penetrating glance.

A single wave of his hand was sufficient. No spoken command, yet that hateful gang who had made me prisoner departed, hastily, as though glad to get away.

Those behind his throne and to either side barely glanced at me, for to them I was but an Earthling; and they, one and all, were nobles and dignitaries of the court of a terrible regnant prince of the powers of evil. And they were too great, in a way, to descend to petty levels.

"What sent thee to my realm, Earthman?"

His voice was quiet, low, pleasantly modulated. He gazed at me with no manifestation of aught save such mild curiosity as might be expected from a ruler granting audience at any newcomer in his territory.

For a fraction of a second I was at a loss for the right words in which to reply without arousing suspicions that might result awkwardly for me—then I remembered a bit of advice I had once received long ago: "When wishing to deceive—tell the truth. No one will believe it!"

"It was a woman sent me," I replied sulkily, playing my part, and noted an expression of wearied disdain flicker momentarily over his almost classically regular countenance.

"Only that?" he murmured, contemptuous. "So many Earthmen—" and a wave of his hand finished the remark for him. Then, as though having decided to get what poor sport from me might be had, he probed farther.

"But what did she do to thee?"

"Let me love her," I growled as if envenomed by bitter memories.

"Ah," he commented, gravely courteous. "I see! She let thee love her; then—refused thy love?"

"No!" I retorted savagely. "She accepted it!" Which was all true enough, but might be interpreted two ways.

"Then, since, because of her, thou hast suffered?" One, hearing, would have deemed him pitying, sympathetic.

"I have recently suffered very greatly," I replied, sulkily, as at first. Then I added, deliberately, insolently, moved thereto by one of those bursts of inspiration which at times come to even the dullest—"And now, O Prince of Hate, I have said all I will!"

He stared, as did his courtiers thronging the dais! Very probably, not in ages had any ego dared defy him thus, show such independence. It seemed, strangely enough, to please even while it apparently angered him. An enigmatic light glittered in his eyes, and he nodded reflectively.

I braced myself, expecting some terrific outburst; but again I was disappointed. He made no reply to my insolence, nor did he comment thereon. Merely he caught the eye of one standing near; and that one hastily bent the knee before him.

"Take this Earthman and find for him quarters here in the palace," he commanded. "Let him have such comforts as may please him. He has my favor. I will make him my personal attendant! Depart!"

As this last evidently meant me as well, we left the throne room together; and as we went, I fancied I heard a quickly suppressed, low-pitched murmur of amazement from the assembled courtiers. My guide's first remark to me fully confirmed this idea.

"Never before has our Master showed such treatment to any who have stood before him, let alone an Earthman; for above all others he hates thy world the worst!"

"Why?" I queried.

"Nay," he responded, grumpily, "I know not. Nor," he added, as afterthought, "do I care! Nor is it any affair of thine!"

I returned his ugly stare with interest, and in mutual animosity we reached the rooms that were, for so brief a time, to be my abode. And here with no word of farewell nor other courtesy, my guide left me to shift for myself.

There was a comfortable couch, and a table spread with viands, and wine stood in a tall beaker.

Food and drink! I had not thought of them since I had left my physical body lying at the foot of the black cubical altar away back there on earth. They had not since then been necessities; nor were they so here, but they were luxuries; and as such I appreciated them. And, of their sort, they were good. Then I reclined upon the couch, and for a time I slept.

For quite a long while I dwelt an inmate of the palace pleasantly enough—speaking strictly in a negative sense—for I was in nowise annoyed nor molested by anything or anyone.

My quarters were comfortable; I had all the luxuries which an honored guest might have expected placed at his disposal; the raiment furnished me was little short of sumptuous. And I was puzzled by it all.

Had I made such an impression upon him, the Lord of Hate, that I had won his actual regard? Or was it all but a prelude to some particularly and peculiarly devilish form of torment he had devised for me as reward of my temerity in replying so insolently during that one brief interview? I could not figure it out, so decided that the only sensible course was to accept the situation as I found it and await developments.

I even had the hardihood to leave the palace and wander about the infernal city at will, on several occasions. It was a chancy thing to do; but aside from several minor disagreeable adventures, too trivial to set down in this relation of more important events, nothing happened to me during these rambles.

Then, finally, when I was becoming so bored that once I caught myself seriously contemplating participating in the vice and depravity so prevalent in the city, a messenger came to summon me to the throne room. Fortunately, I was in my quarters at the time.

The mighty prince surveyed me with somewhat of approval in his gaze — or so I imagined.

"Earthman," he greeted me; "thou art improved in appearance since thine arrival. Henceforward thy place is here at my side."

I expressed my appreciation as best I might, but he waved the matter aside, as courteous as ever, treating the favor he showed me as a merest nothing.

I noted from time to time that messengers came and went — all of them apparently of some importance. They naturally varied greatly in appearance and types, as among them were representatives from practically all the realms and regions of space.

Not being wholly a fool, I judged them for precisely what they were — emissaries from the princes and rulers of evil, bearing tidings from their fiendish masters — who, doubtless, were his allies and who intended joining him in his projected war of aggression when all plans were complete.

I was right. For later, as I stood beside the prince, he turned to me.

"It is my will that thou goest with me," he commanded; and I cooly queried: "Where?"

"There is, in a great hall in this, my city, a council now assembled. It is formed by the Lords and Princes of the Powers of Wrong from all the many hells," he replied, smiling a trifle indulgently at my obvious interest.

"I shall preside," he went on; "and as thou art high in my estimation, Earthman of mine, I shall have need of thee immediately our deliberations are ended."

"It is thine to command—mine be it to obey," I responded, outwardly servile, but inwardly delighted at my luck.

"Come then," he said quietly, rising from his throne of bronze.

I was a bit puzzled at his going forth to such an important gathering unattended by any retinue; and he read my thought.

"It is of too great moment for any but the highest to be allowed to attend," he stated, "but thou art my personal attendant, and as such, I shall need thee presently. Moreover," he added graciously, "I have no fear thou wilt ever betray me, no matter what thou mayest learn."

He had paced slowly in the entrance while he had been talking, and now we stood upon a balcony overlooking that side of the city. He raised a hand and pointed out a huge, square, dark building.

"There," he said, "is the great council hall, where, at my command, convene the Lords of Wrong whenever I have need of them."

"Do they all yield obedience to *thee?*" I questioned.

An expression so utterly damnable came upon his usually controlled features that I shrank back a pace in stark terror—and I am not easily affrighted.

"They do well to obey," he snarled. Then, turning upon me the full strength of that awful hell-glare suffusing his eyes, he demanded in a chill voice:

"Who dost thou think *I* am—some subordinate, petty princeling? Nay, thou blind earthworm—*I am the Adversary himself!* Knowest thou *now* whom thou dost serve?"

"*Lucifer!*" I gasped. This was more than I had calculated upon! Lucifer, the Archfiend; the Fallen Angel; the Rebellious One—he who was formerly the chiefest and fairest of all the Seraphim; and was now but a banished rebel against the Supreme Will.

And he it was who was planning—and the bare idea of what those plans must be made my spirit shudder, appalled. He had been watching my face intently, and now he nodded as if well pleased.

"Come," he said simply, mastering the momentary rage which had dominated him. I must say that, despite my knowing him now for what he was, he forced from me an unwilling admiration by his display of will dominating inherent nature.

Suddenly as an earthly rocket, he shot into air, and with no effort of my own, I was drawn after him precisely as a bit of steel might be drawn to a rapidly moving electro-magnet.

As we approached the great council building, I recognized it. I had seen it from every possible angle during my wanderings about the city; and I knew it for an immense, hollow cube, with no visible entrance on any face.

Never had I traveled at such high speed before! I had barely time for the fleeting thought that the tangible envelope I was wearing as a body would be splattered against that massive stone structure in a single smear as soon as we passed through it—dense, solid as it was—with our forms intact!

I caught my breath and blinked in amazement. That proud prince, Lucifer, was already seated upon a richly jeweled throne, far and away more gorgeous than the one of bronze in the throne room of his royal palace. And I found myself standing in my regular place close to his left elbow.

But what caused me to actually gasp was the semicircle of seated forms, occupying each a throne scarcely less splendid than the one wherefrom Lucifer faced them. Yet theirs were reared not quite so high as was his; as was but fitting, for they were, after all, his tributary vassals, high though their rank might be in their own realms.

A way back in the medieval days upon Earth, someone with an imagination approximating that of a little child's tried to describe the different Lords of Wrong. And the best he could do was to endow them with the physical appearances of a horde of beasts and monsters, actual and mythological. And such has been the accepted idea ever since!

What puerile folly—merest piffle! They were, and are, masters of powers and forces such as Earth even yet knows nothing of. And is it to be supposed that, with such at their command, they could not weave for themselves whatever forms and semblances were pleasing to their notions?

I say emphatically that never in all my universal experiences have I looked upon a grander, statelier, or more beautiful assemblage.

True, there was one thing they, for all their powers, could not do. They could not wholly disguise their true characters. I saw infernal pride stamped on every countenance there; besides which, each face wore an expression of strange, wearied *patience* as of those immortals whose lots are fixed, unchangeable, immutable, for all eternity.

But there common resemblance to type ended. Just as on Earth every man has one besetting sin or vice or dominant desire, so was it with these. Only, precisely as their natures are more intense than are those of Earth-mortals, so too, their predominant evil was stronger and marked them each with his own peculiar expression.

I shall not describe them farther. Let each one imagine them as he or she may please. We all know the look of avarice; of hate; of envy—but why amplify? This is enough for illustration.

That Infernal Council opened as formally as any lodge on Earth. And, long before it was ended, my soul was sick within me. Yet, oddly enough, I sincerely believe that despite the fact that these were archfiends and I a mere mortal, I was the one who, in all that vast hall, felt the greatest wrath!

But it was against them, one and all, that my hate burned. I had listened to the unbelievable—the unspeakable—the unthinkable! In truth, I know not how the very soul of me—the spirit itself—escaped shriveling to nothingness from horror—or kept from becoming even as they were from venomous rage in presence of such damnability!

I dare not write what I heard and learned!

I have made report to the Shining One who sent me. I have been commanded by an authority to which even she yields implicit obedience, to remain silent forever on this matter. And I certainly will not disobey the clear injunction I received before I was permitted to set down these events for my fellow mortals to read. Were those things written out, the very pages would burst into flames as the penpoint traced the horrific phrases! And mortals, reading, were I to grave them in stone, or scrawl them on asbestos, would pray in vain for annihilation!

Finally the deliberations ended. Ensued a brief pause. And over me swept such aghast fear as never before had I know. I realized that *I* was the focus of attention!

The fallen Archangel turned to me with jeering, softly sardonic words on his lips and a mocking smile in his eyes.

"O Earthman of such great courage—and even greater folly; well and faithfully hast thou played thy part! Doubt not that she who beguiled thee into attempting to match thy feeble wits against mine own, will be much beholden to thee—*when thou dost make to her thy report!*"

I knew what he meant by that last sentence! Only too well I understood! He meant that my report would be made sometime after eternity itself had ceased to be!

If I had hated before, I now was like a dog suddenly gone mad. I had no weapons! I had nothing wherewith to smite!

Emitting something between a snarl, a howl, and a shriek, I hurled myself straight at that evilly, luridly beautiful countenance!

The distance was less than arm's reach, yet ere I could overpass it, without the slightest gesture on his part, not even pointing a finger, I was stricken into immobility; smitten with a paralysis that was anguish untellable!

I had less power of motion left me than a stone image. Yet I was anything but stone. That is insensate. But I—I was a mass of little else save sensory nerves and perception. And what play those fiends made with me can be imagined; but never can I bear to describe it!

It was too agonizing, too awful for words. And the terrible part lay in the fact than not one of them left his seat. They did but *think*—and I suffered! It was humiliation unbelievable to realize that they were not even enjoying themselves but held me as being too trivial a subject to afford them amusement. Why, they were scarcely interested! Yet every one of them was as fully aware of my torments and excruciating anguish as was I myself!

As a final refinement of cruelty, the Arch-Enemy removed from me the paralysis; left me free to wince and writhe and shudder—to moan, shriek, groan, and howl. And I, with all pride and strength sapped, in frenzy availed myself to the fullest of the capacity!

Suddenly all pain departed and was followed by the most exquisite sensations. I felt my tormented nerves and tissues tingle with a life and vigor such as are undreamable. The relief was so great that at first I could not believe it. But then I realized that it was real, and in the conscious thrill of that power of life flowing through me, I smiled! But that smile was a trifle premature!

Why, what was this? I was no longer standing on the floor,

but was suspended above the center of the hall, about equidistant from all the seated members of the Infernal Group. I could feel no cruelty emanating from them—there was not either curiosity or anticipation. What was coming next? I found out!

About me was gathering a faint mist of a grayish hue. It was more like a cloud of dust-particles very finely sifted. It did me no harm. I did not even notice the dust as I breathed.

Then it commenced to *swirl;* apparently in all three dimensions at once. The motion became faster; the particles became more plentiful—I could no longer see clearly, although still I could see.

Faster yet the swirling became—friction soon set up—the density increased—centripetal and centrifugal forces came into play—attraction and repulsion balanced each other—there commenced to grow about me a dim light—I understood suddenly!

I was ensphered in a ball or globe of etheric particles. The fiends were sealing me up in the hollow center of what might, centuries or eons later, become a world, a planet in space!

But just then it was more like a comet or a sun—incandescent. Being burned alive is one thing, and being *baked* alive is another matter; the more especially when to it is added the certitude that by no possibility could death intervene to put an end to suffering. No matter how long I might roast, I knew I could not die!

Apparently, I was accounted for and there was no use wasting farther efforts upon me. The hollow sphere suddenly shot upward through the roof and departed forever from that plane.

Whirling and spinning, it tore on its way into outer, remotest space, where was never a gleam of light from planet or sun, and where the terrific absence of temperature was so great that presently the incandescence of my vehicle perceptibly lessened. And over me swept the nightmare conviction that it was cooling, would soon grow cold! Then contraction would ensue and—

It did! It contracted until it was pressing upon me in all directions at once. It grew colder than any iceberg ever was or will be—and still it contracted in that unimaginable chill of outer space.

The worst thing of all the Arch-Adversary had done to me was in endowing me with that terrible power of life. It had affected that body I was wearing until, no matter how great the pressure, I did not crush. But how it did hurt!

By then I was some milliards of miles from his realm; but suddenly, through the solid walls pressing so awfully upon me, I saw him still seated in full council; and I knew that for a fleeting moment he had allowed himself to think of me.

I knew, too, as soon as I caught his thought, that he was aware of that, also. And I saw a faint, mocking smile shine ever so briefly in his eyes. Then darkness and horror for what seemed eons untold.

I remember that at times I shrieked, raved, whined, and implored—begging mercy from the Merciless! Then again I would strive to reassert myself, trying to endure, to keep steadfast, and not give the proud Archfiend the satisfaction of knowing how deeply I suffered.

A terrific shock, the impact of which well-nigh stunned me! My whirling prison stopped, hung suspended. Some new form of torture, and I would have to endure it as best I might, I thought with a queer, resigned apathy.

Another shocking, jarring impact, worse than the first one. Another and yet again. The blows came faster and faster until there was no distinguishing one from another. Faster and harder still—and my prison globe was commencing to give out a strangely musical humming note. Suddenly comprehension dawned upon me.

"Power is not great in proportion to weight of impact, but to number and regularity of impact." Undoubtedly, some new vibratory force or energy was assaulting my shell—but why? Did it mean what I had first thought—fresh torment? Or could it—*could* it mean that—

The globe burst! Burst in all directions, simultaneously, as if from internal explosion. *And I burst apart also!* Flew asunder, outwardly, from a common center. Disintegrated with an instantaneous thoroughness that left nothing to be desired in its finality.

Why not? The pressure upon that body I had been wearing had been of tons and tons. And it had been too suddenly released. Expansion was but a natural consequence. Too much expansion—pressure too suddenly withdrawn!

Of course it will be understood that that self which is the real "me" did not burst. It was, as I have said, but the acquired body alone. But at last, after experiences as hideous as though I were in truth one of the eternally damned, I was once again *free*.

The crowning joy came when I found myself surrounded by a throng of dazzling, shining beings—beings whose type I instantly recognized. And, at once, I saw *her*, the Silver One!

She had not forgotten, had not abandoned the Earthling whose chiefest wish had been to serve her. Through space uncharted, where never before had light gleamed; where never before had even the exploring Archangels passed, she had traced my prison cell in its appalling flight; had finally overtaken it, for all its amazing speed and—

Despite the Arch-Adversary himself, I would, after all, make to her my report! And I did, then and there. At first, she bade me wait until we were once more in her shining city. But I boldly insisted that she hear me immediately. She graciously yielded the point in recognition of what she was pleased to term my claims upon her for meritorious service.

Well that I did report at once. When I had finished, she was, for all her supernal nature, plainly disturbed; aghast at the awful menace threatening the universe.

I thought I knew the laws of etheric vibration fairly well. And, for earthly requirements, I do. But all I had ever known put together was but the prattle of an infant, compared to the wisdom of the Silver One.

How far-reaching, how all-comprehending, how all-inclusive must have been that power of sight she controlled, to enable her to keep track of my arrival on the plane of Hate; and to know when I departed therefrom, and the manner of my going. How accurate, too, that she could follow that shell so closely. And how stupendous her ability; that she could and did disrupt it so promptly!

And that Lucifer, the fallen Archangel, was likewise one of the masters of the ether, is understood almost without saying. Already I had had more than one demonstration of his abilities; and I was to receive others very shortly.

It was a joyous throng that swept in a brilliant, gleaming cortège through that black vault of Tartarus. And after my lengthy exposure to the vibrations of Hate, I fairly *soaked* up all the loving pity and sympathy that they so generously bestowed. I felt that I needed it to cleanse me from the pollution of that realm where I had dared venture like a spy into an enemy's chiefest citadel.

There was not even a preliminary glow of lurid light to warn us! One instant, ahead of us, still the void of outer space—and the next instant, hordes and legions of fiends, demons, imps, and goblins; swarming all about us, above us, below us. Everywhere, save in our very midst!

Once again—as while imprisoned in the shell—to me there came that far-reaching clairvoyance, and I could see the Great Adversary himself sitting on his brazen throne in his palace dwelling. He was guiding, controlling, directing, from that incalculable distance, his infernal host he had sent to intercept us.

Why, I could even sense his thought waves—not directed to me, but to the Silver One herself.

"What I once have held is mine throughout all eternity! Yield to me that Earthling's spirit, and go thy ways in peace—for this time!"

I was in for it! That I could see plainly. I had incurred the personal animosity of one who never forgave; one who forever remained relentless; one who would not be deprived of his vengeance, once begun! He wanted me—and there was no hope. I knew my doom. Yet it was I who would finally triumph, of that I was assured, for I would yield myself to him, give myself over to his tender care—and what that might be I could easily guess.

But in defying him, mocking him, flouting him even in the midst of his worst torments, *I* would be the tormentor—his tormentor—even while he tortured me! I could not, would not let harm come to her I served because of me. Why, who was I—?

Before I could demand of her that she give me up to him; I caught her answer.

"Lucifer, I yield not one of those who cleave to me. If he be thine—come take him! Cease malingering there on thy brazen seat; come in person—thou who wast formerly of our Celestial Host—*thou*, Fallen Seraph; Arch-Rebel; *Supreme Coward of the Universe!*"

That supernal defiance rang through space that heard with bated breath! The very atoms of the ether shuddered and wavered in their eon-old steadiness of flow; shocked and aghast at that most stupendous final insult! And I—I gazed spellbound at her whom, previously, I had deemed a gentle spirit!

Where now was that softly shimmering, silvery tint of living light that had composed her matchless form? It shone now with a vivid coruscating radiance far more like white-hot iron superheated; yet had all the hardness of appearance characterizing highly polished, chilled steel!

The soft gentle roseate flushes—color of love—which had faintly tinged her entire aura, had changed to the clear bright scarlet of wrath celestial. The serene brow was still calm, but bore an expression of awful sternness, lofty, implacable, unyielding. The great pools of light—her eyes—now blazed with indignation. And the smiling, tender mouth which had been so mobile, quivering with loving, yearning wistfulness, had subtly hardened—the lips were curled with scorn and contempt—

A shriek burst from the regnant figure seated on its brazen throne! That hellish ululation rang through all the illimitable Etheric Ocean till the wave of Life itself well-nigh changed and became a tide of Death instead!

That supreme taunt had stung the Lord of Hate beyond all his demoniac endurance. It had cut straight to the very wellsprings of his being! It could be replied to in but one manner.

In a blinding, dazzling, lurid flash of crimson and hectic purple he sped straight from his throne-seat to the very forefront of his hellish host which swarmed and swirled all about us; as yet not daring to attack.

His arrival and the opening of the war were simultaneous. His first act was to launch direct at me a streak of greenish-white luminescence that barely missed me, and would have taken me full, had not one of those who followed the Silver One interposed herself.

The shining being shrank, shriveled, seemed to wither; grow smaller, deformed; the splendid beauty of her aura turned dull gray and leaden in hue—she writhed and quivered in an agony excruciating to behold. Had that streak of Infernal Energy smitten *me*—I doubt if my supposedly indestructible self could have survived it!

I shame to confess it! I shrink from the admission as never have I cringed in self-loathing before, but I must tell it! There is that within me that compels me and will not be denied. Before that terrific battle was over, fifteen of those beauteous ones, male and female both, had interposed their unselfish selves;

had been my preservation; rather than let me fall victim to the wrath of the Archfiend!

And I could not fight him back! Why, I was but a helpless babe in this most stupendous strife! The worst—or best—powers I knew how to utilize failed to affect the most puerile and impotent of the least of the goblins in the Arch-Enemy's array!

But now, if I seem to digress, in truth it is not so. I find that I must shift from one thing to another, keeping as best I may to the thread of my narration; yet covering certain points of grave importance, in order to make some matters clear.

The self is indestructible, was never born, can never die. But it can know suffering, can be hurt, not permanently, yet terribly while the hurt endures. It may not be affected thus by any means known to Earth. But, as I have said once and again—in the Etheric Ocean of Space, which is the Storehouse of Universal Energy, there are strange powers and forces latent which may be set into activity by that chiefest and greatest dynamic energy, "Will."

All the universe is but ions and electrons—atoms. The solid rock, the yielding flesh, the intangible smoke, or the impalpable gas—atoms, all of these! Atoms, too, are electricity, chemistry, radium—

All that differentiates one thing from other things throughout all the universe is—vibratory rate! Certain vibrations are pleasant, soothing, gratifying, because they are harmonious, in attunement.

Then, given a vibratory wave of sufficient intensity, *out* of attainment with its objective—and injury is quite possible! And of such nature were the weapons used in that spatial warfare!

Again to revert—when she, the Silver One, turned from her gentle attitude, realizing that thus only could she maintain her integrity and insure the safety of her followers; they too, had promptly altered. Not so high, so potent as she, perhaps; still, in their ways, they were anything but weaklings!

So, indescribable as was that strife, and banal though the strongest words are for purposes of description, I still will try in my poor way to tell what I may of its progress.

The lesser host, that of the Silver One's array, held closely together, despite the most determined assaults against them. At her command, they had assumed a strange geometrical formation, and from this they hurled forth flickering rays of clear lights, scintillant sparklings, coruscating whirls and spiriting puffs and jets of gases and vapors, faintly luminous, but devastating in effect.

Incessantly, from the forefront of that gleaming cohort where blazed the Silver One herself, there burst sheets and flares of blinding white, violet-tinted light which was almost solid in its atomic intensity of impact! It was shot through with sparks and bursting points and darting tongues of super-iridescence, And wherever that awful vibration smote, the unlucky fiends howled and yelled, and some even wept in anguish — so terrible was the result of her wrath!

And ever as she smote, clear as a strain of music heard amidst the turmoil of an Earthly tempest, her challenge rang above all the hellish riot from that Infernal Army.

"Come and face *me*, Lucifer! Thou, who didst swear once, eons ago, to drag me down lower than the lowest goblin damned of all thy far-flung outposts! Leave off assailing my followers, and face *my* power, thou Scum of the Nethermost Pit!"

But he came not. Rather, he kept carefully on the farther side of her cohort; and in this one matter he had her at a disadvantage. For she, with those terrible sheets of celestial flame, was blasting for her attendants a path in a fixed direction — back toward her shining city, while to him and his demoniacal legion, one direction was as good as any other.

And he and his hellish hordes were anything but passive!

Their weapons were, in a way, more dreadful than were those they were facing. For they were using the vibrations of their kind. And between the two hosts played such display as no earthly pyrotechnics could ever hope to approximate.

Against us they launched whirling spirals and vortices of scarlet and crimson fires; flares of sulfurous blues and yellows; jets and gouts and splashes of flames of all colors, but all shaded with dark impurity; foul with wrath and malice and all indecency.

There came, ever and again, gusts of fetid odors; blasts of stifling, mephitic vapors of green and leaden and purple; and thick, black clouds, filthy, revolting to touch and smell; shot through with jagged sizzling darts and streaks of hell's own essence—which is a vibration indescribable to earthly concept.

Had I to choose, I had far rather have faced the worst that the Shining Band could do to me—for their weapons were clean, at least, however dreadful the effects might be. But the noxious, virulent emanations from the enemy array were pollution itself. They well-nigh choked the souls of us who faced them!

Again I shame to say it, but so far as possible, I had been kept in the middle of that geometrical figure. Yet, it was against me, as much as he could, that the Great Adversary directed his most detrimental efforts.

But following close on a particularly biting taunt from the Silver One—a taunt which held more than a hint of mocking merriment—he shifted his position enough so that he could launch straight at her one of those virulent greenish-white streaks of phosphorescence—a streak far more intense than any he had so far condescended to waste upon me!

Straight at her noble breast it sped—and for a brief second I grew sick with apprehension. A faint, soft, rose-colored glow shone on her bosom for a mere moment—but the awful vibration, touching it, lost its power! Again he hurled one of those frightful darts; but again the soft, rosy glow foiled him. Again and yet again he smote, and ever as they struck, impotent, her jeering challenge retorted, maddening him.

I know not how it happened. It was all too quickly done for me to follow; but I found myself suddenly before her—and the baleful glance of the Adversary was quick to perceive his opportunity!

But because of his position, her form partially intervened. He changed location still farther and shot at me one terrific streak! I saw it start—and saw, streaming from the fingers of her left hand which she swiftly interposed before me, a shield, oval in shape, of that wondrous rosy glow. The hell-dart fairly *crackled* as it impinged upon that defense, but harmed me not at all.

I sensed the wild, thrilling exultation of her triumph—and realized that she had deliberately used me as a lure to entrap him!

Her magnificent, shapely right arm shot straight upward, full length, swept downward again in a superb gesture, her strong, slender tapering fingers pointing full at him; and from their tips there leaped a single flash of Black Light transcending all *Light!*

Concentrated to a spot no larger than an Earth-child's hand, it smote him full on his wrathful brow! And at its stabbing impact he screamed as never fiend nor imp nor lost soul ever screamed in direst tortures of his devising!

That ghastly yell of anguish rings yet in my memory! The coronal of lurid flames about his head went out. He turned a livid, sickly hue, suddenly grew limp, weaker than the weakest member of all his hideous host—

He turned and fled! Fled, slowly, painfully, moaning and wailing in futile misery and humiliation! And, fleeing, was overtaken and passed by his entire army who broke and scattered when they witnessed their leader's defeat! But he could not flee fast enough to escape from her derisive mockery.

"Go, proud prince! Go, without this Earthling whom thou

didst demand from my hands! Go, without taking me prisoner—me whom thou didst threaten to degrade! *Lucifer, thou hast my pity!*"

I think that last hurt him worse than all else!

We were annoyed no farther. Space was but empty space until we reached the shining city. There were many of that bright band sorely hurt, and even in that Abode of Light it was some time ere they wholly recovered.

I was unhurt, but the very self of me was inexpressibly wearied, almost to exhaustion. Despite this, I would have returned to Earth, for I feared for that mortal body I had left so long lying in the Temple—asleep in the Black Shrine, but the Silver One forbade.

"Thy brethren care for thy body by my express command," she assured me, adding: "And as for that futility thou dost name thy 'business affairs' upon earth—fear not thou! Bide here yet awhile. It is my wish."

Now, who was I to refuse?

It was pleasant enough there, and finally I asked her outright to grant me permission to remain, permanently, forever. Over her serene features—now once more gentle-hovering on her lips there crept an enigmatic smile.

"Wait!" was all her reply.

I was wondering what that might mean when a blaze of sapphire and gold filled all the place about her throne. Momentarily dazzled, I then became aware of a Radiant Being by contrast with whom even *she* appeared obviously of lesser rank. Nothing and no one told me, yet I knew it for one of the great Archangels who abide in the immediate light of the Presence Itself. He surveyed me a trifle curiously.

"Earthman," he stated bluntly, "thou art the greatest fool who ever left thy world."

I bowed my head abashed. Yet I was aware that the Silver

One was smiling approvingly on me.

"But," continued the Seraph, "it is such daring fools as thou who serve the Inscrutable Purpose."

I felt even more abashed, for this was praise. From an Archangel!

"Wouldst thou dare alone face the Great Adversary once again, there on his dais in the heart of his realm?" he queried as if desirous of finding out just how bold a fool I really was.

I raised my head, looked at him, despite his blazing splendor, straight in the eye.

"If it serves," I replied humbly.

"Give heed, then," he commanded. "It is thy right to hear and judge if thou wilt go or not. Ages ago, this Lucifier sought to corrupt thy world. Thou knowest that it is far from perfect now! It was because of that that he was reduced to his present estate. Wherefore it is that he hates thy world, the Green Star, the worst.

"Now he has dared transgress again; has been prevented for a time; but still he mediates rebellion. And so, I have a message for him! But because he hates thy world so viciously, it is fitting that thou shouldst bear him that message — thou, an Earthman from the star he hates; thou, the one Earthman whom above all Earthmen he has greatest cause to hate! Well?"

"I serve," I replied simply.

Oh, the stupendous powers under the control of those Celestials! There was no message given me; no command to 'go'; there was not even perceptible transition — it was instantaneous transposition!

I was standing on the dais facing the Archfiend on his brazen throne! The very sight of me seemed to madden him, giving him the spur he evidently needed; for the jaded look faded from his worn-appearing countenance, being replaced by a wild ferocity.

"Thou?" he snarled, half incredulous. I suppose I should

have quailed before that frightful rage, but somehow I did not do so.

"I have a message for thee," I stated bluntly.

In sheer mockery he assumed the manners at once of a gravely courteous, suave prince receiving an envoy.

"I listen," he replied, with but the faintest hint of irony in his tones.

"Lucifer," I commenced sternly, "once thou didst rebel against the Presence. As punishment, this is thy estate! Thou, too, dost serve the Purpose; as does the eternal conflict! But lately thou didst o'erpass the boundaries of thy province; and what that brought thee, thou knowest! O'erpass thy boundaries once again, and thou wilt o'erpass the limits of the Patience! And then—no worm squirming beneath the dust of the Green Star from whence I came can be so low as thou shalt be abased. *Heed ye the warning!*"

It was not of myself that I had spoken. That *I* knew. But the Archfiend was blinded by his hate, or he, too, would have known it. He leaped to his feet. In his eyes the hell-glare blazed as never before.

"Thou presumptuous—" he yelled, but never finished his remark, whatever it was. Facing him from the center of the throne room stood the Archangel who had sent me. Never a word he spoke; his eyes looked—but did not even seem to notice the Prince of Hate. Had he gazed at nothingness, his eyes had held that same expression—serene, aloof, indifferent. Yet Lucifer sank back upon his throne, cowed, beaten once again.

"I hear—and—and—" he well-nigh choked on the final words—"I—obey!"

There was no throne before me; no fallen Seraph promising abject submission! Again that Celestial's supernal power! We were hovering just above the "couch of dreams" whereon still lay my earthly body.

"Man of Earth," said my companion, "we have need of such as thee in Space. There is a planet of which thou hast never heard, where things are far from what they were ordained to be. We can use thee there. Well?"

"Still I serve," I replied gladly.

"Re-enter thy body," he commanded. "Thy brethren will not attempt to question thee. Arrange thy earthly affairs as may please thee, but in such wise that if the call comes, it will find thee waiting in readiness—for when *I* come for thee, thou wilt 'die' as do all thy race."

"I will be ready at any moment," I promised.

Everything grew dark, I felt a strange strangling sensation—I gasped, opened my eyes wearily. I heard a startled exclamation. I turned my head slowly, for my neck felt queerly stiff and moved with difficulty.

That same "Temple Dove" who had woven for me the spell of the Temple-sleep was kneeling beside me.

"Oh," she exclaimed softly. "You have come to life again. I am so glad!"

"You have not been here all this time, I hope," I said.

"No, no," she replied, shaking her head emphatically. "Why, you have been gone more than five weeks! But always someone has watched over you, waiting for your awakening. It has been done by the command of the Hierophant of the Order."

"Help me up," I said, for I felt unable to rise by my own unaided efforts.

I got to my feet and stood swaying unsteadily. In fact, had not the girl placed her arm about me and supported me I should probably have fallen. But after a bit, as the circulation improved, I grew stronger.

"I'm all right now," I said.

"I'm so glad," she repeated, her eyes shining joyously. "I—I—prayed—for—you," she whispered diffidently.

I stared! *She!* Prayed—for *me! I who*—! Then comprehension dawned in my arrogant mind! After all, within her limits, she, too, served! Very gently I bent and kissed her on her smooth brow.

"Thank you, Little Sister," I said humbly.

Then I left the Black Shrine, and, a few minutes later, dressed for the street, I passed out of the Temple building.

AFTERWORD

I retired from business. I have money enough and more than I shall ever use. I made a will, leaving everything to that kindly little maid who also serves. No one else had ever manifested any regard for me. Yet—she had "prayed".

A week ago I awoke from out a sound slumber. The room was so black that there might as well have been no room. There came a soft gleam of radiance! Clearly against the blackness, I saw the Silver One herself. A question passed from my mind to hers.

"Not yet," came her gentle, pitying reply. "It is another than I who will come—even as he said."

"Tell me," I implored. "May I write these matters out for the dwellers of earth to read?"

"You may—if it be your wish," she consented.

"When shall I—" I recommenced, but she shook her head in negation, and I did not finish that query. She smiled and was gone! But I lay awake awhile, staring into the darkness; and as I stared, a vision formed.

I saw a small, barren-looking planet, as yet scarcely cooled, whereon dwarfish, distorted creatures, low in the scale of evolution, yet strangely *aspiring;* strove ever with a race of giants, malignant, brutish, stolid, stupid.

But what it was they strove for; or what part I was to take in their affairs—I saw not then, nor do I know as yet.

Only, I wait. Wait, that I may once again *serve* —

And, somehow, I do not think my waiting will be very long!

He Refused to Stay Dead

Ghosts? We think of them as pale, faintly luminous doubles or counterparts of people who have departed from this life. But are these the only true ghosts? Isn't it possible that ghosts of the dead sometimes evade the powers that watch over them? May not phantom wraiths sometimes slip stealthily into the bodies of new-born infants? — to take up again some love or hate not consummated?

Was I myself such an infant so chosen to fulfil the destiny of some dissatisfied ghoul? At times I doubt it. Comforting thoughts come, and I deem it all my imagination. Yet, at other times I feel positive that such an one I surely am! For I have, at intervals, remembrances of that which I dare not admit, even to myself.

My hair is white, my face is lined with the deep furrows due to shock; my eyes reflect within their staring depths something of that awful terror which has made of me an old man long before my time. For as years are counted, I am still fairly young, being on the near side of forty; yet I look and conduct myself more like a man over sixty.

My experience has been terrific. But let the facts speak for themselves:

During the World War I was with Allenby's forces in the Mesopotamia campaign, and I saw things then which I do not like to think about. Yet when I returned to England I was in no wise altered in appearance, save that I had been considerably browned by exposure to sun and weather. I took up the threads of civilian life precisely where I had dropped them, and was, as life goes, a contented and happy man. And why not? I was my own master once again. Furthermore, I was engaged to a most charming girl, even before the War, and she waited for me faithfully with that same sweet, half-shy graciousness.

She was dark haired, dark eyed, exquisitely formed; her face one of that rarely-seen but never-to-be-forgotten type which artists and others romantically inclined describe as "Oriental," perhaps because of the combination of dark eyes and hair, and slightly olive-tinted complexion.

Edwina was quite the antithesis of myself; for I, Eric Marston of Falconwold, English born and English bred, am typically English in appearance. I stood, before I acquired this feeble stoop, nearly six feet in height, was rather bony in structure, florid featured, gray eyed, and with light, almost yellowish-brown hair.

Was it memory on my loved one's part that, even as a child, she would have none of the good old English name of "Maud" bestowed upon her by her lady-mother — insisting that, instead, her name was Edwina? I am sure of it now. She was, as I have just implied, a trifle peculiar, given to reading odd books, studying forgotten languages, positively reveling in folklore, in tales of witchcraft, and in legends of the various historical places nearby.

She questioned me eagerly regarding the scenes and traditions of the country through which I had passed with Allenby's forces. Naturally, I could tell her but little. A trooper on active service has small time to post himself on such topics. Foreseeing this, however, I had brought back with me such few mementoes as could with ease be transported.

An old Arab, dying, gave me as a last token of esteem, a small stone amulet, which he assured me solemnly was a very potent talisman. Both sides of the little octagonal tablet were intricately carved with queer characters. I call them "queer" advisedly, for a very distinguished savant assured me that they were in no known language, ancient or modern, of which he had ever heard.

But Edwina, the instant I showed her the talisman, gasped, murmured a strangely musical phrase, and went off into a dead faint.

Naturally I was appalled, horror-stricken. Had this occurred before the War, I doubtless would have resorted to the usual methods of lovers, and taken her into my arms, covered her face with kisses, murmuring fond and foolish endearments.

But my late experiences had taught me the value of practical methods. Despite my perturbation, I promptly brought her out of her swoon. And as soon as she came to herself she demanded the talisman. I was not overly pleased at the idea of her having anything more to do with the confounded thing, and expressed myself plainly, telling her out-and-out that if I'd know the effect it was to have upon her, I'd never have brought the amulet from the Near East.

She smiled all that away, as she did my request that she translate for me the phrase she'd uttered before she fainted. All in all, I was a badly puzzled man, and a somewhat angry one as well, when I took my leave shortly after.

But from then on, Edwina wore that talisman as a thing sacred.

"It helps me to know myself, for I lost that charm ages ago," she would state with a look in her eyes I did not at all admire. It was as though she gazed into infinity and saw something which, while it evidently pleased her, left me completely out of her calculations and out of her life.

"She'll get over her notions, once we're married," I'd assure myself. But at times I'd wonder if she would. "And if she didn't get over her notions?" "Oh, well, I'll make allowances!" Every lover has indulged in the same sophistry.

I was a proud and a happy man when I took her, as my wife, over my ancestral home, the gray old castle of Falconwold—from then on, to be her home likewise. Romantically inclined as she was, there was enough romantic history attached to the place to satisfy even her seemingly insatiable nature. And as for legends, both historic and supernatural, there was goodly supply of both.

Although Falconwold had a ghost, there was but little known about it. Once only had it ever manifested itself, and that was many, many years ago, away back in the time of King Charles the First. An event that occurred during that period gave rise to the belief that "our" ghost dated back to at least the time of the First Crusade.

There were two brothers of the house of Falconer, according to the story told me. Hotheads, both, given to dicing, gaming, carousing, and all the follies of that period. Touchy, too, upon points that pertained to their "honor."

Filled with wine and self-esteem, these two brothers—and to make a black matter even blacker, be it said that they were twins—came to words late one night over a notorious beauty of the court.

To such hotheads there was but one course open. In less than no time the center of the floor was cleared, swords were out, and with but a valet each for seconds, the madcap brothers started to finish each other off as deliberately as Cain slew Abel.

Their slim rapiers had no more than touched when, without sound or warning, there appeared suddenly a mighty arm with broad bands of gold gleaming around it, and in its mighty hand was an enormous sword—such a blade as those two foolish brothers could scarcely have lifted, together.

In sheer mockery that terrific, spectral long-sword played between the would-be fratricides; played around them and about them, brandished lightly as a feather in that huge hand. Gleaming and flashing with a lurid flicker, it swept in dazzling arcs until the brothers, appalled, dropped their silly splinters of rapiers to the floor and clung to each other in their mutual fear. At which, in final, supreme mockery, the great blade saluted them in different fashion than that in vogue at their period. A deep, bellowing gust of derisive laughter pealed in their aghast faces—and the apparition vanished as abruptly as it had materialized. So the story ends.

Needless to say, Edwina was gifted with a considerable

share of that strange spiritual faculty called "intuition." I related the tale of our family ghost to her, and asked her what she thought about it. Her reply rather surprised me.

"Surely," she exclaimed, "that was no Crusader's ghost! The spectral long-sword apparently gave birth to that idea. But the Crusaders wore armor, and that spectral arm was bare, with great torques of gold gleaming about it. And that seems more like one of the ancient Northmen. I think, Eric, that the ghost of Falconwold dates far back beyond the First Crusade."

But her mind refused to stop at that point. Would that it had! Her next question came direct.

"How long has this castle stood as it is? And when was it commenced?"

"Allowing for additions and renovations, it was first begun by a Saxon Thane in the time of Alfred, which would be about the year 800 or 900 A.D.," I replied. Then, struck by a sudden thought, I added: "Incidentally, there are old monkish scrolls in the library, handwritten, in black-letter—"

After that chat, whenever Edwina was missing from the usual living rooms, I knew exactly where to locate her. She became a veritable bookworm, seemingly engrossed in her researches amongst the musty old parchments in the somber library of Falconwold castle.

There came a day when I glanced up from my desk, where I was going over certain rentals and other business accounts, to see Edwina standing before me, a strangely exultant look in her dark eyes.

"Oh, Eric!" she exclaimed, all excitement. "The most wonderful, amazing discovery—"

In her hands she held an old, yellowish-stained scroll of parchment which she opened and spread before me on the desk. It was in black letters which I could not read. To her it was as plain as everyday print, and she proceeded to render its bad Latin into good modern English for my benefit.

It would take too long to give it in detail, and would seem too prolix, for those old monks were not sparing of their words—but briefly, the scroll revealed to us an heretofore unknown page of the history of Falconwold. Allowing for brevity, I give it almost literally:

I, Rolf the friar, who am Chaplain to Count Hamo Falconer in this his castle of Falconwold, have, by virtue of the power vested in me as an humble servant of our Lord, this day placed upon the oaken door which closes the burial mound of the Norse Viking, Thorulf Sword-Hand, that symbol which all such as he—Trolls, ghosts, vampyrs, witches, warlocks, and their ilk—fear and avoid.

With proper exorcisms, with bell, book, and candle, and with earnest prayers, I affixed the charm, carved upon a silver plate to the door, so that that evil being should be thereby bound, obliged to await in his own proper grave-mound the coming of that final great Day when all bonds shall be sundered.

But until that time, no more shall the revengeful ghost of Thorulf the Viking be reunited to his unhallowed body to the sore travail of the countryside, for I affixed the silver seal, the symbol of power, at a time when his ghost wandered in the castle, leaving his Troll's body still seated at the table within the barrow-mound.

Let no mortal hand disturb the Silver Seal that holds him fast, lest that be liberated which may not again be restrained—

From that point onwards, the scroll told that Thorulf the Viking was buried somewhere on the lands of Falconwold; that he had landed on our coast with a strong following of Northmen at his back and had promptly attacked the castle, some ninety years before the scroll had been written. After a bloody resistance, the garrison had been conquered. Thorulf with his own long-sword had slain the Saxon Thane Eric, and had taken Eric's beauteous wife for his—Thorulf's—leman.

So, with his Northmen Thorulf had held Falconwold, terrorizing the countryside with sudden, fierce raids. But Eric left a son, which boy Thorulf had spared at his mother's pleading. This son, coming to man's estate, fled the castle. He, Harold, son of Eric, in his turn gathered to him a great force of Saxons, stormed the castle, and in the fierce affray which followed Thorulf Sword-Hand was slain by Harold.

But Harold seems to have been a merciful man, according to those wild times, for he forbore to slay all the Northmen. Instead, he suffered those who had survived the actual fighting to inter Thorulf after their wild, heathen Norse fashion, and had then allowed them to sail away wherever it might please them; only, he exacted from them a solemn oath that never again would one of them set foot on English soil.

Thereafter, Edwina never rested content until she located the exact place where Thorulf had been buried. It proved to be a low hillock which I had always supposed to be natural; and located only about a thousand yards from the castle. And that added fresh fuel to Edwina's enthusiasm.

She coaxed so earnestly that I detailed a small party of workmen to start excavating. They had better success than I had anticipated, for in a couple of days John, the head gardener, came to me late one afternoon reporting:

"We've uncovered what looks to be a door of some most mighty hard wood with stone doorposts and lintel. Door's got a queer plate of some black metal fixed on't, and lot of odd letters burnt into the wood above the plate and on each side and below, too. Will you come and inspect it, sir — or shall us break in the door first? Although" — he added dubiously — "it's going to be none so easy a job, breaking in that door. That wood do be as hard as iron, a'most."

"Leave things as they are," I replied after a moment's consideration. "Send the men about other matters until I tell you to resume work there. Get them all away from that vicinity. Do you understand?"

He departed reluctantly, obviously consumed by curiosity, but I gave him no explanation. I meant that Edwina and myself should be the first ones to see what lay hidden within that burial mound. And if any breaking in was to be done, I considered my own muscles fully adequate to the task in hand.

It was late in the afternoon, as I have said, and for once Edwina was reasonable, agreeing with me that it would be better to wait until morning before commencing on that door. But she was in a high state of excitement, as I was myself, for we both realized what a wonderful thing was this finding of the actual tomb of one of those daring Northmen who in their time had so thoroughly stamped their seal of terror upon the little island Kingdoms of the Angles.

That night I dreamed a strange dream, if it indeed was a dream. Rather I should say that the gates of the past had opened and allowed me to know somewhat of a former life, wherein I had sown causes that were soon to bear strange fruits for Edwina, for myself, and for another...

I saw myself, clad in much different garb than that of this present time. I knew that I was I, yet also I knew that I was that same Eric the Falcon, that Saxon Thane who had built him the strong, fortified castle of Falconwold as a defense against forays of the wild, Northern sea-thieves.

In the dream-vision I sat in my great hall. Outside a tremendous tempest was raging. Presently there rushed in a shock-headed serf. His hair was dripping, his jerkin was saturated, but his manner betokened wild delight.

"A foreign ship—such as never before saw I the like of—in distress!" he panted. "She will strike the rocks—soon! Rare pickings—from the—sea! In such storm she—will—surely—strike."

I came to my feet in wrath, cursing him for his impudence. Thanes were no lily-fingered, mealy-mouthed gentry in that far-off time. I knocked him asprawl with a hearty buffet from my fist.

"Thou dog," I roared, enraged. "Since when has Eric the Falcon been named a scavenger-bird? There is a foreign ship in distress—and will surely strike, eh? Then will her people be in sore need of help! Get thee to thy feet, oaf, and summon thy fellows—"

A well-planted kick did the rest, and he scrambled up from among the rushes strewing the floor and left the hall much more rapidly than he had entered. I heard his voice raised against the tumult of wind and rain. To enforce his summons, I seized a great war-horn and blew blast after blast upon it. Then I tore out of the building and raced down to the beach where presently I was joined by my men, serfs and freedmen together.

Black squalls and a torrential downpour of rain made sight a difficult matter, but dimly through the murk we could at intervals catch glimpses of the doomed stranger. A long, low ship she was, slender, evidently build for speed. She showed the ragged stumps of two masts. Her prow bore no effigy of dragon nor of serpent, which fact we all noted with relief. At least, she was not a long-ship of the dread Northmen.

In that frightful gale time seemed to stand still. I had no idea how long we watched that doomed ship striving to claw off-shore and win its way back to open sea again, but suddenly the end came. A black squall, worse than any so far, rushed landward—there was an interval during which the keenest eyes lost all sight of her—then as the light, feeble enough at the best of times, grew a trifle brighter—behold! there was no ship struggling upon the tumultuous waters.

Some of my followers cursed bitterly because the sea-demons had robbed them of all hopes of flotsam and jetsam; but I cursed them in turn for their heartlessness. But in the midst of it all, I saw a gleam of white flesh, an arm, momentarily revealed in the surf.

"One lives," I shouted, and dashed into the boiling, roaring waves that thundered our rocky strand. To his credit be it said, that same serf who had brought me the tidings of the wreck about to take place, and whom I had stricken to the floor, took to the water only a pace behind me. Later, I remember, I rewarded him for that bit of loyal service by giving him his freedom, and a hide of land to boot.

Had it not been for his help, I would never have won to the kindly land again. Undertows dragged at me, sand and pebbles slipped and rolled beneath my feet, foam and spray stung my eyes, blinding me; yet somehow I managed to grasp that which I knew by sense of touch alone to be a woman—a woman, and still alive, although well-nigh sped.

Hardly had I seized her when two great hands clamped fast hold upon me, and that shock-head serf bawled in my ear:

"There be no more—back to land, Master!"

He spoke truly enough. No other body, living nor dead, came ashore, then or later. Nor was any wreckage ever picked up from that lost ship, although I sent men up and down the coast for half a day's journey, searching.

In my arms I bore her to the great hall, where I laid her down upon the wide bench before the bright fire in the broad, deep hearth-place. Then, and only then, did I observe that she was young, also very fair to look upon, despite the cruel buffeting she had endured from storm and wind and wave.

I called the women of the household to attend to her needs and comfort. Late that night one of them reported to me that the stranger-woman slept but had first spoken, briefly, in a language none of the women could understand.

For that matter, neither then nor ever could any be found who could understand her musical speech, which sounded to our ears more like singing. But, she, being quicker of wit than we dull Saxons, gradually mastered our rough tongue. "Edwina," she named herself; daughter of an Arab *rais,* or ship-captain. And many were the strange tales she told—tales of her own land, and of other lands and of races of men about whom not I nor any I knew, ever had heard…

Then my dream changed.
I was conscious that a considerable lapse of time had transpired. The sea-waif, Edwina, had grown more beautiful with returned health and strength. She was given to practices that had already caused the members of my household to murmur that she was a witch. Much she consorted with an old woman, one Elfgiva, who was, all knew, still a worshipper of the old gods—and from that same Elfgiva, most assuredly, Edwina learned nothing good.

Yet, in my dream, I loved that dark-eyed maiden from the seas; and, although by our Saxon law, what I had torn from the sea was mine, I would in no wise constrain her. Wherefore, instead, I wooed her and, later, wed her. The clergyman who wed us bestowed upon her by my wish and her consent the good old Saxon name of Alrica, which name had been well and honorably borne by my mother in her time…

So my dream ended.

At breakfast the morning following my glimpse into my forgotten past, I greeted my wife half seriously, half jestingly with:

"Edwina—Alrica—which are you? Are you Arab—or Saxon—or English?"

She stared at me, amazement writ plainly on her flawless features, and in her darkly luminous eyes a look of dawning comprehension.

"So, you know! What do you know?" she queried earnestly.

In detail I related my dream, and she followed me attentively.

"It makes me very happy—that you do know," she stated gravely. "All this I have known for a long while; even before we were married—in the Twentieth Century. But, oddly enough, just as I ceased being Edwina and became Alrica, there my knowledge ends; nor can I remember what came after—"

"Unless the record of Rolf the friar is at fault or misstates," I said, "we know fairly well what came after. You were kidnapped by this Thorulf Sword-Hand and—"

"B-r-r-r!" she retorted. "I am glad I cannot remember, if that's the case. Let us forget that part, Eric. Let the dead past remain buried!"

It would have been well for us both had we done that very thing, literally! But curiosity, that fatal curse of mankind, drove us on; and—as I now think—something else, a terrible mind, unhuman, outside the pale of kindly humanity, was working on our mind for purposes unholy—evil purposes that had held to one fixed course throughout a thousand years and more. The demoniac mind of that fierce Northman, Thorulf Sword-Hand, who, according to the scroll of the chaplain, Rolf, had become a Troll—and who, slain, had refused to stay dead, but whose unhallowed body could in no manner pass the magic symbol that held him prisoner; while at the same time, his revengeful ghost could not get back to its material frame—

It all sounds mad enough, I know, but—let the ensuing events tell their own story.

That door was, as John the gardener had stated, almost as hard as iron. The wood, buried and sealed from air throughout all the long centuries, had slowly seasoned instead of rotting. Furthermore, it was built of thick, square-hewn means fully nine inches through. In its center was a plate of blackened silver which I rubbed with dirt until it shone a trifle brighter. Edwina scrutinized it closely.

"Oh, look, Eric!" she exclaimed. "The old monk was no mere dabbler in magic! It is the seal of Suleiman the Wise—that same seal with which the great King of old bound the races of the Djinns."

And a moment later:

"Oh, bother! That silver plate is fastened squarely over a lot of the words branded on the door. Eric, those characters are Norse runes; the old, old magic letters and words. I cannot read them all, but I can read enough… I wish that plate did not cover so many of them."

To please her, before she was aware of my intention, I drove the sharp edge of a spade under one corner of the square silver plate, and wrenched. It came partially loose and sagged askew, held by one spike only. I grasped it and tore it completely free. Edwina emitted a warning cry.

"Stop! It is the Seal of Suleiman! It may not be tampered with, lightly. You are too bold, Eric."

"Nonsense!" I smiled. "What do you suppose I care about a few queer triangles engraved on a silver plate—if its removal pleasures you?"

But the smile died out on my lips even as I spoke. A ghastly chill pervaded the air. Even though the sun shone so brightly a moment before, somehow the light had become awesomely dulled, as when an eclipse occurs. A feeling of such horror as never until then had I known, not in all my war experience, surged through me; and, to crown that horror—through the great oaken door I thought there came the sound of low, rumbling, mocking laughter. We stood appalled, staring at each other. Then with an effort I regained my self-control.

"Clever grave-robbers we are," I jeered, humorously. "This is the Twentieth Century, the era of materialism, and in broad daylight—"

I swung up a sharp, heavy axe and attacked that massive door at one edge. Where, as we both noted, was something very like a great lock of greenish metal that was unquestionably formed of hammered bronze. I was no weakling, yet before I had chopped all around that lock it was growing dusk. And I had started on it considerably before noon. I suppose I should have become exhausted by my exertions long before I finished the job, but instead, a strength almost superhuman seemed to possess me. It was precisely as if I were anxious to get within for some motive far above that of mere curiosity — almost as though I had an appointment with that which dwelt within.

Edwina suggested that I stop, and resume once again the next day, but that suggestion I flatly vetoed.

"By no means will I stop now!" I exclaimed emphatically. "It will be dark inside there at any time of day or night. We'll go and refresh ourselves with supper, get flashlights, and I at least will come back. I've just gotten fairly started, and things will become interesting from now on."

But after all, it was nearly midnight before the last barrier was down and our way cleared. Edwina had asserted that she would stay with me to the end of the adventure, and I had not the heart to make her return to the castle. So, together, each holding a flashlight, we entered, and looked about us cautiously.

In a way, it was an impressive sight we gazed upon. Or, rather, it must have been so when first that Norse sea-thief was walled within the tomb.

Picture to yourself a thick oak table some nine feet long and over four feet broad. At the head of the table, facing the doorway, was placed a great chair, also of hewn oak, and seated therein —

He had been a veritable giant in his day, and seemed but little shrunken despite the ages since he had departed this life. On his head was a helm of metal, from the sides of which, just above his temples, there curved upwards like a crescent moon, two horns, and from the dull yellow gleams they gave off, they were wrought from gold.

In his left hand he held an enormous drinking cup of gold, gem-encrusted; but in his right hand he grasped the thick handle of a huge long-sword that lay extended on the table, point toward the door.

His shoulders and his torso were covered with chainmail;

but then, as we first viewed him, seated, we could not see his body at all. A bristling, matted beard covered most of his face.

"Was he embalmed, then? And if not, why has he not crumbled to dust long ago?" I said, breaking the dead silence in which Edwina and I had been staring at this strange and awful relic of a long-forgotten age.

She shuddered. "I do not think the Northmen understood the art of embalming. Oh, Eric, it's too terrible! Let us go, quickly. I am afraid. It kept itself—in preservation—for a time at least—Rolf the friar did well to warn— *That* is why he made exorcisms and placed the seal of the Wise King— Oh, come away, Eric, before it is too late! Oh, Eric, Eric—*it – is – too late – now!*"

Her voice rose gradually to a horrified shriek; she ended on a gurgling, choked note, sighed, and, smitten into merciful coma by sheer terror, Edwina crumpled in a tumbled heap to the floor.

I well-nigh joined her! Man though I was, soldier though I had been, materialist as I had always held myself, I, too, very nearly screamed at what followed. The closed eyes had slowly opened. The wide, ugly mouth opened cavernously in an amazing yawn, disclosing blackened tushes more like those of a wild boar than anything resembling human teeth.

A low chuckle sounded though the charnel-chamber. Then, haltingly, as one renewing acquaintance with a long-disused tongue, the hideous Troll-thing spoke in a voice whose every tone sounded in my ears precisely as if filtering through glue or slimy ooze.

"What? After all these ages? It is Eric the Falcon—the Bright Falcon of those accursed dogs of Saxons—come again to earth? Eric—whom long ago I slew, taking his lands and his very beautiful wife for my own! And now Eric came again, and opened for my spirit the way back to my body— Ho! a rare jest, Saxon dog! Thine was the hand that pulled away that silver plate I dared not pass! Great haste was thine, fool, to enter my barrow and bring back to me that same fair woman—

"Why, Saxon, it is kind of thee! Long have I waited. Yet thou hast come—even as that Devil-goddess I visited in Hela's Halls swore to my raging soul—she swore, too, that if I would yield her reverence and service I should await thy coming throughout the ages, still in mine own body. Saxon, I claim my bride! Get thee hence, swineherd!"

Oh, now I knew why I had been so determined to cut through that door. That *I* which is greater than I, knew that the Troll-thing dwelt therein, and had a heavy score to settle... I heard my own voice, hoarse with wrath, speaking in frenzied words that came from I knew not where.

"Thorulf Sword-Hand! Sea-thief, murderer, ravisher in life! And in death, Troll, Vampyr—I, Eric of Falconwold, name thee *Niddering*—"

But at that word, the worst that could possibly be applied to a Northman, the Troll, who had risen, slowly, lumberingly, from his great chair and taken his first stride towards me, stopped short.

"*Niddering? A coward? I?*" His gluey tones held a note of unbelief, incredulity, as though he could no longer trust his hearing.

"Aye, Niddering! *Thorulf Niddering,*" I cried ferociously, almost into his matted beard. "Niddering—and worse! Art armed, hast a long-sword, and I am empty-handed! Art clad in armor, and I in cloth, yet thou dost threaten, bid me hence! Thou, Thorolf Niddering, dare not fight me, whom once thou didst slay, with weapons! Had I but a knife, I'd send thee yelling with fear, back to that Devil-goddess who rules in Hela's Halls with a fine tale—"

He heard me out, standing motionless, his ugly head nodding reflectively; while in his vampyr eyes the hell-lights flickered and flared.

"Behind my chair—a battle-axe," he growled. "It is a good axe. Long ago I took it from a Christ's-man. I will not touch it—but thou—get it, Saxon! I will fight thee once again—for her," and he pointed, leering evilly, at Edwina, lying there so still and white.

For a single second I mistrusted—and why not? It was no man, but a demon I stood facing. That great brand, his long-sword! But as if reading my thought, he lowered the point to the floor and folded his huge hands on the ball-shaped pommel. I knew I must chance it—for Edwina's sake.

In a single bound I was past him, had grasped the axe from where it leaned against his chair. I whirled about, leapt between him and my unconscious woman.

"Now, Sea-thief, Troll, Vampyr," I shouted, defiant.

"Harsh names, Saxon," he grumbled, "after I gave thee a good axe!"

My flashlight I had placed on the table, so its rays would be cast on us as we stood. Edwina's had slipped beneath her when she fell. There was a gruesome, greenish-blue half-light that pervaded all the charnel-chamber; I know not whence it sprang. But in that weird light I could see the Troll-thing's eyes shine lurid as he lashed out at me with his ponderous brand. I parried it easily with the axe-head, for as yet Thorolf's arms were awkward and stiff, as well they might be.

Then began, full-swing, one of the strangest battles ever fought—a battle between man the soul-bearer, and that which had lost its soul's heritage, becoming one of the horrible Undead—one who, slain, had sold his right to dwell in Valhalla for revenge and a life that was not life! And the prize of that fierce conflict between us twain was the body, and soul, of her who lay there so motionless, so waxy-white that I surely deemed her dead, and silently thanked God that such was the case. For it could then possess only the inanimate body—yet from that horror, too, I must save her!

Once that thick voice rumbled *"Thor Hulf!"* The old, wild, Northman battle-cry! And I retorted "God's Help!" Then jeered the Thing with biting scorn.

"Thor will never heed thee, Troll," I mocked. "Thor sits in Valhalla with the honorable brave, and holds no traffic with Hela's brood!" And thereafter we fought in a grim silence.

Quicker of foot I was, but the Troll had advantage of reach both of arm and weapon. Wherefore he did most of the attacking, while I could but parry the sweeps of the enormous longsword, dodge and swerve, and, at rare intervals, swing a futile blow at his arm with the heavy, double-bladed axe.

Where the thought came from, I have no means of knowing, but into my mind leaped, full-born, the certitude that could I once get the Thing out of his burial-mound and into the open, where was greater room, I might yet have a chance.

To that end I used all the craftiness I could command. Feinting, swerving, leaping backward and ever sidewise, I worked toward the entrance. Somehow, as by mutual consent, unspoken but understood, we both avoided trampling on Edwina as we fought past where she lay...

We were outside! A thunderstorm was raging, and in my soul I thanked Heaven for it. The rain refreshed me, and I had the kindly lightning to see by. It was Nature's own light, and not that greenish-blue hell-light that shone, unnatural, within the charnel-chamber.

My foot struck against something! I staggered. The battle-axe flew from my grasp as I strove wildly to regain my balance. The Troll's great sword, swinging, barely brushed my shoulder with its flat—well for me it was not the edge! But lightly as it touched, it was enough to finish my stability. I went asprawl!

The Demon-Thing strode heavily forward, grinning hideous joy, intending to make an end! My hand touched something hard and smooth. In desperation I clutched it, swung back my arm, and flung whatever it was I had picked up fairly into the middle of that triumphant leering abhorrence of a face —

God's mercy — and His help!

A wailing yell that turned me sick to hear — and the Troll threw wide its arms, crashed backward, lay prone and forever still! I scrambled to my feet, seized the axe I had let fall, ran to the monster, whirled the axe aloft to behead — but there was no need.

Even as I looked, the Thing began to crumble into dust. Aye, even the bronze and leather, the great long-sword, and, likewise, the horn-hafted battle-axe I was holding, slowly but surely disintegrated! There was no longer a hell-preserved body — only a gleaming skeleton, gigantic, white in the lightning's flare. Then that, too, dissolved into a soft paste from the falling rain. I saw a shine of metal where the head had lain on the ground. I picked it up —

God's help — and His help is very potent!

Falling, I had grasped and flung at the Troll the silver plate which the monk of old, Rolf, had fastened to the door of the barrow! The dark hell-charm that had preserved that Troll-Thing throughout the ages, was not proof against the White Magic of Rolf, servant of the powers of light. His silver seal had done that which not human arm nor heavy battle-axe had availed to achieve.

I crept within that accursed charnel-house, and, weeping and wailing like a frightened child, I sought and found the still form of my beloved. Stumbling through the storm, I bore her to the castle. The dawn was breaking.

Then — I collapsed.

Edwina recovered consciousness shortly after the noon of the third day following. Her hair is as white as mine but her beauty is unimpaired. She did not see what happened after the Thing opened those eyes of red fire.

She was badly shocked at my aspect when she beheld me, as

I was also when first I looked at myself in a pier-glass, after I'd somewhat recovered from my collapse.

Only once did she seek to question me. We were idly sunning ourselves on a bench in the garden at the time, and she asked, a trifle listlessly:

"Eric, what occurred? Did Thorulf—"

But I looked her squarely in the eyes and—lied!

"Oh, Thorulf crumbled into dust shortly after you fainted. Ask no more, Edwina."

I had the burial-mound blown up with high explosives. Specialists assure me that I may eventually recover wholly from—whatever it is that has made me as I am. But they are badly puzzled by my case, for I tell them nothing.

Edwina promised to ask no more questions. She has kept her word; yet, woman-like, she has very nearly violated it.

Yesterday she slipped her hand in mine as we walked, saying:

"Eric, though my body lay in a swoon—yet I somehow know and remember all that happened! I think—Eric—that the soul—never loses—consciousness."

The Dark Lore

As an occultist of some thirty years' standing, it has been my lot to listen to some strange stories and tales, for I have been called upon to hear confidences, some of which were horrifying in the extreme—things which almost appalled me, but never quite, for two reasons. One is that once I myself passed through an experience so frightful that nothing happening thereafter has ever availed to wholly upset my equanimity. And the other and more important reason is simply this:

The Great Law is *just!* Equal and opposite vibrations cancel each other. Sin as deeply as one may, still redemption is possible, nay, certain, after the equivalent proportion of suffering has been experienced. Thereafter, whoso has sinned may build Sin's opposite of Good until the last scars of Evil are erased from the sight of men and angels, and the soul once again shines stainless...

Repeatedly I have emphasized this to those poor, sick souls who have crept to me, sobbing out their griefs, fear-stricken, all hope vanished, yet desirous of relieving their sadly overburdened minds by "talking it over" with one who could at least sympathize because he could understand, and who, they knew, would not shrink from them, poor spiritual outlaws though they might be.

So, to me has been granted a privilege that has brought tears of humility to my eyes many times; the highest and holiest privilege to which the eternal-living spirit may hope to attain while still inhabiting the body of the flesh—that of sometimes reassuring and comforting a fallen soul that has been drawn into the abomination of desolation, clutched by the grisly hands of the powers of darkness. And because I have been, perchance, of some slight help along such lines to them, there are a few who speak of me as a "soul-doctor."

Yet never, I say this truthfully, have I betrayed a confidence reposed. True, I have given some stories to the world, as I may give others. But always with the consent of the principal character involved — never otherwise.

And now, by her actual, expressed wish, I release the terrible story told me in her own manner by her who was once upon earth named Lura Veyle.

I can recall, dimly, a time when I was innocent, spotless of soul, and with a mind unstained. But that was ages ago, if time be measured by experience rather than by the hands of a clock. Yet now, as earth-years are counted, I am but forty-one.

Oh, this hideous burden of memory! Can it ever be lightened? Horrific thoughts swarm up from the lowest depths of my consciousness wherein I have tried to bury them — stifling, choking me till speech becomes an overwhelming exertion.

Great sin have I wrought, power and triumphs unearthly have I known, arrogance has made of me first an evil-doer against all spiritual laws; and afterward an abject slave, exposed to the insults, jibes and derision of the leering legions of the Haters and Mockers infesting the outer voids!

Through hells unnamed till now I have passed, tortured and harried. From Flaming Furies I have fled in a blackness so dense it could be felt. Alone, I have wandered over the rocky face of a burned-out world, devoid of any inhabitant save myself.

Deep has been my suffering — and I have merited it, every bit! Nor has all of it sufficed to blot out my sin. Atonement is very far from complete. Yet, with soul laden with shame, I have struggled so high already that I dare say "Thank God," without shuddering in terror lest even worse befall me for venturing to breathe that Ineffable Name.

Behold me as I am! A dwarfed, bent, crippled, warped, hunchback. Hair hanging in wild elf-locks, gray and stringy, about my face. My face! It more nearly resembles that of an ape than of a woman. Blear-eyed, wrinkled, with evil writ so plain on my features that children run screaming and dogs bristle, snarling, as I pass. Yet I was, at twenty, considered the most beautiful young woman in a city noted for its examples of feminine pulchritude.

That beauty which was mine was my curse, yet not that alone caused my undoing and downfall. That was due to my unholy pride and self-conceit. Mortal happiness and the joys of earth were insufficient to gratify my inordinate ambition. Wherefore, in a world beyond this world I accepted pomp and power and dominion, and reveled therein; to the height of my desire and beyond, to horrors inexpressible.

I had a sister. She loved me. And so did I — love myself! She was my diametric opposite. Blond whereas I was brunette. Slender and petite whereas I was tall and voluptuously modeled. She was gentle and humble, and I, to my shame, was stern, cold, proud and haughty. She was kindly where I was cruel — ah! fill in for yourself all that was good as contrasted to all that was evil, wicked; and whenever the finer quality was manifest, be very sure that while it was descriptive of her, never by any chance would it apply to me.

All that was good and holy she was, and I, filled with the seeds of all that was bad — unsprouted, then, it is true; but soon, all too soon, to crack open and rear a writhing crop of clinging hell-weeds that eventually well-nigh strangled my immortal soul.

One loved her, and she adored him as only a pure and good girl can adore the man of her choice. And I adored him too, or thought I did, from the first moment I set my eyes on him. I had been prepared to ignore "her Edwin." She had enthused too much about him. "What a good man—" until I was nauseated at the sound of his name. Once, in a tantrum, I snapped:

"The sooner you two fools are married, the better for all concerned! After the honeymoon, when full acquaintance is established, perhaps we'll get a vacation from 'Edwin' and his multifarious perfections. He's just plain man like all the rest; and if you want my candid opinion, he's very much a 'he-sissy'!"

Even yet I can see the hurt look she bestowed upon me. But all she said was: "Wait, sister, until you've seen him. You'll love him, too."

I did—but not in the way she, in her innocence, meant!

There came a time when, during an interview which I deliberately schemed to bring about, I sought to turn his allegiance from her shrine to myself. And in terse, scathing phrases, he let me see, plainly, what a really honorably man thought of me and my attempt!

Humiliation, followed by a cold, deadly rage, suffused my entire being. Without further words I walked away from him. Nobody, observing us as we met at breakfast next morning, would have suspected that aught untoward had ever passed between us. Only he and I knew, and I knew, too, that very soon only I would ever know...

I'd heard the servant maids talking. There was an old gipsy woman, too old to travel longer with the caravans. Her sons had purchased for her a tiny plot of ground and a small cottage near where Lost River enters Deadman's Swamp. The maids had whispered of love-philters, charms, spells... One said: "She will only see those who love when the moon shines... those who hate when the dark o' the moon prevails."

That old gipsy was a disappointment to me. She heard me out, patiently. But she shook her head. Nor could a proffered bribe of a thousand dollars move her to change her determination.

"You do not belong in my circle," she said. "Nor does any that touches mine touch yours. I may not, dare not, help you. Yours is a strange fate. You must work out your magic wickedness or leave it alone. Yet if you desist from your purposes you will die from the hate-poisons in your blood. You had best go home and pray, then lie down and die. Otherwise, great evil will you wreak, although never on earth shall you be punished therefor."

In disgust, I left her presence, wordlessly.

But all that night one sentence ran through my mind, excluding all else:

"You must work out your magic wickedness or leave it alone."

An ignorant, illiterate, uncivil old gipsy! There must be a higher, stronger magic. I wrote to dealers in antique books. They mailed me lists such as they compile for collectors. So, I gained insight into ancient arts; such lore as it were well for all the world had it never been known!

Two photographs I took to a sculptor of my acquaintance. In exchange for a smile and a few low-spoken words, meaning less than nothing to me, but which went to his head like a powerful wine, the poor, infatuated fool made me two figurines from a white clay. And the likenesses, though small, were very perfect. I'd assured him they were intended as a wedding jest, and he believed me. What did he know of the Dark Lore? He considered himself overpaid when I allowed him to kiss my hand as I left his studio.

The terrible methods I employed in utilizing those figurines are best unrelated. None shall ever learn of that frightful sorcery from me, directly or indirectly. But—there was, within a month, a terrible auto accident. Edwin was unrecognizable. And she, my little sister, lived but ten days thereafter; a helpless, shuddering, apathetic wreck; vaguely moaning: "Edwee... Edwee..."

And I—exulted!

This is the curse of the Dark Lore—no sooner is one triumph achieved by its sinister aid than the drunken soul craves even greater conquests! And I was no exception.

Edwin? Was dead—through my spells, and lost to the world and me. But was he lost to *me?* True, his body I might never see more—but his spirit! Once again I turned to the forbidden books. And the Evil Powers beheld—and chuckled. On the night when I found that which I sought, there was mirth in many hells.

"Thus is the Mystic Lamp of the Adept prepared...

"But when ye shall come to light it, use ye not fire nor flame. Fairly in the center of a darkened chamber shall ye place it. Then must ye, circling about it, with woven paces and waving arms, whisper at low breath the Spell to the Fire-Sprites; until at length, streaming from all fingertips shall a flickering flame be seen. So, hold ye one hand each side of the holy lamp in such wise that the streamers of lambent flame do unite at that spot where is the wick fashioned from the thrums of the *Lapis Asbestus*. And if all be well and duly prepared, ye shall behold a marvel indeed.

"Yet observe the color of the flame the Lamp gives out, for it will be the color of the soul of whoso made that Lamp. And should the flame be silvery, know that high spirits love and guard ye. Shall it burn blue like the vault of heaven, then steadfast shall ye stand against all evil, sin, or shame. If it be of golden hue, deep is the knowledge to which ye shall attain, and wisdom worthily used is good to have. But should it blaze scarlet, know it emanates from a wrathful soul. Crimson shall betoken a nature filled with wicked desires. Purple shall tell of pride and of high command, although this may be well or ill; for there be colors holy as well as unholy, which may be known by their softness or by their glare..."

Vivid, glaring crimson, tinged with hectic purple rays, flooded that darkened chamber when I completed that experiment. And my lip curled in scorn of all consequence as I read in that illumination my secret nature revealed. To an humbler soul it might have served as a solemn warning. To mine it was but proof that I was great, and would be greater.

Thereafter, for eleven days I made another lamp each day,

which totaled a dozen. And on the twelfth night, I lighted them all at once. And each gave off that same glorious yet sinister brilliance as did the first with which I had experimented. Grouped together they filled the room with intense vibrations, much as the overtones of some great organ would thrill the soul of a musician. I had dared much; but had succeeded thus far in all I had attempted. Always the drunken soul seeks further conquest...

So, I drew the circle and the triangles, and at each angle save one I placed a lamp. The draperies of earth I removed from my person and tossed them aside indifferently. I was above all conventions, had cast off all inhibitions which hamper the mediocre. For I knew that power more than mortal was henceforth mine to wield as best pleased myself.

Then, with the remaining lamp, the twelfth one, held high in a hand which did not shake or quiver, I entered the magic circle — and only then did I close the gap in the mystic figure with that twelfth lamp. For several minutes I stood thus, reveling in the sense of my own importance and splendor, for I felt — royal! Then, with a wave of my hand I began the spell that should drag back the soul of lost Edwin from whatsoever dim realm it had reached. Once it had beheld *my* glory — knew *my* — power...

It came!

That command was too potent to be disregarded. And I beheld a white specter that gazed at me with eyes mutely reproaching me for that which I had done to him and his... Disillusion!

That? The poor, feeble, important, contemptible ghost — it was not worth summoning! Its love? Absurd! With a wave of my hand and a curt order I banished it from my presence. But what, oh! what was left?

In my mind, unbidden, unsought, there formed another incantation. I swear that never had I read *that* in any book. It was the clarion call of a soul athirst for love — the call of a soul high enough to be greatly daring — for that call would summon no lover from earth's weak children... I uttered it in clear, full tones. And I would that brain had shriveled and tongue withered ere I thought, and dared, that unholy evocation.

Yet what ensued was anything save terrifying! Came a blaze of regal, splendid, somber purple and dusky gold; and, lo! just outside the magic circle stood one whose lofty bearing and prideful look bespoke him no lowly, common spirit.

His great, luminous eyes met mine and in their depths I read full understanding and mutuality of purpose. On his lips a slow smile hovered, proclaiming louder than words the extent of his admiration of myself.

But back of him!

Rank on rank, stretching away in space as though no chamber walls existed, were ranged a throng, hardly less glorious than was he in appearance. Who or what he might be, I knew not—then. But one thing was very evident, would have been clear to a duller wit than mine—he was their Master, their Leader, their Overlord.

And mine!

None who has not faced such a being can comprehend the subtle urge which I knew then. Never thereafter for me could there be inclination toward mortal man, not though one such should lay at my feet all the treasures of Golconda.

That mighty being was kneeling just without the barrier of the protecting circle. His arms were outstretched, his fingers barely avoiding passing above the mystic lines traced upon the floor. And I—I laughed in his face. But not the derisive laughter of scorn—nay! it was the laugh with which a woman greets her well-beloved.

"Thou art a—demon?"

"Call me that, if thou wilt—thy 'demon-lover', and I'll be content!"

"But what, then?"

"A rebellious Angel—I!"

"Lucifer?"

"Not so—yet his co-equal!"

"Who, I said?"

"Hesperus!"

"And *I*?"

"Shalt share my throne and power!"

"On earth?"

"Here—and hereafter!"

Again I laughed. Triumphant. Thrilled at my evident power over such a being. But not thus easily was I to be won. I would make certain of his love.

"Nay, not tonight!"

He rose to his full height, folding his arms across his breast. His brilliant eyes flamed into mine—there was not a yard of distance between us, for I had unknowingly drawn close to the edge of the ring "Pass Not".

"Thou wilt summon thy Hesperus again, O Beloved?" The cadence of his tones thrilled me as never had I thrilled before.

"Assuredly."

"Soon?"

"Perhaps."

"A token from thee, my Queen, ere I depart?"

What had I to bestow? Then I remembered. On my finger I wore a ring set with a black opal. It had been my mother's and her mother's before her. But surely, it was mine now. It should have been sacred. But what was sacred to me—then? I stripped it from my finger, *kissed it*, and tossed it to him. And by that one piece of folly gave him a focus whereto he could always direct his thoughts, so, reach me, invariably, at his will! But I knew not that, at the time. Would that I had! The blaze of splendor—triumphant—from his eyes, well-nigh intoxicated me! I reeled backward to the center formed by the interlaced triangles. It was a genuine physical effort to keep from rushing forward again—to his embrace!

For a full hour I stood there, still guarded by the power of those protecting symbols I had traced upon the floor; accepting homage, as one by one his attendant host of lesser fallen angels and fiends and demons filed past me; each in his turn bending the knee and bowing his head in subjugation to their Lord's choice—their Queen to be! He, last of all his subject throng, saluted precisely as had the least of his followers. Then, he, too, vanished, and I was alone.

That night I slept fitfully. Visions of pomp, and pride, and power filled my mind to drunkenness. Little could I recall of them when daylight filled my room, but while the dreams lasted, they were gorgeous. No one had entered my room, that I knew, for the door was locked on the inside. Yet on my dressing table I found a necklace the like of which never was known on earth before.

It was a long chain of some dusky yellow metal, neither copper nor gold. The links were strangely wrought and intricately twisted. Pendant from every link hung a transparent, ruby-colored stone; each one fashioned artfully to the semblance of a small human heart. And, most peculiar feature of all, while each heart-shaped stone was in reality smooth, yet at a casual glance each one seemed to be actually sweating drops of blood!

A jeweler to whom I showed them said it was due to some peculiarity of crystallization; but he could not for all his skill and his experience of years name the stones; and he was a sorely puzzled man. Nor was he at all pleased when I refused to tell him whence I had them. All I would vouchsafe was: "Oh, a gift from a ruling Prince—an admirer..."

I wore the gift of Hesperus, for such I knew the necklace to be, to a ball that night. I was never popular with the members of my own sex, but on that night it seemed to me that many who had at least formerly pretended to be nice to me acted as though they actually feared me. There was a truly great statesman there. I had never formally met him. But as I passed him during the course of the evening, I saw such involuntary admiration betrayed in his eyes that I favored him with a dazzling smile.

I heard him query of the lady to whom at the moment he was talking:

"Who is that superbly beautiful creature?"

"Lura Veyle," she snapped, all out of patience with him. "Stuck-up thing..."

He contrived to get himself introduced to me. It was easily accomplished. There were mutual acquaintances. We did not dance. We sat—and *he* talked. He was a brilliant conversationist, and on that occasion he fairly outdid himself. Inwardly I smiled. It was so obvious. Later he wheedled me into accompanying him to a dimly lit balcony—"for a breath of fresh air," he said.

I'll admit I was flattered by his attentions. What woman wouldn't be? Hardly were we alone than—it was highly improper, especially from one such as he, with his social status—he attempted to slip his arm about my waist, murmuring: "I know—dear—it's presumption on such short acquaintance, but—Lura—I—"

It was as far as he ever got! Even in that half-light I saw his eyes protrude; while over his face came a look of unqualified terror. His knees gave from under him and he slumped down, whispering, "My—heart—"

Naturally, I shrieked! He lived barely long enough to gasp, audibly, so that others as well as myself heard him: *"The—Devil—"*

Truly, I knew myself the beloved of Hesperus!

Of course, the tragic episode broke up the ball. It was then just a few minutes past midnight, and naturally, all the guests went to their respective homes. I, however, had no intention of losing any sleep because of the regrettable circumstance. Wherefore, by 1:30 I was in my bed and sound asleep. But before 2:30 I was once more wide awake. Moved by an impulse I did not pause to analyze, I arose, donned a light kimono and slipped from my room to that empty chamber wherein I was accustomed to perform my strange and unhallowed practices.

Deliberately I caused the mystic lamps to ignite, and equally deliberately I refrained from drawing the protecting lines of the mighty ring "Pass Not," although I knew full well that unless I stood in the center of the potent dodecagon formed by the interlaced triangles, there would be no protection or safety for my spirit from the Haters who Haunt.

Yet I, in my arrogance, ignored that awful danger. It was well enough for lesser souls, I thought, contemptuously, to take all due precautions; but for me they were superfluous, puerile.

Was not I the beloved of the great Hesperus? Most assuredly, yes! Then what lesser powers dared molest *me*, when to do so would be to incur the full wrath of their puissant Overlord, whose terrific vengeance could nowise be escaped or averted?

Even more rashly, that I might emit no single detail which could aid in filling my cup of folly brimful and running over; after I had cast aside my earthly habiliments, with the exception of that wondrous necklace of ruby-colored, bleeding stone human hearts, I once more voiced that same incantation that had first brought my Dark Angel to my presence.

I had not uttered a third of the spell ere he arrived! And wondrous power that was his, for one moment he was a mighty spirit, devoid of material substance; and the next moment, his was a form as solid as my own, into whose arms I yielded myself! Our lips met — and in the next instant — I was in the halls of Hell!

Nor have I ever seen that body which was Lura Veyle since!

But I presume that they — my relatives and friends — interred the inert form with appropriate ceremonials; and praised the departed soul; and mourned my loss, after the fashion of Earth's dwellers.

I suppose I should have been either terror-stricken or else enraged, because of what had happened to me. But in truth I was neither angry nor frightened. I say it honestly — my sole reaction to that stupendous change was a certitude that I had reached home! For I actually felt thus. I had attained to my own proper place, my true environment!

To my added satisfaction I found that I was robed in splendor far surpassing the fairest dream of any earthly costumer. On my brow was a scintillant diadem of many-colored jewels. In my hand I was holding a scepter of gold, gem-studded, tipped with a great amethystine stone which was carven into a symbol strange to me; but which, I knew in some indefinable way, possessed in itself some very potent properties.

Obviously I was in a palace — the palace of Hesperus, Ruler of one of the realms of Hell. Equally obviously, I was in a chamber which had been prepared against my coming, for it was virtually a duplicate of my own personal room back upon Earth; excepting that the furnishings and fittings were of more splendid material and finer workmanship. I was standing before a great mirror, and reflected therein I could see myself as I was in all my glory.

Kneeling just before me, but one at each side a trifle, so as not to interfere with my view, were two shapely, nude, coppery-colored female slaves whom I rightly took to be there in the capacity of hand-maidens to my own royal self.

Oh, my soul knew where I was, and all that had happened, yet I pinched myself in several places — then I grasped one of the maids by the hair and tugged! The abject creature emitted a whimpering yell. I released her.

"But — but," I said, uncertain if they could understand my speech, "I seem — solid — as ever. You seem — solid..."

One, not her whose hair I had pulled, replied:

"O Regal Lady! Let this slave explain. Only your Earth-body have you departed from. When *you* are not in it, it cannot feel. You are now here. That which *felt* while in the Earth-body now feels *here*... Only one envelope have you abandoned; and the self has many envelopes yet remaining. Each resembles, but more — *this* — the outer one. Only it is really the other way about — for each one, going *outward,* is like the inner one, but coarser as one becomes more thick, until the greatest thickness is found upon Earth...

"But when the Earth-thick body is hurt, scars remain. Here no matter how badly the form may be injured, the wounds close again shortly — unless one is condemned to — destruction — by our Master..."

The slave faltered in her speech, while a look of ghastly fear overspread her intelligent features. Very low she whispered: "Before — *destruction* — are many — horrors to be undergone — then — the self is — *thinner* — in a different, but not less awful — Hell..." and again that look of ghastly fear hinted at the untellable...

There ensued for me all the splendor which lay within the power of Hesperus to bestow. Feastings, revelries unholy at which I presided co-equal with him; glories and triumphs unimaginable; ecstasies so thrilling that mind cannot in soberer moments comprehend such; and I was taught control of powers and forces stupendous; received homage from beings splendid, beings grotesque, and beings — or fiends — of malignancy so hideous they nearly appalled even my over-bold soul to gaze upon. These, all these and more, were mine for a period covering several Earth-years; for in full compliance with his given promise, Hesperus proclaimed me his Queen, and I shared his throne and his authority.

However, these matters I do not enter into detail about, for it is not of my triumphs and the gratifications of my inordinate ambitions, vanities, and arrogance that I would tell, but of what came after. But even before the crash occurred, I should have been warned, for there were times when I deemed, vaguely, that I detected a fleeting sneer on more than one countenance as some spirit, or fiend, bent the knee before me and bowed the head in token of subjugation.

But ultimately I could not conceal from myself that Hesperus was neglecting me; stating quietly that important affairs which concerned me as well as himself were demanding all his attention. And, perforce, with that meager explanation I must needs content myself. Finally, though, at a great banquet held in celebration of a victory over some band of Angelic Ones from a higher plane, my fate came upon me with a certainty leaving nothing to be hoped for.

As I entered the great hall by one portal, through another came Hesperus, and at his side glided with serpentine grace one who—I recognized the fact at a glance—had originated on some planet far different from that Earth whence I had fallen!

The mocking smile on her curling lip was all too unmistakable. Rage suffused me. All the Hell-nature that was mine rose up, rebellious; gone were all the fears of consequences to myself, and naught remained but hate and—revenge!

Long ere this happening I had learned one of the uses of that amethystine-tipped scepter. What injury it could inflict—if any—on the actual spirit, I knew not; but to the various layers, or shells, or souls—call them as may be most suitable—I knew that it could do much. With wrath sufficiently intense suffusing the bearer, simply by pointing at the hated one with that symbol, annihilation of all which was visible ensued, abruptly.

And it was full at the towering figure of the Arch-Liar Hesperus himself that I directed its full potency, rather than at the beguiled fool swaying so gracefully triumphant, serpentlike, at his left side.

And nothing happened!

Only, a yelling, screaming, hooting, howling tumult of demoniacal laughter rocked that vast hall to its very foundations.

The merriment of the utterly damned, rejoicing at the humiliation and the shame of her to whom, formerly, they had rendered abject homage!

Reverting to earthly methods, I drew back my arm and hurled that accursed scepter at the gravely smiling countenance of the Arch-Liar. Languidly he held up a hand, and the whirling scepter floated, light as a feather, into his grasp.

And a moment later, with no validation of my own, I found myself, denuded of all my regal robes and ornaments, crouched like any abject slave at his feet, helpless, unable even to move! While all about us crowded and jostled and swirled that fiendish throng, mocking, jeering, reviling me, gloating, appraising that beauty which was mine, so ruthlessly revealed.

Suddenly Hesperus singled out one from amongst that hideous mob. "Thou," he commanded.

The monster approached, bent the knee in fealty. I shuddered with horror at his aspect. A dreadful premonition overwhelmed me, and with it there came despair absolute, unleavened by any hope! I knew my fate.

I cannot adequately describe that—oh! *what* shall I term it—or him! All that I can say is—it was a huge, hairy-appearing brute, altogether bestial; yet in a way a most amazing travesty on the human type. Its back was furry, but what seemed to be hair, I learned later, was in reality more closely allied to the quills on a porcupine, although longer, thicker, and more sharply pointed. Its front was scaly skin like an alligator's underparts; and its awful, cruel face and head were of some horny substance closely resembling the upper shell of a turtle.

Add to all this two round, black, lackluster eyes, staring lidless, with a dull red glow showing beneath their inky surfaces; and two upper eyeteeth so long that they hung always bared nearly to the chin of the Thing—and you will have then but a poor and feeble word-picture. Its sole weapon was a ponderous, spike-studded bronze mace, nearly as long as the monster was tall.

"Thy name?" Hesperus demanded.

"Grarhorg!"

"Thy rank?"

"Guardian of thy watchtower of Nak-Jad, standing where thy north frontier o'erlooks the Gorge of the Gray Shine."

"A lonely, a drear, and a dangerous post," Hesperus said reflectively, while the rabble ceased its clamor in anticipation of that which was yet to come.

"All that," growled the beast-fiend, truculently. "Yet I hold it fast, under thee. Naught from the north has ever passed thy border unbidden since thou didst commission me the Guardian of Nak-Jad."

"The force under thee?"

"Composed of Vobwins, Sogmirs, and Miljips. A mixed array, a bare ten score; but sufficient, under me."

Hesperus nodded approbation of this modest speech.

"Thy recreations are—?"

"Holding thy line inviolate, as bidden."

"But thy followers?"

"Find it suffices them that I am not displeased. Nay, are they nobles of thy court, that they should know delight in soft dalliance?"

"Thou art bold, Grarhorg," Hesperus reproved sternly, but a moment later he fairly smiled with delight when Grarhorg, nowise abashed, retorted grimly:

"There is need of boldness in him who can hold Nak-Jad secure!"

"See, my Grarhorg"—Hesperus indicated miserable me crouched there between them as they faced each other—"here is some slight recompense for thy labors, a comfort in thy loneliness, and a toy for thy idle moments."

"Mine?" The monster seemed incredulous.

"Aye," nodded Hesperus, "a toy for thee."

A huge paw, with claws as long and as sharp as those of a bear, clamped down on my bare shoulder. I was tucked under the hideous fiend's arm as though I were an inanimate bundle. In a voice as harshly reverberating as the bellow of a great bull alligator, such as I have often heard by the river near our family home upon Earth, the monster roared, exultant: "Grarhorg, for this, will hold Nak-Jad safe though thou wert—pardoned!"

Even Hesperus laughed outright at the absurdity of that possibility; but that usurper Starling, swaying serpent-fashion beside her new Lord, asked, furthering the jest: "But why, Grarhorg, after he were pardoned?"

"Because he would soon return," retorted the brute. "What, do I not know my Lord by this time?"

"Enough of this," exclaimed Hesperus when the laugh died down. "Let the feast commence." He would have led the way to the long tables but Grarhorg spoke once again.

"Thy leave to return to Nak-Jad—now?"

"Small honor dost thou do us and our feast," Hesperus replied. "Why such haste?"

"This—my 'toy'," explained Grarhorg succinctly. "There is meat to be had in Nak-Jad for the eating, as well as here. Let this *infant* depart with his plaything, O mighty Hesperus."

"Farewell, sweet babe," mocked Hesperus. "Thou hast my permission."

Grarhorg, with no further words, turned from the festivities and strode out of the great hall to a wide, high-walled courtyard where he opened his ugly gash of a mouth and emitted a raucous howl. Came the swishing of mighty pinions, a fetid odor, and, swooping down from the air above, a winged nightmare descended.

It had the head of a crocodile, the neck of a serpent, a lizard's body, the legs and talons of a vulture many times magnified, and the wings were those of a gigantic bat. It towered above the huge Grarhorg half again as high. Grarhorg caught me by the neck in one great paw and held me out to the nightmare.

"Carry this—thou," he rumbled. "Harm it not—or *I* harm thee!"

The sinuous neck arched, the ugly head shot downward, and the bony jaws seized me by the middle. I felt every sharp-pointed tooth sink deeply into my waist, piercing me through and through. Writhing and screaming in agony unbearable, but which yet I had to endure, I beheld Grarhorg clamber to the back of the nightmare and seat himself where serpent neck joined lizard body. Smiting his frightful steed a heavy thump with his bronze mace he yelled:

"Back to Nak-Jad!"

I was but a sickly, whimpering, moaning, semi-conscious *limpness* when the Blood-Red Tower was reached. And that edifice I cannot describe at all. I was barely aware that that nauseating breath was no longer scorching my middle at the same time that both extremities were almost freezing from the intense cold of the air through which we had flown at a speed incredible. Dimly I could perceive a building and that its color was scarlet-red; but thereafter I never saw again its outside.

Grarhorg, descending from his seat on the nightmare's back, received me in one capacious paw and strode through a narrow door...

It is not within the scope of the human mentality to comprehend an infinitesimal portion, even, of the soul-nauseating outrages and degrading debaucheries to which I was subjected... Grarhorg—eventually tired—then—

Ensued a period so dreadful I lost even the concept of time. There were... Vobwins; Sogmirs; Miljips... each worse than the preceding ones... argh! I—I—

An abominable Sogmir, who, at his best, was fouler, more cruel, viler even than Grarhorg was at his worst; wearied, too...

as a new amusement, grasped me by the ankle, whirled me about his head, and, sufficient momentum established, he released his hundred-clawed clutch, sending me hurtling headlong, through a window in the lower story of the Red Tower of Nak-Jad, out into empty space! I fell as falls a shooting star, down and adown into the ghastly Gorge of the Gray Shine!

Actually I could hear the *squelch* as my form struck bottom! Saw the frightfully mangled form which had been so sickeningly tormented in Nak-Jad lying there, writhing, twitching, in feeble, expiring convulsions; until slowly the final quivering twitch indicated that the end had come. And realized that I myself had stood apart during all this, and had, in fact, but lost another of my shells; had now a new one in which to functionate; and was, in reality, but become more *thin*.

And oh, the relief of it, after Nak-Jad and —

Shrieking, sobbing, wailing and moaning in hopeless horror afresh, I whirled about and fled down the sloping bottom of the Gorge; for close behind me, with shrill whistlings and high-pitched pipings there raced a dozen or more luminous-shining skeletons, remarkably human in appearance; except that upon Earth any one of them would have measured at least twenty feet in height, yet not one of them would have spanned, at the waist, to the bigness of a fourteen year old boy.

The bottom of the Gorge was for a long way as slippery-smooth as glare ice; and I skidded and slithered and slid as I ran, while behind me came that skeleton hell-brood, and they experienced not the slightest difficulty in maintaining their footing.

By what method can Earth-time be measured in the many Hells? Was it an hour — or a day — or an eon that I fled, and those ghastly things pursued? How may I tell? If horror is any criterion, it was an eternity of flight, spurred on by a nameless dread of consequences beyond even my concept, should I be overtaken. But oh! that Gorge seemed endless between those towering walls wherein that lone and sorely affrighted soul that was myself fled, wailing.

How or when or whence it came I had not noted, but I discovered that I was, for the first time since Hesperus cast me openly aside, once more arrayed in a robe. It was of some grayish, shining texture. It floated behind me like a filmy veil as I sped along on fear-driven feet. Then, suddenly, the robe was tight against my back as an icy wind blew shrieking down the Gorge.

That robe acted somewhat as a sail, which helped me, as it held part of that ponderous wind which swept me onward and forward. But that same wind helped my pursuers not at all, as their more *open* structures failed to catch or hold any assisting pressure from it. I began to have hopes...

And as usual, in those infernal regions, hope springs up but to add another and keener torment when the hope dies horridly... Abruptly I came to a halt. Incredulously I gazed, as well I might. For a very few more steps would have precipitated me, all asprawl, into a vast lake of dark blue slime or ooze! The Gorge of the Gray Shine had terminated. And that lake had no beach. Sheer cliffs rose on both sides of the mouth of the Gorge. And behind came on, avidly, that luminous skeleton crew. One, evidently fleeter than his fellows, was even then within reaching distance. His bony claw caught me by the throat. The piping whistling he kept uttering resolved itself into words:

"Thick—thick—like you! I shall draw strength and be *thick*..."

Desperation and nausea aroused wrath within me. Wrath such as I had thought was obliterated completely from my nature, slain beyond all possibility of re-arousal during the loathly depravities to which I had been subjected while in the power of the demoniacal vilenesses who inhabited the Blood-Red Tower of Nak-Jad.

There, at first, I had tried to fight against my fate, in regal indignation, for I had not then lost my pride and arrogance, even though I no longer queened it by the side of Hesperus.

But such awful punishment had been dealt me by Grarhorg that it very effectually slew the last temerarious thought of resistance. So that thereafter I had dared do naught else than tamely submit to whatsoever of humiliating degradation he might choose next to inflict upon his—"toy." And after he had become wearied of me and had cast me to his legion—I had been in even worse plight, likewise endured inertly, indifferently at times, when the overtaxed spirit could no longer recognize varying degrees of agonized, excruciating suffering.

All this was flashing through my mind as that bony grisliness clutched me by my throat. But at that chill touch, the rapidly mounting wrath within me exploded. Exerting a strength I knew not before that moment that I possessed, I struck violently at that pallid white forearm. It broke! Broke like a brittle twig! The fleshless, thickless fingers fell at my feet. In my turn I grappled that elongated animate skeleton and lifted! It was feather-light. I hurled it from me out into the Lake of the Dark Blue Ooze!

"You would be *thick!*" I screamed. "Wallow there, then, and soon shall you become thick indeed!"

The skeleton fell on the surface of the slimy lake, but did not sink, for the stuff was too dense; although it was not exactly solid, either, being more like the gumbo mud of my natal region upon Earth. After considerable struggling the animate abhorrence got to its feet, but it no more resembled a skeleton. I had plenty of time to watch; as the other members of the pursuing band had halted in a hesitant group.

I laughed, openly, mocking them. Actually, I had at last encountered some *things* that were afraid of *me!* Yet, I knew that, did I attempt to retrace my steps and go back up the Gorge, they would be upon me like so many ravening wolves; and against such odds I could not dare to contend. Also, doubtless, there would be many others like them, and probably things even worse to be encountered should I escape them, so long as I should stay in that Gorge.

I turned again to observe the thing I had flung into the lake. It was no longer pallid white. Rather, it more resembled a corpse decaying and blackening from putrescence. It was not a pretty sight, even to eyes such as were mine, inured to horrid sights. It had accumulated all the thickness it could carry, and too much; albeit not of the sort it had desired so avidly. As I watched, its knees buckled, overweighted, and it went down and stayed prone. Slowly, very slowly, it partially settled into the gummous ooze.

A wild idea possessed me. Upon Earth the suicide disposes of one shell at least, speedily. Already I had lost two, and could have not so very many more remaining. Behind me were the animate skeletons who waited... and before me the Lake of the Dark Blue Ooze. Well, I would intentionally cast myself upon the bosom of that sinister-appearing Lake, and if the ooze swallowed me, then I would have rid myself of all my woes at a single stroke. And if I should find that I had but lost another shell, with others still remaining, I'd no longer flee from any menacing Things; but would, rather, welcome them as unintentional deliverers.

I rushed out upon the surface of that ooze and found that it would bear my weight so long as I kept moving rapidly. I sank barely to my ankles in most places, although at times I would go down halfway to my knees. So I decided that I'd not lie down and quit, but keep going. Who knew? Perhaps even Hell had its limits! Occasionally I stood on one foot and scraped the sticky stuff from the other and then reversed the operation. And so, went on, and on, and on.

Two red suns hung in the sky, close together, revolving about each other slowly. Apparently they never set, for the plane of their orbits seemed to be parallel to the surface of the lake. As I looked back, the cliffs where the Gorge of the Gray Shine debouched showed but as a dim, dun cloud. Ahead I could faintly see another shore showing as a purplish-black bank of cliffs. Was I at the bottom of a huge bowl with unscalable sides? Or would there be a way out—and if so, into what would it lead me of further horrors unguessed?

But I was thinking too far ahead, borrowing trouble when real trouble was awaiting me but a few yards ahead of where I then was. If the evidence of my sight was to be relied upon, I was approximately halfway across the lake. And just in front of me was a genuine pool, a lesser lake of clear, limpid fluid within a greater lake of viscous ooze.

The pool mirrored the red suns, and, vanity not yet wholly dead within me, I bent above its surface, desiring to see how I appeared after all my many vicissitudes. And a long, whiplike tentacle whirled upwards from the depths, barely missing my face! Another instant, and that pool was aboil with squirming, writhing snaky feelers that came over the edge and secured fast anchorage on the surface of the ooze. Another instant still, and great purplish-pallid globular bodies hove themselves up from below and pulled themselves out upon the ooze which easily supported their weights. Great, round, black, lackluster eyes, horrifically reminiscent of the baleful eyes of Grarhorg, were glaring into my own wildly staring orbs!

I howled—*howled*—in maniac frenzy, and, catching up my robe, for I sorely needed free use of my members, I departed, full speed; howling at every jump! And those damnable things, octopods, or rather, polypods; for each had many more than eight legs; swarmed over that slimy surface much faster than I could run.

Short indeed was the distance I covered before I was overtaken. One clammy tentacle had me by the waist, hauled me back so violently that I went sprawling flat—and was at once the nucleus of a heaving, feasting mass that was drawing through many rubbery suction cups, wherewith each tentacle was provided the substance composing that form or shell serving me as a body. I could feel ropy strips of substance pulling away from me to the accompaniment of such rending and racking tortures as I had never before then undergone. Nothing which Grarhorg and his myrmidons...

The globular, many-tentacled ghouls were slowly crawling back to their limpid pool, leaving me lying there. With a shock I realized how *thin* I had become. Then realized that I no longer *hurt*. Slowly I comprehended what had actually happened. The ghouls had depleted so much of my *thick* that I had become invisible and intangible to them; so that, to them, I was as one wholly devoured, leaving nothing more to be assimilated.

Then I noted another fact. In actuality I was no longer in contact with the surface of the ooze; but was floating at an appreciable height above that gummy slime. I was in a horizontal posture, but as soon as I attempted to assume the perpendicular I was successful. So, off I set once more, heading for the black cliffs ahead. My progress, for I was literally walking on, or through, the air, was so restful after my wild race from the ghouls, that it seemed no time at all ere I was looking up the towering walls and wondering how I was to surmount them.

I caught myself wishing that I could fly. Dimly, somewhere in my consciousness an earth-word was urging remembrance... what... again... "Levitation..." what was that? But even as I was thinking—as the meaning came—so I began to float upward, slowly at first, but as conscious will took charge, faster and faster—I was atop!

Even at the cliff-lip the light was so dull it was a dusky twilight; and but a short way inland, it was black as black could well be. Nor, try as I would, could I levitate myself above it. Yet I dared not go back the way I had come, and the narrow strip of twilight zone seemingly terminated but a few yards in either direction from where I stood. With no alternative I walked directly away from the cliff-lip and into that dense pall of blackness.

Hark! What was that rumbling, rolling reverberation? Thunder, of course... Again! Thunder? Perhaps... And once again. And that time I became positive that whatever it might be, thunder it certainly was not! Peal on peal that heavy rumbling shook that dense blackness — peal on peal of Gargantuan laughter!

At me? And if so, why? It simply couldn't be directed at, or caused by, my own small and thin self. There was not sufficient of importance about one poor, disconsolate, lost soul to occasion all that disturbance!

I decided I would head directly toward its source. But that was more easily decided upon than accomplished. It was ahead! It was back of me! Only it wasn't back of me at all! It was off to the right — no! it was close by, to the left — but, it was overhead and very, very near — no, again! It was straight beneath me, down, away down — except that it was everywhere at one and the same moment...

And I was more afraid of that awful laughter than I had been of the many-tentacled ghouls which had risen from the limpid pool in the Lake of the Dark Blue Ooze!

It shook one so! It aroused imaginings of beings monstrous; beings such as had never known light-rays; beings that had lived in Chaos and Old Night! And with that last thought, I knew to what realm I had arrived.

I was in that original Great Void which was, long before the shining worlds were created; beyond the Last Frontier; remote even from the scope of the Ultimate — *Mercy!*

I commenced speculating: "Mercy... Mercy... Ultimate Mercy... and what is it, this — "Mercy"? But try as I would, I could make nothing intelligible of that word "Mercy". Yet I had heard that word — but where, and when, and under what circumstances? ... although I could not recall what it meant, nor how it was to be reached — won — nor of what use it would prove to be, once it was — was — "granted!"

No wonder that then I could not understand. Two abstractions these, which I had never rendered concrete in all my selfish, cruel existence upon Earth—the universe's training school for souls.

Not that I thought out at that moment the last part of what I have just said. That is only a recent realization. All I was capable of actually comprehending at that period, was the lost and hopeless condition in which I found myself. One thing, however, I could not well ignore—that fearsome laughter!

My progress was slow, dreadfully so. Just that! For every step was taken in dread of the unknown; which—considering my experiences during what seemed to my wearied soul to have lasted for eons past—must necessarily be "dreadful." Why! How could I even foresee what frightful calamity the next step might precipitate me into? For that matter, I could not see anything at all! That blackness was so dense I could feel it! Save for the fact that it was dry, it was virtually as dense a medium as water, calling forth as much exertion as would swimming in order to make appreciable headway through it. Yet in reality I was not swimming, but as I have said, I was walking.

There were times when I trod on what I knew to be bones— old, dry bones that broke, crackling, beneath my feet. There were times when I stepped on things that wriggled and squirmed, sluggishly, underfoot. There were occasions when I felt long, soft, furry somethings drifting aimless through the air; that brushed against my face and body, sickeningly. There were long spells when I seemed to be part of a multitude of invisible beings, not even so solid as was I; chill, feeble beings that did but weep and wail, low-voiced, while over, and under, and through, and all about, reverberated that shaken laughter.

And then again I would wander alone in stygian darkness; alone save for that terrible merriment that was not mirth, nor anguish, nor sorrow, nor any other emotion known to human concept; but which yet bespoke a horror greater than all other horrors—the Horror of Great Darkness itself, as mentioned, guardedly, in the Ancient Books.

It became unbearable, totally so! Nothing could be worse! Rather than endure my fears alone another moment, I would cheerfully have welcomed Grarhorg and his hellish crew in the Blood-Red Tower of Nak-Jad as dearly beloved playmates!

The last vestige of what—borrowing an Earth-word—I must perforce term "spunk" quitted me. For, after all, the self can endure only so much and thereafter it capitulates, regardless. As did I!

I opened my mouth, and all the repressed terror which was stifling me found expression in a prolonged series of howls, yells, and shrieks! Not mere whisperings and low-voiced wailings, either; but a perfect pandemonium of discordant vocalization that for the time at least, to myself, forced the terrible shaken laughter into taking second place in volume.

My screams were replied to by screams even louder and more horrific than were those I had emitted. A horde of bipedal beings, apparently formed of fire, for they glowed as if internally they were in a state of combustion, rushed at me swifter than the swooping of hawks dropping from above.

A horde of women, naked, the most beautifully modeled figures I ever beheld; but with their classically perfect faces writhed into the most damnable expressions of malignancy imaginable. Three-headed they were, every one of them; with twisting, squirming knots of coils of slim serpents atop their heads in lieu of hair. And long jets and flickers of flame issued from their straining mouths at every screech, while from their lurid eyes streamed rays of baleful, cold, green fire! Aghast, I fled! I was not immune from terror at such a visitation as I myself had invited!

Ah well! They soon caught me, for they were long of limb and fleet of foot and much *thicker* than was I, and of strength prodigious. I was surrounded by them. They screamed— words, at me. They clasped me in their arms, hugging me fiercely to their burning breasts. They—*kissed me!* Kissed me, avidly, with lips that scorched, while they breathed searing sighs into my nostrils and between my lips. They tore me from one another's embrace, jealously, each shrieking, maniacally, that she loved me!

They pushed, clawed, and fought with one another to obtain momentary possession of me; and all the while the writhing serpents of their hair struck, and struck, and struck again at my face, and neck, and shoulders, and breast; infusing at every touch their venom into that shrinking, anguished, naked thing that was "I."

What abominable poisons entered into me, whether from serpent-stings or Furies' breaths, or from both together, I cannot say; but—ere long I—*I was kissing them in return;* avid, panting, drunken, knowing that I was fast becoming as they were! Aware too, that I was commencing to *glow;* was full of flame delighting while it hurt excruciatingly—and, worst of all the many terrible things which had happened during all that period elapsing since I had received the first embrace of Hesperus, I was aware that I was fiendishly glad to be at one with them!

Likewise, I knew that I was rapidly becoming *thick*—almost if not entirely as thick as were they, for they were actually endowing me with their substance. And I could feel that, starting at each cheekbone and reaching to about the back of my neck, another face was growing out of my head! Knew, surely, irrefutable, that my long, fine hair which upon Earth had hung nearly to my knees, was turning—nay, had turned—into thin, venomous serpents that writhed, hissing soft wickednesses into my ears, which thrilled, joyously, at the enticing music of the sibilant sounds!

Sudden as leaves before the breath of a wind, the Flaming Women, or Furies, released me, scattering as blown leaves, into open order; and promptly, clasping hands, they formed a ring having me as its center; then, slowly at first but with ever-increasing swiftness, they swirled into a dance, amazingly graceful, yet, in its way, terrible, too; because of its utter, voluptuous abandonment.

They burst into song—the most dreadful song in all the universe. A chant of initiation and welcome into their ranks. A song of instruction revealing to me depravities and loathly delights of abandonment such as I, who had been the victim of much that is foul, could not wholly understand the meaning of.

Even now, so deeply were those burning words branded upon my innermost self, I could recall, if I would, every horrifying word as well as every alluring, nauseating sweet tone of that frightful song.

Catching fire from their fire, I swayed and swirled and swung with abandonment equaling theirs. I spun and pirouetted wildly, frenziedly, until the serpent-locks upon my heads stood out horizontally, rigid; as I postured more vilely, if that were possible, than they; and, gradually finding my voice again, I too, took up the burden of that song.

That song I will not, dare not repeat! Were I even to *think* it from its tempting beginning to its sinful end this Earth would become polluted beyond all hope, and would become but one more of the many Hells in a long chain of Hells. For that song, in full, would summon hither that entire flaming horde to ravage this fair planet until the Angels of the furthest spheres would shed tears of unavailing sorrow over its wo!

But the refrain of that chant terminated with:

"Sister, Sister, Sister, Sister,
"Sister, Sister, ha-ha-*hah!*"

That word—"Sister!" What stirred within me? It shook me, not at all pleasantly, nor evilly. Rather it was agonizingly, mournfully saddening. Again! *Sister!*

Rose an inward vision, fleeting, lasting but a brief moment, of a pale, white face; clear blue eyes; soft, tenderly smiling mouth; a small, gracefully poised head surmounted by sunny, golden, wavy locks... *Sister!*

Something swelled within my burning breast until I deemed it would burst asunder from the internal pressure. I stopped swirling and ceased from participation in that song—a—a—something—rose—in my—throat—it—it sounded like—"*glub!*"... forgive me, but it cannot be expressed in any other way!

Something, not burning but *scalding*, gathered in each of my six eyes and ran adown my three faces! I—I—whispered:

"*My* little sister knows naught, in her spotless innocence, of such frightful things as I do in my sin. Thank—God—she is—spared..."

A howl of rage arose—a chorus of hate voiced from every fiery throat of that most abhorrent, malignant band.

"She *weeps!* Has dared whisper the name forbidden in all these realms!"

As one they hurled themselves upon me, clawing, kicking, biting, gouging, tearing, rending me apart, limb from limb, ripping me into shreds—oh anguish untellable, unthinkable—my last conscious idea...

"Oh, that I were where—naught—was—but—*myself*..."

I was nothing but Spirit; all trace of form had vanished, and but a dingy spark was hurtling through Space! It was so black, so black, above, and below, and ahead of me; but yet it was not that Great Blackness wherein I had so long sojourned. Naught but a Spark was I, soulless, only remained to me the Spirit; the ever-living Spark from the Eternal, Ineffable Flame. Yet still was I conscious of identity and remembered all the torments through which I had passed since Hesperus had bestowed me upon Grarhorg...

Away and away ahead of me I "saw" a tiny point of light. After flight lasting for a few more ages I knew it for a-star! Back in the known universe once again! Until the skies were ablaze with myriad lights that were not — Hell-lights!

On and on, past planets and suns and constellations, galaxies and nebulae and asteroids; into, through, and beyond the great solar system hurtled that Spirit-Spark that was I. Until, finally, at the furtherest limits of the universe, my Spark hovered, swooped, and settled on a little whirling globe.

It was a dull, barren, burned-out world. A world devoid of vegetation, lacking in moisture, without heat, and weak of illumination. A globe that once had been a fair planet, eons and eons ago — but which was now but gray, harsh rock, and sad white ashes, and blackened, scoriated lava-beds.

And then I noted a strange thing. At the time I did not understand how it had happened nor why it was necessary. Although now I know that no matter where in all the infinitude of Space the Spirit may be, by operation of a natural law it promptly attracts to itself — or sloughs off from itself — matter, or atoms, until it is covered by an envelope, a proper vehicle through and in which to function to its best advantage within such environment as it has attained to.

All I did know then, was that I had in some manner accumulated a tenuous body. And I did not want that form. Formless, I had little to fear save extinction of that spark which was my "Self". And that same extinction was naught to be feared by such as I, but was rather a hope; for annihilation would be a boon; a wondrous rest; a perpetual cessation of consciousness, identity, and — worst torment of all — the ending of *memory*.

For that faculty of "memory", abiding when all else is stripped from the sinful Spirit, constitutes the truest and most terrible torment; is, in itself, the greatest hell! A hell from which none may escape, though they flee to the outermost star; yet will such a spirit bear along its own peculiar hell, for that hell has become an integral part of the Self who evolved it. Nor is *absolute* extinction ever possible!

But I knew that, once I were again possessed of a definite form, tenuous though it might be, and were on a tangible world, there was no guessing what new and very terrible torments were in store for me. Doubtless, however, tortures afresh of some sort there would surely be. And I was so wearied of agonies and horrors inflicted.

"What had I done to deserve—?"

And then and there hell let loose!

Such hell as never yet had I undergone. Pictures, thrown outward from the seat of memory; taking visibility at a little distance, against the curtain of that dull air. Sounds, emanating primarily in my consciousness, impinging upon that same heavy air; echoed and thrown back again to my outward hearing; to penetrate in turn deeply into consciousness once more, laden with stinging anguish worse, far worse, than any virus instilled into my system by kiss of Flaming Furies or stroke of serpent-hair from Flaming Furies' tripled heads.

All I had thought, said, or heard, or did, or desired! Not one infinitesimal thing, however trivial, but what, with merciless exactitude, I was obliged to witness. I tried covering eyes and ears with my hands. And to no avail. Too tenuous! So *thin* I must, perforce, look through all attempts at self-blindness and see, and hear…

And again and again, repeated, circumstance by circumstance; episode followed by episode. On Earth, from childhood to maturity—from evocation of the Dark Angel Hesperus to my present isolate estate. And repeated yet again!

"What had I done to deserve—?"

That which I had done deserved ten thousand fold…!

And that denunciation came from no god, nor angel, nor demon, but from—*within!* It was the fiat of that last great judge, my *Self*, whose sentence, though long delayed, is inexorable! For it is very just.

The sole moisture that burned-out world had known for countless ages past burst from my eyes in ineffectual tears. Whence the moisture came I cannot explain. Do *I* know the

Universal Laws? Nay, hardly do I know myself — except as very sinful, very vile, immeasurably fallen, and, were it not for the Ultimate Mercy, as one *lost* beyond all hope of redemption.

Gradually the fountain of my tears dried up. No moisture left wherewith to weep. Yet the haunting, torturing fantasmagoria continued. I could no more bear it, despite my innate conviction that it was all fully merited.

I rose to my feet and realized as I rose that I was become still more thick. Had, in fact, a body nearly as solid as I had possessed while in the halls of Hesperus. A lingering trace of self-pity told me that if I walked, and walked, and walked, fatigue would eventually assert itself; and I knew that a tired consciousness receives but poorly any extraneous impressions.

Why, I thought to myself, I might even *sleep!* Which was a thing I'd not done since first I gave myself over to the will of Hesperus. Not in all the many Hells has ever one lost spirit slept! My idea was good. I wandered until my feet ached and my limbs ached, while every part of me reveled in pain that was for once wholly physical.

Until, finally, exhausted, I laid me down by the side of a great rock, on a soft bed of ashes, and then — at last, I slept. And it was but a terrific nightmare, compounded of all the past experiences I had endured; but by no means in any sort of conceivable sequence. Rather, it was a jumble worse than the actual events. And awoke, weeping anew; awoke to the realization that I was even thicker, was as solid as though I still dwelt upon my native planet.

Like a child I sought to wipe my streaming eyes on the sleeve of my robe, and saw, to my amazement, that the tears I was shedding were of blood. And then the fantasmagoria of my sins and sufferings recommenced in merciless detail. And still those tears flowed. Tears of hopeless anguish. Tears of impotent weariness. Could I never be freed from the torment of my deed?

"Oh, that I were back upon Earth in the most hideous body

ever beheld! I would be so—so—g—g—good!"

Came a flash of rose and gold more beauteous than Earth's fairest dawn-rise. Before me there stood, stately, serene—

I leaped to my feet. Shrieking in terror I turned to flee.

"*Stay!*"

Those tones so commanding, yet so—*gentle*. In desperation I faced about. Although within me I was sick with a ghastly fear.

"Thou art a *demon*—well do I know thy sort! What torment hast *thou* in store for lost me? Let it begin, swiftly! Since needs must, I can endure..."

Never a word that radiant one spoke, but the light shining all about It became brighter, more glorious; and the pity I read on that serene countenance—

Awe-stricken I sank to my knees: "Thou are one of the Celestials, a—Helper of the Lost? Forgive..."

"Poor, sorrow-laden child!"

I looked up into that countenance. I was well-nigh incredulous; finding it hard to realize that for such as I there was pity. But what I saw was unmistakable—and then, I *did* weep.

"Thou wouldst return to Earth, hideous where formerly thou wert beautiful—why?"

"Can you ask?" I sobbed. "To escape—this!" I meant that haunting fantasmagoria.

"For that reason?"

"Aye!"

The Shining Helper vanished.

After prolonged grieving I knew my fault. And while I grieved, still the fantasmagoria continued, hammering home the lesson I was slowly commencing to assimilate. For now I knew that each past agony had but counterbalanced some evil deed, some wicked thought...

Yet it was a long while after I began to comprehend ere that

Helper came the second time to where I sat in self-loathing inexpressible. Boldly, with the courage of the hopeless, than which is no greater desperation possible, I said:

"Earth I shall never behold again. That I know, for such were too great mercy for me. But were I only worthy, one boon alone would I ask—"

"I listen."

"Is there not some borderland wherefrom I can—mayhap—*help*, in some small way, some other sinful soul lest—lest—it, too—"

No comet ever shot through Space so swiftly as did that Helper, bearing me!

And how or why I knew not, but I was a Spark once more; shining not so brightly, it is true; yet not dingy nor lurid. There was even a slightly yellowish tinge—

Above a great city of Earth, we hovered finally. I could see, oh, what could I *not* see? Earth-life, its familiar evils, its sins, its hatreds, and its self-caused woes!

"Is not here work enough for thee?"

"Too much, too much," I wailed, knowing my own unfitness. "I cannot—"

"*One* soul, thou didst say…"

"Let me descend—and try."

On a bed of rags in a barely furnished chamber in a decaying house located in a dirty slum, lay a woman, dying. Dwarfed, crippled, worn and wasted. Not in any wise a pleasing sight, even were she not at the last extremity. And, while I watched, I saw the vital spark fade out. Very clearly, gratefully, I realized my most glorious opportunity.

"What have I done to deserve—?"

"Naught hast thou done—yet! But thy slain sister made intercession for her slayer; so—this!"

"And yet she knew?"

"It was because she did know that she interceded, besought mercy — for thee!"

"*Oh! What have I been?*"

The Helper indicated that twisted, stunted body from whence the Spark of Life had so recently departed…

"Well?"

"I am content."

"With *that?*"

"Aye!"

"So low…"

"Leaven rises from beneath…"

"Thou hast said!"

Death may be painful, but such birth as I then experienced was — there are no words adequately descriptive… The Helper had vanished.

Slowly that new body I had been granted, as fit instrument through which to atone, grew well again, gained strength. On a street, one day, I heard someone speaking of a "soul-doctor"; and — I — would — *work*. For thus far, I have sought in vain…

* * *

What I said to that grieving soul I may not reveal. Yet never will I forget the look in her eyes, nor the expression on her features as she departed.

"You give me — hope," she stated simply.

But I do not think that she who was Lura Veyle sinned, suffered, and repented in vain. To believe thus were to doubt the Infinite Wisdom. Just and perfect is the working out of the Great Law.

For I believe that the world is nearing the dawn-light of a great spiritual awakening. Science, with its inexorable exactitude, will — nay, has commenced to — investigate, and is finding that many things heretofore labeled "superstition" have in reality a solid basis of fact as foundation.

The powers and forces and potentialities latent in the universe are manifold, limitless in possibility. But as there are true, good spirits dwelling within these our bodies of the flesh; so, too, are there others—evil, self-seeking, unscrupulous. Armed with intangible yet very real forces—against such, the Powers of Light, even, may not avail nor suffice to guard this world...

Yet, mayhap, the story of Lura Veyle will help to deter some such unscrupulous ones. As it may suffice to turn away, perchance—should any such read it—some erring soul who has already held, or who seeks to hold, intercourse with the Destroyers Who Tempt with Bribes.

So may it be!

The Oath of Hul Jok

"*Kah-plang!*"

The Kalion tablet on the wall above my scribble-table rang out its sonorous summons. I raised my eyes, giving vent, as I did so, to an impatient expletive. I hate interruptions when I am attempting to compose a poem. But the message which flamed out in luminous letters on the tablet's dull gray surface made me change my tone from impatience to amusement, although I repeated the same expletive.

In the ragged script I beheld was traceable no resemblance to the usually perfect characters distinguishing our greatest Venhezian scientist, Ron Ti. It did not need that I read the message to assure me he must be terribly perturbed; and the words themselves but confirmed that impression. The message ran:

Hak Iri: I must see you at once. I am in sore trouble, and need your advice.

RON TI.

I rose to my feet and caught up the scribble-stick where it hung at the end of its thin gold chain below the tablet. The flaming letters of Ron Ti's message had already faded as soon as read. He was my friend, had stated that he needed me. What was to write save:

Shall I come to you, or will you come here? Am, as ever, at your command.

HAK IRI.

Touching the tablet with my forefinger, I will-wafted the reply, saw the letters flame and fade, and waited but a brief second before the clanging sound repeated and once again there shone out a sentence:

Am coming to you. Wait.

RON TI.

I reseated myself, in my mind a queer mixture of curiosity and sympathy.

Ron Ti, despite all his wisdom and poise, in trouble, and needing advice from humble me, Hak Iri, writer and recorder of the deeds of greater men? What could be untoward? This our planet Venhez was all too well regulated for strange occurrences to take place; as, for that matter, were all the other inhabited worlds of the Planetary Chain.

Was it war? I asked myself; and replied to myself that that idea was nonsense! For war, that colossal folly, was a thing of the remote and barbarous past on and between the known Inhabited Planets. It cost too much in lives and misery for aught accruing of gain.

True, the Planets each maintain a colossal war-fleet, armed with terrific disintegrators—great ak-blastors on the aethir-torps and the tiny but not less proportionately deadly hand-size blastors for individual encounter; as we reason that the best method of insuring peace is to make war so frightful that no race will prove temerarious enough to venture its hazards.

Still, within scope of my own memory was one war. But that was, really, only a brief affray, what time Ron Ti, Hul Jok, Mor Ag, Vir Dax, Toj Qul, Lan Apo, and myself had gone to the Green Star, Aerth, and had found there an appalling state of affairs prevailing. On our return to Venhez we had stirred up first our own Venhezian Supreme Council, and, after, the ruling minds of the other worlds to an aggressive expedition which resulted in the destruction of the Lunarion Pollution—as our historians now term it. But that was the only strife recorded for ages back...

"KAH-PLANG!"

That slamming note could emanate from but one inhabitant of our world. It was entirely characteristic of his fierce impetuous spirit. And the flame-symbols, as they flared, proved me right as I read:

Hak Iri: I am coming to your abode, for I need your brain to help me.

HUL JOK.

But this was serious. Ron Ti in trouble and needing advice meant no ordinary matter; but when Hul Jok, War-Prince and Commander in Chief of all our Venhezian Planetary Forces of Offense and Defense was likewise in need of my brain!... And those two were positively the most self-capable men I knew, and should be able to cope with any and all problems pertaining to themselves without enlisting outside aid... It was all beyond me... yet, war perhaps it was... intuition...

"*Kah-plang!*"

Short, terse, incisive. Vir Dax, this, he who juggled successfully with the powers of Life, the shrewdest and wisest dispenser of remedies, powders, and decoctions in our capital city Ash-Tar. And I swore again as I read his flame-words, for he, too, was in mental distress and desired to see me forthwith.

Well, I was in my own abode, and presumably master therein; and Our Lady of Bliss forfend if ever I denied myself to a friend who needed me. So I replied to Vir Dax precisely as I had done to Ron Ti and Hul Jok—that I, and all that was mine, were his likewise. And had no sooner finished than:

"*Kah-kah-plang-ang-ang!*"

It was only by mercy of the Guardian Powers that my sorely abused Kalion tablet did not fuse from the intensity of the three superposed flame-messages blazing on its surface! I said things—uncomplimentary, very—about my friends and their lack of consideration; for no Planetary reason could excuse such precipitancy! And then I paused, aghast, as well I might, for those last messages were from the rest of our group—namely: Toj Qul, Chief Diplomat of Planetary Affairs; Mor Ag, who knew the races, languages, habits, manners and customs, ancient and modern, of every inhabited world as no other man ever did know them; and young Lan Apo, whose gift was unique, in that he could unerringly detect, when listening to anyone, be it Venhezian, Markhurian, Satornian, Mharzian, or even from far-flung Ooranos, Planet of the Unexpected—Lan Apo could, I repeat, detect infallibly whether the speaker spoke pure truth or calculated falsehood. More—he could even read the truth held back while seemingly listening attentively to the lie put forward! A valuable asset, he, to our Venhezian civilization, but somewhat an uncomfortable friend to have about, at times!

I know, I have already described these my friends, in that record I have set forth for the benefit of the future generations, that record entitled *When the Green Star Waned*; and I know, too, that that record not only reposes among our Venhezian archives, but has been copied into every language spoken on every one of the major inhabited planets, and is preserved thus, for all time; but it does no hurt to repeat their descriptions as—but I digress.

They arrived well-nigh simultaneously, and gazed at one another in somewhat of bewilderment, for each had supposed that he, and he alone, had wanted to see me. It was I who broke the spell which had come upon them.

"It seems," I said, "that you each have a grief and have done me the honor of seeking my advice—"

And at that point Hul Jok, the practical, interrupted.

"Right," he growled, adding, "and speaking for myself, I care not if you all know my trouble. We seven—"

"Are even as one," suggested Toj Qul, smoothly.

"True," nodded Ron Ti. "It is so with me."

"So, I think, is it with all of us," ratified Lan Apo.

A unanimous sigh of relief went up. If Lan Apo had spoken thus, no need existed of reticence among us. He had, as usual, read our true thoughts.

But then Lan Apo doubled up in a sudden spasm of mirth, straightening his features promptly, however as he beheld Hul Jok's unpleasant scowl fixed upon him.

"Suppose we allow Ron Ti to speak first," I proposed. "He it was who notified me first that he desired to consult with me on an important matter."

Again Lan Apo, despite his lugubrious expression, snickered; whereat Ron Ti flushed painfully; while Hul Jok made a queer snarling sound deep in his throat.

"It is Alu Rai," began Ron Ti. And at that, catching the eye of Lan Apo, I grinned, too, for I began to see, also — or thought I did.

"She was gentle, tender, affectionate," Ron Ti groaned. "What has come to her, I comprehend not at all; but she has become a veritable goblin of perverseness. I cannot devote myself to my experiments for Planetary Benefit as I should, for my mental perturbation! She is a disturbance incarnate; nor is she amenable to reason; nor will she explain her attitude. Seek I her arms for rest and inspiration, she delights, instead, in tormenting me—"

"Precisely my trouble with Ota Lis," said Vir Dax gravely.

"Mine, too, with Cho Als," vouchsafed Toj Qul sadly, adding: "And I, who am accredited with being able to talk a bird off a bough, cannot persuade her, my Love-Girl, to tell me why this state of affairs should prevail."

"My fix, exactly," stated lugubrious young Lan Apo. "Kia Min, gentlest of her sex, is so obdurate that I cannot read her mind!"

The others groaned, looking exceedingly glum at this; from which we all understood that in every case the trouble was identical. All but mine! I—I was exempt! And I swelled with pride thereat.

"*I* am untroubled," I boasted. "I will see Esa Nal and instruct her to visit your Love-Girls and ascertain—"

"*Kah-plang!*"

And the message we all read, although meant for me alone, left me in a state of perturbation worse even than all the other six of our group put together.

And once again Lan Apo, the irrepressible, snickered. But I was aghast. Esa Nal, *my* Love-Maid!

Then that hereditary temper bequeathed me by my turbulent namesake Hak Iri who lived two thousand years agone, flamed within me, and what I indited and flashed to Esa Nal should have blinded her soft golden-brown eyes for hours, once she gazed upon those sentences. Words are my trade. And I know that upon that occasion I surpassed myself, rising to heights of objurgation and invective hitherto undreamed.

Ron Ti sighed in envy.

"Hak Iri," he murmured, generous as ever, complimenting me, even in his own distress, "could I but express myself thus to Alu Rai. I'd cheerfully pay as price for that ability that reputation I hold as the greatest living scientist on all the worlds."

"I, too," growled Hul Jok. "But after all, what are words? Less than nothing, where Love-Girls are concerned! Although," he continued grumpily, "I cannot say that my method was any improvement."

"*Your* method?"

Lan Apo's eyes were dancing with mirth as he caught Hul Jok's hidden thought, albeit his face stayed sober.

"Aye," rumbled the badgered giant, "*my method!* I did lay Hala Fau face downward across my knee and—"

But that was too much! And we all burst into a shout of laughter as we each pictured that strapping termagant, Hala Fau, in the predicament of a naughty child. Yet the mirth died, abruptly, as is usual with ill-timed merriment, and we gazed at each other even more blankly than at first.

And then Jon the Aerthon, without stopping at the door to

announce himself, burst, incontinent, into the room and crossed it straight to Mor Ag, who, aside from Ron Ti, was the only one of us who spoke his Aerth-tongue fluently. And what Jon gasped out in his excitement turned Mor Ag's face a deathly white.

"Great Power of Life!" Mor Ag ejaculated blasphemously. "That accurst Lunarion!"

Lan Apo's face was a study in horror and grief, although the rest of us were puzzled, bewildered, and, as is usual when the untoward intrudes itself into well-regulated lives, we were more than a little angry. But then, simultaneously, realization came to us, one and all. Not in detail, of course, but enough.

When we returned from Aerth on that momentous first trip, we had brought with us a captive Lunarion. By decision of our Supreme Council "It" had been kept confined in our Planetary Museum of Strange Things, held prisoner in a specially devised cage, from which, despite all Its evil will-force, It could in nowise liberate Itself. Ron Ti had designed and constructed that cage, charging it with restraining vibrations in some mysterious manner known solely to his profound scientific brain. But whatever had been the method he'd employed, it had so far worked.

But now!

It was apparent that the Lunarion had escaped. And we all knew Its fiendish malignancy, and Its even more demoniacal hatred for everyone and everything not of Its own type. And being of at least average intelligence, we all knew, irrefutably, that It had doubtless already revenged Itself.

But how?

Then Mor Ag spoke, slowly, dully, setting forth in plain words what Jon the Aerthon had reported in broken, excited phrases. And in substance, without quoting Jon's exact words, thus it was:

When we brought Jon with us to Venhez, Ron Ti, learning

that Jon was accustomed to working in metals, had given the Aerthon place in the Experimental Laboratory over which he, Ron Ti, presided.

It had been Jon's custom, when his tasks were ended, solely as recreation to go to the Museum of Strange Things and jeer at the last survivor of his hated Master-Race. It did him good, so Jon said, to swear at the Lunarion and behold Its impotent fury at being thus mocked by one of Its former slaves.

Jon had arrived somewhat earlier than usual one night not so long back; and had observed Alu Rai standing gazing at the captive "Moun-Thing." Again, upon another occasion Jon had found several other girls whom he recognized accompanying Alu Rai. Jon had thought nothing of it, as to him it seemed but natural that the girls should be interested in the captive their men had brought to Venhez, where nothing like It had ever before been dreamed of...

And at that point, Ron Ti groaned again, in anguish of spirit.

"That demon, that demon! It has will-witched them all. Our Lady of Venhez only knows—"

But Mor Ag continued as though no interruption had occurred:

"Tonight, not an hour ago, Jon saw all seven of our Love-Girls stand before the cage again. Alu Rai in some manner neutralized the imprisoning vibration, and the Lunarion *oozed* out—free! Knowing himself as being impotent to cope with It, Jon did the next best thing, and followed It and our girls. By the darkest ways It went, Alu Rai guiding and the other girls following. They went straight to the Great Central War Castle.

"There, Hala Fau, displaying the diamond Looped Cross, Hul Jok's symbol of authority, caused the guards to bring forth the great aethir-torp *Victuri*, Hul Jok's own fighting-craft. Into this they entered, and then that Lunarion, becoming in some manner aware of Jon's espionage, will-forced the Aerthon to Its presence and gave him a message for Hul Jok! After which It, too, entered, and the aethir-torp, with Hala Fau at the controls, shot away into outer space. After which, again, Jon hastened back to Ron Ti's workshop hoping to find him there; thence to his abode; and, finally, here."

"But that message for me?" demanded Hul Jok truculently.

Mor Ag stammered, hesitant, ill at ease. But Hul Jok was in no mood for evasions. His voice held a strangely repressed note as he spoke slowly.

"That—message—Mor Ag! I speak not again!"

"But—but—" began Mor Ag.

Hul Jok rose to his feet. In his eyes—

Lan Apo interposed, saved the situation:

"Hul Jok will hold *you* blameless, Mor Ag. As well punish Jon! It is the Moun-Thing's defiance, not yours. Transmit it, hurriedly, and you, Hul Jok, hold your wrath until you have the proper cause of it within your reach!"

Hul Jok threw one great arm about Lan Apo's neck, bowing the slender boy nearly to the floor beneath his weight.

"Always I held you a flighty-minded youngster, Lan Apo," he rumbled. "But this time you speak with the wisdom of a Supreme Councilor. For it I will hold you ever as a younger brother. Very near was I to violence upon the wrong object. I am myself once again. That message, Mor Ag!"

But despite his assertion that he held full control over himself, Hul Jok's face belied his words when the full purport of the evil Lunarion's insulting defiance dawned upon him.

"Tell that gigantic fool, Hul Jok," so the Moun-Thing had charged Jon the Aerthon, "that I have repaid him, and his fellow-fools, for their deeds against myself and my race. Tell him that I hold their women in the thrall of my will. Tell him that his woman stole, at my desire, his diamond Looped Cross of which he is so proud, as well as his own especial fighting-craft—the mightiest aethir-torp on all the worlds.

"Say to him that I know I am the last Lunarion in all the universe; but that with seven such women as I now hold—"

The remainder of that message is unfit to write!

Hul Jok's face, as I have said, was a sight to behold—and quail from. His eyes, always aglow with the light of his proud, high spirit, now shone with a lurid, implacable wrath. His heavy black brows were drawn into a frown, ominous, lowering, His wide, full-lipped mouth was but a thin, grim, straight line, pallid and sinister. His entire features seemed at the one and the same time to be convulsed and frozen into a mask of hate above and beyond aught I had ever dreamed could be depicted on any countenance anywhere. Not even the demons that, ages agone, dwelt in our Venhezian deserts could have looked one half so terrible as looked our haughty War-Prince in his consuming rage.

I state it truthfully—he frightened even me, and I had known Hul Jok since we played as children together. And when, after an heroic struggle to master his emotions, he finally spoke, the tones as they issued from his throat bore such dread menace that we all shuddered, friends of his though we were.

"My Hala Fau—*my woman!* A traitress? Sooner would I believe that Our Lady Venhez herself were false to her own planet! Nay! Hala Fau's will was overborne. That Lunarion devil! We did permit It to live too long. And now!

"But It shall not escape, though It flee beyond the furthermost limits of the known universe and into the Outer Voids—even there will I pursue It and exact such vengeance as no mind in all the worlds can now conceive. Aye! Though I tear the Sun from its place and plunge the entire Planetary Chain back to what it was uncounted eons ago, into the limbo of Chaos and Old Night in order to do so!

"Not the Love-Girl of the lowliest Venhezian may be stolen without a frightful reprisal—it has been our Venhezian Law for ages—and shall it be told on the worlds that *seven* Love-Girls--?

"Hak Iri! Will-waft my command to every member of the Supreme Council and bid them assemble at the great Hall of Conference at the Central War Castle within one hour. Say that it is my imperative order. Add that I will slay with my own hand any one of them who comes one instant later than the given time! And you others—"he turned the full glare of his blazing orbs upon us who gazed spellbound at him—"do you prepare, even as once before we made preparation, for a long spatial journey—save that ten times the quantities will be needed of all supplies. In two hours we leave Venhez—to return triumphant or—to return no more!"

We had no trouble with our Supreme Council. Hul Jok is not the sort to request foolish things. And this time, even had his demands been folly absolute, one look at his grim face blazoning forth the wrath of his raging soul would have effectively nullified any opposition, had any been stupid enough to raise such issue. But the Supreme Councilors have common sense, and they were commeasurably angry at the stupendous shame done to all Venhez by that accurst Moun-Thing.

Hul Jok took barely a quarter of a Venhezian hour to set forth the case, and the Council took barely a quarter of that, again, to grant him, and us who were chiefly concerned, a free hand.

The only suggestion proffered was that we take a dozen aethir-torps of the Venhezian War Fleet, each fully manned and armed with the very latest in ak-blastors. But that proposal was rejected, flatly, by Hul Jok, who snarled:

"*One* Lunarion—and seven Venhezians whose women have been ravished away? Nay, Councilors; be the expedition ours alone!"

And we all were fully in accord with him in that.

So, as rapidly as could be done, messages were outcast to every known inhabited planet to be on watch for the great Venhezian aethir-torp *Victuri*. Albeit that was a superfluous measure, for never once was it sighted by watchers of any of the planets from Markhuri to Neptuan.

Yet we had no sooner descended to the courtyard of the Central War Castle and boarded the craft awaiting us than we found that Ron Ti had preceded us and was already busily engaged in installing a queer-looking contraption. Still, it was amazingly simple in construction; and without it! ... I shudder to think what might have been the outcome of our affair had Ron Ti's brain not held that appliance within its scope.

He had not completed his adjustments when with a *swoosh* we shot into the air, and in no time at all we were hurtling into space. But hardly were we clear of the atmospheric envelope about our planet than he lifted the thing bodily — a square box it was, with a disk of Kalion atop — and set it where Hul Jok, standing at the controls, could see the disk without distracting his attention from his steering.

Perturbed and enraged as he was, Hul Jok, always profane, swore admiringly. For on the surface of the disk was depicted, shooting through the darkness of interstellar space, an aethir-torp, easily recognizable as the *Victuri*, the Standard-Craft of the Venhezian Fighting Fleet.

At the moment, it showed near the rim, at Hul Jok's left. With no explanation from Ron Ti, the giant Commander seemed to grasp the principle; for he deflected the nose of our aethir-torp a trifle, and the pictured quarry swung slowly to the center of the disk. Hul Jok growled his satisfaction thereat.

"Let that Moun-Thing escape us now, if It can," he exulted. And thenceforward that image, as well may be believed, was held exactly in the disk's center.

Once, seized with a brilliant idea, I asked Lan Apo, whose telepathic powers we all knew, respected, and trusted implicitly, if he could not contact with Kia Min. Of course, I remembered that, on that night when we had first become apprised that the girls were under the Moun-Thing's spell, he had stated that he could not do so any longer. But within me was the hope that mayhap that spell had weakened, as the Lunarion might have his thoughts too much taken up with other matters to have time to devote toward holding the girls in steady thrall during their flight into space.

Well, Lan Apo tried it, but to no avail. Nor could he so with Hala Fau; nor with Alu Rai; nor with Ota Lis; nor Cho Als; nor with Esa Nal—although in that last attempt I had no faith anyway, knowing her as well as I did, and do! But so it was with the remaining victim of the Lunarion—the merry, laughing Lue Jes, Mor Ag's love-maid.

Yet the idea was not so foolish, after all. For Jon the Aerthon, who had accompanied Ron Ti from his laboratory, carrying the appliance we were even then using to follow our quarry by, and who had raised such a terrific *howl* at being left behind that not even grim Hul Jok had the heart to bid him stay—Jon, I say, once he realized why Lan Apo had laid himself flat on his back and closed his eyes, volunteered to do for us what Lan Apo admitted he could not accomplish.

Jon made his astounding offer through the medium of Mor Ag; and we all grinned a trifle derisively when Mor Ag translated. But Jon waxed insistent.

"Once I, and my forefathers for ages before me, were creatures of the Moun-Things' wills," he explained. "We became, inspired thereto by terror, accustomed to reading their thoughts, even when not intentionally directed at us; lest, did we fail to anticipate their wishes, divers inflictions might become our portions. So now, perhaps, I can make my mind think Moun-Thing thoughts—"

"Pity he could not have caught the Lunarion's thoughts before all this happened!" Hul Jok sneered.

But Ron Ti spoke up for Jon the Aerthon, reproving the giant Commaner.

"That speech is unworthy of the great War-Prince of Venhez," Ron Ti asserted flatly. "As well accuse Lan Apo of the same thing—negligence. Or me—"

"Aye," Hul Jok made amends. "Best that I accuse myself for permitting the Lunarion to survive, what time we thought we had cleaned Aerth when we exterminated the rest of his hell-brood fellowship. Let the Aerthon try—and should he succeed, rich shall be his reward should he and I survive this expedition."

What filth poured from Jon's lips in a hideous babble of broken phrases, words, and even whole sentences, Mor Ag would never, either at the moment nor afterward, wholly repeat. But we ascertained from out the jumble, that the Moun-Thing intended dodging about in space for a while, then dashing direct to Aerth, and taking refuge in some subterranean retreat he knew of.

And for a single moment we exulted, but alas! prematurely. For we thought that, by steering direct to the Green Star, we could reach there first, intercept the stolen aethir-torp *Victuri*, and—then we realized that, should we attack it and destroy it with our ak-blastors, we would at the same time destroy our own Love-Girls who were aboard. Nor would the Lunarion Itself be injured by the disintegrating power of the ak-blastors, as we had found out long ago.

Then, worst of all, from Jon's lips, Mor Ag still translating, there came the final reason why we might not attack the Standard-Craft of the Venhezian Fleet. Namely, that it mounted ak-blastors superior in intensity and range over our present ones—and also, that, under imperative dominance of the Lunarion's evil will-force, our own Love-Girls would be compelled to work fighting-craft and destroying batteries of ak-blastors against *us!* And from what would ensue, because of such an affray, Our Lady of Venhez spare us all!

So we gazed at each other, wordless and hopeless, as full realization dawned in our minds.

Hul Jok, however, refused to stay long daunted. War-Prince

of a planet, the one man to whom an entire world looked as leader and strategist extraordinary, it was but natural that his brain worked more quickly on such a problem than would ours.

"We must get to Aerth first," he decided. "Not too hastily, but we must be within its atmosphere when the stolen aethir-torp makes its landing. And we must land promptly thereafter, within seeing distance, yet remain ourselves unseen. Thenceforward we must even be guided by circumstances, until we, in our turn, can guide circumstances to serve our ultimate purpose."

It was the same dull, lurid, reddish-glowing atmosphere, yet not quite so dense, as we had noted upon our first visit to Aerth, into which we drove headlong; but the surface of the planet, as we gazed upon it with mixed emotions, presented to our eyes the same deadly, drear monotony. Yet we had, vaguely, expected to see some signs of change; as to our minds, the Aerthons, once freed from their demoniacal Lunarion oppressors, should have immediately commenced to improve their degraded conditions. But, instead, things appeared precisely as when we had left Aerth last time.

No birds in the air, no animals on the ground, and no cities of men could we descry. Only dull gray-brown dirt and sad-colored rocks, with here and there a dingy grayish-green shrub, stunted, distorted, isolate.

Naturally, a second visit would reveal the same familiar scenery; still, so depressing an effect did it have upon our spirits, that I cannot but describe it again, even at risk of seeming to repeat, to some extent, my previously recorded statement of our former adventure.

But we did not land just then. That disk of Ron Ti's devising showed that the aethir-torp we awaited was as yet a considerable distance outside Aerth's murky atmosphere. So we put in several Aerth-days surveying the inhospitable surface beneath us for suitable places whereon to land whenever occasion warranted.

Whether or not the accurst Lunarion realized that It might be pursued was a question we debated frequently. But that, too, Jon the Aerthon soon resolved for us.

"Too big hurry," he stated decisively. "I caught the Moun-Thing's thoughts once more. Got good place, underground. Got whole race, men like me, to serve as slaves, to eat, if It pleases. Got idea to be King over all Aerthons, *Yakshas* and *Yakshinis*—"

This last we did not comprehend for a bit. But as Mor Ag questioned and Jon replied, we for the first time became aware that there was yet a terrible hell-brood left upon this unfortunate world—a race of beings sprung from the unholy union of Lunarions and Aerthons, yet quite different from either. And then Jon's concluding words droves us to frenzy afresh as he said:

"Lunarion think he now got fine chance to rule alone; and got seven fine queens—"

It was the final infliction. After that, nothing mattered but rescue for those we loved above ourselves, or—extermination for us in a group.

True, we bore the means of communication with Venhez, and did we call for help, not solely the Venhezian War-Fleet would respond, but unquestionably those from the other planets would join the expedition should they be needed.

But, as Hul Jok had told our Supreme Councilors, we held that seven Venhezians in one aethir-torp were fully adequate to deal with one Lunarion; and whose should be the delight of vengeance, if not ours? And our thirst therefor was very great!

Then, even as we were discussing the affair for the hundredth time, and were far too much interested to be as watchful as we should have been, there came a lurid glare of light upward from Aerth's surface, and—

Our aethir-torp was out of all control! Worse, it was falling rapidly, caught, presumably, by the planet's gravitational pull. Soon its plane altered from the horizontal, the nose dipped, inclining yet more steeply, still more, clear to the perpendicular. Then the stern overpassed the upright—in a minute more we were falling, falling, whirling over and over, apparently in all three dimensions at once—over and over, and end over end, sickeningly, until—

Crash!

When consciousness once again asserted dominance in me, I was aware, first, of a most terrific headache, and secondly, of a full realization as to what had occurred; although how I knew it, I could not then have told, had I been asked. But to adhere strictly to truth, neither can I now wholly account for it. Only—*I knew!*

Jon's statement that the Moun-Things had left a numerous progeny to still afflict the Aerthons was rampant in my mind. Also, I was assured that, apprised of what had befallen their progenitors, they had busied themselves, inventively, and were prepared, after their own fashion, to protect what they doubtless considered their own planet from further hostile invasion.

And we had reaped the benefits of their efforts. I was not bound in any way; so, despite the throbbing anguish in my skull, I sat up and attempted to see what sort of surroundings I had. But for a bit everything spun about so giddily that I could not believe aught I gazed upon. Then my head cleared somewhat and I could believe my own eyes—but did not want to!

There lay my companions, every one; and not one of us had on a single rag of apparel. Every particle of clothing gone, our blastors gone; and, for aught I knew to the contrary, gone likewise was our aether-torp. Truly, we were in a mess!

Then Lan Apo sat up—and what that gentle youth said was almost sufficient! At least, it availed to awaken the others, one by one, Hul Jok last, oddly enough, considering his great size, prodigious strength and intense vitality. Wofully we stared about us, as well we might.

One comfort alone remained to us. After a hasty questioning, we were assured that, aside from minor bruises, bumps and scratches, we all were intact! But where were we?

Apparently in a cavern or other subterranean place. And what we saw in nowise exhilarated us. I say "saw," and I mean just that, for the place was illuminated by a light the source of which we could not determine, as it seemed to glow from walls, roof, and floor alike. Ron Ti, scientist as he is, commented at once upon that phenomenon.

"Cold light," he stated. "Wonder how they do it?" But as none of us know as much about such matters as did he himself, no reply was forthcoming.

"They've quaint ideas of art," said Lan Apo, striving to put a facetious aspect upon our plight, and dismally failing therein.

"*Art!*" snorted Vir Dax. "Do you think those ghastly figures we behold all about us are but statuary? Deceive not yourselves. Once those were living beings! Obviously, after tortures nameless, unguessable to normal minds like ours, they have been thus preserved, *mineralized*, by some process best known to the race of underground devils who hold us here, in all likelihood, naked as we are, for like torment and a like preservation."

"Probably their Museum of Strange Things," suggested Mor Ag, with deep interest.

But for my part, I simply stared in horror; although I wished to avert my gaze but was so hideously fascinated that I could not do so.

Staring, or shrinking in horror, however, did us no good. And Vir Dax—who is first a body fixer, and afterward a Venhezian, as even his own Love-Girl said once upon a time—was wild with curiosity about those gruesome relics, even to the point of total forgetfulness of his, and our, peril. He rose to his feet, approached one, the most abhorrent specimen of them all, and ran his skilled hands over it, while a look of amazed incredulity overspread his usually immobile features.

"Ron Ti," he said, excitedly. "Come here! This touches your province quite as much as it does mine."

Ron Ti, the moment he felt the gruesome thing, nodded, saying in a surprised tone: "Metal—and Sclenion, at that. I wish I knew how it is done. Transmuting flesh to inorganic metal is beyond my scientific attainments. That I know!"

No one explained, for none of us could, and just at that moment something occurred which took our minds off an unprofitable speculation; for a faint slithering sound we heard behind us, and as we turned, simultaneously we beheld—

Oh, none who have not *seen* one of the damnable creatures can ever wholly form a concept of, much less believe, the description of what we were looking at.

It had the head, shoulders, arms, breasts, and torso of a woman; and in a fierce, wanton way, its features might even have been called beautiful—by those admiring that type. For it had bluish-silvery hair—a snow-white skin with a slightly golden tinge shimmering over it; lips so darkly red that they held a purplish tint in their crimson; and eyes that were greenish-yellow with a lambent light aplay in their unholy depths. But from the hips down all resemblance to womanhood—as we know it—ceased. Instead of the bipedal form, it was a serpent agleam with iridescent armor-plate of scales as big as Hul Jok's thumbnail.

The lower, or serpent-part, was fully as long as was our giant Commander tall; but the upper, or woman-part, was small as any average ten-year-old Venhezian child. Yet it was anything except an infant, as was written plainly in its strange, disquieting eyes, wherefrom looked forth, unashamed, exultant, temptingly even, all ancient evil and original sin.

Its eyes played over us as we stood, appraising us openly,

and I saw Lan Apo shudder as he read all too clearly the creature's thoughts. In a voice as silver-sweet as a love-flute's notes, she poured forth a stream of words in a language none of us understood. Yet Lan Apo—

Hastily I formulated a thought-wave and strained to will-waft it to him: "Do not betray your inestimably priceless gift of mind-reading! Later it may serve us well in time of extremity, if they know not of its power." And I felt immeasurably relieved as he nodded almost imperceptibly.

Realizing that her words were but wasted, she tried again, this time employing the tongue spoken by the Aerthon slaves, although she conveyed by her expression how repugnant to her notions it was to stoop to this. Even her voice sounded not so liquid sweet, but took on a harsher, raspier quality; more imperious, too, as if she found it needful to impress us with a sense of her superiority. Sensual, crafty, vain. Aye! that was it—vanity! I had a brilliant idea.

"Flatter her, Mor Ag," I said hurriedly. "It is her vulnerable point!"

"Toj Qul could do better than I," he retorted. "But I will do my best."

"Translate to him, then, and after, translate to her his replies," I suggested. "Act you simply as spokesman between them."

That devil-spawned Daughter of Sin was staring at us with rapidly mounting suspicion and hostility flickering in her glinting eyes.

"Speak quickly, Mor Ag," I advised.

"What would you with us?" he queried, bowing to her. I must say he did it well, for I saw a look of gratified importance gather on her wickedly beautiful features.

"From what world came ye here, O strangers: and why came ye here to this planet Aerth for the third time? Lie not; as well we know ye for those who once came, took one of our Moun-

Lords away; came yet again with a mighty fleet of destroyers, and annihilated that godlike race who begot us, their sons and daughters. But fools ye were to come for a third time! And as fools ye fell by our arts! Now, why came ye this third time? Lie not, I say! That Jon, that renegade Aerthon slave ye took away and again brought with ye, has, true to his slavish nature, betrayed ye, in your turn..."

"She it is who lies," muttered Lan Apo. "Jon has proved obdurate, and from him their questionings have elicited no gain."

She had noted the start of surprize we had all manifested at the mention of Jon's name, but evidently she thought it was because we believed her statement. So, with added confidence and more than a trifle of arrogance she awaited our spokesman's reply. But Ron Ti had been whispering softly to Toj Qul, meanwhile, so her questions were met with counter-questions.

"Tell us first, O Beauteous One, who and what you may be? Never before have we beheld your like, although we have visited all the known planets."

"Does that one ask?" And she pointed to Hul Jok. "Let him tell me I am beautiful and—"

Hul Jok leaped! Caught her by her slim neck, and squeezed, hard! Her eyes nearly popped out of her head. A slap from his huge, open hand sent her spinning clear of the floor, to bring up with a solid-sounding *thump* against the farther wall, to drop thence, limply, to the floor, where for a moment she writhed feebly, then became still.

Vir Dax bent above her, straightened up again, and shook his head, reassuringly.

"Not dead, but badly jarred, although no bones are fractured. She will live," he reported.

"So?" Hul Jok grinned, pleased with himself. "We have had enough of this dissembling. Am I Commander? Then obey! Toj Qul, we need not your smooth tongue—you take too long to get results with your flowery phrases. *I* will question this—whatever it is; and do you, Mor Ag, translate with exactitude. Now! Lan Apo, is she shamming?"

The boy nodded. Then, warningly: "Have care, Hul Jok! Her *bite* is poisonous! Even now she meditates waiting until opportunity presents—"

I have seen that giant Commander of ours move quickly ere this; but never so swiftly as when that warning came. Not away from her who lay there supinely, but toward her!

She, too, had moved like a lightning-flash, but not—for all her serpentine qualities—quite quickly enough. And when our eyes caught up with their motions, she hung by the neck in Hul Jok's grasp, held at arm's length, where, despite her writhing and thrashing about, she was harmless. Twice she attempted to fling a coil about his arms or legs, but each time he *squeezed*, very gently, yet meaningly, and she soon desisted.

"Now," he commanded, "you talk to her, Mor Ag. It is not needful to translate her every word. Just tell her what I say, and tell us the substance of her replies. First, who is she? And secondly, has she any status or authority among her sort?"

Followed a volley of question and answer, until Mor Ag nodded his satisfaction.

"She claims to be a princess, Idarbal by name—says that she rules, now that the Lunarions are become extinct, but admits that a sort of devilish priesthood styled the 'Wise Ones' exercise a drastic supervision over her entire race, herself included. She herself is, according to her statement, daughter of a full Lunarion father and a mother but one-sixteenth Aerthon. Says that when the Interplanetary fleets invaded, only the full Lunarions were allowed to participate in the fighting. Their variously admixtured offsprings had been reared to luxury and debauchery, and had not, at the time, the proper warlike spirits nor the scientific training; as the Lunarions, normally undying, kept these matters as their own monopoly. They probably knew their spawn too well to trust them!

"But after the Moun-Things were obliterated, their progeny were obliged to do for themselves or perish at the hands of their slaves, the Aerthons. The great calamity could not, of course, be long kept a secret. And, as soon as the tidings filtered down to the Aerthons, there followed one insurrection after another.

"Even now one is raging in the underworld caverns. And this time the Aerthons are not only holding their own, but are making some slight headway. She says that the Aerthons have naught wherewith to fight save their swords, while her race have light projectors—"

And at that point Mor Ag broke off to smile at a grim jest she'd betrayed without realizing that she'd done so. As he elucidated, Hul Jok burst into a bellowing shout of laughter that frightened his captive worse than anything he'd so far done.

"You all will recall," Mor Ag's explanation ran, "that when the Lunarions attacked the interplanetary fleets with aethir-torps, following the destruction of their Selenion globes, they rammed a Satornian craft, completely wrecking it? Of course, the fragments fell to the ground. And the Satornians use an alloy of Berulion and Iron. Magnetic; yes.

"This hell-brood experimented, built light-projectors that attracted Iron and Berulion, believing that thus, should another hostile fleet ever hover over Aerth, it could be *crashed* without any of the defenders being obliged to sally forth to do battle. Instead they could send out the Aerthon slaves to finish with their swords any who might survive. A most splendid scheme!

"Well, when these Aerthons started their last rebellion, an army of their master-race marched against them, bearing as weapons small, powerful light projectors intended to attract the steel swords from the very hands of their slaves. Another most wondrous scheme, but it worked altogether too well! The swords were attracted so violently that over half of the pursuing army were slain by a perfect rain of steel blades traveling their way at incredible speed."

And at that explanation, we all laughed.

The Serpent-Woman princess stared in fear of us.

"What manner of beings are ye?" she demanded, quaveringly, of Mor Ag; "what manner, indeed, who, knowing your interplanetary ship is wrecked and your weapons gone, yourselves captive, naked, unfed, and facing the most ghastly torments ere ye die—if indeed, ye may be slain—can yet laugh at a jest told by one of yourselves? Oh, release me," she begged suddenly, abjectly. "I will struggle not against ye. I will not *bite!* Nay! I will *love* ye, all seven; will be submissive wife to ye, all! Oh, let me down, great Lord!" And she turned her pallid face and frightened eyes to Hul Jok with a look of appeal which needed no translating for our giant to understand.

Hul Jok, as Lan Apo nodded that she was sincere, very carefully set her down, giving her mute but empathic warning against any treachery she might contemplate, by clenching his great fist and holding it suggestively within an inch of her nose.

Six of us snickered as she very humbly *kissed* that animate bludgeon. And Lan Apo, irrepressible as ever; cackled:

"She's beginning her wifely attentions promptly."

"If she's so anxious to please," said Hul Jok, "we'll make her tell us where Jon is."

"They've got him in a different cavern," she stated. "Not as yet have they tortured him. They so far do but question him, and he replies always that ye be actual gods from another planet which he insists is a part of Heaven, the Abode of the Blest; and that, ere ye depart from this world of ours, not one of the race of the Moun-Beings' children will ye leave living. Aye, great is his faith in ye. As is mine," she finished. And the glance wherewith she favored us did actually bespeak love—her sort—for us all! Very obviously, she was completely ours to do with as pleased any one, or all, of us.

For my part, I cared not a pinch of Cosmic Dust for her amorous glances, nor her too readily proffered caresses. But I realized, suddenly, that I was most abominably hungry.

"Make her get us some food," I suggested. "I feel empty clear down to my feet!"

Mor Ag explained, carefully, and Idarbal acquiesced immediately, seemingly delighted at the idea of serving us.

"But we'll have to let her go," demurred Ron Ti. "And," he added, "we may be sure she'll either not return at all, or else — she'll poison what she fetches!"

We all looked blankly at one another. But Lan Apo spoke up for her.

"You cannot understand all her mental reactions, and neither can I. But she's sincere; actually in love with us, collectively. Probably for the first time in her life she's telling the truth without any reservations. She'll do precisely as she promises."

And with that we had, perforce, to content ourselves. That boy was never mistaken since he was born. Plenty of Venhezians would like him better if he would be mistaken once in a while!

So we stood and watched her glide over to one corner where was a little hole close to the floor — a hole so small that Lan Apo, slenderest of all us Venhezians, could not have thrust his shoulders into it had it been possible to save all our lives by so doing. But into that hole she slipped as freely as an aethir-torp might traverse interplanetary space. Nor was she gone for very long.

"Now I wonder why she came here alone? What could be her object in so doing?"

It was Ron Ti who made the remark, and Lan Apo replied:

"Simple female curiosity, abetted by hate. For we — in her estimation — are the actual murderers of her 'god-like' race, the Lunarions. So she came to gloat over us, revile us; anticipated the delight of seeing us tortured — "

"Never mind that," Hul Jok interrupted. "What we most

need to know is: How did they put us into this cavern-cage? Not through yon snake-hole, surely. My fist would nearly suffice to stop that entrance."

Immediately we investigated, but no trace of door or other opening could we find. And while we were busied in that futility we heard a silvery ripple of laughter, spun about as one, and stared at Idarbal who had returned.

Behind her were two attendants, likewise female, but quite evidently inferior in the racial scale to herself; for, whereas she was part serpent, and a gorgeously glittering one, they were lizard, from their waists down. Covered they were with a garish, unwholesome purplish skin, blotched unevenly with greenish-yellow spots as large as the palm of my hand. And even their features were lizardlike. Why, their very hands were those of lizards! The skin of trunk and arms and face was lizard. Only, as I have said, from their waists up were they shaped as she.

I heard Vir Dax mutter: "Oh for a free hand, a few sharp dissecting tools, and plenty of time!"

But even he, despite his scientific mania for studying grotesque mistakes of nature, was ready to eat. And we seven, our systems fairly shrieking for nourishment, gathered about our self-elected "mutual wife" avidly awaiting the food her attendants bore. They placed their burdens on the floor, unrolled a bundled skin, very finely dressed and ornately painted, spreading it out as a surface whereon to place the viands. Then they set before us the various portions, both cooked and raw, *of an Aerthon!* Even the head was there, baked, yet easily recognizable!

It required many words before Idarbal understood that we did not care for man-meat, or that we would not drink blood instead of wine, though poured from golden bottles. And she only laughed at us when she did comprehend.

"But what, then?"

We explained that, coming from another planet, we could

only assimilate the foods we had brought with us.

"All, everything, was saved and brought below," she stated. Something she said to her attendants. They obediently bundled up our untouched "feast" and departed through what Hul Jok had termed the "snake-hole."

Idarbal was a strange compound of woman and demon, and for all that the demon mostly prevailed within her, still, she had her good qualities. I dare say it, now that the Serpent-Princess is no more; although Esa Nal will doubtless fly off the handle when she reads this and knows that I have so recorded my opinion.

Still, maugre Esa Nal's displeasure, I still say that Idarbal was whole-hearted in her own queer way. For when the lizard-attendants returned they bore not only our own Venhezian foodstuffs and wine-bottles, but also — oh, priceless restoration! — our garments. Had they but brought our little blastors likewise! But as it was, we were immensely pleased. And Idarbal noted this and was commeasurably happy, so much so that she imperiously dismissed her attendants and then insisted upon waiting on us with her own hands. Meantime, between mouthfuls, we questioned her.

"What will your people do with us?"

"Like that," she explained succinctly, indicating the horrors ranged on pedestals all about.

"How is it done?"

"Ask the Wise Ones," she shrugged. "I am the Princess Idarbal. It is no task of mine."

"No escape possible?"

"Where to?" Finality, futility even, was in her very tone.

"To the Aerthons?"

"They would kill me, your wife, as they would destroy, if they could, all my race. Am I a fool that I should help you so?"

"How were we brought here?" This from Hul Jok, one-ideaed as ever, where anything for our welfare was concerned.

"Never shall ye learn that from me!"

Lan Apo snickered almost inaudibly, and as one man we understood why! Nor did Hul Jok need any prompting. For the second time his broad hand slapped Idarbal into a complete coma!

Lan Apo rose to his feet, walked over to one of the metallized horrors, and indicated it.

"Tip it over," he ordered, and Hul Jok heaved with a will. As it overset, a yawning hole showed, slanting downward, whereat Hul Jok grunted his pleasure. Then his eyes lighted. He stepped to one specimen of gruesomeness, caught hold of its legs, one in each hand, and wrenched, twisted, and tugged until both came away from their jointures. The same attention he paid to the arms, and four serviceable clubs were the net result. Two more arms and another leg completed our weaponizing. They were metal clear through, and correspondingly heavy.

With a grim and mirthless smile, Hul Jok caught up our somnolent "wife," wrapped her long nether extremity about her torso until only her white face showed, so making her into a compact bundle which he coolly tucked under his left elbow. Then, holding a metallized leg, the ankle gripped in his huge fist, he stepped to the edge of the downward-slanting hole and dropped into it, boldly. Apparently it was a smooth chute, for he vanished very rapidly.

One after another we each caught up food-bundle or wine-bottles, and followed our giant, sliding adown an unknown passage, to find at the end—

Hul Jok's bellowing voice rose to meet me as I, following him, slithered and skidded downward—the old, wild Venhezian battle-cry, handed onward from forgotten eons back: *"Hue-Hoh!"*

I heard the *thud* and *crash* of his improvised war-club, a confused medley of rapidly moving, shuffling feet, and then a shattering, blood-curdling, screeching shriek that fairly *ripped* into my eardrums. And then I shot feet first into space, fell a short distance, staggered as I lit on a floor, and blinked as I beheld — whirled up my club, also a sizeable, hefty leg, and jumped in to help Hul Jok as best I might.

That thing with which Hul Jok was fighting was a total reversal of the structural anatomy of the Princess Idarbal. It had an Aerthon's legs and trunks and arms; although instead of hands it had great claw-tipped paws at the end of its wrists. And it stood nearly as tall as our giant Commander. Nearly as heavily built, too. But its head! Covered with tawny, reddish-yellow hair it was, with small, pointed ears laid tightly back against its skull. Brilliant yellowish-greenish eyes it had, glaring, yet *slitted*; a yawning cavity of a red mouth with long, dazzlingly white teeth — in short, it was, from the neck up, what the Aerthons later informed us was called a *"Lyon-Kat."*

Hul Jok was bleeding from a scalp-wound where the beast-man had clawed him with a slashing paw-stroke. I got in a whack at it, and was repaid by a lightninglike *rip* that left three blood-spurting lacerations on my left shoulder. As I spun about from the impact of the beast's blow, I saw Ron Ti shoot from a hole in a wall above me, saw him swing back his arm and hurl the bludgeon he carried, squarely into the man-brute's open mouth. For a moment, at least, that monstrosity's breath was shut off completely. It emitted a choking *gurgle*, clawing at the protruding club with both paws.

Hul Jok dropped her he'd been holding fast under his left elbow, grasped his leg-club with both hands and swung heartily.

Crash!

Never was skull made could withstand that! The way before us was unobstructed. Then, one by one, the rest of our party arrived. An adoring voice behind us caused us to glance back at Idarbal.

"I *knew* ye were worthy of my love. Very mighty men are ye."

Hul Jok pointed to his victim, then shook his bludgeon suggestively her way.

"Mor Ag," he ordered, "tell her to guide us to where Jon is kept. We need that Aerthon. Speak, I say!" He reached for Idarbal, but she slitheringly eluded his grasp.

"Is no need, O Mightiest," she assured him, with a ravishing smile. "Shall not leave ye—fear it not. Enjoying myself too much with ye. If ye want that Aerthon-slave, shall have him. Come!"

Really, it looked as if Jon would have a fit when he saw us. Oh, no! we had no trouble at all in locating him. Idarbal led us directly to where he was imprisoned. True, before the entrance of the cavern, wherein he was confined, was stationed another of the ugly Lyon-Kat guards, but the thing was attacked and slain before it even started to fight. It was dozing, half-asleep. And before it could gain an erect position, Hul Jok jumped squarely on the small of its back, landing with both feet. And Hul Jok's feet are no light matters. One smashing blow from his club, and the way was all our own. Idarbal chuckled.

"So it cannot tell tales," she approved.

Jon started an excited gabble to Mor Ag, but Hul Jok put a stop to that waste of time.

"Shut that big mouth of yours, Jon, and come along," he growled.

Jon was too full of delight to obey for long. So he soon attached himself to Ron Ti and commenced giving him an earful regarding the Princess Idarbal, her sinful disposition. He said too much, in fact, for the Serpent-Woman caught at least part of it, and became thoroughly enraged.

I was afraid the Aerthon, in his joy at finding himself among us, his Venhezian friends, would blurt out something, in her hearing, about our actual mission there on that afflicted planet; but some Guardian Power must have inhibited his mind along that line until, through Ron Ti, I could caution him regarding the need of secrecy.

Hul Jok grew bored with trudging along one corridor after another in this subterranean maze, apparently getting nowhere at all. Suddenly his arm shot out and gathered the Serpent-Princess in its viselike hold.

"Whither go we?" he snarled menacingly.

"To my palace," she responded readily. "Is the only place where ye will assuredly be safe. So far ye have not met any of my people—only slaves who dare not tell of seeing ye, lest *I* be displeased. The time of the Moun-Festival draws nigh, and my people are busied in preparations therefor."

"This Moun-Festival," queried Mor Ag, his interest aroused in a new custom. "How is it conducted?"

As I am a living Venhezian, that Serpent-Woman shuddered in horror! Her face, even, turned a livid gray, and her vivid lips blanched.

"Thank whatever gods ye believe in that *ye* shall escape ever knowing how it is conducted," she whispered brokenly. "Those—*things* in that cavern where I found ye—they died—learning how we—worship the Moun! And, had I not given myself to ye, all seven, as wife, ye too—"

And again her great eyes expressed the awfulness of the untellable.

I think that we Venhezians have our share of boldness, but as we caught sight of Lan Apo's face we realized that he, at least, had correctly caught the thought-forms conjured up in her mind as she spoke—and we all felt sick from horror, too. We asked no more questions along that line. The details had suddenly lost all interest.

Idarbal had stated that she was guiding us to her palace, wherever that might be, but after all, we never reached it. For then that occurred which changed everything for us.

Came a terrific jangling sound, much as if all the bells, gongs, and other sonorous instruments on all the worlds had all been tumbled together adown an immeasurable height to bring up with a dissonant *slam* at the bottom! Again—and yet again—until our eardrums ached in misery inexpressible. Hul Jok's bellowing voice sounded like an infant's *coo* as he demanded explanation. But Idarbal was as puzzled as were we.

"Never sounds *that* warning," she declared, "unless great happenings are toward. Yet, I cannot imagine…"

"That Lunarion has landed," Lan Apo spoke up, confidently. "The thought-waves from her rejoicing race are so strong that even here, deep beneath Aerth's surface, I catch them plainly."

Hul Jok decided instantly on changing our plans.

"Tell that she-devil," he commanded, "to guide us to the Aerthons, directly, if she wants not her slim neck twisted until her eyes look down her own spine!"

That threat, I think, wholly disillusioned the Serpent-Princess Idarbal, changing all her self-aroused love for us into intense hate. That we should seek the Aerthons! It was too much! Her face betrayed her thoughts. Such utter, venomous malignancy I never saw depicted on any countenance before. Not even her Lunarion progenitor could have looked more virulent. Yet strangely commingled with her hatred was an expression of intense fear. With a *swish* she shot ahead of us along the passage and so vanished around a bend. So fast she went that none of us, although we immediately gave chase, could overtake her.

"Ends *that*," snapped Hul Jok. "Now ahead, and fight our way."

"This place *I* know!" It was Jon, the Aerthon. "So, from here, I can lead to where are many of my people."

That *was* a relief. We all were pleased at that, Hul Jok especially.

"If we can contact with the Aerthons and form an alliance," he said, "mayhap we can yet upset this world and reshape it for its own good. Jon, how numerous are your people?"

And when Jon assured us that his people outnumbered the Yakshasin race by fifty to one, Hul Jok saw the possibilities even more clearly. As he put it:

"All that these Aerthons need is leaders in whom they can put full confidence, in order to regain control of their own world and again evolve to their former high evolutionary status. We were grievously at fault, long ago. We should have promptly returned here as soon as we eliminated the Lunarion Pollution, and helped them, instead of leaving them to their own devices. Now we have it to do, anyhow. So! This time there will be no turning away until our task is wholly accomplished."

He was right. In our hearts we acknowledged it. And felt inspired to do our best. Ron Ti added the final inspiration, were such needed.

"Great are the mercy and the wisdom of the Ineffable Power! Once were we permitted to become the instruments whereby Its will was carried out. But we, in our short-sightedness, did but half our work. Now will we, seeing more clearly, do the remaining half. So shall we acquire merit! Perhaps, even, we may yet regain our loved ones, unharmed."

And somehow, thereafter, the outcome was never for a moment in doubt, in our minds.

How long it was we wandered in those infernal underground passages, following Jon's guidance, before we contacted with the Aerthons, we had no means of knowing. But every last one of us was fairly aching with fatigue when we finally came into an enormous cavern, man-made, and found there a great crowd of them gathered. At first it looked as if we were due to be butchered by their long, sharp swords which they whirled in unpleasant proximity to our noses.

Jon shouted and cursed at them until finally they commenced to pay some slight attention. Well, we had a staunch advocate. Then we had two!

A gaunt, red-haired woman burst through the ring of menacing warriors, embracing him with ardor. Plainly his wife! Few and terse were the words he shot at her, but they sufficed. She outyelled them all!

Very shortly, the long blades were sheathed, and we were eating, heartily, from our own supplies. Then we seven Venhezians and Jon the Aerthon held a brief council, surrounded by a curious, staring throng of his people. Strategy those Aerthons knew not at all. Direct attack best suited their primitive, barbarous minds. But that, as Hul Jok promptly pointed out to Jon, was but a suicidal mania. Jon proved an apt pupil, grasped our ideas easily. Evidently, travel had broadened his mind.

"What first?" he queried.

"Explain in detail to your people how wonderful you think we are," Hul Jok ordered, regardless of all appearance of modesty or lack of it; for it was necessary to impress them thoroughly with our importance, if we were to use them as allies. "Then, when they are willing to follow and obey us, send out armed parties to capture—not kill—a number of your enemies, and bring them to us that we may question them."

Jon caught that idea, too.

"And then?"

"We ourselves do not know, until after that has happened," Hul Jok admitted frankly. "Now we would sleep. Find us a quiet place, if such may be had. Then go among your people and do as you have been bidden. When you have several prisoners, awaken us that we may interview them. That, for now, is enough."

Oh, that Ron Ti!

I learned, afterward, that he'd barely slept an hour; then, because he could converse fluently with the Aerthons, he'd gone among them and made friends. Above all, he'd sought out their metal-workers, from whom he'd learned where their workshops were, and had been immensely gratified when he'd been told that none of the dominant race did any actual work, ever. That part they'd always relegated to the Aerthon slaves.

Learning also that, since the insurrection started, no one was in any of the shops, Ron Ti had taken an armed party of Aerthons and set out on a tour of investigation. As he told us when he returned:

"Little time have I for experimentation; but if all goes well, I feel certain that very shortly our Aerthon allies will have more potent weapons to their aid than their own sharp swords. Neither blastor nor ak-blastor can I produce; for the materials are not to be had, nor do I know where to seek for the proper minerals. But"—and his eyes lighted confidently—"I have found a number of light-projectors which do but need repairing to make them again effective, the rays from which will crumble rock, dirt, and metal to dust for a couple of thousand feet ahead. Evidently it has been by use of those that these stupendous caverns have been hollowed out.

"Should our enemies attempt to use their death-ray projectors on our Aerthon allies whenever we do attack, those instruments, being principally of metal, will be promptly rendered useless by our Crumble-Rays. And, should they attempt to barricade themselves against direct attack, we can shatter their defenses faster than they can build them up. And at close quarters, the Aerthons, with their sharp swords, being in numerical superiority—"

"It is absolute extermination, then?" Lan Apo asked, horrified, for he had caught Hul Jok's and Ron Ti's thoughts. "With all their outward defenses pulverized, their light-ray destroyers rendered powerless, these Lunarion-spawn, bad as they are, will be wholly at mercy of their Aerthon-slaves, and what that mercy will prove—"

"Little girl, be still," gibed Hul Jok. "Remember, this hell-brood you are wasting pity upon are but intelligent animals—or reptiles, rather—they are un-naturalisms, depraved; given to loathly debaucheries; unfit to survive; for whom is no place in a decent universe! Once we allowed one Lunarion to live. You, as well as we, now reap the consequences of that colossal folly. Do you, Lan Apo, advocate that we repeat our former mistake?"

The boy flushed.

"You are right," he admitted. "So let it be."

Certainly, it was war, unrelenting, ferocious even, and we could tolerate no thoughts of mercy. Yet when the Aerthons brought in a dozen or more captives, as they did shortly, we could not but dread that which we knew must inevitably ensue.

Those captives were an amazingly queer-looking lot. There was one much like the Princess Idarbal in appearance, only bulkier from the waist up; evidently masculine. There were two who walked upright, had great, horny scales all over their bodies, had elongated heads, somewhat lizardlike save that upper jaws lifted as well as lower jaws dropped when they opened their mouths. And both sets of jaws were provided with long, white, spikelike teeth. One who stood erect had the head of a bird, beak and all, was covered with leathery skin, had long, cruel talons at ends of arms and legs—ugh! Monstrosities, every last one; yet fair examples, save in detail, of all the hell-brood begotten by their Lunarion parentage. For those who wish further knowledge of that now exterminate race of Yakshasins, there are the writings which Vir Dax has but recently completed, wherein he has gone to further lengths than there is space for in a brief narration of this sort.

"It sounds heartless, I know," Hul Jok told Vir Dax, grimly. "But *you* know bodies, brain, nerve, tissue, bone, muscle and blood as none other can know. So! I command you by that Looped Cross we all serve, that, should torture prove needful in order to make them talk—"

Vir Dax smiled vindictively.

"Apologize not, nor command," he said quietly. "It will be a pleasure—nor am I at all squeamish. I hope," he added emphatically, "that they will prove obdurate! Let you, Hul Jok, question that one, first." And he pointed to one perfectly gigantic fellow, huger than was our War-Prince himself.

The prisoner indicated had a face not at all bestial, structurally, although his expression, while denoting a high grade of intelligence, denoted also a most horrifically cruel disposition.

Question after question Hul Jok, with Mor Ag and Ron Ti interpreting, hurled at the captive. But all he would vouchsafe was that he was one of the Wise Ones, obviously a warrior-priest, and that he held himself too wise to tell us anything.

Vir Dax, in a voice which fairly *purred* with pleased anticipation, ordered them all, bound securely, to be laid flat on the cavern floor. Coldly, deliberately, with a short length broken from the pointed end of an Aerthon's sword, he tested each and every one for sensitivity to pain. One of the Crokhadyl-headed Yakshas proved to be the *least* sensitive; and I saw the cold eyes of Vir Dax light suggestively.

What followed, none of us Venhezians, except Vir Dax, likes to remember. Yet, ere that Crokhadyl-headed nightmare died, there was inspired in the others, who watched his gradually increased agonies, a most dreadful fear of that quiet, cold-eyed, gently smiling, softly moving Venhezian, Vir Dax—so much so, that whenever his eyes flickered in the direction of any one of them, that captive *winced!*

Very deliberately, as one who prolongs a delight, Vir Dax selected as subject number two that leather-skinned, birdlike monstrosity.

Its squawks of fright and anguish helped it not at all. Vir Dax went on as if he were accustomed to disarticulating such beings, still living, every day. Why, when he finished with that second specimen, and rose to his feet, even the Aerthons who had watched, shrank uneasily from meeting his gaze, and we Venhezians were shuddering with horror, Hul Jok not excepted.

And when Vir Dax bent above that "Wise One," who had at first defied us, the cold sweat of terror burst out all over his naked body, and he screamed, panic-stricken, as might any weak woman.

He talked! No question about it! Told us all we needed to know. Would have—had we permitted—turned against his own people and fought for us, would have betrayed them, singly or in a mass, into our ruthless hands, gladly, if only, he whimpered, we would keep that awful tormentor from even touching him!

Were I to set forth in detail all that he told us, it would use up too much space, and would be out of place in this narrative, besides. But, in effect, we learned that Lan Apo was, as usual, correct, when he'd declared that the Last Lunarion had landed. We learned that our Love-Girls still lived, and—joyous news!—were as yet unharmed; were safe, in fact, until the time of the Moun-Festival.

We learned, too, that, indirectly, we had our former "mutual wife," the Princess Idarbal, to thank for their immunity since the Lunarion had arrived on Aerth. For It—or he—who had intended making our seven Venhezian Love-Girls for his queens, had promptly abandoned that idea from the instant he'd set eyes on Idarbal, who suited his notions even better. But she had stipulated as price of their union that the Venhezian women be given over to the Wise Ones as sacrificial victims at the forthcoming Moun-Festival.

"And this Moun-Festival occurs, when?"

Hul Jok roared his delight as our captive informed us that it was as yet nine nights off. And Ron Ti was equally pleased.

"They might fully as well give us a thousand years to prepare in," he chortled. "In seven days I will have every unarmed full-blood Aerthon provided with a good sharp sword. Us Venhezians I will equip with those repaired Crumble-Ray projectors I mentioned. Seven will be sufficient."

Hul Jok motioned to the Aerthons standing about us, and — well! Our remaining captives did not continue to survive; that is all! Nor, from then on, were any more captives brought in by the Aerthons. We did not need any.

Thenceforward, Aerthons and Venhezians alike became busy beings, hardly pausing by day or night, save to eat hurriedly, snatch a wink or two of sleep, and again resume our labors. And daily and nightly, more and more Aerthons came in from remote caverns…

And what were their Yakshasin master-race doing, all this while?

Feasting, reveling, indulging in every debauchery their depraved desires prompted, in accordance with their unnatural natures, and rejoicing, generally, over that stupendous miracle of all unexpected miracles — the survival and return of one of their "godlike" Lunarion begetters.

Oh, assuredly, they knew that we Venhezians were somewhere on, or in, their planet, and so had apprised the Lunarion himself. But they knew, too — or thought they knew — that we had naught wherewith to stir up trouble, save, mayhap, clubs or rocks. And they? Did not they have once again a Lunarion to guide and rule them? Plenty of time in which to attend to our case, after the great Moun-Festival was ended. Then they could hunt us down, capture us, and hold us for the next one.

As Ron Ti had promised, the night of the seventh day found all in readiness.

We knew, because of what we'd learned from the Aerthons and from our captive Wise One, that the Moun-Festival was held in the great Temple of Lunarah, which was, in reality, but a vast, dome-shaped, hollowed-out hill with a hole in its top which let in the direct Moun-beams when that orb, at its full, hung at its greatest height in the night skies. And we knew, likewise, that it was located on Aerth's surface in the middle of a broad, flat, rocky plain. As Hul Jok remarked, sardonically, when first we were told of it:

"What, for our purposes, could be more convenient than that?"

Even more to our purposes was it that none of the Yakshas or Yakshinis would be armed, during the ceremonials—aside from a lot of Lyon-Kat guards whose duty it was to surround the victims until the Wise Ones took them over into their clutches. So far as we could see, figuring ahead, it was nothing less than a slaughter we were planning—very unpleasant, but very necessary! Yet on one point Hul Jok waxed emphatic to the Aerthons. Which was:

"Every Wise One possible must be kept alive. I must have at least a dozen, intact! And that Lunarion I will attend to, myself. Wo to that Aerthon who disobeys me in this!"

But he needed entertain no worry along that line. The Aerthons were rapidly losing their fears of their Yakshasin masterrace, thanks to Jon's excellent work in telling amazing yarns regarding the great prowess of us, their Venhezian allies. But not an Aerthon of them all but dreaded, with a dread unspeakable, facing one of the demoniacal Moun-Things again. They were only too willing to leave the Lunarion to Hul Jok!

Very early on that ninth night we seven Venhezians, each accompanied by a dozen Aerthons bearing the Crumble-Ray appliance of Ron Ti's finding, started upward to the surface of Aerth, and debouched on the rocky plain. And behind us swarmed hordes of armed Aerthons, fairly lusting for the coming fray. Long, heavy, and terrible was the account standing between them and their master-race; and short, sweet and final would the reckoning be! One look at the savage features, hate-distorted, was sufficient to vouch for that, the crowning proof being, were such needed, that they marched silently, instead of yelling, as might have been expected from hordes of barbarians. But they took no chances of giving untimely warning!

Jon the Aerthon, who had developed marked ability as a leader, and who had in consequence won Hul Jok's unqualified approval, remained underground. He and that red-haired, screeching fury, his wife, in command of some two thousand Aerthon men and women, were to close every exit beneath the Temple of Lunarah, so that none should escape that way.

"Two thousand is too plenty," Jon assured us with a cheerful grin, and his gap-toothed terror of a wife added a reassuring smile of her own that sent cold chills running up my back.

Before the Moun had climbed halfway to the zenith, we Venhezians, with the Crumble-Ray projectors assembled and focused, were placed as Hul Jok would have us, and our Aerthon allies were simply a-quiver with murderous anxiety for the attack to begin. And we Venhezians were fully as anxious as were our allies, to tell the truth about it; only, we awaited the proper signal. Ironically enough, it would be our intended victims who would sound their own death-knell. That same jangling *crash* of dissonance we'd heard when the Lunarion landed, while yet we were wandering in the underground passages with the Princess Idarbal, would once again be sounded as announcement that all were present, and that the Moun-Festival was ready to start.

So we settled down and waited. There remained naught else to do. But finally it came...

My Crumble-Ray projector slammed its viciously crackling brilliance against that hill the instant the first vibration of sound smote upon my suffering eardrums.

A shattering yell sounded behind me as the Aerthons rose to their feet and charged straight for the yawning passage I'd driven into the side of that damnable hill-temple.

One thing we hardly figured on came into my mind and rather frightened me for a bit, although it was too late then to do anything about it, even if I'd tried. Which was, that with the enormous mass of hill being pulverized by the Crumble-Rays from seven projectors, what could save our Love-Girls from being smothered in the heap of dust ensuing? It was an appalling thought, and it brought the cold sweat of horror out on my forehead, albeit the night was warm enough.

But then I bethought me that even such a fate was more merciful than what awaited them during the ceremonials. And then I saw, with infinite relief, a huge, featherlike cloud of dust spout upward from the hole in the apex of the hill, and realized with joy that, with seven holes being driven inward with the speed of light, air was rushing inward too, as fast as the rays could make way for it; and that as soon as the shell of the Temple of Lunarah had been penetrated the combined air-currents had sought outlet through the opening at the top. Actually, the dust was spouting upward like an extremely active volcano.

Strictly speaking, there was very little fighting. It was, rather, even as we had anticipated, merely an overwhelming catastrophe for the Lunarion and the Yakshasin race. True, the Lyon-Kat guards died fighting valorously, and it must be recorded that they took nearly thirty times their number of Aerthons with them! But aside from that, the rest was but a butchery. Nine Wise Ones and the Last Lunarion were all that were left, some time before the Moun had reached that point where it had shed its cold light into the opening, bathed in its effulgence the naked, sacrificial victims, and so given the signal for their atrocious torments to begin; ere death gave the signal, in its turn, for their transmutation from organic flesh into inorganic metal.

I was inside practically as soon as our Aerthon allies. The work of my Crumble-Ray apparatus was finished, and for all that Esa Nal had her faults—glaring ones, too; more especially, a temper—still she, such as she is, is yet all mine; wherefore I had my own feud to settle, my own vengeful feelings to glut.

I'm not the smallest Venhezian on our planet, although neither am I a giant like Hul Jok. But—for close quarters I have learned to love a hefty war-club. And I had a fine one. Ron Ti had made it for me with his own hands. And it balanced splendidly.

The first trial I gave it was on an enormous Lyon-Kat guard. He made a sidewise swipe at me with something he gripped in both paws, a something that flashed dully through the swirling dust infiltrating the air, a something that fairly *sang* as it cleft the air.

Instinctively I sidestepped and lashed out, two-handed, with the plaything Ron Ti had devised for my enjoyment. It connected, satisfactorily, with the Lyon-Kat's nose just in alinement with its greenly glaring eyes—and I passed on, well pleased. A wonderfully sweet little toy I had!

Then a thing like a fat, white worm, erect, snapped at me with its slavering, pink mouth—and *squelched* to a filthy mess as I caressed it with my war-club. A snakish being flung a few coils about my legs, like lightning—and unwrapped itself much more rapidly as I reproved it by butting it in the abdomen with the head of my bludgeon.

A bellowing voice tore its way to my ears through the din and the dust: *"Hak Iri – to me!"*

I saw our gigantic War-Prince, armed with a great club, twice the size and heft of mine, striving to smash his way through a ring of Lyon-Kat guards, six deep, in the center of which I caught brief glimpses of soft, womanly, nude flesh. Our Love-Girls, at last!

I needed no further invitation. With a yell which would have done credit to Jon's wife at her best, I jumped to Hul Jok's side.

Those infernal Lyon-Kats were every one of them armed with long, thick metal staves surmounted by disks, convex on both surfaces, a *metar* in diameter, and sharp as knives all around the edges. Moun-symbols they were but deadly weapons at close quarters. I saw one Lyon-Kat shear a bulky Aerthon clear through at the waist, with a single swipe. My club caught that same Lyon-Kat alongside of his ugly head at practically the same instant, and he sheared no more Aerthons!

Then, out of the top of my head, as it were—for both of my eyes were otherwise busied in watching those shimmering, swiping disks—I saw a sight which made me gasp in amazed horror and dread.

Straight up, out from the center of that ring of Lyon-Kats, there shot into air, levitationally, the Last Lunarion! In his hands he grasped one of the Moun-disk weapons such as the Lyon-Kat guards wielded. Once above the ruck of the fighting, It made straight for Hul Jok, poised above him, and swung his keen weapon viciously downward at our leader's head.

Hul Jok must have seen that blow coming—apparently through the top of *his* head—for he flung up one arm, and caught that awful weapon just back of its *razhir*-sharp disk head in his mighty grasp. One terrific downward *yank*—

Hul Jok hurled his ponderous war-club into the face of a Lyon-Kat and wrapped both arms about that "godlike" Lunarion. In his inexorable grasp the Moun-Thing turned a dirty leaden-gray from fear.

"In! In, I say, Hak Iri! To the Girls! I've *this* to hold!"

Then occurred the well-nigh unbelievable.

The instant the Lunarion went *grey*, his will-witchery spell over our Venhezian Love-Girls was broken!

I heard the clear, clarion voice of Hala Fau, Hul Jok's woman, ring out in the old Venhezian battle-chant:

"*Hue-Hoh! Venhez and the Looped Cross! For Life and Love! Slay! Slay! Slay!*"

Heard, too, the high, shrill voice of Esa Nal:

"Hak Iri! Hak Iri! *My Man!*"

Saw Esa Nal drive forward, catch a Lyon-Kat around the legs

with her arms, spilling him to the ground. Saw Hala Fau stamp on the back of his head, jamming his ugly nose into the hard-packed dirt floor, and, bending forward, snatch his disk-weapon from him, make sure with it that he would never attempt to regain it; saw her split with another blow the head of another Lyon-Kat—and saw *my* Esa Nal promptly equip herself and set to work like any old veteran of many affrays—which, in a manner of speaking, she was! *You* never—whoso reads—got into dispute with her. I have! Why, even gentle, tender, timid Kia Min, Lan Apo's Love-Girl, fought with a ferocity that out-vied any Lyon-Kat!

It marked the end. With seven thoroughly enraged Venhezian Love-Girls armed and athirst for revenge and liberty in their midst, the ring of Lyon-Kat guards was soon but a memory...

Never could we ask aught from the Aerthons we could not have. Less than four days sufficed Ron Ti to erect a plant, crude, 'tis true, but powerful enough to signal Venhez. We knew, without awaiting reply, that a Venhezian War-Fleet was on the way to Aerth as soon as that message could be read.

The only way in which we could be sure that the Last Lunarion would remain innocuous, we adopted, cruel though it might seem. We turned him over to the Aerthon women and children to amuse themselves with. Well, they invented a new one! In a place where a cavern-wall was very thin, and formed a sharp corner, they bored several holes to the outer air, letting in sunlight, such as it was; shining ever into that Lunarion's face and eyes. Also, they had fire, and sword-blades, and took turns, continuously, day and night... I do not think that the Lunarion's kingship pleased him...

Vir Dax, Hul Jok, Ron Ti and I held sessions with those nine captive Wise Ones. At first they were stubborn, would tell us naught. But—Vir Dax, his methods!...

Finally Ron Ti ended his satisfaction, and Hul Jok's blazing eyes were agleam with triumph.

"It is even simpler than I had thought," Ron Ti said. "I can do it myself—with improved variations. Even better in my Workshop back on Venhez than I can here."

The Wise Ones, or what Vir Dax had left of them, we gave, likewise, to the little Aerthon children—the first playthings Aerthon children had had for eons past, doubtless. And the little imps certainly appreciated their new-found sport!

Then, one morning, a hundred Venhezian fighting aethir-torps hurtled into Aerth's atmosphere and effected landings in such haste that the well-nigh infusible Berulion plates of which the hulls are made were red-hot almost, from atmospheric friction. And their crews nearly went *fran-tak* from delight when Hul Jok rated them soundly for careless—not to say reckless—navigating! But it was Hul Jok! And listening to his tongue-lashing sounded good to ears that had never hoped to hear his heavy voice again.

A hundred Venhezian aethir-torps. Six ak-blastors to each craft, and a crew of one hundred Venhezians aboard each one of the fleet, each carrying one of the tiny, deadly disintegrators—the hand-size blastors—and each man aching to use his toy!

In another two days, poor, afflicted Aerth was truly clean. That hundred Venhezians left not even a spider nor a toad, let alone those loathly *Blob-Things* we'd encountered on that first momentous trip of all.

Hul Jok, at request of the Aerthons themselves, left a dozen aethir-torps and a Venhezian sub-commander to govern, educate, and assist them until they became, in actuality, self-sustaining.

Then we returned to Venhez, where an entire planet went mad with delight. Not one Love-Girl of the lowliest Venhezian may be stolen without the most frightful penalties being exacted…

𝔐idnight! And in Ron Ti's great laboratory were gathered a silent, grimly waiting group. All seven of us were there, as were our lost and regained Love-Girls. Also were present all the members of the Venhezian Supreme Council.

The Last Lunarion was there, likewise. Caged again, in so narrow a space It perforce had to stand erect, and without ability to will-witch Itself out, this time. Never, since Hul Jok had *pawed* him out of the air above the fighting, back on Aerth, had the Lunarion lost his leaden-hued gray color of fear. Yet I do not think he really guessed how Hul Jok meant to deal with him; in truth, I do not think that Hul Jok himself knew the precise method he'd employ — until after he'd actually gotten his hands on the Moun-Thing.

Coldly, all emotion lacking from his heavy voice, Hul Jok, in plain, terse terms, explained to that fear-quivering thing in the cage that Its day of punishment had arrived — and why!

The Moun-Thing shuddered, whimpering, glaring out of Its horror-haunted eyes at us who watched. Still, It tried to defy us:

"I cannot be slain…"

"True," assented Hul Jok. "Nor do we wish your death…"

Ron Ti swung a lever over.

A stream of softly glinting particles from one of Ron Ti's queer mechanisms sprayed through the bars of the Moun-Thing's cage. The particles seemed to do It no hurt. In fact, for a moment It did not appear to notice what was happening. Then comprehension dawned upon Its consciousness. Although even then, none of us Venhezians who were watching, save Hul Jok and Ron Ti, fully understood.

The scintillant stream which flowed so softly, gleaming so *prettily*, was gradually impregnating that Thing in the cage, was turning Its entire body, *while yet alive*, to a statue of solid metal — impregnating It with Selenion, the Metal of the Moun!

The terrific transmutation was finally accomplished…

O Our Lady Venhez! What a fate! Although metal, and thus

immobile, *the Thing still lived — had consciousness!*

In the center of the great public square in our Venhezian capital city, Ash-tar the Splendid, there stands an enormous cube of inky-black rock. Atop of this is another cube, but little smaller, of crystal-clear glass. So clear it is, indeed, that air itself is scarce more lucid.

Imbedded therein, a sight for all to behold, is sealed forevermore that Selenion Statue which cannot die...

The Last Lunarion...

Surely, the oath of Hul Jok was no light threat!

And Venhezian men and women — also those who at times come to our fair planet from other worlds — gaze thereon and turn away in the full assurance that nevermore shall the universe be menaced by the malignant activities of a pollution incarnate and unspeakable...

The Red Witch

Is there a past, a present, and a future; or are they in reality all the same state, being merely differing phases of the same eternal "Now"?

Are our lives and deaths and the interludes between them naught but illusion; and are we ever the same beings, yet capable, even though we do not recognize the fact, of experiencing two or more states of consciousness of personal identity—I mean, under certain exceptional conditions?

Times there are when my recent terrific experience impels me to adopt that hypothesis. How else may I explain the events wherein I played so strange a part—together with another who is far dearer to me than aught else in the universe?

Am I Randall Crone, a scientist connected with a great public museum, or am I Ran Kron, a youthful warrior of a savage tribe in the eon-old Ice Age? Is my wife, Rhoda—the gently nurtured, highly cultured Rhoda Day—the modern product of this Twentieth Century; or is she Red Dawn, the flaming-haired daughter of a red-headed witch-priestess of a devil-worshipping tribe of skin-clad Anthropophagi in that same remote Ice Age?

What is true, and what false? By what strange laws are we governed, we mortals, that we can see neither ahead nor backward, and are only aware of a limited "Here"?

My brain reels as I seek to solve the mystery—and to what account? Truly has a great poet said:

> Of all my seeking, this is all my gain—
> No agony of any mortal brain
> Shall wrest the secret of the life of man,
> The search has taught me that the search is vain!

I first saw her in the museum where I was on duty, and hard-headed scientist that I prided myself on being, I admit that my heart did a flip-flop, and I knew I beheld the one woman for whom I'd ever truly care. But that is a mild word for the love I felt. Love, I say; and I mean just that. In the holy emotion that possessed me there was no faintest throb of passion, no taint of desire. Beautiful? Yes, the most superbly beautiful woman on earth, I thought then, and still do think, and will continue so to think long after wrinkles and gray hair and decrepitude shall cause others to say "Old Hag", should that ever come to pass.

For soul has spoken to soul, and we twain know that we belong to each other; and though menaced as we were by the frightful ghost of the implacable savage chieftain, Athak the Terrible, yet we have overcome his menace, and no longer has he the power to afflict and harass our love and happiness through his eon-old malicious hatred.

Yet while he still had the power, he surely availed himself of it, measure full and running over; as my beloved knew from her early childhood up to the time we were married; and as I myself had several samples of, after that event; although, thanks to some benignant power, Athak's final attack was his undoing. But I am in danger of anticipating and must set down my account in a more logical sequence.

As I have said: I loved Rhoda Day from the first; and later I learned from her own lips that her feelings toward me were identical. At the time we neither of us knew why, but eventually we found out. Yet when I asked her to be my wife she burst into tears, sobbing:

"Oh Randall, if only I could say 'Yes'; but—but—I—dare not!"

"Don't you care for me?"

"More than for life itself..."

"Then why not—surely there must be some reason?"

"Oh, Randall, a terrible one..."

"Tell me," I urged. But I coaxed for over an hour, holding her close in my arms, her head with its coronal of red-gold hair resting on my shoulder, her soft cheek against mine, before she finally gasped out her fears in broken phrases.

I'll not attempt to render her exact words. It simply cannot be done. We both were in the grip of one of life's greatest emotions; and at such times I do not think that memory reproduces exactly. But in substance, thus the matter stood:

From a child, she'd been cognizant that, no matter where she was, or what she did, always there seemed to be another present, invisible, but very real nevertheless. A very terrible presence, too, inspiring her with loathing and dread, although it did not seem antagonistic to her welfare or her life. Rather it seemed to gloat over her with an air of proprietorship which she found indescribably horrifying.

Times there were when the presence exercised a very real power to protect her; as for example—when in her eleventh year she had a nerve-shaking experience with an ill-natured brute of a dog that snarled and menaced her with bared fangs. She knew, irrefutably, that the beast would have sprung in another moment, and stood paralyzed with terror, unable to cry out for help.

She sensed a storm of ferocious wrath sweep past her, enveloping the dog; and—unbelievable as it appears—that dog died! Yet on its body was evident no mark of violence. Apparently the brute died in a paroxysm of terror. But even after that episode, for a long while she had no idea as to what the Presence was.

As she grew older, she noted more frequently that that same power, or force, or influence, was exerting itself in her behalf to guard her—sometimes too zealously—a something too fiercely possessive, and capable of emitting a wave of such malignant hostility that she was for the most part devoid of the friends such as a young girl usually has.

And as she ripened into the first blush of young womanhood, drawn by her beauty there was no lack of young men who sought to do her homage and court her with their attentions—but none of them ever sought long. Doubtless, the air of hostility they felt about her, enshrouding her like a garment, they attributed to her; believing her to be of a disagreeable, if not an actually repellent personality; instead of realizing that it was an alien nature, emanating from a source outside itself, and certainly quite apart from her desires.

At that same period she became aware that the Presence was even more strongly possessive in its attitude; and, worse, again and again it made her sense its proximity even in the sanctum of her own room. But up until the day we were assured of each other's feelings she had not seen the thing—whatever it was. That night, however, after retiring, she awoke with the hideous feeling of being not alone—awoke to see the two eyes staring down at her; eyes aflame with wrath; eyes set in a vague, nebulous blur that might or might not have borne the semblance of a human face.

Of course she was frightened. Anyone would be, under the same circumstances. She was so frightened that, try as she would to call out and arouse the household, she could emit no sound louder than a moan, barely audible to herself. She could not even move a muscle; could only lie still in an agony of apprehension, staring wildly up into the blazing orbs not a yard above her face.

Oddly enough, the apparition contented itself with glaring at her, striving to impress something on her mind, indelibly. All the impression conveyed, however, was that in some manner she had angered the "Thing", although how, or why, she could not comprehend.

But as we met more frequently, and our minds as well as our hearts became more filled with each other, the unholy visitant, appearing nightly, became more and more enraged. It was easier to see, assuming density of form and features with its rapidly growing wrath. After such visits she felt as if she had been beaten, physically, with a thick stick, wielded by a strong hand and arm.

Always it strove to impress upon her consciousness a very definite command, but always it failed to make its will register. Yet with each visit it became more visible until it was easily seen to be a huge man, long-armed and thick-legged, inclining more to the blond type than to the swarthy; skin-clad, carrying a huge knotted club, and a great stone-bladed knife stuck through a narrow leather thong tied about his middle.

"He—he—looks so—*savage*," she shuddered.

I stared down at the lovely, tear-bedewed face, my mind in a queer jumble of commingled amazement and fear. Those wondrous blue eyes looked straight back into mine, reading my unspoken thought.

"Randall, my beloved," she said gravely, mastering her emotions with a superb manifestation of will-power, "it all sounds crazy enough, I know; but please do not think your Rhoda is crazy. *She isn't!* I know what I've been subjected to ever since I was old enough to remember anything."

Ashamed of my momentary suspicion, I hastened to make the only amends within my power.

"If you're crazy, then I'll go crazy, too," I stated seriously. "How soon will you marry me? You love me, and I love you. That being the case, to whom but me should you turn for sympathy, understanding, and protection; insofar as lies within my power to give them... why, Rhoda, what's a husband *good* for, if not to stand between his woman and the whole world, and the Powers of Hell, too, for that matter, if she needs his aid? Once married, we can be together at the very times your danger is the greatest. I don't know what I can do, if anything; but I'll guarantee that whatever this skin-clad giant is up to, he'll have me to dispose of before he harms you. I want you, and you need me, and that brings us back where we were—*How soon do we get married?"*

"Randall! Randall! Stop urging me, or you'll sweep me off my feet! I cannot and will not let you become involved—"

"Try keeping me out," I defied, my whole being aflame with a loving sympathy and pity. Suddenly over me swept an unalterable certitude—that I was already involved, fully as much as was she. Nay, more: I felt that I always had been; only until then I had not known it. But in that one moment I knew that my fate and Rhoda's were the same; and that whatever this being was which menaced, it was likewise a menace to me, and would be so forevermore, unless in some manner as yet unguessed by me I could put an end to its unholy machinations. So I told her of my sudden conviction, and when I'd concluded, I saw stark worship replace the fear-haunted expression in her eyes.

"Randall,"—her voice was vibrant with all the love a good woman feels in her soul and cannot express with mere words—"you'd dare that awful being, risk your life, perhaps your very soul for—me?"

"Risk my life, perhaps my soul, for you, Rhoda? Mine would be but a pitifully weak love if I hesitated to do so. I most certainly am going to do that very thing, if need be. Your troubles henceforth are my troubles too, so that's that! Now let's drop all this cross-purpose talk and talk sense for a while. I've already asked you to marry me, and now I'm saying it differently—we two are going to get married right now, at once, immediately, today! Get me? You've got absolutely nothing to say about it. *I'm* Boss, with a big 'B'! And how do you like *that?"*

"Oh, I—I—give up," she faltered. "Only you will simply have to wait at least a week. We've simply got to conform somewhat to the standard conventions and tell a few people; otherwise tongues are sure to wag, unfavorably."

I was too well pleased to argue. After all, that day or a week later, mattered but little. The monster had not slain her up till then, and had had plenty of time in which to have done so, had such been his purpose. So I let it go as she stipulated, with one amendment.

"If that 'What-you-may-call-it' reappears in your room, you tell him my name and address; try and make him comprehend *me*, then tell him to come and annoy *me* for a change and let you take a rest. I've an idea that I can cope with him…"

That night things did happen!
Rhoda told me later what her experience was that night. Unpleasant, very, but fortunately brief; and in a way it was merely the preliminary to what I went through immediately afterward.

She had no sooner retired than the Thing appeared, seemingly more tangible than ever before. It made no attempt to actually molest her, but was obviously in a towering rage. It did everything but rave aloud. It stamped about the room, gnashing its teeth in the perfect frenzy; frowning and grimacing intimidatingly; shaking a huge fist in her face; pantomiming strangling her with its enormous hands; and plainly conveying through sheer force of wrath, that she'd gone to the ultimate limit of its patience. Above all, it made her understand that it was *jealous!* Which gave her her cue. It speaks well for her brave spirit that she faced the ugly apparition with a smile of contempt, jeered at it, and demanded in a whisper:

"If you're jealous of Randall Crone, why don't you go and try to bully him, instead of acting like a coward by tormenting me all the time?"

To make a good job of it, she exerted all her will to picture me and my abode so clearly that he could catch her thought-images. And after a bit she succeeded; for a look of comprehension and hatred came over the savage features, and a second afterward the apparition vanished from her room.

I'd been reading and at the same time hoping that the Thing would pay me a visit that night. I had no idea as to how to cope with it. I do not claim to be a great hero, but had the Devil himself threatened Rhoda's peace of mind, though he came to me with horns, barbed tail, talons all sharpened, cloven hoofs, flaming eyes, breathing sulfur fumes, and with his white-hot pitchfork raised to strike, still I would have fought him to the best of my ability and trusted to luck to defeat him somehow. But I didn't intend to be caught asleep and off guard if I could help myself. Hence I sat and read.

And it came!

The same huge, savage warrior that Rhoda had so graphically described. And the instant it assumed visibility, I knew that I was in for a most unpleasant time. The utter malignity of its expression proclaimed that here was a being to whom the very ideas of mercy, reason, or even caution, were completely unknown.

It had the power of rendering itself visible, but could not make itself audible, although if it had spoken, I'd have been none the wiser, for I could not have understood whatever uncouth language might have been its native tribal tongue. But it certainly could and did make its thoughts register on my brain. He—for there's no need to longer call the Thing "it"—warned me very emphatically that *he* owned that red-headed woman; had owned her since the world was young, and always would own her till long after the world died of old age; and that if I wanted to remain all in one piece I'd best never go near her again. All this was punctuated by flourishing an enormous knotted—spectral—club which he wielded in one huge fist.

I never did like being bullied!

And the more that infernal savage phantom raved, the less I liked it. A slow anger began to burn within me. I had my own ideas about his asserted ownership of Rhoda. I wasn't conceited enough to think that I owned her, but I was quite sure that *he* didn't! While as to me staying away from her simply because he bade me do so—

I came to my feet, "seeing red" literally, and hurled myself at him with all my inhibitions inherited from my civilized ancestry wholly in abeyance. I was fully as much a savage as ever he had been! My entire being was filled with but one desire—to get my hands, aye, my teeth even, to working on him; to batter, to rend, to tear, kick, bite, gouge, and strangle until he was—

Something seemed to burst within my skull; a terrific blaze of scarlet light which blinded me for a bit—in my ears was a roaring like to the four winds of the world colliding simultaneously—a queer rushing sensation as if I were hurtling through the boundless abyss of space—

I regained consciousness...

I was in a village of some fifty-odd stone huts. Low round buildings they were, wherefrom smoke rose lazily into the air through holes in the high-pitched peak-roofs. It was late in the day, for the long shadows stretched almost eastward. Skin-clad men and women moved about the huts. White of skin they were, the majority light-haired, with blue or gray eyes. The women for the most part were short, broad, stocky of build; none of them really bad-looking, yet none really comely, let alone any of them having even a remote approach to beauty. Their faces were too stolid, and their voices were too harsh to render any of them attractive.

The men were proportionately taller, equally as broad, their faces more savage in expression; and all, even in the comparative safety of their own village, were armed with various weapons—a stone knife in a skin girdle, or a short stone-headed spear carried in one brawny hand; or a stone ax; or a knotted club; but I saw no missile weapons such as bows and arrows or slings; nor did any of the warriors bear shields.

I saw myself as one of their number; knew myself as Ran Kron, a savage youth, a mere stripling not as yet a warrior; still untried, longing, yearning, looking eagerly forward to that time when I might stand with these hard-faced warriors in the whirl and tumult of a battle, that I might prove myself a man.

Wherefore I exercised at all the war-like pastimes and practices and in my spare time haunted the abode of old Juhor the Snake, the tribe's most highly skilled weapon-maker.

To return to this present time in which I now write—I realize how difficult it is to make plain just how I knew all this which I've just described. All that I can say is—I did know. The same difficulty is confronting me in regard to what now follows. I can only write it as I knew it to be occurring while I was living in that phase of my existence. I knew my own experiences. But I knew, too, the experiences of others, insofar as those were intertwined with my own. So from here on, for a while at least, I must write in the third person instead of the first person, singular...

Juhor the Snake, old, bent, crippled, and incredibly wrinkled, looked up from his work of chipping and polishing at the head of a green-stone war-ax he was making. A crafty gleam shone, transient, in his one good eye, as he beheld the tribe's mightiest fighting-man passing some few yards from where he, Juhor, sat at the door of his stone hut.

"Ho, Athak, Great Warrior! Athak the Swift! Athak the Strong! Athak the Terrible! Come and see!"

The gigantic, frowning war-chief turned shortly and strode to where sat the tribal weapon-maker.

"Well?" he snarled.

Juhor the Snake indicated the well-nigh completed jade ax-head.

"What of that, O mighty one?" he asked with the pride of a master craftsman.

Athak inspected it critically, with the shrewd scrutiny of another master craftsman, which he was, albeit no weapon-maker but a user of them instead.

"Put a handle to it," he commanded.

"Not yet," Juhor objected. "It is too heavy for its size. No warrior could wield it for very long. In steady fighting it would soon tire the strongest arm."

"A lie," snarled the surly giant. "It could not tire *my* arm to use it through a whole day's fighting!"

"Not all men are as Athak," flattered the old man.

"That is true," nodded Athak. "Put a handle to it, and we will see how heavy it is. Soon I shall return. Have it waiting." And with that he strode off.

Juhor the Snake smiled slyly to himself. Things were going well for him, very well indeed. So, carefully and skillfully and patiently too, he tugged and strained at the wet rawhide lashings which, drying, would shrink and bind helve and head till both were as rigid as if but one piece.

Some two hours later the shadow of Athak fell again athwart old Juhor's gnarled and twisted body. The old weapon-maker looked up in feigned surprize.

"The ax," Athak demanded, shortly.

Juhor indicated it where it leaned against his door-post. Athak closed his huge fist about the thick, tough oaken handle. A smile of ferocious pleasure came over his usually stolid features the instant he lifted the weapon, while into his eyes came a covetous light such as nothing in all his life had ever aroused before.

"Truly, a weapon worthy of even me," he rumbled. "Its price, O Juhor?"

"Canst thou pay it, O Athak?"

"Whatever be the price, I will pay it. That ax shall be mine!"

"Thine after it be paid for," nodded the cripple. "Neither thou, O Athak, nor any other in this tribe shall own that war-ax till it be paid for."

"No?" Athak sneered. "Look now, Juhor the Snake. In my grasp is thy handiwork. Since the price be so great, what shall hinder me, Athak the Terrible, from testing it on that old skull of thine? So shalt thou lose ax, price, and life all together!"

Juhor gazed calmly up at him.

"What shall hinder, O Athak the Fool? Only this! With every stroke, as I worked I breathed a charm, a curse, on the head of him who should possess that ax unearned. Strike if thou wilt. Juhor is old and crippled, and cannot prevent thee!"

Athak hurriedly stood the ax against the wall and squatted down by Juhor.

"Nay," he rumbled," I did but jest, old man! Name me the price I must pay for that wonder-ax. It will go hard with me if I earn it not."

"It is a long tale, Athak the Chief," said Juhor. "I must tell it in mine own way. Hast time and patience to listen?"

"Aye," grunted Athak. "Time enow, patience too, so be it ends in my ownership of that ax."

"Harken, then!" Juhor settled himself more comfortably, relaxing perceptibly indeed, for up till that moment he had not been sure if Athak would prove to be the man he, Juhor, had hoped for; or if it would be necessary to tempt some other mighty warrior with the bait of that great jade-headed war-ax. For a long moment the gnarled old cripple sat silent; then:

"As a little boy, O Athak, dost recall that in those days Juhor was tall and straight and a warrior even as thou art now?"

"War-chief thyself, for a while," Athak nodded, "if I recall aright."

"True, O Athak! And now—Juhor the Snake, as thou seest! Broken, twisted, old and ugly. Maker of weapons and—dealer in magic, among other things. But in those days whereof I now speak, I was young strong, and restive. In war, Juhor was the foremost; in peace, unable to sit day by day while the women worked. Nay, I hunted big animals, and was a crafty hunter, too. Also I traveled much, visited other tribes, and strange sights did I see.

"One soft summer I journeyed far to the northward. Into a country of hills came I finally. Snow-crowned were those hills, robed in forests of pine and spruce and hemlock; and the lakes of water, which were many, were very beautiful to behold. So pure were the waters that they seemed black to one looking down into them from a height. Oh, a very fair country, Athak, but inhabited by a race of devils in the semblance of men.

"For as I slept one night on the banks of a small lake, all unaware that foes were nigh, the light of my fire was observed by watchful eyes. And I awoke at the dawning with two strong warriors atop of me! Of course I struggled, but to what avail? Two had leapt on me, but a dozen more stood ready to aid them, were there need. So they bound Juhor, and bore him, trussed like a wild beast, to their tribal village.

"A hundred houses of stone were in that village. A high stone wall enclosed them safely. Only one gateway pierced that wall, and it was so narrow that two men with spears might easily hold it against a strong war-party.

"Into the largest building they bore me and threw me into a stone-floored room. Afterward I learned that the building was their temple, where, with horrible rites, they worshipped their devil-god.

"For a day and a night I lay there, bound hand and foot; hungry, too, although I was filled full with rage; but to tell truth, fearsome also, for I knew not what fate lay before me; albeit I could guess, to some extent; and my guesses were not of enjoyable matters — to me, at least.

"When on the second morning there entered one bearing food and drink, I believed for a moment that I was dreaming, or had gone mad and was seeing that which was not.

"But then *she* spoke...

"And to my enchanted ears the sound of her voice was as the song of birds in the golden springtime of the world. The sight of her was like to the glory of the sun in the first bright hour of the day. Tall she was—not squatty as are our women—full-breasted, strong, yet shapely in body and limbs. Blue were her eyes—blue as were the waters of the mountain lake where I was captured. Pink were her cheeks as are the blooms of the wild roses. Scarlet were her lips, even as the blood from a fresh-dealt wound; no snow ashine in the light of the full moon ever gleamed so brightly as did her strong white teeth; and her head was crowned with a great mass of hair red as the flames from a burning pitch-pine log—hair that fell almost to her feet.

"Forgotten were food, drink, hunger, captivity, apprehension; and I knew but one desire...

"Her I wanted, and her I would have; aye, though afterward I died ten deaths of torture before I were finally slain.

"With one powerful surge I burst the rawhide bonds against which I'd struggled in vain all through a day and a night! And she did not flinch, nor did she manifest aught of fear as I rose to my feet. Her blue eyes lit with a flame matching my own fire! Her scarlet lips smiled approval and she laid one finger, cautioningly, on her lip, in token of silence. Setting down the vessels of food and drink, she came, unfalteringly, straight into my opened arms.

" 'O Man of Might,' she whispered—for their language is very like to ours, and I could understand her fairly well—'you have taken my heart in your keeping. Yet how shall it profit us? I am the Red Witch of Ugdarr, the 'God-Who-Eats-Human-Hearts!' I am sworn, virgin, to his service; and you, O Strong One, are destined to provide his next meal!'

"For a bit I stood afraid. To die in battle was one thing, but to die helpless, a sacrifice to some devil-god named 'Ugdarr', who ate human hearts... Then I caught fast hold on my waning courage.

" 'When and how do I?'

" 'Three moons hence,' she said sadly. 'Four times in the year—and the last time was but a few days before you came. You will be fettered by one ankle atop of the great stone altar at the feet of the image of Ugdarr. You will be given any weapon you may select—ax, club, spear or knife. Three young warriors, desirous of proving themselves before the assembled tribe, will attack you, one at a time, armed with a similar weapon to your choice, but their ankles will not be bound! If you wound one so that he falls to the ground, his heart will be torn at once from his breast and given to the village dogs as something unfit for Ugdarr. But even should you slay all three, still are you doomed. You have but one advantage. They may wound you till you cannot stand longer, but slay you outright they dare not. To be acceptable to Ugdarr, your heart must come from your yet living breast while you still breathe, however feebly. And—the tribe will eat your flesh!'

" 'No hope of escape,' I whispered through dry lips.

" 'None,' she replied drearily.

"In my heart I swore that if I might not escape Ugdarr's hungry maw, at least I would make a mock of him... And I did, Athak!

"Each day thereafter she came bringing food and drink, for part of her service to Ugdarr lay in feeding Ugdarr's victim. And the devil-god wanted his sacrifice well nourished, that his heart might be more of a dainty morsel.

"Not long dared she tarry at any one time during the daylight hours, but again and again in the dead of night, when none suspected, she crept to my side and we lay in each other's arms till the first gray hint of dawn... and I knew, finally, that I had made a mockery of the devil-god Ugdarr...

"Young was I in those days, Athak! I had no thought for the woman, whether or not her tribe would mete out vengeance upon her for daring to give herself to me—me, the captive destined for Ugdarr's gullet; her, the virgin priestess who had violated her office; but later I was to think—oh, many, many times!

"For one night we were discovered, despite all her imagined caution. An old, old man, servant also of the devil-god, whose office it was to cut out the hearts of the sacrifices, became suspicious. Nay, he came not alone, but with a dozen ugly-faced warriors at his back...

" 'The man-captive is no more fit for Ugdarr's sacrifice,' he said sternly. 'He shall be tortured thus—he shall be tied to a post and each member of the tribe, from the youngest child to the oldest man or woman, shall throw at him one stone each. If he still lives, then he is free to go whither he will, save to return to this village. But should he crawl back here, then he shall be burned, slowly, to ashes.

" 'For the woman who was a maid—this! Witch of Ugdarr she was, and Witch of Ugdarr she shall remain till the child reach adolescence. Then shall she rear it to serve the god. If a boy, he shall become a priest. If a girl, she shall take her mother's place as Witch; and then this evil-doer who preferred the caresses of a captive to the favor of the great Ugdarr shall be bound at Ugdarr's feet and there she shall be stoned to death by the tribe—and the village dogs shall devour her body. I have spoken.'

"So, O Athak, you behold Juhor the Broken One! 'Snake' they name me, partly because I have wisdom and magic of a sort. But at first they so called me because I *crawled* one day into this my native village—how I made that long, terrible journey, broken, shattered, maimed, warped and twisted as I am, I know not. It was all a horrible torment like a dreadful dream of the night. Yet I did it, my brain aflame with but one idea— vengeance!

"Now, O Athak, Great War-Chief, thou knowest the price of the ax—the beautiful green-stone war-ax! Not with that ugly wooden handle either, but with this—" and Juhor held up a long, finely carved handle of pure ivory! Athak's eyes fairly blazed at the sight. He could hardly speak.

"Ax and handle, *mine*, if—"

"If thou wilt make war upon the tribe of Ugdarr, slaying man, woman and child, save only the Red Witch and her—my—*our*—child; bringing her and the child, if both still live, here to me…"

Athak nodded briefly.

"I am War-Chief," he said quietly. "The warriors and the young men will follow where I lead. I take the ax with me. Wielding that, not even this 'Eater-of-Hearts' Ugdarr himself shall withstand the war-frenzy of Athak the Strong!"

"I said," old Juhor pointed out, "that the ax must be earned ere it be possessed. Otherwise a curse—"

"Athak has never lied yet! He does not begin now, even to gain that wonder-ax! It will be earned! Thy price will be paid as soon as I can rouse the warriors and reach that devil-god's village. But I use that ax in the fighting, or I stir not a single step on thine errand!"

For a long while Juhor stared at Athak. Then he nodded as if fully satisfied at what he read in the eyes of the great war-chief.

"The ivory handle from a mammoth's tusk shall be fitted ere morning," he promised. "In Athak's grasp shall the magic war-ax earn its own purchase price. Juhor has said it!"

The exultant yell pealing from Athak's throat startled the entire village.

And Ran Kron, the untried stripling who aspired to the status of a warrior; sitting anigh and hanging breathless upon every word falling from the lips of Juhor the Snake, saw his opportunity and promptly grasped at it.

"Ho, Athak the Great Chief," he cried boldly. "Here is one for thy war-party!"

Athak stared contemptuously at the slight figure.

"Girl with the semblance of a boy," he jeered. "Thy mother made a mistake..."

And a lightning-swift lunge with a slender white flint knife in the hands of the infuriated youth well-nigh despoiled old Juhor of his long-plotted vengeance, then and there.

"Thou fool ten times accursed," shrilled the old weapon-maker. But Athak laughed, a hearty, roaring bellow wherein was no trace of anger.

"Nay," he told Juhor. "Let be! None are born full-grown and proven! The boy has the heart of a warrior. Even thus would I have replied to a like insult. He marches with the *other* fighting-men!"

The next night the old men sat in a circle, thumping on the snakeskin-headed war-drums, and the old women in a still larger outer circle banged and clattered cymbals of flat bone plates from the shoulder-blades of larger animals.

The old men chanted and the old women shrilled at intervals, while every male of fighting size and age danced and leapt and pranced and shouted boastfully, waving and brandishing their weapons. Finally, as the fire in the center of the circles died down, each man tossed his weapon on to a pile in the dancing-space in token that even as the weapons were all together, so would each man be at one with all the others of the war-party. Athak, as leader, tossed his newly acquired jade-headed war-ax atop of all the rest, so that when the weapons were lifted, his would be first, even as he as first in command. As his wonder-weapon—the tale of which had already been bruited about the village—fell atop of the rest, the warriors broke into their deep-voiced battle-cry:

"*A-Houk! A-Houk! A-Houk!*"

Athak was a good leader. Never once did the war-party see any one, nor were they seen by any wandering hunter from the morning they left their native village until they sighted the walls of Ugdarr's people. It called for craft and strategy to achieve this, but Athak's brain was equal to the task.

The first intimation in the gray dawning that the people of Ugdarr had of enemy proximity was the deep-toned:

"A-Houk! A-Houk! A-Houk!"

Into the undefended gate surged the men of Athak's band — for two skilled spear-throwers, at Athak's command, had crawled close an hour previously, while yet it was dark, and had made sure that the two men guarding the gateway slept the last long sleep.

Counter-yells arose of:

"Hah-Yah! Yah-Yah!"

And out from their huts like a swarm of angry hornets poured the men of Ugdarr. After all, it was not an all-day battle. At most, there were some hundred or a hundred and fifty savages locked together in one wild whirl of clubs, knives, spears and axes — a struggle in which quarter was neither asked for nor proffered.

One savage fight is very much the same as another, the only thing which distinguished that one being that for the first time in his life Athak the Strong One was laid prostrate on his back. A fallen enemy had stabbed him in the calf of his leg at the same moment that another man of Ugdarr had hit him on the head with a club.

Ran Kron, fighting madly at the left side of his gigantic chief, promptly repaid the clubman by practically eviscerating him with the sixteen-inch stone knife which formed the young warrior's sole weapon, and then bestriding Athak's body, swinging in both hands the club he'd wrested from his victim as he fell. It was but a moment in which Athak lay dazed; then he was on his feet again, bellowing "A-Houk" as lustily as ever, and smiting even more furiously with the great jade ax. But he found breath between blows to shout to Ran Kron:

"No longer art thou an untried youth, but a warrior! Shalt be made Athak's blood-brother when this fighting ends!"

If the stripling had fought madly before, after that promise of Athak's he became like a youthful demon unleashed. And, in consequence, he was bleeding from a dozen minor wounds by the time the affray ended.

And its ending was complete. The huge war-chief had made a definite pledge to Juhor, and as he himself had declared, it was no habit of his to deal in lies. Wounded or whole, those of Ugdarr's people who survived the fighting were dragged before their own devil-god and knocked on the heads; all save a few strong-bodied women who were kept to act as beasts of burden and carry loot for their captors on their homeward journey; and even those would be slain as soon as the trip was ended.

From these women, questioned by Athak, it was learned that Juhor's Red Witch of Ugdarr had been slain a few years previously. But she had left a daughter, Red Dawn...

"Where—"

Nobody knew...

Athak picked up one woman and flung her, bodily, into a fire blazing near at hand. By the time the shrieking wretch crawled out, the other women recalled that in the Temple of Ugdarr there were a number of hidden rooms...

It was Ran Kron who found her. What magical words he used, none knew, but she listened to him without fear, and came forth from the building hand in hand with the youth. Nor did she relinquish her hold when he brought her before Athak.

"Which is the captive?" shouted the chief, in high good humor. Made bold by Athak's friendliness, Ran Kron grinned and replied:

"I am, O Athak!"

The chief stared a second, then grinned back.

"Had I the right, I'd say 'Take her, lad!' But she goes to old Juhor. It is for him to say what disposal shall be made of her."

Juhor the Snake heard the welcoming tumult heralding the returned war-party, and smiled his wry smile. When the gigantic form of Athak stood before him, the old weapon-maker looked up calmly, although deep within himself he was in a storm of emotion. Athak's right hand grasped the great war-ax, while his left he held fast-clamped on the shoulder of a slim, beautiful girl whose hair was a flaming red-golden glory.

"Ax and purchase-price, O Juhor the Snake. Athak keeps his word!"

"The ax is paid for, and is all thine, O Athak the Mighty! Upon the ax is no curse. Nay, so long as thou shalt hold it in battle, none may overcome thee. Dost want the maid, too, O Athak? None better could I give her to. As my son—with thy might, and my wisdom—"

"Not I, Juhor! The ax fills my one desire. Rather, I would that thou give her to my blood-brother, Ran Kron. He wants her, and I think he has her favor."

"Give *her*—to—that—*cub!* Athak, dost jest?"

"Cub?" roared the chief. "My blood-brother, I said! None braver than he ever went forth to war from this village. Swift of foot, great of heart, fearless, and a deadly killer with that long knife of his, I myself saw him account for five in the fighting at Ugdarr's village. Saved my life, too, *mine*, Athak the Chief! Young he is yet, it is true. Had he greater war-wisdom, and more years, I'd make him second in command under me. And *you* call him—cub!"

"Girl," said Juhor, hastily veering away from the subject which had aroused Athak's wrath, "thou art my daughter. Hath thy mother—"

"I heard him"—she indicated Athak—"name thee Juhor the Snake. My mother, before they stoned her to death in Ugdarr's village, told me a tale of a captive, Juhor the Strong One, who was stoned by the tribe because of her, who was borne into the wilderness, and there left to live or die even as Ugdarr chose.

Art thou in truth that same Juhor?"

The old cripple could only nod, for words failed him. The girl looked too, too like another and elder Red Dawn... The girl flung herself on her knees beside him, drew his old head to her young breast, smoothing his sparse white locks with her slim soft hands, crooning over him... The warriors turned away at a grunt from Athak.

"This is no time to forward thy suit, my brother," the chief told the young Ran Kron. And the youth nodded, understandingly. He could wait.

Red Dawn was the most beautiful woman the tribe had ever beheld, and many were the young men who sought her from old Juhor. But to one and all he gave the same reply:

"Her heart and her desire are all for Ran Kron. She is my daughter and shall please herself."

So in due time the day came when before the whole people Juhor tied Red Dawn and Ran Kron together with a strong cord, calling down curses many and horrible upon the head of whoso should attempt to sever that bond. And the tribe, with feasting, and mirth, and jest, celebrated the wedding. Yet some there were who reasoned that as the girl was the most lovely, and Athak was the most mighty, she should have been mated with the great chief rather than with the youthful warrior.

But when some, made bold by drunkenness, ventured to hint thus to Athak, he roared with laughter. Then, for he had imbibed largely of strong drink himself, he became inspired with a most wondrous idea.

"Juhor," he shouted, "in thy hands lies the power to bind the cord of wedlock, where thine own offspring are concerned. Thou hast wed Ran Kron to Red Dawn. Now, haste thee and wed me to thine other child!"

"My — other — child," Juhor stared in wonderment. "Nay, O Athak! I have no child other than Red Dawn."

Athak held up his jade war-ax.

"This," he shouted, so that all heard. "The child that thou didst create. Wed me to her, for I love her more than I ever could love my woman of flesh and blood."

The grim fancy caught the imaginations of the people, and they clamored for the ceremony. Juhor, knowing Athak's disposition, and seeing that he was at that pitch of drunkenness wherein good humor abruptly changes to fury when crossed, took a fresh cord and performed the rite with all the needful words and curses.

Again Athak tossed the weapon high in the air above his head.

"Athak's wife!" he bellowed. *"A-Houk! A-Houk! A-Houk!"*

Catching fire from his fire, the warriors responded in savage chorus: *"A-Houk! A-Houk! A-Houk!"*

Yet one old hag there was—own sister to Athak's mother who had died giving a man-child to the world—who dwelt in Athak's hut and cooked his food for him, who sat and glowered while all others made merry. She was getting old and lazy, and had long urged the giant chief to bring a younger woman into the hut as his wife. All through the feasting, the old woman said naught about what was in her mind, but next morning, well knowing that Athak's head was aching fit to burst, she queried with her tongue laded with venom:

"Was your stone bride kind to you in the night, O Athak, and were her caresses sweet?" Then, with a cackle of derision, as he glared at her: "She can never give you a son to boast that Athak the Mighty was his father. She cannot cook for you. She can deal wounds, but she cannot heal wounds with the poultices of soothing leaves... better had you taken Juhor's *other* daughter—" And with that, dodging a chunk of wood hurled at her by the exasperated chief, she fled the hut, still cackling evilly.

And thenceforward she lost no chance to prod Athak about

his folly in "choosing the wrong daughter of Juhor" until in time her evil hints and slurs bore fruit. She was helped in her work by the fact that since Ran Kron had had one taste of war, he'd found it so greatly to his liking that twice afterward he'd gone out with small parties of young and ambitious men; and in both cases had easily proved himself the foremost. And the hag hinted to Athak that his prestige as chief was seriously threatened by this young upstart—as she termed the youth.

Came a day when Athak harkened and took her gibing seriously; so that thereafter he began casting meaning glances at Red Dawn whenever they met. Worse still occurred when, in one of his drunken spells, he sought to drag her into his hut against her will.

His girl-wife's shrieks reached Ran Kron's ears where he sat in converse with a group of other young warriors. With a cat-like rush he hurled himself at the would-be ravisher. Twice and thrice his long flint knife stabbed, lightning-quick, drawing blood and eliciting a yell of pain each time he struck.

Completely lost to all thoughts of blood-brotherhood, and driven by a two-fold lust—to have Ran Kron's wife and Ran Kron's life, Athak let go his hold on the shrieking, struggling Red Dawn and drew his great jade ax from his belt. Ran Kron, seeing, leaped back, snatching a spear from the hand of a bystander, and promptly lunged with it at the face of the giant chief.

For a while it was either man's fight. Mighty as Athak was, enraged, too, so that flecks of foam dripped from his lips, still Ran Kron kept him busy; dodging, leaping, parrying, or evading the sweep of the great green-flashing ax; from time to time getting in a thrust with his spear that drew blood each time, but never deep enough to reach a vital spot and end matters.

Yet despite all his efforts, step by step the lighter man was forced to retreat—suddenly a yell arose from the onlookers, partly in triumph, partly in warning, according to their sympathies. With a feeling that the end was nigh, Ran Kron realized that he'd reached the brink of the river, and that back of him lay a fifty-foot drop to the swift, swollen, muddy waters below. In sheer desperation he hurled his spear straight at the face of his giant opponent.

Athak saw it coming, too swift for him to dodge it. He threw up both arms in front of his face. The stone spearhead drove deep into his right forearm, and a spurt of blood followed, staining the ivory helve of his battle-ax a bright crimson.

In despair, Ran Kron whipped out his long stone knife, prepared to sell his life as dearly as possible. Athak bellowed his rage, and moved a step closer. The great ax swung up above his tousled head and swept down again on its death-dealing arc. Ran Kron, summoning up his fast-waning strength, dodged again, bending his torso far back. Athak's hands were too blood-smeared from the wound in his forearm. The ivory ax-handle slipped in his grasp. Flying through the air, it struck Ran Kron a glancing blow on the side of his head, stunning him. The young warrior, his balance overborne, went backward over the edge of the low bluff; and, with a sullen double splash, Ran Kron and the great jade ax that had overthrown him to his death disappeared together beneath the surface of the swollen stream…

Now how I, Randall Crone, know this latter part which ensued after Ran Kron fell into the river, I cannot tell; for I do not understand. But know it I do, however.

Athak sank to the ground, gasping from his last terrific exertion. Red Dawn would have thrown herself into the river, there to join her man, Ran Kron, but was seized and held by certain ones who sought to curry favor with Athak.

Juhor the Snake hobbled up, stood in front of Athak, and shook his gnarled old fist in the giant's face. The old man was fairly a-quiver with the rage consuming him. Twice he opened his mouth and twice he closed it again before he could find words to express himself.

"Was it for this, thou fool, that I made for thee that magic ax? Did I not wed thee to the ax at thine express command, by thine own choice? Did I not lay curses many and deep upon the head of whoso should part ye twain who were one in wedlock? And now, it is thine own hands which have flung the magic ax into the deep, deep river!

"Now I, Juhor the Snake, prophesy to thee, O Athak the Fool! Thou shalt go accursed for all thy remaining days upon the earth. Evil shall befall thee ever, and when thou shalt die, in outer darkness shalt thou wander till once again the magic ax which thou thyself didst name 'Athak's Wife' shall return to thine embrace! Athak the Accursed, I Juhor, have spoken thy doom!"

Athak staggered to his feet and clutched one great hand upon the old man's shoulder.

"Aye," he snarled, "thou hast spoken—thine own doom, Juhor the Snake!" One shove he gave the old cripple, and Juhor, with a single quavering cry, vanished over the edge of the all-devouring river...

One might say that I'd been dreaming; or that I'd been in a trance state and had left my body and gone into the astral plane—but neither hypothesis would account fully for the facts.

For I learned, upon my return to my Twentieth Century personality, that I'd been gone for a considerable time, *body and all!* My room had been found vacant and my bed unslept in, the morning after I'd been visited by the phantom of Athak.

Then as totally unproclaimed as my absence had been, I reappeared. And I had considerable difficulty in explaining matters to those most interested in my movements—business associates, and others. Of course I hastened to Rhoda as quickly as possible, and from her lips I had full confirmation of my strange experience. For she, too, had "vanished" insofar as her everyday environment was concerned, and she, too, had just reappeared. I did not have to make any explanations to her. She knew! She'd been through the same sort of adventures as had I. In other words, she had suddenly awakened from a sound sleep to find herself Red Dawn, the young Witch of Ugdarr! In fact, she was able to tell me the part I did not know, and describe the episode after Athak threw old Juhor over the bluff. Yet what she told was but little after all.

Athak had dragged her to his hut, where she naturally anticipated just about the worst fate that could happen. In a frenzy of fear, she had tried to stab herself, but Athak prevented that by hitting her with his fist the instant she caught up a knife.

But he had struck too hard, and thereby cheated himself of the woman he coveted so greatly that he'd slain his own chosen blood-brother in order to get her for himself. She recalled the terrific concussion of his fist against the side of her face. Ensued a brief period of unconsciousness, naturally, and when her consciousness returned, she was again Rhoda Day, in her own room, and her mother was bending over her, demanding a trifle crossly:

"Rhoda, where in the world have you been for the last few days, and why did you go away without saying anything about it to me, before you started?"

As to what happened to Athak, we neither of us knew; but could easily imagine, knowing him as well and unfavorably as we did. To use Rhoda's words:

"He probably went from bad to worse, just as Juhor had predicted, until someone did the world a service by ridding it of his presence; and he has since, to use Juhor's very words, 'dwelt in outer darkness'. But in some manner he — or his spirit, rather — located my whereabouts, and he seems determined to assert his imagined ownership. Probably he doesn't even know that he is dead and hasn't a body in which to function any more."

Wherein she was wrong. Later again, we learned that Athak knew quite well that he was devoid of a body. All he was waiting for was a good chance to acquire one, in order to resume his age-old devilment just where he'd been compelled to leave off by reason of hitting Red Dawn too hard and thus cheating himself of her possession.

Apparently old Juhor's curse had taken effect, and Athak had, in truth, dwelt in outer darkness instead of coming back to earth via a rebirth, as we two had done. But the more we speculated, the more intricate and involved the problems became; so that finally we quit all speculating and preserved a policy of watchful waiting instead.

Meantime, at my urgency, Rhoda capitulated and we were married. For a brief while we managed to fool the savage phantom. Travelling on our honeymoon trip, we kept to the crowded cities, knowing that for us to isolate ourselves would best please the vindictive ghost who so hated us. In modern hotels and amongst throngs of people, he'd be out of his element.

But honeymoons end eventually, in this workaday world, and dollar-chasing is a very necessary pursuit if one would continue to enjoy life in its modern phase. So, regretfully, we returned home, not, of course, to Rhoda's parents, but to a little place of our own.

And Athak turned up the first night we were there!

His fury, when he grasped the situation, was something to tremble at. His futile attempts to wreak either or both of us bodily injury, had they not been so frightful, would have been ludicrous. For over half the night he carried on his antics. It was of no avail to turn off the light, so I left it burning. Rhoda was so unstrung that I feared a permanent shock to her nervous system would result.

I was angry, not with the ordinary type of wrath common to everyone at times, but that same savage ugliness I'd experienced once before. Much more of it, and I'd again become Ran Kron, the young savage warrior... But Rhoda sensed the change taking place in me, and begged so earnestly that I control myself, that somehow, to please her, I succeeded in fighting back my rage. At that, I could not have done it, had she not whispered:

"Randall, my husband, for my sake be very careful! Cannot you see that you are rapidly getting into a state such as will best please him, and render us accessible by translating us again to his plane, where he *can* function?"

It was a hard task, even then, but I did it. Then I had what I considered to be a happy thought, and carried it out; and it did win for us a modicum of rest from Athak's rage, if only for a short time. Deliberately I kissed Rhoda, then grinned triumphantly at the frenzied savage ghost; and for a second, I thought that Athak the Terrible would disintegrate from the hell-storm of wrath and jealous hate that simple act aroused on his part. But then he turned sulky, withdrew until he seemed to merge with the wall itself, and there remained, glowering. And finally we fell asleep and left him to sulk all he would.

But the next night he was back again, twice as ugly as before. And for many a night after that.

Then I thought up another bright idea, or deemed it one until—

It was summer, and the nights were warm, so we took to sleeping in a rose arbor in the garden. For the first night there was absolutely no sign of Athak. But on the second night, Rhoda wakened me from a sound slumber with the startled exclamation:

"Randall, what *is* that repulsive odor?"

One sniff told me instantly that it was the acrid, decayed-cucumber scent of a copperhead snake! Very cautiously, holding my breath in stark fear, I pressed the switch of a flashlight and swept the nearby ground with its bright rays. Luckily I managed to reach a stick with which I broke the reptile's back before it could—*ugh!* I shuddered at the thought of what might have happened. And, somehow, in my mind, I associated that snake's arrival into our garden of peace with Athak's hatred. And instantly, although I heard no sound, I was aware of a burst of unholy glee that fully confirmed my conviction.

Next day I bought an automatic pistol equipped with a silencer, and a box of cartridges. Then I did that which would cause any alienist to suspect my mental condition; for I had every bullet extracted from the loaded shells and replaced by silver ones. I'd read somewhere that silver bullets are efficacious against such as Athak; and I was open to conviction. But when I laid in that equipment I unwittingly played into Athak's hands, completely.

Nightly thereafter I kept the loaded pistol within reach, and for several nights we were undisturbed. Yet always we had an uncomfortable sense of Athak's presence, albeit he kept himself invisible. Actually, I began to think that in some manner he'd sensed that I was organized for him with a potent weapon, and that he was correspondingly cautious about bringing matters to a definite showdown; which proves how little I know about the unseen world and still less about the abilities of those who dwell therein.

We had gotten so that we could fall asleep almost immediately after retiring in our rose arbor. It was around midnight one night that I awoke with the certitude that we had been outwitted and that even then we were exposed to some unutterably ghastly horror. Instinctively I grasped the pistol and threw off the safety catch. Rhoda had awakened at the same time, and we sat up simultaneously. She screamed, once, and I felt the cold sweat of fear break out all over me.

Not ten yards away was the phantom form of Athak. A leer of cruel, anticipatory triumph was on his ugly face, and he had reason for it, too; for although he himself was but a phantom, there was nothing intangible about the monstrous dog he had somehow introduced into our garden. It was just a dog; yes; but such a dog! It loomed as big as a cliff! I learned, later, that the brute was a Tibetan mastiff belonging to a dog-fancier dwelling some twenty miles distant. And that breed of dog is one of the most ferocious of the entire canine species.

Its eyes were aflame with fury, and as they were fixed unwaveringly upon me, it was not difficult to imagine what was coming next. Its jaws dripped slaver, and its lips were drawn back in a soundless snarl. Its whole body was a-quiver with pent-up energy.

And even as I noted all this in one horrified glance, the phantom chief waved an arm in a gesture of command, and the huge beast launched itself straight at me! One bound brought it halfway, but then I brought the pistol into action. I'd had a gunsmith do a little juggling with the inner works of that automatic; so that in a way, it was more a miniature machine-gun than a pistol. Once the trigger was pulled, provided it was held back, the shots were continuous till the magazine was empty. I intended, when I had it fixed like that, to put sufficient of those silver bullets into, or through, Athak, to make a thorough job of it, or him. But as things turned out, it was the dog that got the entire load; and it needed them all, too, squarely in its big skull, to stop its ferocious rush.

Even at that, the brute didn't die instantly, but fell on the ground almost at the entrance to the arbor, writhing and twitching in a fast-spreading pool of blood.

Athak's opportunity had arrived! That infernal savage had waited for just such a chance for ages! The blood furnished him with the medium for materialization, and he promptly utilized it. Before I could reload the pistol by inserting a fresh-charged magazine clip into the butt, the metamorphosis was achieved. It was, to all intents and purposes, a flesh and blood savage from out the distant Ice Age who hurled his huge bulk at us, whirling a heavy bludgeon in one knotted fist!

Rhoda gasped, moaned feebly, and slumped to the floor of the rose arbor in a limp heap. And I, feeling that this was the end for us, and the consummation of Athak's triumph, nevertheless flung myself off the bed in one wild leap, to meet him and have it over with.

I had naught save that empty pistol still in my hand wherewith to put up a battle, and that was a poor and futile thing beside the club Athak flourished. Yet in some manner I dodged his first stroke, retaliating by throwing my empty pistol into his face as hard as I could slam it. Luckily for me, it landed just where eyebrows and nose meet. For a second it dazed him, and he paused, even in his frenzy, to shake his head to clear his sight, I suppose. And, in that one second of reprieve, a miracle and naught else came to my aid, or I should not be here now to tell this tale...

Out of nowhere, apparently, appeared the gnarled, twisted, crippled form of old Juhor the Snake! Into my hands he thrust the ivory handle of a green-stone war-ax!

"Heh-heh-heh!" laughed the incredible apparition. "Once he stole your wife! It is only fitting that now you should have his!"

What strange power lay in that ancient war-ax? I know not, even now. But this I do know: No sooner had my hands closed in a firm grip on the handle than a terrific surge of commingled hate and strength suffused my entire body! I felt that my muscles had doubled—nay! infinitely multiplied in power to smite. I heaved the heavy ax aloft and moved toward my enemy. He saw the weapon, and hell flamed in his face and eyes. In a low, dreadful tone he spoke:

"Now! Long have I waited for this day! Red Dawn, and the green ax! Once again are both within my reach! O Fool, who thinks to stand against Athak the Mighty with his own war-ax; now shall I slay thee, and take both weapon and woman! Then shall she and I together eat your heart, raw, torn from out your yet warm body..."

He had no time for further boasting. With all the new strength that had flowed into me, I struck out at him. Skilled warrior that he was, he parried the ax-sweep with his club. Very craftily he struck just back of the stone head, turning the stroke aside thereby. The shock of his blow jarred my arms clear to my shoulder-sockets. And swiftly following came his counterstroke. He delivered it horizontally at my head, but I bent my knees quickly, and the club barely grazed my hair. The momentum of his blow turned him a trifle, and I swiped back again with the ax, and that time, despite his backward leap, the ax drew blood from his side; not a deep cut, but still enough to madden him.

With a snarl of pure fiendishness he drove in a blow I could not evade, so lightning-swift it had come. Fairly on my left arm it landed, and my whole side went numb as if suddenly paralyzed. I had only my right arm then with which to wield that ponderous stone war-ax, while my eon-old enemy still had two arms with which to swing his no less ponderous club.

The derisive sneer on his hateful face drove me beyond all semblance of caution. As if it had been naught but a light throwing-hatchet, I whirled up that great stone-headed ax in one hand and hurled it! So quickly did I move that he had no chance to raise his club in order to ward off that hurtling weapon.

Edge first it struck him in his barrel-like chest, driving deep in through flesh and bone. With a bubbling grunt the breath went out of his lungs, followed by a gush of bloody froth. He threw both arms across his torso, hugging the ax-handle in his agony...

The cracked voice of old Juhor rang out: "When Athak's wife returns to Athak's embrace, then shall the age-old curse lift; and Athak shall cease to dwell in outer darkness! *Athak the Mighty, get thee hence to the place appointed for all such as thou!*"

The giant stood swaying, his arms still clasping the handle of the ax. Bust as Juhor spoke his doom, he tottered and fell!

Unheeding aught else, I staggered wearily—for my strength left me even as Athak fell—over to where Rhoda lay, lifted her to the bed and turned—to see only a faint haze where a moment before had lain the gigantic materialized form of Athak the Terrible! As I looked, the haze vanished, too. Of old Juhor the Snake there was no sign. There remained only the carcass of an enormous, dead dog; an empty automatic pistol; and a great, ivory-handled war-ax lying where I had dropped it. Oh, yes! And a great bruise on my left arm…

What is real, and what illusion, in this universe? Nobody knows, I least of all.

Juhor handed me that ax. I used it. Next day it hung on the wall in my study. And that same evening I read in the newspaper that a jade-headed, ivory-handled battle-ax had been mysteriously abstracted some time in the night hours from a glass case in a scientific museum located over eight hundred miles from where I dwell, and had been missed the same morning I hung it on my wall! And the glass case had not been broken into, nor unlocked.

The news article went on to state that the weapon owed its remarkable condition of preservation to the fact that it had been found fast-frozen in a huge fragment of ice that had "calved" from a glacier up under the Arctic Circle…

Oh, my very soul faints when I try to make coherence of my jumbled data! Yet out of it all, dimly I get this for my comfort: Time, and Space, both are as naught to the Self of man. Justice endures and Love is eternal; nor shall all the Powers of Darkness ever prevail against them!

The Sapphire Goddess

Suicide as a means of escaping trouble never appealed to me. I had studied the occult, and knew what consequences that course involved, afterward.

But I was fed up on life. I was destitute, and had no friends who might help, even were I to appeal to them. At forty-eight, one does not easily regain solvency. And, gradually, I'd lost all ambition. Not even hope remained.

If only there were some other road out—a door, for example, into the hypothetical region of four dimensions... it certainly couldn't be worse there than what I'd borne in the last three years. Well, I could try...

I seated myself cross-legged on the floor. If I concentrated hard enough, perhaps the miracle might occur... at least I should have tried... a last resort... Gradually a vague state ensued wherein I was not unconscious, for I still knew that I was *I*; yet a queer detachment was mine—there was a world, but of it I was no longer a part...

Click!

Like a movable panel a section of the wall opened, revealing a most peculiar corridor—a strange Being stood smiling at me. It did not speak, yet I caught the challenge: "Dare you?"

With a single movement I rose and stepped into the opening...

Oh, the agonizing, excruciating torment of that transition! Every nerve, tissue and fiber flamed and froze simultaneously. My brain seethed like a superheated cauldron. My blood turned to corrosive, searing acid. Tears suffused my aching eyes. I choked, unable to utter the groans my sufferings constrained me to emit...

Had I landed in Hell? It certainly seemed so!... Then abruptly it was all over. I was still *I*, yet vastly different. I was *free*—and with senses above the dull senses of Earth, with power beyond Earth's muscular strength. I realized that I was in a different realm where the Laws were strange to me, and that I must be careful lest I be caught in some trap from whence escape might not be so easily achieved. But where, I wondered, was the Being who had dared me?...

"*Here!*"

"But—you seem not the same... there was a vague, misty, red haze—now you are distinct..."

"Many high-speed light waves formed a veil through which earthly eyes cannot see clearly."

"Hence—the agony during transition?"

"Precisely! The vibrations altered your atomic structure. But you are still your true self."

"Perhaps," I assented. "But who are you, and why did you make it possible for me to come?"

"I am Zarf; and your subjects need you, to say naught of—"

We were interrupted by a most discordant howling, and abruptly some two dozen hideous dwarfs surrounded us. They bore long straight swords, were clad in iridescent scale armor, stood about five feet in height, and had the ugliest faces I ever saw.

"King Karan of Octolan—and the commander of his bodyguard, Zarf!" Their voices were shrill with maniacal glee. Evidently they considered our capture a big event.

I did not like their looks. I did not approve of their air of insolent triumph. Back on Earth I had lost all material ambitions, but suddenly I regained one, and proceeded to realize it.

With all my new strength, I drove my clenched fist right into the face of a particularly burly dwarf standing about two feet away. His head snapped back, he went limp; I snatched his sword from him and set to work. Once and again I struck, caught the true balance of the weapon and saw a head leave its body—shouted:

"A sword for you, Zarf!"

Before the blade touched ground he caught it, then set his back against mine... A wild delight filled me, yet through it I felt a vague wonder—where had *I* learned swordsmanship? For never on Earth had I held one in my hand!

Those dwarfs fought like fiends from Hell. More than once I felt the stinging kiss of dwarf steel. Once I heard Zarf gasp as a sword bit deep, and once he groaned in agony. It was a wild mêlée while it lasted; and never did I enjoy myself more... Through a red haze of slaughter I saw that only two dwarfmen remained facing my blade. Lunge—slash—parry—slash and lunge again—but one left—I gathered myself—dimly saw another blade than mine pass through that last dwarf—heard Zarf as from a far distance crying exultantly:

"Lord King, you fight even better than in the other days! It is well—for you will have many a fight ere you sit once more on the Chrysolite Throne of your race."

Then I slid to a limp heap on the ground, exhausted from loss of blood—I could not speak—heard Zarf cursing furiously, virulently, then all consciousness flickered out...

I regained my senses slowly. I lay on a pallet, a hand's breadth off a hard-packed earthen floor. A feeble lamp barely showed walls of stone chinked with moss and mud. Obviously a hut—but where? Then I saw Zarf. He sat on a low stool, chin on fist, elbow on knee, head bandaged, and his left arm in a sling. Looking at myself, I saw I was swathed even worse than he in bandages.

"Zarf," I said weakly. "We look as if we'd been in a fight!"

"We have been," he nodded at cost of a twinge of pain. "But none of those Vulmins will ever take part in another—while we were just getting a little practice!"

"Zarf," I demanded, insistent. "Who are you, and why did you call me 'Master'? Surely there is some mistake. You know that I am but an Earthman upon whom you took pity and opened for him a door into this realm of Space..."

Somberly he stared at me, then:

"King Karan, what pity was in the hearts of those Vulmin dwarf-devils when they strove to cut us into gobbets for their cook-pots? Yet they knew you and named you 'Karan of Octolan, Zarf's royal Master'. Is it possible you have no memory of the past—no knowledge of who and what you are? Do you not remember the rebel sorcerer, Djl Grm, who blasted your body and drove your self through a bent corridor down to the Earth, where you acquired a new body as an Earth-babe? Have you no recollection of your Imperial Consort? Shall that regal lady—so loved by all in your far-flung realm that she was deemed a goddess—be unavenged?

"What disposal that accursed sorcerer made of her, none knows. It is known that he sought to seduce her, and when she withstood him in that, she vanished! Yet sure I am he did not force her to the Earth, for then you twain might have found each other, and so defeated his major purpose. Nay, King Karan, she is *here!* In the nights her spirit whispers to mine:

" 'Zarf, I am still your Queen. Find my lord, wheresoever he be... watch over him... whenever possible, open for him a door. He will find me—free me—out of his love...'

"King Karan, must that regal lady's spirit wait in vain, believing Zarf a traitor, and you a recreant spouse?"

"*I cannot remember,*" I groaned. I was convinced—believed Zarf fully; and oh! the anguish that was mine in that moment! Amnesia, it is called back on Earth, this inability to remember, with its concommitant of lost identity... Then in the gloom of my mind, one insurmountable objection reared its ugly head, "If this sorcerer blasted my body, and drove my self down to the Earth, where through the medium of birth I regained a body and grew to my present stature—how shall any here recognize me as Karan the King of Octolan? Zarf, I still say you must be mistaken."

"My King," he replied pityingly, "you *are* sore bemazed! On Earth your body was shapen by parental influence; but *here* — when the agony shook you, the body reassembled about the self in its true semblance and substance. Nay! Karan of Octolan you are, and none who ever saw you during your reign would deny your identity, albeit there be many would gladly slay you to prevent you from regaining your throne.

"Lord, evil rules where once was good — and a fair, happy land has become a veritable antechamber of Hell. Vampyr and ghoul prey on the bodies of your people. Foes assail them from without, and devils plague them from within the borders. Your subjects, afraid, disheartened, hopeless, have fallen from their allegiance to the Karanate Dynasty. Scarce may we find a hundred loyal souls in all the eight provinces of Octolan. I myself am but a fugitive; and rich is the reward Djl Grm would pay for the head of Zarf the Proscribed! And as for our gracious Queen, Mehul-Ira —"

He groaned in heaviness of spirit; and I felt two scalding tears run adown my cheeks.

"I cannot remember," I wailed. "Karan I may be, but I have not his memory! A great King would I be, and a wondrous leader — with Karan's body and an Earthman's mind!" And I sank back on my bed all atremble from sheer, impotent fury at myself.

Zarf pondered for an interminable while; then:

"Lord, it would seem that Djl Grm, ere he drove your self to the Earth, laid an inhibition on your memory-coil. And if so, we may be sure he will never release it. But, Lord, it comes to my mind that afar from here dwells another magician — Agnor Halit — fully as evil as Djl Grm, and also fully as powerful. It may well be that he can restore your memory — but it remains to be seen if he will. It is said that they hate each other as only two sorcerers can hate. And in that lies our hope. I think we would do well to start as soon as we are fit to travel, seek out this Agnor Halit, and try to enlist his aid."

"So be it," I assented. "Only, we start at dawn. Are we women, that we should lie at ease because of a few scratches?"

"But you are weak from your wounds," he objected.

"No more so than are you," I retorted. "As I say, we start at dawn. If I am indeed your King, it is for me to command — yours to obey! But for tonight, we sleep — if it be safe to sleep here."

"You will never be safe," he replied, "waking or sleeping, until you are once again on the Chrysolite Throne, surrounded by your own bodyguards. Still, we can take some small precautions to prevent a complete surprize."

He picked up a metal basin and two sticks, with which he rigged a device against the door, which would fall and make a noise were the door tampered with.

"There," he grunted. "Now we can sleep — and we need it!"

The clatter of the falling basin awoke me. I came erect, sword in hand, although I was wavering on my feet. Zarf looked at me in pity, but said naught. Slowly the door swung open, and a most grotesque visage peered in. Zarf audibly sighed his relief.

"Come in, good Koto," he invited soothingly, as one might speak to a timid child. "King Karan will do you no harm. Nor will I." And out of the corner of his mouth Zarf muttered — "Koto owns this hovel. He is a Hybrid, born of a lost woman of the Rodar race and an Elemental of the Red Wilderness. Yet Koto is very gentle and timid. Nor is he such a fool as he looks, for when I told him your identity, the poor creature wept because his hovel was no fit abode for royalty, even in distress. All his life long, Koto will be proud — "

"These 'Rodars'?" I asked, softly. "And this 'Red Wilderness'?"

"The Rodars? Gigantic savages, running naked. Gentle enough, and with child-like brains; and the Red Wilderness is a vast and dreary desert, all yours, but totally worthless."

"Enter, good Koto," I commanded. "I, Karan, King of Octolan, bid you enter and kneel before me."

With a snivelling howl the poor wretch of a Hybrid blundered in awkwardly and flopped asprawl before me. He grasped his head in both ape-like paws, looked at Zarf out of terror-filled eyes, opened his ugly gash of a mouth, and emitted a raucous howl. In a perfect paroxysm of fright he gabbled:

"*I knew it! I knew it!* This hut is unfit for King Karan the Splendid! And now he will cut off Koto's head with his sword—cut off Zarf's head, too, King Karan! He made me take you in—"

"But you are mistaken, good Koto," I assured the poor fellow. "I have no intention to cut off your head—nor Zarf's."

Then I tapped him on the shoulder with the flat of my blade.

"Rise, Baron Koto, Lord of the Red Wilderness and of all the Rodar-folk that therein dwell. Thus I, Karan, reward your service in giving us succor in our need!"

Zarf became angry at the audacity of my act. To him it was nigh to an insult to the entire order of knighthood. Then, abruptly, he laughed.

"Lord," he gasped, "had another than yourself wrought thus, I'd slay him with my own hand. But such pranks were ever your wont in the other days. Mad as is this one, still it may yet serve you well. You are too weak to travel, despite your bold heart, and we needs must wait in this castle of Baron Koto's until strength returns to us both. Perchance by then Koto may be able to secure for us riding-beasts on which we may travel faster than on our own legs."

At that last argument I capitulated. It was a good reason for waiting. But then I began to question Zarf about our intended journey.

"What manner of territory must we traverse, once we start? What sort of inhabitants dwell along our ways? Savage, or civilized? Wild, tame? Hostile or friendly? And will our swords be sufficient for our protection?"

"It will be a long and dangerous trip," he replied soberly. "Our way lies across this same Red Wilderness you just presented to Koto; thence across the Sea of the Dead, where evil ghosts arise from the foul waters; then over the Hills of Flint to the Mountains of Horror, where demons and vampyrs abound; and thence onward again to a city of devils who adore the lord of all devils. There, if we are fortunate, we may hope to find the sorcerer we seek."

"Cheerful prospect!" I commented acridly. "But are these assorted Hell-spawn sufficiently solid to be cut with good steel, or are they immune to injury?"

"Some are solid enough, while others are intangible, yet dangerous for all that. And there be various tribes of savages, none friendly to strangers. Oh, we may anticipate a most enjoyable trip!"

"Zarf," I demanded abruptly, thinking longingly of the guns and pistols of Earth—"Can you return me to Earth for a brief visit, and then bring me back here, together with certain heavy bundles? Also, can you provide me with gold or gems in quantity?"

"Lord," he mourned, "naught have I to give you saving my life and my love. Nor gold nor gems do I possess, or you should have all with no need of asking. Nor can I return you to Earth—but why do you so suddenly wish to go?"

I explained, and he understood, but reiterated his inability to do as I requested.

"Those *'ghunz,'*" he marveled, enviously—"What a pity we have them not. Throwing-spears and knives are our nearest approach."

"Koto," I interrupted Zarf, a new idea arising in my mind. "Do you have a wood that will do like this, when seasoned?" I drew my sword, bent it in an arc, and let it spring swiftly back.

Koto nodded, then shambled from the hut. I heard sounds of

wood being split, and presently Koto was back with a long strip of hard wood which he handed me deprecatingly. I was overjoyed, for it was precisely what I needed.

"Bows and arrows," I exulted. "Now I feel better! Zarf, we have reason to remain here for a while."

Rapidly I explained, using a pointed stick to make clear my meaning, by drawing in the dirt of the floor. I had been an archery enthusiast on Earth, and knew my subject, even if I had never handled a sword.

Despite my earlier urgency, it was three weeks before we three men set forth from Koto's castle on the edge of the Red Wilderness. Three men, because Koto had protested with lugubrious howls that he wasn't going to be left behind. I'd made him a Baron, he claimed, and it was his right to ride with me when I went forth to war! Zarf chuckled in grim approval, and I, too, endorsed Koto's claim.

We rode the queerest steeds imaginable. Huge birds they were, more like enormous game-cocks than aught else I can compare them to; with longer, thicker spurs and bigger beaks. Ugly-tempered, too. Zarf said they'd fight viciously whenever it came to close quarters. And how those big birds could run!

I asked Koto where he got them, and he replied that he'd gone out one dark night and taken them from a flock kept by a petty lordling some distance away. When I laughed and called him a thief, he said seriously he was no such thing:

"Was not Karan the King in need of them? And did not the kingdom and all that therein was belong to the King?"

So we rode forth, all three mounted and armed with short, thick, powerful bows and thick, heavy arrows. Zarf and I had the swords we had taken from the Vulmins, and Koto bore a ponderous war-club fashioned from a young tree having a natural bulge at the big end. Into this bulge he had driven a dozen bronze spikes all greenish with verdigris — a most efficient and terrible weapon, if he had the courage to use it in hand-to-hand fighting. Zarf maintained that Koto would be so anxious to please me that he'd fight like a maniacal fiend, should the opportunity present.

The crossing of that Red Wilderness was no pleasure jaunt. There were dust storms and blistering heat by day, and an icy wind o' nights that howled like all the devils of Hell let loose. But in time we came to the shore of the Sea of the Dead; and a most fitting name it was for that desolate body of putrescent water.

Dull grayish-greenish water, sullenly heaving and surging to and fro sluggishly and greasily; beaches of dull grayish-brownish sands; and huge dull grayish-blackish boulders and rocks — oh! a most nightmarish picture, taken all in all.

"Zarf," I shuddered, "may it not be possible to ride around this Sea?"

"Perhaps," he returned, dubiously. "But we can cross it in one quarter of the time it would take to ride around."

"But," I queried skeptically, "how shall we cross? I see no boats, nor any way of making any."

"I have heard of a tribe hereabouts," he replied slowly, "and it may be that we can barter for, seize, or compel them to make for us a craft that will bear us over this pestilential sea. But now we had best think about making camp for the night."

We rode back from the beach until the sea was lost to view — and smell. A pleased cry from Koto finally caused us to halt. Where a mass of boulders had been piled up by some ancient cataclysm, there was a cave-like recess sufficiently large to afford safe refuge for all three of us and our mounts.

What had pleased Koto particularly was the presence of a lot of lumps resembling amber, but of a queer red color. After he had collected sufficient to satisfy his ideas, he laid a line of the stuff across the entrance, and set fire to them. They burned like coal or gum, and gave off a clear pale white flame, and a most pleasant odor, with no smoke.

"This region is infested with devils at night," Koto said seriously. "But no devil will ever dare pass that line of fire."

He was right. No devil did pass, but after darkness came, a lot of them tried. Failing in that laudable attempt, they drew anigh the opening, and stared in avidly at us...

We divided the night into three watches. Zarf and I wrapped ourselves in our cloaks and slept, nor did aught disturb our rest. But Koto, when he wakened me, said he had seen plenty of devils moving about beyond the line of fire. Then he rolled himself up, and so became immovable. But I, hearing no snores, grew suspicious of such somnolence, considering that he had snored like a thunderstorm incarnate since we started from his castle. Finally I tricked him into betraying himself. With a jerk of my head I summoned him to my side.

"Koto, do you think your King unfit to keep guard, that you lie awake?"

"Lord," he replied, "there be many devils about, and some be very dangerous — tricky, too. I know their ways better than you do, and can better cope with them. Also, I await the greatest one of all, for I would talk with him on a certain matter."

"Your father, Koto?"

"Yes, my King. Koto sent him word by a lesser devil, and he will surely come."

"Koto," I demanded sternly, "would you betray your King?"

"Nay, I seek to serve my Master." He stared at me in hurt surprize. Ashamed of my suspicion, I made amends.

"I thank my Baron! Koto, have I your permission to see this father of yours?"

"So be it," he assented, after pondering the matter for a while. "But first I must tell him, or he will be angry."

A long interval passed. Out of the blackness beyond the fire two enormous crimson eyes glared balefully. Koto calmly arose, stepped across the glowing line of the Fire of Safety, and walked off in the darkness toward those glowing orbs. A thousand misgivings assailed me. I strained my eyes, but could see naught. Even the crimson eyes had vanished. Only one comfort did I have—if harm came to Koto, his howls would surely apprise me of his danger. So I strained my ears, but no faintest whisper came. Then, after an eon of suspense, Koto calmly returned, and muttered:

"Now if King Karan wishes to see Koto's father—come! He is very terrible to behold, but he has promised Koto that King Karan shall be unharmed. But do not awaken Zarf—yet!"

It took all the hardihood I could muster to step across the line of fire and walk out into that fiend-infested dark. Koto minded it far less than I. There was evil in the very air. Strange, terrible faces stared at me, half-heard voices moaned and gibbered in my ears, clammy hands grasped at my arms and clothing, yet could not hold. Once a pair of icy cold lips kissed me full on my mouth; and oh! the foul effluvium of that breath!... Abruptly, Koto halted. A huge mass of black seen against the murky blackness of the night barred further progress. We stood immovable, waiting—for what? After a bit I grew impatient, weary of standing like a rock, and reached for my sword.

"Well," I demanded of Koto. "What is this holding us here? And where is this mighty father of yours? I am minded to try my sword on this black barrier and find out if it be impassible."

Before he could reply—the black barrier was not! Only, two eyes that were crimson fires of hellishness were staring into mine from a distance of mere inches... no face, no form... just vacant air—and two eyes. With a snort of disgust, I turned my back to the phenomenon.

"Koto," I said severely, "I am Karan, rightful King of Octolan. I am not interested in child's play, nor am I to be frightened by any Elemental, devil, goblin, or fiend in all my realm. I am *their* King as well as yours! Let this father of yours show respect, or we return to our shelter..."

A Being stood facing me! It was taller than Koto or I, albeit no giant. Yet I knew that an Elemental was capable of assuming, at will, any form it might choose. Its features were wholly non-human; at the same time its expression was in nowise repulsive, nor was it fear-inspiring. But there were unmistakable power and mastery stamped thereon and shining in its great, glowing eyes.

It was staring at me coldly, impersonally, with no sign of hostility, friendliness, or even curiosity; and I stared back at it with precisely the same attitude. If it sought to overawe me, it was badly mistaken. Then I realized it was telepathically reading my soul. And strangely, I began to grasp some insight into its nature, likewise.

"Truly, you are King Karan of Octolan, returned to regain your own. And I, to whom past, present and future are one and the same, tell you that you will succeed in all you undertake. Aye! And more than you now dream. And because you have treated Koto as a man, and will eventually make of him one of whom I may yet be proud, I will transport you, Koto, that grim Zarf of yours, and your mounts as well, across the Sea of the Dead, and beyond the Hills of Flint. But across the Mountains of Horror you three must fight your own way. Certain powers of Nature I control, and naught do I fear; but there is an ancient pact between that magician whom you seek, and me. Therefore I will not anger him by taking you into his realms, uninvited.

"Yet this I will tell you for your further guidance—he will demand of you a service. Give it, and all shall go well with your plans. Refuse it, and all the days of your life you will regret that refusal. At dawn, be in readiness, and I will carry out my promise. Fear not, whatever happens, for my ways are none that you can understand, even were I to explain them. And now, farewell till dawn!"

And with that—I stood, facing nothing! Koto's father had simply vanished.

Returning to the cave, we found a badly worried Zarf awake and cursing luridly. But he became considerably mollified when I explained, although he shook his head dubiously regarding Koto's father and his proffered assistance.

"His aid will more likely get us in trouble than help us out of it," he grumbled. "Still, as no better course presents, I suppose we will have to accept and run all chances."

At the first flush of dawn we were mounted and waiting. We noted that the air held a peculiar quality, indescribable, yet familiar, somewhat like the odor caused by a levin-bolt striking too close for comfort. Also, there came a strange, murky tinge in the air—a faint moan—icy winds—a howling, shrieking, roaring fury like all the tormented souls in Hell voicing their agonies—sand, dust and small pebbles tore past us— the world abruptly vanished, together with my companions, so far as I knew—naught remained—I was choked by dust and my eyes were blinded—I was dizzy and bemazed—I knew not for certain if I were alive or dead and buried—acute misery was the sole thing I was conscious of.

My mount stumbled and fell asprawl. I lurched to my feet, gasped, retched violently, and presently felt better. I stared about me, bewildered. Zarf and Koto were just scrambling to their feet, and facing us was Koto's father. And the great Elemental had a smile on his lips, and in his eyes a light of actual friendliness.

"Lord Karan, back of you are the Sea of the Dead and the Hills of Flint; and before you lie the Mountains of Horror. I have kept my promise to the King my son follows and honors. Farewell."

And before I could voice my gratitude, he was gone—as seemed a habit with him. One instant visible, then—vacancy!

"I know much about my father," Koto said slowly. "But I never knew he could do this."

𝕬 faint trail ran down into a wide valley, on the far side of which loomed the mighty ramparts of the Mountains of Horror. And they merited the appellation. They were evil, and evil dwelt in them.

Soon the dim trail became a wide road, albeit ancient and in dire need of repair. I do not believe it had been traveled for ages, until we came; the natural conclusion being that whatever race built it had passed into oblivion, leaving their handiwork to mark their passing.

As the day drew to its close, the road led us into the ruins of an ancient city. Not one stone stood atop of another. We decided to camp there for the night, and while Koto pitched camp and prepared a meal, I strolled about the ruins.

Everywhere I looked were slabs that were covered with petroglyphs. Whatever the race, they had a written language, and moreover, they had been prone to embellishment. They must have been, like the old Egyptians, dominated by a priesthood, to judge by the character of the many pictures illustrating the graven text. But if those same pictures were aught to go by, their gods must have been born from a union of a nightmare and a homicidal maniac's frenzy! It gave me the chill creeps just to look at those pictures, so foul and unholy were the rites and acts depicted.

𝕴t was during my watch. My companions snored in a most inharmonious concert; and while I was in nowise asleep, I had drifted into a sort of revery. Slowly I became aware of a pair of eyes gleaming with opalescent lights, staring across the fire at me. Thinking it might be Koto's father, I spoke low-voiced in greeting. But as no reply came, I grew angry and asked who it was and what it wanted. Again no reply, so I snatched up my short bow and drove an arrow beneath those glowing orbs.

A silvery laugh was my only reward. A hard-driven arrow is no laughing matter, but anything could happen in this accursed land, I decided.

"The little death-wand has no power to harm me," a voice asserted in those same silvery tones. "Nay, O Stranger; how may you slay one who died ages agone—but who still lives—and rules?"

"So that little 'death-wand' may not slay you," I snarled. "Well, we'll see what this will do!" And my sword leaped in a whistling cut across the tiny fire. Had there been a head and body there, they must have parted company! But the blade encountered—air!

Across the fire, smiling indulgently, as might one tolerantly amused by the tantrums of an otherwise interesting child, there sat a resplendently beautiful woman, a vivid, gorgeous brunette, with a slightly greenish tinge shimmering over her slender gold-bronze hued body. Her attire, a merest wisp of some pearly glimmering gossamer fabric, accentuated every personal charm of her exquisite form.

"Who are you?" I demanded.

"A Princess of Hell I am, yet having dominance here on this region, likewise. Ages agone I ruled in this city when it was in its height and glory. But there arose among the priests a mighty magician whose power became greater than mine. Quakes and fire and flood he loosed upon me and my people—and we became that which no more is—yet destroy us wholly he could not.

"So it is but a city of ruins you now behold, wherein, as ghosts, my people dwell; and I, a ghost, too, abide with them part of my time, and rule over ghostly people and a wrecked city."

"If you are a ghost, you look like an extremely tangible one," I stated bluntly.

"Yes?" and she laughed in derision. "Was it an 'extremely tangible' ghost against which you tried two different death-wands? Still you are correct, in part. I am tangible enough now, as you may prove for yourself, should you care to do so. I build my body as I need it, or revert it to vapor when its use is over. Child's play, to my magic, O Stranger... You disbelieve? See!"

She arose, a vision of alluring loveliness, passed deliberately through the fire, and seated herself at my side so closely that I could sense the magnetic radiations of her.

"You may touch me, take me in your arms if you will, kiss my lips till your blood is aflame, and cool your ardor in my embrace, nor shall you find me unresponsive!"

Her rounded arms stole about my neck like soft, satiny serpents.

"So," she murmured. "Am I not tangible? Desirable, too? Take me, and I will be to you as no other, woman, or spirit, or ghost, fiend, devil, or angel in all the universe can ever be! Power and wisdom and rulership will I place at your command... love and passion undreamed hitherto—"

I had sat immovable, silent up to that point—but suddenly I made up for lost time. A violent shove sent her asprawl, squarely into the fire; and from my lips came a word so descriptive that Earth's vilest would have blushed in outraged modesty had that epithet been applied.

But the seductively lovely Princess of Hell evidently took the word as a compliment. And if she were angry at being shoved into the fire, she showed no sign thereof. Out from the flames she glided, more alluring than ever; not a hair of her dusky tresses disturbed; with never a blemish on her gold-bronze skin; and with a provocative smile on her curving lips.

"What you have called me—I would be even that, for you," she sighed languorously. "You and I were meant for each other since ever Eternity began—"

But at that, I exploded! Meant for that she-devil? *I?* My hand shot out, seizing her slender throat in a vise-like grip, mercilessly.

"You—!" The word was even worse than the first epithet I

had used. "Since arrow and sword fail, let's see what choking will do!"

I tightened my clutch, putting forth all my strength. For good measure, I drove my fist into her face—and nearly dislocated my arm! For the Princess of Hell, she-fiend—ghost—woman—or whatsoever she really was, or had been, simply wasn't there! In fact, I wondered if she'd ever been there, or had I dozed, and dreamed?...

"It was no dream, King Karan!"

The voice was full, sonorous, pleasant. Glancing up, I saw a tall, stately old man, bareheaded, smiling in amity.

"Zarf! Koto! *Up!*" I shouted, leaping to my feet, sword in hand. The old man raised his hand in protest.

"Nay, King Karan, they will sleep unless *I* release them from their slumber. That she-fiend put them into a trance from which only someone with power greater than hers can arouse them. Nor will I do so until after you and I confer to a matter of mutual benefit."

"Who are you?" I demanded. "And what devilment do you plan against me and my comrades?"

"Yon sleeper—Zarf—told you of a magician; and you set forth to seek that one, did you not? Well, I am he whom you seek, and your journey is at an end, King Karan. Knowing of your coming, I was prepared to greet you as soon as you entered my domains—and this ruined city marks my borderline. So, I am here!

"King Karan, you are naught to me, nor I to you. But we have a common enemy—Djl Grm! Between him and me there lies an ancient feud. You he has wronged. There is a service—I get that from your mind—which you hope I can and will render you.

"Karan, King afar from your crown, throne, and kingdom, you are a bold and resourceful man, and your two companions are worth an army of ordinary folk. Render me one service, faithfully, without evasion or quibble, and I will release your locked memory! Well?"

"Arouse Zarf and Koto," I commanded. "If you be the one I seek, they will identify you, nor will they harm you. I, Karan, give you protection!"

He actually laughed at that, although there was more of admiration than derision in his laugh.

"Bold as ever, King Karan," he complimented. "As you have said, so will I do." He made a slight gesture, murmuring something I could not catch. "Now, speak, in a whisper if you will, and see if they be asleep."

As I complied, they came abruptly to their feet, fully alert... they took one look... on Koto's ugly face came such an expression of ghastly fear that I hastened to assure him he was in no danger. Zarf bowed in respect, albeit he showed no fear. Our visitor spoke, in a courteous manner:

"You know me, Zarf? You, too, Baron Koto?"

"You are Agnor Halit, the mighty magician I persuaded my King to seek," Zarf responded gravely.

Koto nodded vehemently. "My father says you have more power than the devil himself, O Agnor Halit."

"Is King Karan satisfied?"

"I am," I confirmed. "But why do you meet me here, rather than making me journey all the way to your abode?"

"For this reason—the service I ask, if I am to release your inhibited memory, will take you back on your path, even to the near shore of the Sea of the Dead. And so, I save you many long, weary days of travel, hardship, and danger."

"And this service?"

"Give heed, then, and I will explain. There is a treasure I would fain possess. There be good reasons why I may not go after it myself, yet those reasons would not affect you. Truth to tell, it is hidden in the territory ruled by another magician who knows not it is there. The one who hid this treasure is another magician... long ago he hid the priceless thing for some dire reason of his own. It is the statue of a naked, beautiful female; yet it is an enormous jewel—a flawless sapphire, a trifle over half life-size—"

"No sapphire in all the worlds was ever that big," I objected. But Agnor Halit merely smiled as he assented:

"True! But magic works wonders, King Karan. Your throne is made of a huge chrysolite, albeit not in all the worlds was a chrysolite ever that big! Still are you 'King Karan of the Chrysolite Throne.' Magic made your throne from certain substances, yet a trader in gems would tell you it is genuine chrysolite!...

"This sapphire statue was made from flesh and blood by enchantment. It is the actual body of a witch who dared withstand a great magician, long ago, until he conquered her by treachery. For punishment he transmuted her to sapphire, reducing her size to that of a half-grown child, and so left her a beautiful image in which her soul is still prisoned. But once I have that image in my possession, I will have a hold upon him...

"He hated her so greatly that after turning her to crystal, he could in nowise abide to look upon her constantly; wherefore he hid her in a submerged cavern near this shore of the Sea of the Dead. But that cavern can be entered—at times."

"And if I bring to you this statue—"

"Then will I release the bonds that hold your memory in abeyance. So be it that you release the Sapphire Image to me, without any reservations or quibble—your memories of all the past will be perfect. I, Agnor Halit, magician, do pledge you this, Karan of Octolan. And my pledges I do keep to the last atom. I have wrought every known sin, and many nameless evils—but of one thing is Agnor Halit thus far guiltless—a broken promise!"

"It is well," I answered. And not to be outdone by him, a dealer in all unholiness, I gave pledge in return: "I, Karan, will deliver to you that treasure if I succeed in carrying out my venture, nor will I claim part or parcel in it. For aught I care, you may shatter it to blue slivers the moment I deliver it to you."

A demoniacal light flickered momentarily in that dark sorcerer's eyes as he said vindictively:

"I may do an even stranger thing than that, once the thing is in my possession!"

"I am not concerned with your mysteries," I shrugged. "All I need to know about you is that you and I have an agreement which we both intend to keep. Now, tell me all you can, that I may surely find that place where the Sapphire Image is hidden."

So for the rest of the night we three sat listening while that gentle-seeming old man told us in detail all he knew about our course—while at the same time he warned us frankly that we were going direct into the worst antechamber of Hell when we reached the entrance to the cavern. And, as we later found out for ourselves, he understated...

"Lord Karan," Koto said, pointing—"unless Agnor Halit lied, yon place is the entrance to the cavern we seek."

We dismounted after one glance, for the marks were unmistakable. Five huge boulders indicated the angles of a pentagon; in the center, a pool, evidently filled with water from the Sea of the Dead through some underground channel. To substantiate this supposition, the surface of the pool heaved with the heaving of the surges along the beach some few hundred yards distant.

Even as we watched, the surface became violently agitated; a vortex formed, became a miniature whirlpool, making queer sucking noises, strange gurglings and whistling moans. This lasted for upward of an hour. After that, the surface became level and still.

Then abruptly came a change. In the very center a huge bubble rose and burst, polluting the atmosphere with a most unholy stench. More bubbles rose and the stench grew worse. Bubbles came continually, and the pool boiled like a cauldron, filling the air with horrible odor. Then again the surface stilled.

Now my courage well-nigh forsook me, and without shame I admit it. For I knew I'd have to dive into that loathly pool while the vortex pulled downward; and come up — if ever I did come up — while the bubbles arose! And it was in nowise a pleasing prospect. After we'd been studying the pool for some time, Zarf evidently came to the same conclusion I had reached, for he said bluntly:

"My King, that old devil, Agnor Halit, laid a trap for you! It is well known that King Karan does not lightly break his word. But if I, Zarf, have aught to say about this matter, here is once Karan of Octolan breaks a pledge, nor gives it a second thought. To plunge into that pool is the act of a madman. If that damned sorcerer wants that image so badly, let him come and dive for it himself. He will only go to Hell a little sooner, through a most befitting gateway, and this region of space will be that much improved because of his absence!"

"But my memory, Zarf?"

"Once you've gone into that filthy hole, you'll have no need for it, as you'll not come up to use it! Nay, let us rather go back to Koto's hut and plot to regain your kingdom. If successful, we can then force Djl Grm to undo his foul sorcery — "

"Not so fast, Zarf," Koto interrupted. "My father warned our King to comply with Agnor Halit's request, and said that if he did, all would go well with his plans. But my father said, too, that if our King refused, he'd regret it all his life long."

Now Zarf and I looked at each other blankly, for there was truth in what Koto had just said.

"I wonder if there is any other way to regain that statue," I suggested tentatively.

"I know a good way," Koto said simply. "It is just this: Koto goes down, and comes up with the image, or stays down there with it. And if aught goes wrong, Koto can well be spared—"

"Nay, my Koto," I said huskily, for I was deeply moved by the faithful fellow's loyal and courageous proffer—"I can ill spare—"

A gurgling noise from the pool. Koto rose abruptly, and said no word and gave no sign, but dived in like a frog, head first, into the center of the rapidly forming whirlpool. Neither Zarf nor I had been alert enough to prevent him, for he had moved too quickly. We stared at each other, open-mouthed in amazement.

"King Karan," Zarf's voice rang like a clarion—"when you regain your kingdom remember that brave fool, Baron Koto of the Red Wilderness, and sometimes think of—Zarf!"

Splash!

I stood alone, gaping stupidly at the spot where two splendid, loyal noblemen had disappeared. The vortex was growing weaker—it would cease ere long—then an eternity of waiting, hoping—perhaps they would never come up—I'd be alone—never see them again—I, a King minus crown, throne, realm, memory, wife, subjects—why! the only *subjects* I knew or cared about...

I took a deep full breath, and dived.

That vile fluid that stank so abominably hurt worse than it smelt. It was actually corrosive. It *bit!* Raw potash lye is its nearest comparison... I was still head down and going deeper. I was spinning with the swirling until I grew dizzy. My eyeballs felt as if burning out of their sockets from that acrid solution—down, down, and down! A faint, dimly seen blue light struck horizontally through the whirlpool—two vague, shadowy figures barely seen as I whirled in that mad headlong dance—a powerful grip clamped fast on one of my ankles and I thought I was being rent apart—the vortex hated to let go—but that mighty pull at my leg would not be denied—I looked up into Koto's ugly face—then Zarf's voice, heavy with reproach:

"King Karan, is this well? Go back, I pray you, as soon as the bubbles rise!"

But at that, I flatly refused, standing on my royal dignity; and I made them yield the point, maugre their stubborn insistence.

A tunnel stretched away into the dim distance, and up that tunnel we started—toward what? Steadily the blue light became stronger, and in my mind arose the certitude that it emanated from the Blue Image. Demon faces peered at us from cracks and crevices, but none of the devils of the place found hardihood to attack us.

The tunnel debouched into a great cavern. In the exact center, on a mound of bleached skulls stood the source of the blue radiance—the Sapphire Witch herself. I gasped in awed admiration at the flawless perfection of her beauty—and suddenly, how I did hate that sorcerer Agnor Halit, to whom I'd promised to deliver that exquisite Image of Incomparable Loveliness! Cheerfully would I have bartered the empires of the universe for its possession—did I but own those empires—nor would I have considered the price exorbitant. *I wanted it—I wanted it!* And I'd pledged—

Around that mound, in a ring on the floor of the cavern, lay many stones. Half the size of human heads they were, round as balls, and no two were of the same color. Every one was aglow, softly, with inward lights, as if each were afire deep inside— dark reds there were; dull orange; dusky blues, garish greens and sinister purples. We knew they were sentient, malignant, resenting our intrusion! Koto responded by kicking one stone that was apparently sneering at him and radiating contempt. At the impact of Koto's foot, the smoldering stone gave forth a metallic clang like a smitten gong, rose straight in the air to the level of Koto's face—then hurtled straight at him with a speed that would have cracked his skull, had not Zarf struck at the Flying

Stone with his sword and deflected its course.

A dozen of them promptly left the floor and flew at Zarf—who as promptly turned and fled. But he was actuated by discretion rather than fear. I saw him race headlong into a crack in the tunnel wall—and shortly, the devil who dwelt therein came tumbling out, well-nigh sheared in two by Zarf's sword. Evidently Zarf preferred coping with devils, to the Flying Stones. Koto, having the same idea, hastily retreated to the tunnel mouth—and I went with Koto. In another moment Zarf rejoined us there, grinning sheepishly. The Flying Stones did not follow us that far from the Blue Statue...

We stood disconsolate, wondering how we were to pass their formidable menace—and as if to show us how futile was our quest, of a sudden the entire ring of Flying Stones levitated to the height of a man's shoulders and head, and commenced to swirl about the Sapphire Witch who stood so serene on her altar of skulls. Truly a strange goddess, and guarded by even stranger acolytes!

Fast and faster swirled the Flying Stones, their colored lights glowing more and more brightly—faster yet, until we could no longer distinguish any single stone—they were merely a beautiful, gleaming blur of fire—gradually a humming sound became audible, swelling in volume till it became a roar like the diapason of a mighty organ—soon it became distinguishable as a chant of warning!...

And at that, a sort of madness came upon me. I had come for that image—to bear it away—not to stand and look at it from a distance. And that image I meant to take, forthwith! In my rage, all else faded—kingdom, wife, subjects, memory, Agnor Halit, Djl Grm, Zarf, Koto, even my own welfare mattered not. I ran forward, shouting:

"Fools! I am Karan of Octolan! I have come for that image! It shall be mine! Down and lie still, I say!"

Now who was I, after all, that those Flying Stones should obey me? Yet so it was! The fiery band settled down instantly. I walked confidently forward, picked up the image, and so, back to where Zarf and Koto stood staring in amazed incredulity.

"Somewhat of magic my King knows, it appears!" gasped Koto shakily. I myself could hardly believe it. But the fact remained that I held the statue in my arms. And we three walked down that tunnel, nor did aught bother us all the way to the upper world!

Once at the surface, we wiped the foulness of the pool from the lovely image, and stood actually adoring the matchless treasure in the clear light... looked suddenly up, and saw Koto's father, and with him that utterly damned sorcerer, Djl Grm.

The sorcerer clutched swiftly for the image, but as swiftly Zarf spun his sword in a glittering wheel of defense in front of it—and the magician flinched back. Then he pointed a finger—and Zarf became temporarily paralyzed. Koto snatched up the image, and tucking it beneath his left arm, he waggled his formidable bludgeon under the sorcerer's nose with a meaning gesture.

"Try that trick on me!" he invited grimly. But the magician, for some reason, declined Koto's urgent invitation. Instead, I became aware of rapid interchange of telepathic speech between Koto's father and Djl Grm. The great Elemental turned to Koto.

"Are you my son?"

"That, you should know best," Koto responded with a grim smile. He seemed to know what was coming next.

"Then," his father commanded—"give the Blue Image to its proper owner!"

"No!" and Koto shook his head defiantly. "It is not seemly that my King should carry burdens while I, his follower, go empty-handed. I carry it for him. His it is by right of power—for he made the Flying Stones yield to him their trust, and he bore it away from the Altar of Skulls, unmolested!"

The Elemental grew black with rage. His eyes flamed crimson, and their awful glare frightened Zarf and me. Koto looked perturbed, but a faint reddish spark began flickering in his eyes, too.

"Give that Image to Djl Grm, I said!" The Elemental's voice held a note of awful finality.

Koto's arm flew back and swept forward again, and his bludgeon smashed full in his father's face.

"My father you are," Koto howled in fury — "but Karan is my King!"

Unharmed by the impact, the Elemental gravely handed Koto his great club. But it was to me he spoke.

"King Karan, I said I might yet be proud of Koto — *I am!*" Then to the sorcerer, sternly:

"Djl Grm, I know your power — and I know its limitations. And I know, likewise, what you have in mind. Summon your legions if you dare and I will summon mine. And what that will mean to us both ere all be ended, you know, as do I! To a certain extent, I aided you in this affair, for I wished to see how big my son had grown in the service of his King — and I am proud of his loyalty. So long as my son shall cleave to him, Karan of Octolan is my ally and friend. *Djl Grm, is it peace – or war?"*

The magician seemed like to explode with impotent fury. Suddenly he vanished with a scream of baffled, venomous rage. Then came a terrific sensation, comparable only to the emotion an arrow must feel as it leaves the string of a powerful bow.

· Koto, still holding the Sapphire Image under his left arm and his great club clenched in his right fist — Zarf and I, still holding our drawn swords — and Koto's father, smiling as if pleased that he had broken openly with Djl Grm — stood looking at each other, hardly knowing what to say. But one thing we three realized — Koto's father had once again displayed his control of the forces of Nature, and we were in the city of ghosts, where I had promised to meet Agnor Halit. The Elemental said something to Koto that made him grin from ear to ear; then it vanished.

Night. And we three sat by a brightly burning campfire. Not one of us cared to sleep. We were taking no chances on some unexpected treachery assailing us at the last moment. Again and again I had tried to reach Agnor Halit mentally, holding him come get his Blue Image and give me my price, that I might be done with a distasteful business; because *I* wanted that statue for myself, and also because I liked old Agnor Halit not one whit better than his fellow sorcerer, Djl Grm. And the sooner I was quit of further doings with either or both of those two, the more pleased I'd be... But Agnor Halit came not. A hope dawned in my mind—perhaps he had met with some disaster. Then Koto caught my mind and spoiled that idea.

"Nay! He lives. He will come whenever it pleases him to come—till then—we—can—but—wait."

Koto sagged where he sat, slumped over on his side—and snored! Zarf, a second later, did likewise. Amazed, I shouted at them. As well shout at two solid rocks! I grew afraid at that, for I saw what was toward—they, of their own free wills, would never have acted thus! Some malign power had wrought a sleep-spell on them, and I was left to face whatever might happen.

And it started immediately!

The ruined city was materializing as it was before calamity fell upon it! Stone upon stone, tier upon tier, story upon story, tower and turret and pylon, pinnacle, spire and dome, it grew in might and beauty, albeit the might suggested cruelty and the beauty wholly evil.

The streets filled with people—men, women, and little children; and on no face did I see aught written of good, but only all wickedness. Before I could decide what to do, of a sudden a detachment of soldiery bore down on me, surrounding me before I could rise to my feet. Again I shouted to Zarf and Koto; and deep as was the slumber-spell, Koto's brain must have caught, in part, my warning. For he moved uneasily, flinging out one arm restlessly. That arm fell across the image where it lay wrapped in my cloak.

Roughly I was yanked to my feet. The soldiers disregarded the two others, for some reason. Through the streets they led me, into a splendid edifice that proved to be a temple of the loathly devil-gods I had seen depicted on the various rock-faces among the ruins.

Seated on a resplendent throne was the seductively lovely Princess of Hell, looking more alluring than when first I saw her. Languidly smiling, she addressed me as if naught but utmost amity had marked our former brief acquaintance.

"All this I have wrought for your sake, O Stranger for whom I yearn. I did it that you might have proof it is no weakling wraith who seeks your love, but one truly great, powerful and — if you will have it so — kindly disposed toward you."

"What do you really want of me?" I demanded bluntly. "I'm not a total fool, to believe you're actually in love with me, a mere mortal nobody!"

"A mere mortal nobody?" The Princess smiled, highly amused. "Karan of Octolan, Lord of the Chrysolite Throne, is hardly a mere mortal nobody. You do yourself injustice, for you are very much a man. And not a maid in all my train but would be happy to be your mate — and myself most of all.

"Secretly, you regard me as a fiend. Well, I *am*! But I want you to know me fully. Between such as I, and your sort, exists an almost impassible barrier — unless one of your sort invites one of my order across the border. You have a different magnetism, highly beneficial to us, and we delight to bathe therein, returning in exchange a portion of our own powerful vibrations. Thus impregnated, new powers and capacities are yours for the wielding.

"We 'fiends' do not seek your souls! Most of your souls are not worth having, so weak, so embryonic are they. Not good enough to attain to celestial realms, nor wicked enough to be welcome in Hell, naught remains for most of your race but return, life after life, to some of the material planes. But within you, Karan, are great capacities for absolute Evil or absolute Good. Aye, a fit mate for even me—"

"You've said enough," I interrupted harshly. "Mate with *you*? Give you of my magnetic radiations—draw from *you* strength, power, and capacities? Why, you she-devil, sooner would I spend eternity adoring hopelessly—"

"That Blue Witch you stole," she hissed venomously. "O Fool ten thousand times accursed! You dare compare me to that icy cold crystal that cannot move? I would have crowned you Lord of Hell itself in a century's time, had you accepted my offer; but since you dare to refuse me—you shall pay!..."

And pay I did!

In obedience to some unspoken command from the infuriated she-fiend, a particularly malignant-appearing priest stepped forward from amidst a group of his kind. I had never before seen a face so utterly unhuman. His body was more ape-like than man-like.

The priest laid one prehensile paw on my shoulder—and received a smashing blow full in the face from my fist. The priest did not even change expression, but my fist felt as if I had hit a solid rock. Holding me at arm's length, he jabbed me lightly with one finger. He knew anatomy and neurology, that devil-priest, for that light touch wrung a gasp of agony from me, and brought the cold sweat from every pore of my body, while it sent a terrific thrill like commingled ice and fire along every fiber of my nervous system.

That was merely a preliminary...

A vise-like grip on my temples with thumb and finger—

what sort of uncanny powers did that devil-priest control? And throb after throb of lance-like twinges tore through my brain, each one a solid impact, each impact worse than the preceding one; until at each twinge bright sparks burst within my skull, rending and searing the tissues of my brain, and I, all fortitude lost, howled, moaned, shrieked and yelled like any madman in Bedlam as those awful pulsations continued into an eternity of anguish.

But that became monotonous. My howls were too much alike, and wearied the Princess. The devil-priest tried a new one. Releasing my temples, he lightly slapped me on the chest with the flat of his hand, meantime blowing his breath on my forehead…

A most delightful sense of surcease from torture after anguish unbearable swept all through me, and I sighed my relief; but that devil-priest ran his thumb along my spine, once, and the terrific agony of that caress made all I had suffered previously seem but exquisite delight!

Stepping back a pace, the devil-priest levelled his arm, his stiffly extended fingers pointing straight at me, and I commenced to gyrate, at first slowly, then with ever accelerating speed; fast and faster, and faster yet, until the surroundings became a blur—and faster still, until the surroundings and the blur, too, disappeared, and naught remained but myself aspin on my own axis!

Crash!

The motion was instantaneously reversed, and what ghastly effect that simple action had upon me can never be imagined or described. It had to be undergone to be understood, and what little sense I'd still managed to retain thus far left me entirely…

I awoke! I was stretched out on a couch, suffused with untellable fatigue, acutely conscious of agonies endured beyond all endurance…

"O my beloved! Such sufferings! But never again! In my

arms, O loved man, shall you regain strength and know bliss beyond all thinking."

Hovering over me, holding me in her arms, shielding and protecting me from further harm, was a superbly beautiful woman. Azure was her hair, blue as the midsummer skies was her shimmering skin that shone with a clear luster surpassing any gem; yet in nowise was she a stone statue, but a living, breathing, loving, tender, soft-bodied woman of flesh and blood! I reached up feeble arms about her neck, drawing her down to me—almost had her lips touched mine—a lambent reddish light flickered momentarily in her wondrous blue eyes—

"You infernal hag!"

It was but a putrid corpse I held so lovingly within the circle of my arms—and in it the worms and maggots were acrawl!...

The Princess of Hell, on her gorgeous throne, gave utterance to a trill of merry laughter at the success of that final glamourous torment of the man who had dared refuse her proffered love...

That laugh changed to a shriek of fury ere the last silvery note of her mirth died out! Facing her where she sat surrounded by her guards and courtiers, stood a tall, robed figure, grimly eyeing her in a silence more fraught with menace than any words could have conveyed.

"Agnor Halit!" she screamed in a paroxysm of terror, as she recognized the mighty sorcerer.

"Even so, O Princess of Hell, Queen over a ghostly race and a ghost city that I shattered with my magic, ages agone. And now! For that you have not felt the weight of my hand in the last few centuries, you have grown overbold. You actually dared molest this man, knowing that he was at the time engaged in serving my purpose!"

Agnor Halit drew from the breast of his robe a most peculiar reptile, more like a short, extremely thick centipede than aught else. He held it up between thumb and finger. His words came slow, heavy, laden with doom:

"Into this vileness shalt thou go, nor ever come forth from it until I, Agnor Halit, am no more!"

He flung the small abhorrence on the dais, before the feet of the Princess. It remained there, immovable, its full eyes fixed on her face; and she stared back in awe-stricken, horrified fascination.

The sorcerer stretched out his arms, his quivering fingers aimed at the beauteous, erotic fiend trembling in an ecstasy of fear there on her sumptuous seat. Over guards and courtiers, priests and populace an icy terror fell; they stood staring with incredulous eyes, immovable—I myself could scarce breathe from the suspense of that tense waiting...

The Princess of Hell began to shrink. Small and smaller she became, dwindling visibly before our eyes—she became as tiny as the reptile—every exquisite feature of her loveliness remained intact, in miniature—a gray mist swirled between reptile and Princess—*they became one!*

Agnor Halit snapped finger and thumb, deliberately, insultingly contemptuous. At the *"Tshuk"* he made, the entire scene vanished!

I rubbed my eyes... I could not believe... a tiny reptile, most resembling a centipede, ran before my foot and around the corner of a boulder... but facing me was the sorcerer I sought...

"King Karan, you had a narrow escape," he assured me, earnestly. "But she is harmless now. Not even her devil-friends can enable her to work further mischief. She will be naught but a venomous worm so long as I shall continue to live—and as I may perish only by one method which none knows save me, she is like to endure for ages! Her bite might prove dangerous, but the fear I inspired in her will prevent her from trying that, even."

While talking, we had drawn to where lay Zarf and Koto. At our arrival they sat up as if waking from a natural nap. Zarf stared at the magician with undisguised hostility. Koto, most surprizingly, gave the magician a wide grin of welcome; more, he threw back my cloak and permitted Agnor Halit to see that we actually had the image he so desired. But Koto kept nigh, with a wary eye on the sorcerer's every move. Agnor Halit's eyes gleamed with a baleful light, his voice held a note of repressed, unholy exultation:

"King Karan, I am ready to fulfil my part of our pact. Once again, are you willing to renounce all claim to this Sapphire Image, yielding it to me to do with as may please my whim?"

"I am," I replied briefly. "Take the thing and give my price to me — the release of my memory. I grow weary of this magic and mystery-mongering, and would be about my own proper affairs."

"Not so fast," grinned Koto as the sorcerer turned eagerly to the statue. "King Karan has shown you his part of the bargain. Touch this image, ere you fulfil your part — which is not visible, but must be made evident to King Karan's satisfaction — and you have the father of Koto to reckon with — and, Agnor Halit, his power is greater than yours. If you doubt that — try conclusions with him! Shall I, his son, summon him?"

"King Karan," and Agnor Halit ignored Koto completely — "your word is inviolable, nor do I break promises. Yet Baron Koto is right. I can see your part — and you shall receive mine ere I take my payment. Is that satisfactory?"

"Magician," I exclaimed, impatient, "do more, and talk less! And you, Koto, let him have the thing as suits him best. I have taken his word, even as he accepts mine. Shall we quibble endlessly?"

"Yet will I do even as Baron Koto wishes," the sorcerer smiled. He laid his left hand on the back of my neck. The forefinger of his other hand he pressed tightly against my forehead just between the eyebrows.

A slight tingling flowed from that fingertip, through my brain, to the center of the palm against my neck. A tiny spark like a distant star lit in the center of my brain. It grew and grew, filling my entire skull with a silvery-golden brilliance shot through with coruscations and sparkling, scintillant flashes...

CRASH!

Insofar as I was aware of anything, my head had just exploded!... All the agonies I had ever experienced were as naught compared to that! I was so absolutely stunned I could not even fall down and die! Across immeasurable voids came a trumpet-like voice:

"King Karan, I have kept my promise!"

I blinked, and my dazed mind cleared. *Gods and Devils!* ... In one terrific rush, I knew all! Not one trifling detail of all the long reign in Octolan as Karan of the Chrysolite Throne was lacking in my memory! And thereupon my soul descended into Hell even as I stood facing that damnable sorcerer who openly sneered in my very face, gloating over my mental anguish—for I knew one thing which wrecked all benefits I had hoped to gain by my memory's restoration...

That Sapphire Image was the actual body of my wife and Queen, Mehul-Ira, transmuted by the hellish magic of that rebel sorcerer, Djl Grm, into a flawless jewel, with her pure soul imprisoned within the depths of the wondrous blue crystal—and *I* had renounced all claim to the image, thereby giving my royal spouse to another sorcerer quite as evil as the one I'd rescued her from!...

"Karan, becozened and bejaped King, I claim my price!"

"Take it—you—devil!" I managed to gasp finally, albeit my soul was dying within me, and my anguish was plainly visible to my followers...

"Take the image, magician," Koto grinned.

Almost was I tempted to slay Koto for grinning like that

when my very soul was suffering all the agonies of dissolution without the comfort of death's release.

Agnor Halit moved not from where he stood. Only he pointed his finger at the image. A pink mist enshrouded the statue, turned to a deep rose-red, then to scarlet, and finally became crimson like rich blood. Gradually it faded, and a living, breathing woman, radiantly lovely, arose from where she lay on the hard ground, stood erect, turned, smiling at me with an unmistakable light in her great softly shining eyes — she stretched out longing arms — Koto flung my cloak about her, concealing her exquisite perfection from the avid gaze of the sorcerer — she spoke, and the music of her voice tore my heart with its sweetness:

"Karan! *My* Karan! After all these dreary years! I am still all yours…"

"Nay!" Agnor Halit interrupted harshly. "Karan has renounced all his claim to you! You are *mine!*"

That devilish magician, inspired by the malice common to all his ilk, had perpetrated upon me a treachery so utterly fiendish that even the demons in Hell must have shrieked and rocked in glee upon their white-hot brazen seats!

He opened his mouth to its fullest extent, and peals of gargantuan laughter bellowed forth. In a daze, I noted dimly that Koto had stooped and now held something in his hand — why! it looked like a short thick worm — or a centipede…

"Agnor Halit!" Koto spoke with a sneer more bitter than aught the sorcerer knew how to use — "King Karan gave you the image, to do with as pleased your whim — but he gave not his wife! Upon her you have no claim! But I, Koto of the Red Wilderness, in her place give you — *this!*"

Flung with unerring accuracy, the tiny reptile, writhing and twisting, shot from Koto's hand, disappearing in the yawning cavity of the sorcerer's mouth.

Agnor Halit closed his mouth with a gulp of surprise. He

staggered—his face turned to a ghastly greenish hue—the body that had so long defied the ravages of death dashed itself to the ground, rolling in hideous torture—convulsion after convulsion shook it—then slowly ceased—and a second later we were gazing, incredulous, at a carrion corpse that stank most outrageously and in which the worms and maggots were already at work.

"Somewhat of magic Koto knows," Koto grinned. "While my body lay still, my spirit went with my King and saw all; then, returning, I dreamed the secret Agnor Halit deemed that none knew save himself! The Princess of Hell crawled into my hand that I might use her, and so, she revenged herself! Agnor Halit is now in Hell, where she can deal with him according to her fancy!"

We mounted our great birds. My Queen sat before me, my arm steadying her. Before us, smiling pleasantly, was Koto's father. Koto grinned at him.

"Am I your son?"

"I myself could have wrought no better," responded the great Elemental, generously.

"Your son is sorry his father has lost his once mighty power." Koto's tone was lugubrious in the extreme.

"Lost my power?"

"Aye! My King would rest tonight within my castle on the far edge of the Red Wilderness, my Barony—yet here we sit on these ugly, slow birds…"

Again the fury of the elements were loosed for my benefit… We slept that night at Koto's castle!

The Sea-Witch

Heldra Helstrom entered my life in a manner peculiarly her own. And while she was the most utterly damnable woman in all the world, at the same time, in my opinion, she was the sweetest and the most superbly lovely woman who ever lived.

A three-day northeast gale was hammering at the coast. It was late in the fall of the year, and cold as only our North Atlantic coast can very well be, but in the very midst of the tempest I became afflicted with a mild form of claustrophobia. So I donned sea-boots, oil-skins and sou'wester hat, and sallied forth for a walk along the shore.

My little cottage stood at the top of a high cliff. There was a broad, safe path running down to the beach, and down it I hurried. The short winter day was even then drawing to a close, and after I'd trudged a quarter of a mile along the shore, I decided I'd best return to my comfortable fireside. The walk had at least given me a good appetite.

There was none of the usual lingering twilight of a clear winter evening. Darkness fell so abruptly I was glad I'd brought along a powerful flashlight. I'd almost reached the foot of my path up the cliff when I halted, incredulous, yet desiring to make sure.

I turned the ray of the flashlight on the great comber just curling to break on the shore, and held the light steady, my breath gasping in my throat. Such a thing as I thought I'd seen couldn't be—yet it was!

I started to run to the rescue, and could not move a foot. A power stronger than my own will held me immovable. I could only watch, spellbound. And even as I stared, that gigantic comber gently subsided, depositing its precious living burden on the sands as softly as any nurse laying a babe into a cradle.

Waist-deep in a smother of foam she stood for a brief second, then calmly waded ashore and walked with free swinging stride straight up the beam of my flashlight to where I stood.

Regardless of the hellish din and turmoil of the tempest, I thrilled, old as I am, at the superb loveliness of this most amazing specimen of flotsam ever a raging sea cast ashore within memory of man.

Never a shred of clothing masked her matchless body, yet her flesh glowed rosy-white, when by all natural laws it should have been blue-white from the icy chill of wintry seas.

"Well!" I exclaimed. "Where did *you* come from? Are you real—or am I seeing that which is not?"

"I am real," replied a clear, silvery voice. "And I came from out there." An exquisitely molded arm flung a gesture toward the raging ocean. "The ship I was on was sinking, so I stripped off my garb, flung myself on Ran's bosom, and Ran's horses gave me a most magnificent ride! But well for you that you stood still as I bade you, while I walked ashore. Ran is an angry god, and seldom well-disposed toward mortals."

"*Ran?*" The sea-god of the old Norse vikings! What strange woman was this, who talked of "Ran" and his "horses," the white-maned waves of old ocean? But then I bethought me of her naked state in that unholy tempest.

"Surely you must be Ran's daughter," I said. "That reef is ten miles off land! Come—I have a house nearby, and comforts—you cannot stand here."

"Lead, and I will follow," she replied simply.

She went up that path with greater ease than I, and walked companionably beside me from path-top to house, although she made no talk. Oddly, I felt that she was reading me, and that what she read gave her comfort.

When I opened the door, it seemed as if she held back for a merest moment.

"Enter," I bade her, a bit testily. "I should think you'd had enough of this weather by now!"

She bowed her head with a natural stateliness which convinced me that she was no common person, and murmured something too low for me to catch, but the accents had a distinct Scandinavian trend.

"What did you say?" I queried, for I supposed she'd spoken to me.

"I invoked the favor of the old gods on the hospitable of hearth, and on the sheltering rooftree," she replied. Then she crossed my threshold, but she reached out her arm and rested her shapely white hand lightly yet firmly on my left forearm as she stepped within.

She went direct to the big stove, which was glowing dull-red, and stood there, smiling slightly, calm, serene, wholly ignoring her nakedness, obviously enjoying the warmth, and not by a single shiver betraying that she had any chill as a result of exposure.

"I think you need this," I said, proffering a glass of brandy. "There's time enough for exchanging names and giving explanations, later," I added. "But right now, I'll try and find something for you to put on. I have no women's things in the house, as I live alone, but will do the best I can."

I passed into my bedroom, laid out a suit of pajamas and a heavily quilted bathrobe, and returned to the living-room where she stood.

"You are a most disconcertingly beautiful young woman," I stated bluntly; "which you know quite well without being told. But doubtless you will feel more at ease if you go in there and don some things I've laid out for you. When you come out, I'll get some supper ready."

She was back instantly, still unclad. I stared, wonderingly.

"Those things did not fit," she shrugged. "And that heavy robe — in this warm house?"

"But—" I began.

"But—*this*," she smiled, catching up a crimson silk spread

embroidered in gold, which covered a sandalwood table I'd brought from the orient many years before. A couple of swift motions and the gorgeous thing became a wondrous robe adorning her lovely figure, clinging, and in some subtle manner hinting at the flawless splendor of her incomparable body. A long narrow scarf of black silk whereon twisted a silver dragon was whipped from its place on a shelf and transposed into a sash from her swelling breasts to her sloping hips, bringing out more fully every exquisite curve of her slender waist and torso—and she smiled again.

"Now," she laughed softly, "am I still a picture for your eyes? I hope so, for you have befriended me this night—I who sorely need a friend; and it is such a little thing I can do—making myself pleasing in your sight."

"And because you have holpen me—" I stared at the archaic form she used—"and will continue to aid and befriend (for so my spirit tells me), I will love you always, love you as Ragnar Wave-Flame loved Jarl Wulf Red-Brand... as a younger sister, or a dutiful niece."

"Yet of her it is told," I interrupted, deliberately speaking Swedish and watching keenly to see the effect, "that the love given by the foam-born Sea-Witch brought old Earl Wulf of the Red-Sword but little luck, and that not of a sort desired by most men!"

"That is ill said," she retorted. "His fate was from the Norns, as is the fate of all. Not hers the fault of his doom, and when his carles within the hour captured his three slayers, she took red vengeance. With her own foam-white hands she flayed them alive, and covered their twitching bodies with salt ere she placed the old Jarl in his long-ship and set it afire. And she sailed with that old man on his last seafaring, steering his blazing dragon-ship out of the stead, singing of his great deeds in life, that the heroes in Valhalla might know who honored them by his coming."

She paused, her superb bosom heaving tumultuously. Then

with a visible effort she calmed herself.

"But you speak my tongue, and know the old tales of the Skalds. Are you, then, a Swede?"

"I speak the tongue, and the old tales of the Skalds, the ancient minstrels, I learned from my grandmother, who was of your race."

"Of my race?" her tone held a curious inflection. "Ah, yes! All women are of one race... perhaps."

"But I spoke of supper," I said, moving toward the kitchen.

"But—no!" She barred my progress with one of her lovely hands laid flat against my chest. "It is not meet and fitting, Jarl Wulf, that you should cook for me, like any common housecarle! Rather, let your *niece,* Heldra, prepare for you a repast."

" 'Heldra'? That, then, is your name?"

"Heldra Helstrom, and your loving niece," she nodded.

"But why call me Jarl Wulf?" I demanded, curious to understand. She had bestowed the name seriously, rather than in playful banter.

"Jarl Wulf you were, in a former life," she asserted flatly. "I knew you on the shore, even before Ran's horse stood me on my feet!"

"Surely, then, you must be Ragnar Wave-Flame born again," I countered.

"How may that be?" she retorted. "Ragnar Wave-Flame never died; and surely I do not look that old! The sea-born witch returned to the sea-caves whence she came, when the dragonship burned out... But ask me not of myself, now.

"Yet one thing more I will say: The warp and woof of this strange pattern wherein we both are depicted was woven of the Norns ere the world began. We have met before—we meet again, here and now—we shall meet yet again; but how, and when, and where, I may not say."

"Of a truth, you are 'fey'," I muttered.

"At times—I am," she assented. Then her wondrous sapphire eyes gleamed softly into my own hard gray eyes, her smile was tender, wistful, womanly, and my doubts were dissipated like wisps of smoke. Yet I shook an admonitory forefinger at her:

"Witch at least I know you to be," I said in mock harshness. "Casting *glamyr* on an old man."

"No need for witchery," she laughed. "All women possess that power!"

During the "repast" she spread before me, I told her that regardless of who I might have been in a dim and remote past of which I had no memory, in this present life I was plain John Craig, retired professor of anthropology, ethnology and archeology, and living on a very modest income. I explained that while I personally admired her, and she was welcome to remain in my home for ever, yet in the village nearby were curious minds, and gossiping tongues, and evil thoughts a-plenty, and if I were to tell the truth of her arrival—

"But I have nowhere to go, and none save you to befriend me; all I loved or owned is out there." Again she indicated the general direction of the reef. "And you say that I may remain here, indefinitely? I will be known as your niece, Heldra, no? Surely, considering the differences in our age and appearance, there can be no slander."

Her eyes said a thousand things no words could convey. There was eagerness, sadness, and a strange tenderness... I came to an abrupt decision. After all, whose business was it?...

"I am alone in the world, as you are," I said gravely. "As my niece, Heldra, you shall remain. If you will write out a list of a woman's total requirements in wearing-apparel, I will send away as soon as possible and have them shipped here in haste. I am old, as all can see, and I do not think any sensible persons will suspect aught untoward in your making your home with me. And I will think up a plausible story which will satisfy the minds of fools without telling, in reality, anything."

Our repast ended, we arose from the table and returned to the living-room. I filled and lighted a *nargilyeh,* a three-stemmed water-pipe, and settled myself in my armchair. She helped herself to a cigarette from a box on the table, then stretched her long, slender body at full length on my divan, in full relaxation of comfort.

I told her enough of myself and my forebears to insure her being able to carry out the fiction of being my niece. And in return I learned mighty little about her. But what she did tell me was sufficient. I never was unduly curious about other people's business.

Unexpectedly, and most impolitely, I yawned. Yet it was natural enough, and it struck me that she needed a rest, if anyone ever did. But before I could speak, she forestalled me.

With a single graceful movement she rose from her reclining posture and came and stood before me within easy arm's-reach. Two swift motions, and her superb body flashed rosy-white, as nude as when she waded ashore.

The crimson silken spread she'd worn as regally as any robe was laid at my feet with a single gesture, the black scarf went across my knees, and the glorious creature was kneeling before me in attitude of absolute humility. Before I could remonstrate or bid her arise, her silvery voice rang softly, solemnly, like a muted trumpet:

"Thus, naked and with empty hands, out of the wintry seas in a twilight gray and cold, on a night of storm I came. And you lighted a beacon for my tired eyes, that I might see my way ashore. You led me up the cliff and to your hospitable hearth, and in your kindly heart you had already given the homeless a home.

"And now, kneeling naked before you, as I came, I place my hands between your hands—thus—and all that I am, and such service as I can render, are yours, hand-fasted."

I stared, well-nigh incredulous. In effect, in the old Norse manner, she was declaring herself to all intents and purposes my slave! But her silvery voice went on:

"And now, I rise and cover myself again with the mantle of your bounty, that you may know me, indeed your niece, as Jarl Wulf knew Ragnar Wave-Flame!"

"Truly," I gasped in amazement when I could catch my breath, "you are a strange mixture of the ancient days and this modern period. I have known you but for a few hours, yet I feel toward you as that old Jarl must have felt toward that other sea-witch, unless indeed you and she are one!"

"Almost," she replied a trifle somberly. "At least, she was my ancestress!" Then she added swiftly: "Do not misunderstand. Leman to the old Jarl she never was. But later, after he went to Valhalla, in the sea-girt isle where she dwelt she mated with a young viking whom Ran had cast ashore sorely wounded and insensible. She nursed him back to life for sake of his beauty, and he made love to her.

"But he soon tired of her and her witch ways; wherefore, in wrath she gave him back to Ran—and he was seen no more. Of that mating was born a daughter, also given to Ran, who pitied her and bore her to an old man and his wife whose steading was nigh to the mouth of a fjord; and they, being childless, called her Ranhild, and reared her as their daughter. In course of time, she wed, and bore three tall sons and a daughter...

"That was long and long ago—yet I have dived into Ragnar's hidden sea-cave and talked with Ragnar Wave-Flame face to face. All one night I lay in her arms, and in the dawning she breathed her breath on my brow, lips and bosom; and all that following day she talked and I listened, and much I learned of the wisdom that an elder world termed witchcraft."

For a moment she lapsed into silence. Then she leaned forward, laid her shapely, cool hands on my temples and kissed me on my furrowed old forehead, very solemnly, yet with ineffable gentleness.

"And now," she murmured, "ask me never again aught concerning myself, I pray you; for I have told all I may, and further questioning will drive me back to the sea. And I would not have that happen—yet!"

Without another word she turned, flung herself at full length on the divan, and, like any tired child, went instantly to sleep. Decidedly, I thought, this "niece" of mine was not as are other women; and later I found that she possessed certain abilities it is well for the world that few indeed can wield.

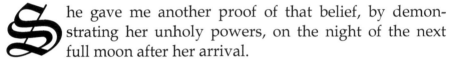She gave me another proof of that belief, by demonstrating her unholy powers, on the night of the next full moon after her arrival.

It was her custom of an evening to array herself as she had done on her first night—in crimson robe and black sash and naught else, despite the fact that her wardrobe which I had ordered from the great city forty miles away contained all any woman's heart could wish for. But I admit I enjoyed seeing her in that semi-barbaric attire.

At times she would sit on the arm of my chair, often with her smooth cool cheek laid against my rough old face, and her exquisitely modeled arm curved about my leathery old neck. The first time she had done that, I had demanded ironically:

"Witch, are you making love to me?"

But her sighing, wistful reply had disarmed me, and likewise had brought a lump into my throat.

"Nay! Not that, O Jarl from of old! But—I never knew a father."

"Nor I a fair daughter," I choked. And thereafter, when that mood was upon her I indulged in no more ironies, and we'd sit for hours, neither speaking, engrossed in thoughts for which there are no words. But on the night whereof I write, she pressed her scarlet lips to my cheek, and I asked jestingly:

"Is there something you want, Heldra?"

"There is," she replied gravely. "Will you get a boat—one with oars and a sail, but no engine? Ran hates those."

"But surely you do not want it now, tonight, do you?"

"Yes, if you will be so kind to me."

"You must have a very good reason, or you'd not ask," I said. "I'll go and get a centerboard dory and bring it to the beach at the foot of the cliff path. It's clear weather, and the sea is calm, with but a moderate breeze blowing; yet it is colder on the water than you imagine, so you'd best bundle up warmly."

"You will hasten," she implored anxiously.

"Surely," I nodded.

I went out and down to the wharves in the village, where I kept the boat I said I'd get. But when I beached the dory at foot of the path I stared, swearing softly under my breath. Not one stitch of apparel did that witch have on, save the crimson silk robe and black sash she'd worn when I left the cottage!

"Do you want to freeze?" I was provoked, I admit. "The very sight of you dressed like that gives me shivers!"

"Neither you nor I will be cold this night," she laughed. "Isn't it glorious? And this is a good boat you brought. Please, let me sail it, and ask me no questions."

She took the tiller, hauled in on the sheet; the sail filled, and she began singing, with a queer, wild strain running through her song. That dory fairly flew—and I swear there was not enough wind to drive us at such speed.

Finally I saw something I didn't admire. No one does, who dwells on that part of the coast.

"Are you crazy, girl?" I demanded sharply. "That reef is dead ahead! Can't you see the breakers?"

"Why, so it is—the reef! And am *I* to be affrighted by a few puny breakers? Nay, it is in the heart of those breakers that I wish to be! But you—have *you* fear, O Jarl Wulf?"

I suspected from her tone that the witch was laughing at me; so I subsided, but fervently wished that I'd not been so indulgent of her whim for a moonlight sail on a cold winter's night.

Then we hit those breakers—or rather, we didn't! For they seemed to part as the racing dory sped into them, making a smooth clear lane of silvery glinting water over which we glided as easily as if on a calm inland mill-pond!

"Drop the sail and unstep the mast," she called suddenly.

I was beyond argument, and obeyed dumbly, like any boat-carle of the olden days.

"Now, take to the oars," she directed, "and hold the boat just hereabouts for a while," and even as I slid the oars into the oarlocks she made that swift movement of hers and stood nude, the loveliest sight that grim, ship-shattering, life-destroying reef had ever beheld.

Suddenly she flung up both shapely white arms with a shrill, piercing cry, thrice repeated. Then without a word she went overside in a long clean dive, with never a splash to show where she'd hit the water.

"Hold the boat about here for a while," she'd bidden me! All I'd ever loved in this world was somewhere down below, in the hellish cross-currents of that icy water! I'd hold that boat there, if need were, in the teeth of a worse tempest than raged the night she came to me. She'd find me waiting. And if she never came up, I'd hold that boat there till its planks rotted and I joined her in the frigid depths.

It seemed an eternity, and I know that it was an hour ere a glimmer of white appeared beneath the surface. Then her shapely arm emerged and her hand grasped the gunwale, her regal head broke water, she blew like a porpoise; then she laughed in clear ringing triumph.

"You old *dearling!*" she cried in her archaic Norse. "Did I seem long gone? The boat has not moved a foot from where I dove. Come, bear a hand and lift my burden; it is heavy, and I am near spent. There are handles by which to grasp it."

The burden proved to be a greenish metal coffer—bronze, I judged—which I estimated to measure some twenty inches long by twelve wide and nine inches deep. And how she rose to the surface weighted with that, passes my understanding. But how she knew it was down there passes my comprehension, too. But then, Heldra Helstrom herself was an enigma.

She re-wrapped herself in her flimsy silken robe of crimson and smiled happily, when she should have been shivering almost to pieces.

"If you'll ship the mast and spread the sail again, Uncle John," she said, surprisingly matter-of-fact now that her errand was successfully accomplished, "we'll go home. I'd like a glass of brandy and a smoke, myself; and I read in your mind that such is your chief desire, at present."

Back at the cottage again, and comfortable once more, Heldra requested me to bear the coffer into her room, which I did. For over an hour she remained in there, then returned to the living-room where I sat, and I stared at the picture she presented. If she had always been beautiful, now she was surpassingly glorious.

Instead of the usual crimson robe, her lovely body was sheathed in a sleeveless, sheer, tightly fitting silken slip, cut at the throat in a long sloping V reaching nearly to her waist. The garment was palest sea-green, so flimsy in texture that it might as well have been compounded of mingled moon-mist and cobwebs. Her rosy-pearl flesh gleamed through the fabric with an alluring shimmer which thrilled anew my jaded old senses at the artistic wonder of her.

A gold collar, gem-studded, unmistakably of ancient Egyptian workmanship, was resting on her superb shoulders—loot of some viking foray into the far Southlands, doubtless. A broad girdle of gold plates, squared, and also gem-studded, was about her sloping hips, and was clasped in front by a broader plate with a sun-emblem in jeweled sets; from which plate or buckle it fell in two broad bands nearly to her white slender feet.

Broad torques of gold on upper arms and about her wrists, and an intricately wrought golden tiara with disks of engraved gold pendent by chains and hanging over her ears, set off her loveliness as never before. Even her red-gold hair, braided in two thick ropes, falling over her breasts to below her waist, were clasped by gem-set brooches of gold.

"Ragnar Wave-Flame's gift to me, O Jarl Wulf," she breathed softly. "Do you like your niece thus arrayed?"

Norse princess out of an elder day, or Norse witch from an even older and wickeder period of the world—whichever this Heldra Helstrom was, of one thing I was certain, no lovelier woman ever lived than this superb being who styled herself my "niece."

And so I told her, and was amply rewarded by the radiance of her smile, and the ecstatic kiss she implanted on my cheek.

Despite her splendid array, she perched on the arm of my chair, and began toying with my left hand. Presently she lifted it to the level of my eyes, laughing softly. I'd felt nothing, yet she'd slipped a broad tarnished silver ring of antique design on my third finger.

"It was yours in the ancient days, O Jarl Wulf," she whispered in her favorite tongue—the archaic form the Norsk language. "Yours again is the ancient ring, now! Ragnar herself carved the mystic runes upon it. Shall I read them, O Jarl, or will you?"

"They are beyond my skill," I confessed. "The words are in the 'secret' language that only the *'Rime-Kanaars'* understood. Nor was it well for others than witches and warlocks to understand them."

"Ragnar took that ring from Jarl Wulf's finger ere she set fire to the dragon-ship," Heldra murmured. "Had those runes been on the ring when your foes set upon you—they, not you, would have perished in the sword-play, Jarl Red-Sword!

"But the sea-born witch knew that you would weary of Valhalla in a day to come, and would return to this world of strife and slaying, of loss and grief, of hate and the glutting of vengeance—and, knowing, she carved the runes, that in time the charmed ring would return to its proper owner.

"It is her express command that I read them to you, for knowing the runes, never shall water drown or fire burn; nor sword or spear or ax ever wound you, so be it that in time of danger you speak the weird words!

"And for my sake—you who are my 'Uncle John' to all the rest of the world, but to me are dearer than old Jarl Wulf was to Ragnar the sea-witch—I implore you to learn the runic charm, and use it if ever danger menaces. Promise me! Promise me, I say!"

Her silvery voice was vibrant with fierce intensity. She caught my right hand and pressed it against her palpitant body, just beneath her proudly swelling left breast.

"Promise!" she reiterated. "I beg your promise! With your right hand on my heart I adjure you to learn the rune."

"No fool like an old fool," I grumbled, adding a trifle maliciously, "particularly when in the hands of a lovely woman. But such a fuss you make over a few words of outlandish gibberish! Read me the rune, then, witch-maid! I'd learn words worse than those can be to please you and set your mind at rest."

With her scarlet lips close to my ear, with bated breath, and in a tone so low I could barely catch her carefully enunciated syllables, she whispered the words. And although her whisper was softer than the sighing of gentlest summer breeze, the tones rang on my inner hearing like strokes of a great war-hammer smiting on a shield of bronze. There was no need to repeat them—either on her part or mine. There was no likelihood of my ever forgetting that runic charm. I could not, even if I would.

"Surely," I muttered, "you are an adept in the ancient magic. Well for me that you love me, else your witcheries might—"

Most amazingly she laughed, a clear, ringing merriment with no trace of the mystic about it.

"Let me show you something—a game, a play; one that will amuse me and entertain you."

She fairly danced across the room and into her own room, emerging with an antique mirror of some burnished, silver-like metal. This she held out to me. I grasped it by its handle obediently enough, humoring this new whim.

"Look into it and say if it is a good mirror," she bade, her sapphire eyes a-dance with elfin mirth.

I looked. All I could see was my same old face, tanned and wrinkled, which I daily saw whenever I shaved or combed my hair, and I told her so. She perched again on the arm of my chair, laid her cheek against mine, and curved her cool arm about my neck.

"Now look again!"

Again the mirror told truth. I saw my face the same as ever, and hers as well, "Like a rose beside a granite boulder," as I assured her.

"You do but see yourself as you think of yourself," she murmured softly, "and me you behold as you believe me to be."

She brought her lips close to the mirror and breathed upon its surface with her warm breath. It clouded over, then cleared. Her voice came, more murmurous than before, but with a definite note of sadness:

"Once more, *look!* Behold yourself as I see you always; and behold me as I know myself to be! And when I am gone beyond your ken, remember the witch-maid, Heldra, as one woman who loved you so truly that she showed you herself as she actually was!"

The man's face was still my own, but mine as it was in the days of early manhood, ere life's thunders had graven their scars on brow and cheeks and lips, and before the snows of many winters had whitened my hair.

Her features were no less beautiful, but in her reflected eyes I saw ages and ages of life, and bitter experience, and terrible wisdom that was far more wicked than holy; and it came to me with conviction irrefutable that beside this young-appearing girl, maid, or woman, all my years were but as the span of a puling babe compared to the ageless age of an immortal.

"That, at least, is no *glamyr*," her voice sighed drearily, heavy with the burden of her own knowledge of herself.

I laid my thick, heavy old arm across her smooth satiny white shoulders, and I turned her head until her sapphire eyes met mine fairly. Very gently I kissed her on her brow.

"Heldra Helstrom," I said, and my voice sounded husky with emotion, "you may be all you have just shown me, or worse! You may be Ragnar Wave-Flame herself, the sea-witch who never dies. You may be even what I sometimes suspect, the empress of Hell, come amongst mortals for no good purpose! But be you what you may, old or young, maid or woman, good or evil, witch, spirit, angel or she-devil, such as you are, you are you and I am I, and for some weird reason we seem to love each other in our own way; so let there be an end to what you are or have been, or who I was in other lives, and content ourselves with what *is!*"

Were those bright glitters in her sapphire eyes tear-drops ready to fall? If so, I was not sure, for with a cry like that of a lost soul who has found sanctuary, she buried her face on my shoulder...

After a long silence, she slipped from the arm of my chair, and wordlessly, her fate averted, she passed into her room. After an hour or so, I went to my own room—but I could not sleep...

Time passed, and I dwelt in a "fool's paradise," dreaming that it would last forever.

The summer colony began to arrive. There were cottages all along the shore, but there were likewise big estates, whose owners were rated as "somebodies," to put it mildly.

A governor of a great and sovereign state; an ex-president of our nation; several foreign diplomats and some of their legation attachés—but why enumerate, when one man only concerns this narration?

Michael Commnenus, tall, slight, dapper, inclined to swarthiness, with black eyes under crescent-curved black eyebrows; with supercilious smiling lips, a trifle too red for a man; with suave Old World manners, and a most amazingly conceited opinion of himself as a "Lady-charmer."

It was not his first summer in our midst; and although when he was in Washington at his legation I never gave him a thought, when I saw his too handsome face on the beach, I felt a trifle sick! I *knew*, positively, that the minute he set eyes on Heldra... Of course I knew, too, that my witch-niece could take care of herself; but just the same, I sensed annoyance, and perhaps, tragedy.

Well, I was in nowise mistaken.

Heldra and I were just about to shove off in my dory for a sail. It was her chief delight, and mine too, for that matter.

Casually, along strolled Michael Commnenus, twirling a slender stick, caressing a slender black thread he styled a mustache, smiling his approbation of himself. I'd seen that variety of casual approach before. As our flippant young moderns say: It was "old stuff."

Out of the corner of my eye I watched. The Don Juan smirk faded when his calculating, appraising eyes met her sapphire orbs, now shining like the never-melting polar ice. An expression of bewilderment spread over his features. His swarthy skin went a sickly greenish-bronze. Involuntarily he crossed himself and passed on. The man was *afraid,* actually fear-struck!

"Ever see him before, Heldra?" I queried. "He looked at you as if the devil would be a pleasanter sight. That's one man who failed to fall for your vivid beauty, you sea-witch!"

"Who is he?" she asked in a peculiar tone. "I liked his looks even less than he liked mine."

"Michael Commnenus," I informed her, and was about to give her his pedigree as we local people knew him, but was interrupted by her violently explosive:

"Who?"

"Michael Commnenus," I stated again, a trifle testily. "And you needn't shout! What he's done—" but again she interrupted, speaking her archaic Norsk:

"Ho! Varang Chiefs of the Guard Imperial! Thorfinn! Arvid! Sven! And ye who followed them—Gudrun! Randvar! Haakon! Smid! And all ye Varangs in Valhalla, give ear! And ye, O fiends, witches, warlocks, trolls, vampyrs, and all the dark gods who dwell in Hel's halls where the eternal frozen fires blaze without heat, give ear to my voice, and cherish my words, for I give ye all joyous tidings.

"He lives! After all these long centuries Michael Commnenus dwells again on the bosom of fair Earth! In a body of flesh and blood and bone, of nerve and tissue and muscle he lives! He lives, I say! And *I* have found him!

"Oh, now I know why the Norns who rule all fate sent me to this place. And I shall not fail ye, heroes! Content ye, one and all, *I shall not fail!"*

Was this the gorgeous beauty I'd learned to love for her gentleness? Hers was the face of a furious female demon for a moment; but then her normal expression returned and she sighed heavily.

"Heed me not, Uncle John," she said drearily. "I did but recall an ancient tale of foul treachery perpetrated on sundry Norsemen in the Varangian Guard of a Byzantine emperor ages agone.

"The *niddering*—worse than 'coward'—who wrought the bane of some thirty-odd vikings, was a Commnenus, nephew to the Emperor Alexander Commnenus... I live too much in memories of the past, I fear, and for the moment somewhat forgot myself in the hate all good Norse maids should hold toward any who bear the accursed name of the Commneni.

"Still, even as I *know* you to be old Jarl Wulf Red-Brand returned to this world through the gateway of birth—it would be nothing surprising if this spawn of the Commneni were in truth that same Michael Commnenus of whom the tale is told."

"The belief in reincarnation is age-old," I said reflectively. "And in several parts of the world it is a fundamental tenet of religion. If there be truth in the idea, there is, as you say, nothing surprising if anybody now living should have been anybody else in some former life... And that sample of the Commneni appears quite capable of any treachery that might serve a purpose at the moment! But, Heldra," I implored her, struck by a sudden intuition, "I beg of you not to indulge in any of your devilries, witcheries, or Norse magic. If this Michael is that other Michael, yet that was long ago; and if he has not already atoned for his sin, you may be very sure that somewhere, sometime, somehow he will atone; so do not worry your regal head about him."

"Spoken like a right Saga-man," she smiled as I finished my brief homily. "I thank you for your words of wisdom. And now, Jarl Wulf Red-Brand, I know you to be fey as well as I am. 'Surely he will atone for his sin'... oh! a most comforting thought! So let us think no more about the matter."

I glanced sharply at her. Her too instant acquiescence was suspicious. But her sapphire eyes met mine fairly, smilingly, sending as always a warm glow of contentment through me. So

I accepted her assurance as it sounded, and gave myself up to the enjoyment of the sail and the sound of her silvery voice as she sang an old English love ballad I'd known as a young man. And under the spell of her magnetic personality gradually the episode of Michael Commnenus faded into nothingness—for a while.

A couple of days later, just about dark, Heldra came down the stairs from the attic, where she'd been rummaging. In her hand she carried an old violin-case. I looked and grinned ruefully.

"You are a bad old Uncle John," she scolded. "Why did you not tell me you played the *'fidel,'* even as Jarl Wulf played one in his time? Think of all the sweet music you might have made in the past winter nights, and think of the dances I might have danced for your delight while you played—even as Ragnar danced for her old Jarl."

"But I did not tell you that I played a fiddle—because I don't," I stated flatly. "That is a memento of an absurd ambition I once cherished, but which died a-borning. I tried to learn the thing, but the noises I extracted were so abominable that I quit before I'd fairly got started."

"You are teasing," she retorted, her eyes sparkling with mischief. "But I am not to be put off thus easily. Tonight you will play, and I will dance—such a dance as you have never beheld even when you were Jarl Wulf."

"If I try to play that thing," I assured her seriously, "you'll have a time dancing to my discords, you gorgeous tease!"

"We'll see," she nodded. "But even as my magic revealed to me the whereabouts of the *'fidel,'* so my spirit tells me that you play splendidly."

"Your 'magic' may be all right, but your 'spirit' has certainly misinformed you," I growled.

"My spirit has never yet lied to me—nor has it done so this

time." Her tone was grave, yet therein was a lurking mockery; and I became a trifle provoked.

"All right," I assented grouchily. "Whenever you feel like hearing me *'play,'* I'll do it. And you'll never want to listen to such noises again."

She went into her room laughing sweetly, and took the fiddle with her.

After supper she said nothing about me playing that old fiddle, and I fatuously thought she'd let the matter drop. But about ten o'clock she went to her room without a word. She emerged after a bit, wearing naught but a sheer loose palest blue silk robe, held at the waist only by a tiny jeweled filigree clasp. Loose as the robe was, it clung lovingly to her every curve as if caressing the beauteous, statuesque body it could not and would not conceal.

She was totally devoid of all ornament save that tiny brooch, and her wondrous fiery-gold hair was wholly unconfined, falling below her waist in a cascade of shimmering sunset hues, against which her rose-pearl body gleamed through the filmy gossamer-like robe.

Again she sat and talked for a while. But along toward midnight she broke a short silence with:

"I'll be back in a minute. I wish to prepare for my dancing."

From her room she brought four antique bronze lamps and a strangely shaped urn of oil. She filled the lamps and placed one at each corner of the living-room, on the floor.

Back into her room she went, and out again with an octagonal-shaped stone, flat on both sides, about an inch thick, and some four inches across. This she placed on the low taboret whereon I usually kept my *nargilyeh*. She propped up that slab of stone as if placing a mirror—which I decided it couldn't very well be, as it did not even reflect light but seemed as dull as a slab of slate.

As a final touch, she brought out that confounded old fiddle!

And on her scarlet lips was a smile that a seraph might have envied, so innocent and devoid of guile it seemed.

"What's this?" I demanded — as if I didn't know!

"Your little *'fidel'* with which you will make for your Heldra such rapturous music," she smiled caressingly.

"Um-m-m-m!" I grunted. "And what are those lamps for — and that ugly slab of black rock?"

"That black slab is a 'Hel-stone,' having the property of reflecting whatever is directly before it, if illumined by those four lamps placed at certain angles; and later it will give off those same reflections — even as the stuff called luminous calcium sulfide absorbs light-rays until surcharged, and then emits them, when properly exposed. So, you see, we can preserve the picture of my dance."

"Heldra," I demanded sharply, "are you up to some devilishness? All this looks amazingly like the stage-setting for witch-working!"

"I have sung for you, on different nights," she replied in gentlest reproach, "and have told old tales, and have attired myself again and again for your pleasure in beholding me. Have all these things ever bewitched you, or harmed anyone? How, then can the fact of my dancing for my own satisfaction, before the mystic Hel-stone, do any harm?"

As ever, she won. Her sapphire orbs did queer things to me whenever they looked into my own gray, faded old eyes — trusting me to understand and approve whatever she did, simply because she was she and I was I.

"All right," I said. "But you're making a fool of me — insisting that I play this old fiddle. Well — I'll teach you a lesson!" And I drew the bow over the strings with a most appalling wail.

And with the unexpected swiftness of a steel trap closing on its victim, icy fingers locked about my wrist, and I knew very definitely that another and alien personality was guiding my arm and fingers! But there came likewise a swift certitude that if I behaved, no harm would ensue—to me, at least. So I let the *thing* have its way—and listened to such music as I had not believed could be played on any instrument devised by a mortal.

I wish that I could describe that music, but I do not know the right words. I doubt if they have been invented. It was wild, barbaric, savage, but likewise it was alluring, seductive, stealing away all inhibitions—too much of it would have corrupted the angels in heaven. I was almost in a stupor, intoxicated, like a *hasheesh*-eater in a drugged dream, spellbound, unable to break from the thralldom holding my will, drowning in rapture well-nigh unbearable.

Heldra suddenly blew out the big kerosene lamp standing on the table, leaving as sole illumination the rays from those four bronze lights standing in the corners.

Her superb body moved gracefully, slowly at first, then faster, into the intricate figure and pattern of a dance that was old when the world was young…

With inward horror I knew the why and wherefore of that entire ceremonial; knew I'd been be-cozened and be-japed; yet knew, likewise, that it was too late for interference. I could not even speak. I could but watch, while some personality alien to my body played maddeningly on my fiddle, and the 'niece' I loved danced a dance deliberately planned to seduce a man who hated and feared the dancer—and for what devilish purpose I could well guess!

I saw the light-rays converge on her alluring, statuesque body, saw them apparently pass through her and impinge on the surface of that black, sullen, octagonal Hel-stone, and be greedily swallowed up, until the dull, black surface glowed like a rare black Australian opal; and ever the dancing of the witch-girl grew more alluring, more seductive, more abandoned. And I knew why Heldra was thus shamefully—shamelessly, rather—conducting! She had read Michael Commnenus his character very accurately; knew that his *soul* had recognized her hatred for him, and *feared* her — and that her one chance to get him in her clutches lay in inflaming his senses… and she'd even told me the properties of that most damnable Hel-stone!

Wilder and faster came the music, and swifter and still more alluring grew the rhythmic response as Heldra's lovely body swayed and spun and swooped and postured; until ultimately her waving arms brought her fluttering hands, in the briefest of touches, into contact with the tiny brooch at her waist and the filmy robe was swept away in a single gesture that was faithfully recorded on the sullen surface of the Hel-stone.

Instantly the dancer stopped as if petrified, her arms outstretched as in invitation, her regal head thrown back, showing the long smooth white column of her throat, her clear, half-closed sapphire-blue eyes agleam with subtle challenge…

The uncanny music died in a single sighing, sobbing whisper, poison-sweet… the clutching, icy fingers were gone from my wrist… my first coherent thought was: Had that spell been directed at me, the old adage anent "old fools" would have been swiftly justified!

And I knew that to all intents and purposes, Michael Commnenus was sunk!

Just the same, I was furious. Heldra had gone too far, and I told her so, flatly. I pointed out in terms unmistakable that what she planned was murder, or worse; and that this was modern America wherein witchcraft had neither place nor sanction, and that I'd be no accessory to any such devilishness as she was contriving. Oh, I made myself and my meaning plain.

And she stood and looked at me with a most injured expression. She made me feel as if I'd wantonly struck a child across the face in the midst of its innocent diversions!

"I don't actually care if the devil flies off with Michael Commnenus," I concluded wrathfully, "but I won't have him murdered by you while you're living here, posing as my niece! No doubt it's quite possible for you to evade any legal consequences by disappearing, but what of me? As accessory, I'd be liable to life imprisonment, at the least!"

Her face lightened as by magic, and her voice was genuinely regretful, and in her eyes was a light of sincere love. She came to me and wrapped her white arms about my neck, murmuring terms of affectionate consolation.

"Poor dear Uncle John! Heldra was thoughtless—wicked me! And I might have involved you in serious trouble? I am ashamed! But the fate laid upon me by the Norns is heavy, and I may not evade it, even for you, whom I love. Tell me," she demanded suddenly, "if I should destroy the vile earthworm without any suspicion attaching to you, or to me, would you love me as before, even knowing what I had done?"

"*No!*" I fairly snarled the denial. I wanted it to be emphatic.

She smiled serenely, and kissed me full on my lips.

"I never thought to thank a mortal for lying to me, but now I do! Deep in your heart I can read your true feeling, and I am glad! But now"—and her tone took on a sadness most desolate—"I regret to say that on the morrow I leave you. The lovely garments you gave me, and the trunks containing them, I take with me, as you would not wish that I go empty-handed. Nor will I insult you, O Jarl Wulf, by talk of payment.

"When I am gone, you will just casually mention that I have returned to my home, and the local gossips will not suspect aught untoward. And soon I shall be forgotten, and no one will suspect, or possibly connect you, or me, with what inevitably must happen to that spawn of the Commneni.

"But of this be very sure: Somewhere, sometime, you and I shall be together again..." Her voice broke, she kissed me fiercely on the lips, then tenderly on both cheeks, then lastly, with a queer reverence, on my furrowed old brow. Then she turned, went straight to her room, shut the door, and I heard the click of the key as she locked herself in, for the first time during her stay in my house...

Next morning, as she'd planned, she departed on the first train cityward. I'd given her money enough for all her requirements—more, indeed, than she was willing to take at first, declaring that she intended selling some few of her jewels.

And with her departure went all which made life worth living...

Heavily I dragged my reluctant feet back to the empty shell of a cottage which until then had been an earthly paradise to an old man—and the very first thing I laid eyes on was that accursed Hel-stone, lying on the living room table.

I picked it up, half minded to shatter it to fragments, but an idea seized me. I bore it down-cellar, where semi-darkness prevailed, and the Hel-stone glowed softly with its witch-light, showing me the loveliness of her who had departed from me. And I pressed the cold octagon to my lips, thankful that she'd left me the thing as a feeble substitute for her presence. Then I turned and went back upstairs, found an old ivory box of Chinese workmanship, and placed the Hel-stone therein, very carefully, as a thing priceless.

I went to bed early that night. There was no reason to sit up. But I could not sleep. I lay there in my bed, cursing the entire line of Commneni, root, trunk and branch, from the first of that ilk whom history records to this latest scion, or "spawn," as Heldra had termed him.

Around midnight, being still wakeful, I arose, got the Hel-stone and sat in the darkness—and gradually became aware that I was not alone! Looking up, I saw her I'd lost standing in a witch-glow of phosphorescent light. I knew at once that it was not Heldra in person, but her *"scin-læcca"* or "shining double," a "sending," and that it was another of her witcheries.

"But even this is welcome," I thought. Then I felt *her* thought expressed through that phantasmal semblance of her own gorgeous self—and promptly strove, angrily, to resist her command. Much good it did me!

Utterly helpless, yet fully cognizant of my actions, but oddly assured that about me was a cloak of invisibility—the *"glamyr"* of the ancient *Alrunas*—I dressed, took the Hel-stone, and passed out into the night.

Straight to the cottage of Commnenus I went, pawed about under the door-step, and planted there the Hel-stone; then, still secure in the mystic glamor, I returned to my own abode.

And no sooner had I seated myself in my chair for a smoke, than I realized fully the utter devilishness of that witch from out the wintry seas whom I had taken into my home and had sponsored as my "niece" in the eyes of the world.

Right then I decided to go back and get that Hel-stone, and smash it—and couldn't do it! I got sleepy so suddenly that I awoke to find that it was broad daylight, and nine-thirty a. m. And from then on, as regularly as twilight came, I could only stay awake so long as I kept my thoughts away from that accursed Hel-stone; wherefore I determined that the thing could stay where it was until it rotted, for all me!

Then Commnenus came along the beach late one afternoon. He raised his hat in his Old World, courtly fashion, and tried to make some small talk. I grunted churlishly and ignored him. But finally he came out bluntly with:

"Professor Craig, I know your opinion of me, and admit it is to some extent justifiable. I seem to have acquired the reputation of being a Don Juan. But I ask you to believe that I bitterly regret that—now! Yet, despite that reputation, I'd like to ask you a most natural question, if I may."

I nodded assent, unprepared for what was coming, yet somehow assured it would concern Heldra. Nor was I at all disappointed, for he fairly blurted out:

"When do you expect Miss Helstrom to return, if at all?"

I was flabbergasted! That is the only word adequate. I glared at him in a black fury. When I could catch my breath I demanded:

"How did even *you* summon up the infernal gall to ask *me* that?"

His reply finished flattening me out.

"Because I love her! Wait"—he begged—"and hear me out, please! Even a criminal is allowed that courtesy." Then as I nodded grudgingly, he resumed:

"The first time I saw her, something deep within me shrank away from her with repulsion. Still, I admired her matchless beauty. But of late, since her departure, there is not a night I do not see her in my mind's eye, and I know that I love her, and hope that she will return; hence my query.

"I will be frank—I even hope that she noticed me and read my admiration without dislike. Perhaps two minds can reach each other—sometimes. For invariably I see her with head thrown back, her eyes half closed, and her arms held out as if calling me to come to her. And if I knew her whereabouts I'd most certainly go, nor would I be 'trifling,' where she is concerned. I want to win her, if possible, as my wife; and an emperor should be proud to call *her* that—"

"Very romantic," I sneered. "But, Mr. Woman-Chaser, I cut my eye-teeth a long while before you were born, and I'm not so easily taken in. The whereabouts of my niece are no concern of yours. So get away from me before I lose my temper, or I'll not be answerable for my actions. *Get!*"

He went! The expression of my face and the rage in my eyes must have warned him that I was in a killing humor. Well, I was. But likewise, I was sick with fear. What he'd just told me was sufficient to sicken me—the Hel-stone had gotten in its damnable work. My very soul was aghast as it envisioned the inevitable consequences...

An idea obsessed me, and I needed the shades of night to cloak my purpose.

Aimlessly I wandered from room to room in my cottage, and finally drifted into the room which had been Heldra's. Still aimlessly I pulled open drawer after drawer in the dresser, and in the lowest one I heard a faint metallic *clink.*

The four antique bronze lamps were there. I shrewdly suspected she had left them there as means of establishing contact with her, should need arise. I examined them, and found, as I'd hoped, that they were filled.

Around ten o' clock I placed those lamps in the four corners of the living-room, and lighted them, precisely as I'd seen Heldra do. Then I tried my talents at making an invocation.

"*Heldra! Heldra! Heldra!*" I called. "I, John Craig, who gave you shelter at your need, call to you now, wheresoever you be, to come to me at my need!"

The four lights went out, yet not a breath of air stirred in the room. A faintly luminous glow, the witch-light, ensued; and there she stood, or rather, the *scin-læcca,* her shining double! But I knew that anything I might say to it would be the same as if she were there in the flesh.

"Heldra," I beseeched that witch-lighted simulacrum, "by the love you gave me, as Ragnar loved Jarl Wulf Red-Sword, I ask that you again enshroud me with the mantle of invisibility, the '*glamyr,*' and allow me to lift that accursed Hel-stone from where you compelled me to conceal it. Let me return it to you, at any place you may appoint, so that it can do no more harm.

"Already that poor bewitched fool is madly in love with you, because the radiations of that enchanted stone have saturated him every time he put foot on the door-step beneath which I buried it!

"Heldra, grant me this one kindness, and I will condone all sins you ever did in all your witch-life."

The shining wraith nodded slowly, unmistakably assenting

to my request. As from a far distance I heard a faint whisper:

"Since it is your desire, get the Hel-stone, and bear it yourself to the sea-cave at the foot of the great cliff guarding the north passage into the harbor. Once you have borne it there, its work, and yours, are done.

"And I thank you for saying that you will condone all I have ever done, for the burden of the past is heavy, and your words have made it easier to bear."

The shining wraith vanished, and I went forth into the darkness. Straight to the house where I'd hidden the Hel-stone I betook myself, felt under the step, found what I sought, took it with an inward prayer of gratitude that because of Heldra's *"glamyr"* I had not been caught at something questionable in appearance, and started up the beach.

The tide was nearly out; so I walked rapidly, as I had some distance to go, and the sea-cave Heldra had designated could not be entered at high tide, although once within, one was safe enough and could leave when the entrance was once more exposed.

I entered the cave believing that I'd promptly be rid of the entire mess, once and for all. But there was no one there, and the interior of the cave was as dark as Erebus. I lit a match, and saw nothing. The match burned out. I fumbled for another—a dazzling ray from a flashlight blinded me for a moment, then left my face and swept the cave. A hated voice, suave yet menacing, said:

"Well, Professor Craig, you may now hand me whatever it was that you purloined from under my door-step!"

An extremely business-like automatic pistol was aimed in the exact direction of my solar plexus—and the speaker was none other than Michael Commnenus!

Very evidently the mystic *"glamyr"* had failed to work that time. And I was in a rather nasty predicament.

Then, abruptly, Heldra came! She looked like an avenging

fury, emerging out of nowhere, apparently, and the tables were turned. She wore a dark cloak or long mantle draped over her head and falling to her feet.

Her right hand was outstretched, and with her left hand she seized the Hel-stone from my grasp. She pointed one finger at Commnenus, and did not even touch him; yet had she smote him with an ancient war-hammer the effect would have been the same.

"You dog, and son of a long line of dogs!" her icy voice rang with excoriating virulence. "Drop that silly pistol! *Drop it, I say!*"

A faint blue flicker snapped from her extended finger — the pistol fell from a flaccid hand. Commnenus seemed totally paralyzed. Heldra's magic held him completely in thralldom... I snapped into activity and scooped up the gun.

"Followed me, did you?" I snarled. "I'll —"

"Wait, Jarl Wulf!" Heldra's tone was frankly amused. "No need for you to do aught! Mine is the blood-feud, mine the blood-right! And ere I finish with yon Michael Commnenus, an ancient hate will be surfeited, and an ancient vengeance, too long delayed, will be consummated."

"Heldra," I began, for dread seized me at the ominous quality of her words, "I will not stand for this affair going any farther! I —"

"Be silent! Seat yourself over there against the wall and watch and hear, but move not nor speak again, lest I silence you forever!"

A force irresistible hurled me across the cave and set me down, hard, on a flat rock. I realized fully that I was obeying her mandate — I couldn't speak, couldn't even move my eyelids, so thoroughly had she inhibited any further interference on my part.

Paying no further attention to Commnenus for the moment, she crossed over to me, bent and kissed me on my lips, her sapphire eyes laughing into my own blazing, wrathful eyes.

"Poor dear! It is too bad, but you made me do it. I wanted you to help me all the way through this tangled coil—but you have been *so* difficult to manage! Yet in some ways you have played into my hands splendidly. Yes, even to bringing the Hel-stone back to me—and I would not care to lose that for a king's ransom. And *I* put it into yon fool's head to be wakeful tonight, and see you regain the Hel-stone, and follow you—and thus walk into my nice little trap.

"And now!"

She whirled and faced Commnenus. And for all that he was spellbound, in his eyes I read fear and a ghastly foreknowledge of some dreadful fate about to be meted out to him at her hands.

She picked up the flashlight he had dropped and extinguished it with the dry comment:

"We need a different light here—the Hel-light from Hela's halls!" And at her word, a most peculiar light pervaded the cave, and there was that about its luminance that actually affrighted. Again she spoke:

"Michael Commnenus, you utterly vile worm of the earth! You know that your doom is upon you—but as yet you know not why. O beast lower than the swine! Harken and remember my words even after eternity is swallowed up in the Twilight of the Gods! You are a modern, and know not that the self, the soul, is eternal, undying, changing its body and name in every clime and period, yet ever the same soul, responsible for the deeds of its bodies. You have even prated of *your* soul—when in fact, *you* are the property of the soul!

"Watch, now!" She pointed to the cave entrance. "Behold there the wisps of sea-fog gathering; and gradually will come the rising tide. And on the curtain of that cold, swirling mist, behold the pictures of the past—a past centuries old; a past wherein your craven, treacherous soul sinned beyond all pardon!

"Look you, too, Jarl Wulf Red-Brand, so that in all the days remaining to you upon Earth, you may know that his doom was just, and that Heldra is but executing a merited penalty!

"And while the shuttles of the *Norns* weave the tapestry of the sin of this Commnenus, I will tell all the tale of his crimes.

"In Byzantium reigned the emperor, Alexander Commnenus. Secure his throne, guarded by the ponderous axes and the long swords of the Varangians, the splendid sons of the Norse-lands, who had gone a-viking. Trusted and loved were the Varangs by the emperor, and oft he boasted of their fidelity, swearing on the cross of Constantinople that to the last man would his Varangs perish ere one would flinch a step from overwhelming foes, citing in proof of their battle-cry:

"'Valhalla! Valhalla! Victory or Valhalla!'

"Into the harbor of the Golden Horn sailed the viking longship, the *Grettir*. Three noble brothers owned her—Thorfinn, Arvid, Sven. With them sailed their sister... her fame as an *Alruna-maid*, prophetess and priestess, was sung throughout the Norse-lands. No man so low but bore her reverence. Sin it was to cast eyes of desire on any *Alruna*, and the sister of the three brothers was held especially holy.

"Between the hands of the Emperor Alexander Commnenus, the three brethren placed their hands, swearing fealty for a year and a day. Thirty fighting-men, their crew, followed wherever the three brothers led. And the great emperor, hearing of their war-fame from others of the Varangian guard, gave the brothers high place in his esteem, and held them nigh his own person.

"Their sister, the *Alruna-maid*, was treated as became her rank and holy repute. Aye! Even in Christian Byzantium respect and honor were shown her by the priests of an alien belief. But one man in Byzantium aspired more greatly than any other, Norseman or Byzantine, had ever dared.

"A Commnenus he, grand admiral of Byzantium's war fleet, nephew to the emperor, enjoying to the full the confidence and love of his imperial uncle. Notorious for his profligacy, he cast his libertine eyes on the Norse *Alruna-maid*, but with no thought of making her his wife. Nay! 'Twas only as his leman he desired her... So, he plotted...

"The three brothers, Thorfinn, Arvid, Sven, with their full crew, in the long-ship *Grettir* were ordered to sea to cruise against certain pirates harrying a portion of the emperor's coasts.

"Every man of the *Grettir's* crew died the deaths of rats—poison in the water-casks! ... They died as no Norseman should die, brutes' deaths, unfit for Valhalla and the company of heroes who had passed in battle! And their splendid bodies, warped and distorted by pangs of the poison, were cast overside as prey for sharks, by two creatures of this grand admiral, whom he had sent with the three brothers as pilots knowing the coast. They placed the drug in the casks, they flung over the dead and dying, they ran the *Grettir* aground and set fire to her—but *his* was the command—*and his the crime!*"

And as Heldra told the tale, in a voice whose dreary tones made the recital seem even worse—the watching Commnenus and I saw clearly depicted on the curtain of the mist, each separate incident... Heldra turned to the wildly glaring Michael.

"There was but one person in all Byzantium who knew the truth," she screamed in sudden frenzy. "I give back for a moment your power of speech. *Say, O fool! Coward! Niddering! Who am I?*"

Abruptly she tore off the somber cloak and stood in all her loveliness, enhanced by every ornament she once had worn for my pleasure in beholding her thus arrayed.

𝔄 cry of unearthly terror broke from the staring Commnenus. His voice was a strangled croak as he gasped:

"The *Alruna-maid*, Heldra! The red-haired sea-witch—sister to the three brothers, Thorfinn, Arvid, Sven!"

"Aye, you foul dog! And me you took at night, after they sailed away, and me you shut up where my cries for aid could not be heard; and me you would have despoiled—me, the *Alruna-maid*, sworn to chastity! Me you jeered at and reviled, boasting of your recent crimes against all that the Norse-folk hold most sacred!

"Yet I escaped from that last dreadful dungeon wherein you immured me—*how?*

"By that magic known to such as I, I called upon the empress of the Underworld, Hela herself, and pledged her my service in return for indefinitely continued life, until I could repay you and avenge the heroes denied the joys of Valhalla—by you!

"And now—comes swiftly the doom I have planned for you... you who now *remember!*"

Heldra spoke truly. Swiftly it came! Sitting where I was, I saw it plainly, a great dragon-ship with round shields displayed along her gunwales, with a big square sail of crimson embroidered in gold, with long oars dipping and lifting in unison—in faint ghostly tones I could hear the deep-sea rowers chanting, *"Juch! Hey! Sa-sa-sa! Hey-sa, Hey-sa, Hey-sa, Hey-sa!"* and knew it for the time-beat rowing-song of the ancient vikings!

The whole picture was limned in the cold sea-fires from whence that terrible viking ghost-ship had risen with its crew of long-dead Norsemen who were not dead—the men too good for *Hel*, and denied Valhalla...

Straight to the mouth of the cave came the ghost-ship, and its crew disembarked and entered. Heldra cried out in joyous welcome:

"Even from out of the deeps, ye heroes, one and all, have ye heard my silent summons, and obeyed the voice of your Alruna from old time! Now your waiting is at an end!

"Yonder stands the Commnenus. That other concerns ye not—but mark him well, for in a former life he was Jarl Wulf Red-Brand! See, on his left hand is still the old silver ring with its runes of Ragnar Wave-Flame!"

The ghost-vikings turned their dead eyes on me with a curious fixity. One and all, they saluted. Evidently, Jarl Wulf must have been somebody, in his time. Then ignoring me, they turned to Heldra, awaiting her further commands. Commnenus they looked at, fiercely, avidly.

Heldra's voice came, heavily, solemnly, with a curious bell-like tone sounding the knell of doom incarnate:

"Michael Commnenus! This your present body has never wrought me harm, nor has it harmed any of these. It is not with your body that we hold our feud. Wherefore, your body shall go forth from this cave as it entered—as handsome as ever, bearing no mark of scathe.

"But your niddering soul, O most accursed, shall be drawn from out its earthly tenement this night and given over to these souls you wronged, who now await their victim and their vengeance! And I tell you, Michael Commnenus, that what they have in store for you will make the Hades of your religion seem as a devoutly-to-be-desired paradise!"

Heldra stepped directly before Commnenus. Her shapely white arms were outstretched, palms down, fingers stiffly extended. A queer, violet-tinged radiance streamed from her fingers, gradually enveloping Commnenus—he began to *glow*, as if he had been immersed and had absorbed all his body could take up...

Heldra's voice took on the tone of finality:

"Michael Commnenus! Thou accursed soul, by the power I hold, given me by Hela's self, I call you forth from your hiding-place of flesh—*come ye out!*"

The living body never moved, but from out its mouth emerged a faint silvery-tinted vapor flowing toward the *Alrunamaid*, and as it came, the violet glow diminished. The accumulating silvery mist swirled and writhed, perceptibly taking on the semblance of the body from whence it was being extracted. There remained finally but a merest thread of silvery shimmer connecting soul and body. Heldra spoke beneath her breath:

"One of you hew that cord asunder!"

A double-bladed Norse battle-ax whirled and a ghostly voice croaked: *"Thor Hulf!"*

Thor, the old Norse war-god, must have helped, for the great ghost-ax evidently encountered a solid cable well-nigh as strong as tempered steel. Thrice the ax rose and fell, driven by the swelling thews of the towering giant wielding it, ere the silver cord was broken by the blade.

A tittering giggle burst from the lips of the present-day Michael Commnenus.

I realized with a sudden sickness at the pit of my stomach that an utterly mindless imbecile stood there, grinning vacuously!

"That *Thing*," Heldra said, coldly scornful as she pointed to the silvery shining soul, "is yours, heroes! Do with it as ye will!"

Two of the gigantic wraiths clamped their great hands on its shoulders. It turned a dull leaden-gray, the color of abject fear. Cringing and squirming, it was hustled aboard the ghostly dragon-ship. The other ghost-vikings went aboard, taking their places at the oars... yet they waited. Heldra turned to me.

"Be free of the spell I laid upon you!" Her tone was as gentle as it had been in her sweetest moments while she dwelt in my home as my niece.

I gasped, rose and stretched. I wanted to be angry—and dared not. I'd seen too much of her hellish powers to risk incurring her displeasure. And reading my mind, she laughed merrily.

Then her cool, soft, white arms went about my neck, her wondrous sapphire eyes looked long and tenderly into mine — and I will not write the message I read in those softly shining orbs. Once again her silvery voice spoke:

"Jarl Wulf Red-Brand! John Craig! I am the grand-daughter of Ragnar Wave-Flame! And once I went a-viking with my three brothers, to far Byzantium. You know that tale. Now, once I said that Ragnar Wave-Flame never died. Also, I said that I had dived into her sea-cave and lain in her arms — and now I tell you the rest of that mystery: with her breath she entered this my body where ever since we have dwelt as one soul. I needed aid in seeking my vengeance, for it was after I'd escaped the clutches of the Commnenus, and had passed through adventures incredible while making my way back to the Norse-lands — and my spirit was very bitter. And when I sought her council, Ragnar helped me...

"This now do I ask of you: Do you, as I have sometimes thought, love me as a man loves a maid? Reflect well, ere you answer, and recall what I once showed you in a mirror — I am older than you! So, knowing that, despite my witcheries of the long, bitter past, and those of tonight, would you take me, were you and I young once more?"

"By all the gods in Valhalla, and by all the devils in Hela's halls: *yes!*" My reply was given without need of reflecting, or counting cost.

"Then, in a day to come, you shall take me — I swear it!"

Full upon my mouth she pressed her scarlet lips, and a surging flame suffused my entire body. Yet it was life — not death. Against my chest I felt the pressure of her swelling breasts, and fires undreamable streamed from her heart to mine. Time itself stood still. After an eon or so she unwound her clinging arms from about my neck and turned away, and with never a backward glance she entered that waiting, ghostly dragon-ship. The oars dipped…

"*Juch! Hey! Sa-sa-sa! Hey-sa, Hey-sa, Hey-sa, Hey-sa!*" and repeated… and again… until the faint, ghostly chant was swallowed by distance…

I left the cave.

The driveling idiot who had been Michael Commnenus was already gone. Later, the gossip ran that he'd "lost his mind," and that his embassy had returned him to his own land. None ever suspected, or coupled me or my "niece" with his affliction. And he himself had absolutely no memory—had lost even his own name when his soul departed!

But within a month, I sold my cottage, packed and stored all my belongings until I could find a new location, where I'd be totally unknown; and then I went away from where I had dwelt for years—and with urgent reason.

The fire with which Heldra had imbued me from her breath and breast was renewing my youth! My hair was shades darker, my wrinkles almost gone; my step was brisker, I looked to be nearer forty than almost sixty. So marked was the change that the villagers stared openly at what seemed at least a miracle… tongues were wagging… old superstitions were being revived and dark hints were being bandied about… So I finally decided to leave, and go where my altered appearance would cause no comment.

I wonder if—

Heart of Atlantan

There are sins beyond the urge of the appetites, beyond the desires of the senses. Sins beside which murder is but an idle pastime, and all lesser evils mankind in the frenzy of bestial passions indulge in at expense of their fellows, pale into the category of mere mistakes.

For Man is a creature possessing two natures, a material one which can only transgress laws of the material plane, and a spiritual one by which he may soar to heights undreamed, or descend to depths unfathomed.

For the sins, follies and mistakes of earth, there is punishment provided, or atonement to be made. But for the sins spiritual there is retribution, grim, lasting, inexorable, and none dare say if it will ever end.

And whoso sins thus, and is punished, had best welcome his fate, and hope to outwear it with the slow passage of the years, nor seek to escape it, for though he may seem to do so, having found, perchance, the method, yet always remains the Law that in effect says: "As ye sow, so shall ye likewise reap!"

And sin they never so greatly, yet will that awful Law, with inexorable exactitude, requite them in just and perfect measure, proportionate to the harm they have done—

As It has dealt with me!

Leonard Carman and I sat in my study, smoking and talking as old friends will after long separation. Our conversation ran along the lines of the ancient civilizations, now veiled in the murk of impenetrable mystery.

"And the veil can never be lifted," I mourned. "Nor will these mysteries ever be solved. There are no more Rosetta stones inscribed in unknown tongue together with one familiar to modern scholars. And some of the great lost races and their works passed so long ago that absolutely no traces, however slight, remain to show that ever they lived and moved beneath the sun and moon and stars. Unless," I added, as an afterthought, "science makes greater progress with some form of radio than is now possible."

"I'm not so sure about that," Carman interrupted. "It's barely possible that some fragmentary bits of knowledge *can* be recovered. Perhaps not to the satisfaction of exact science, but still of sufficient interest to satisfy your prying curiosity as well as my perfectly normal interest."

"Wherein do the two differ?" I snapped.

"Your curiosity concerns itself with how they lived, what they wore, and the progress they made along the lines of material achievement," he replied, smiling slightly at getting a rise out of me; which, by the way, I had never succeeded in doing with him; for a more equable temper than he possessed, I had never encountered, while mine is short-lived at best, and, also, highly explosive.

"While my normal interest is chiefly concerned with their intellectual attainments, the extent of their knowledge regarding the finer forces of nature and their possible uses," he elucidated.

"Just what are you driving at, Leonard?" I demanded, his words arousing within me a rapidly awakening interest.

"Simply that I believe they progressed along quite other lines than we of this modern age, thus giving rise to the tales of an 'Ancient Wisdom,' now lost. And I likewise think that under certain circumstances, it may be recovered, if not wholly, at least in part."

"And the method?" I queried. I was not at all skeptical now. He'd fully convinced me, and I felt, even before he replied that he already had a working basis with which to make an attempt to solve the otherwise unsolvable.

"I can have the method here any evening you may select," he assured me gravely.

"Right now, if that is possible," I stated, and he agreed. He stepped to the phone and called a number, and a moment later—"Otilie?" Apparently the answer was satisfactory, for he asked: "Can you come to where I am, this evening?" Again the response was as he desired, for he gave minute directions for reaching my place. I was curious about this "Otilie," and showed it, and he increased my mystification by smiling enigmatically, and saying, "Wait."

In about fifteen minutes a taxi stopped before the house. Carman went to the door to admit the strangest-looking being I've ever seen. As I had surmised from the name, "Otilie" was a woman, but such a woman!

She was a hunchback; wry-necked, with a pronounced squint in her left eye. Her nose had been mashed flat at some time, her mouth hung slackly open, revealing gnarled yellow fangs, and she walked with a decided limp. Add to all this a muddy brown skin and you have the picture. All in all, she was the most unprepossessing figure imaginable—until I noticed her hands. They were beautifully kept, with long tapering fingers, and seemed those of an artist or a musician.

Later, I learned that Otilie was a Finn, and that she was wholly illiterate. But when one looked at those hands and listened to her voice, a clear, bell-like contralto, one forgot all else about Otilie in sheer, downright fascination.

"Get me a stack of paper and a few pencils," Carman demanded. Rapidly he cleared the top of my library table, placed a chair for Otilie, and escorted her to her seat as if she had been an empress.

"Under normal conditions," he explained rapidly, "Otilie cannot read or write. But under other conditions she does some surprising things with automatic writing."

I felt disappointed, let down. So his "method" was merely automatic writing! I think he saw my feeling reflected in my face, for he smiled tolerantly and told me very gravely:

"Henri, you've know me for a long time, and you know that I do not lie to my friends. When I state that Otilie is phenomenal, and has proven it time and again, to my entire satisfaction, I think that you may well believe it.

"Otilie," and he turned to the queer-looking woman, "do you know anything about Atlantis, or the dead and gone civilizations of antiquity?"

"No," she said. "Otilie knows nothing of those. What do you want to find out? I'll try and see what we can get."

She picked up a pencil, inspecting it critically, laid it flat in her hand, and commenced making long, slow, magnetic passages, stroking the pencil with the fingertips of her right hand. And as she stroked, the pencil, her face, which, despite her grotesquerie, wore an habitual expression of pain and sullen discontent, assumed gradually an abstracted expression, and her usual harsh breathing grew calm and even. The change was so amazing I was dumfounded. She appeared remote, detached, as if between herself and the ordinary world were measureless gulfs of time, space, and condition.

She ceased stroking the pencil, poised it on a sheet of paper, and nodded slightly at Carman. For a minute or so the pencil moved in aimless figure eights, and Carman looked at me with deepest significance.

Suddenly the pencil started off, apparently by its own volition. Watching closely, I am prepared to state that Otilie's hand followed the pencil, rather than the pencil following her hand.

"Atlantan," it wrote, and paused, again describing figure eights. Yet Carman had queried concerning "Atlantis." A second later it wrote "Tekala, priestess of Atlantan." Then, "Kalkan the Golden."

"And who was Tekala," queried Carman softly.

Otilie's face grew rapt, her eyes lit with an inward fire, her entire figure and features were transformed.

"H-m," grunted Carman. "This is a new one. Never saw Otilie like this before. Wonder what's coming."

We were not long in finding out!

"Who is Tekala?" The deep, mellow tones of Otilie's voice became wistful, dreamy, filled with a strange reverent awe. "She is lovely, beautiful, with all the beauty I never had and can never have! But she says I am to let her speak for herself."

Silence reigned supreme in that quiet study of mine, but Carman and I felt the presence of a fourth personality, one of an alien nature, with a will so terrific in its impact that ours were less than naught beside it.

Added to that was a queer impression of incredible antiquity, plus age-long sorrow, patience beyond human concept, and longing unendurable.

Abruptly the lights dimmed, grew dully red, blinked and went out. Otilie gulped, audibly, Carmen whistled softly, and I swore feelingly. Then I noted a faint glow of light close by Otilie and wondered vaguely if she were becoming phosphorescent.

But the glow increased, became a faint aura gradually growing in brilliance to a nimbus whose center was a radiantly, exquisitely beauteous being, formed of tenuous light. It was, at moments, hard to distinguish from its nimbus, while at other moments it became clear and distinct, revealing itself as a form unmistakably feminine in contour, yet robed and shrouded in particles of light, so that its actual apparel was largely a matter of conjecture. Yet there was majesty expressed in that luminous figure, a stateliness shown in the poise of the head, and an air of conscious power compelling respect.

"This," I thought, "is no materialization flummery common to séances, but a genuine apparition—progressed to a stage far in advance of ordinary humanity."

It took me but a second to think thus far, and it took less than that long for our shining visitant to grasp my thought, read it, and appreciate it at its true evaluation. She stared at me for a long minute, then smiled slightly—and oh, the pathos of that smile! It would have wrung the heart of a stone image! It brought a lump to my throat, and caused my eyes to sting and blur with an unaccustomed mist.

And again the radiant vision stared unbelievingly, but then, to my utter surprise, it—or *she,* rather—moved swiftly till the outer edge of her aura was well within a foot of my body, and there she stood, obviously *reading* me as a scientist might study some strange and unusual form of life.

Meantime I gazed up into her face, watching it change from curiosity to understanding, and from that to genuine hope and satisfaction. And I know that I would have given anything and everything I owned could I but lift from her the burden of sorrow, or whatever it was which gave even her smile such wistful pathos.

But apparently our visitor was not as yet completely satisfied, for she moved over beside Carman, her nimbus well nigh touching him. She started, as if surprised, but her expression of doubt lightened somewhat, as does that of one who recognizes an old friend.

One look she cast at Otilie, and that look bespoke absolute pity for the poor ugly travesty, who was watching her with visible adoration writ large in her strange eyes, and again our visitor nodded, as to a friend well liked.

Once more she nodded, vehemently this time, and moved with the speed of light, standing by Otilie's left side. She stretched out her shapely right arm, laying her hand caressingly on Otilie's shoulder. I saw Otilie shudder with ecstasy at the touch, and then her hand began following the pencil, but with a speed I'm positive the poor creature could not have achieved unaided.

But that pencil was bewitched; it was writing in letters and words of liquid golden light! And its first question showed plainly the interest our visitor took in all three of us:

"How are you named, you man of a younger race, who are of so deep intuition that you can read my lost condition in my features; and who holds so great sympathy and pity that you would alleviate my lot, if you could?

"And who are you, man with the calm gray eyes, you to whom emotions are strangers, being replaced by curiosity instead, ever seeking to probe into the secrets of antiquity and the lost lore of the elder races?

"And who are you, little Sister whom I envy, for you have the most precious gift in all the world—freedom, while my body and mind are held helpless prisoners in a dreary prison, and not even on the bosom of the kindly earth, but far down in the dim gloom of the bed of old ocean?"

And at that point Carman interrupted. "Lady," he asked in all seriousness, and his very tone bespoke his absolute belief in what she had caused to appear on the paper, "lady, you speak of yourself as being a prisoner, yet you have appeared *here!* And if indeed you indited that message through the hand of Otilie, I ask you to explain how you know our language, if you are of such a great antiquity as your appearance implies."

"I am an Atlan," flashed the response on the paper beneath Otilie's hand, "and this is but my projected spirit you do now behold. As to my understanding of your language—bethink you: If I be indeed of so great antiquity as I have claimed, and if I wield sufficient powers to be enabled to appear to you here, then in the course of all the long ages, I have had sufficient time in which to learn it."

Carman nodded, fully satisfied, gave our names, Henri d'Armond; Leonard Carman, and plain Otilie. Then he coolly voiced the same question I was about to ask:

"May we be told—"

"Who I am, and why I thus appear before you? For long I have sought the society of wise men of this day and age who could understand and believe, and perchance, help me to escape an eon-old doom. And it seems that at last I have found my goal—or have I, for I dare not hope too greatly.

"But let me tell you three my tale, which will fully clear up the mystery of the Lost Land—and afterward—who knows? At the least, it may entertain you, and may meet with credence, and perchance I shall feel less lonely thereafter in my prison cell—"

And then, as Carman nodded eagerly, the pencil fairly flew across the pages, and Carman read the words aloud, while Otilie and I hung spellbound on every word as the strangest tale ever told unfolded itself:

I am Tekala. I am that woman who with a single motion of her hand destroyed a continent and its inhabitants! Truly, a terrible tale to tell in such few words; therefore I will amplify.

It was late in the day, and the sun was slowly sinking to his rest in the calm waters of the great western sea. In the streets of Kalkan the Golden, sacred city of the sun-god, the lights were commencing to gleam; and overhead the silver stars were adorning the purple skies with gorgeous splendor.

I stood beside old Ixtlil the high-priest on the flat top of the highest tower of the great sun temple. The unearthly beauty of the scene held us both old *paha* [father; priest] and young priestess in breathless enthrallment for a moment. It was a spell I dreaded to break, yet something within me drove me to voice the question which had vexed me for over a year.

"Tell me, O *paha*," I said softly, "who am I, and who my parents, for I never knew them. All I remember is the temple, and naught else know I, and my sister-priestess Malixi taunts me when, daily, we prepare the flowers for the altar. Tell me, O *paha*, and relieve my mind."

Very gravely the old *paha* surveyed me, and I saw in his keen old eyes a twinkle of tolerance for my youth and natural feminine curiosity, which not even the temple discipline could entirely eradicate.

"Tekala, little Daughter of Heaven," he murmured, laying his gentle hand on my bowed head, "it were better that you know not, for it is an evil story; but it is your right to know. Also, there is another reason why you should not, but of that, later. So—

"You are the first-born of wicked King Granat and his no less evil consort, Queen Ayara! But they wanted a man-child, and being what they are, when you disappointed them, you were placed in a boat on a dark, stormy night, and sent adrift, the tide running strongly out at the time. That was some sixteen years gone.

"A fisher-craft picked you up in the dawn, far out of sight of land. The captain, an adherent of the Old Gods, brought you to me, deeming you more than mortal, so beautiful a babe you were, and your robe so richly embroidered.

"The symbol embroidered on that garb of yours told me your identity. So I went straight to the royal palace carrying you in my own arms, whence not king, queen, or the most brutish guardsman dared remove you lest the wrath of the Sun God punish such sacrilege.

"Full into their sneering royal faces I hurled my denunciation of them and their evil ways, prophesying that in a day to come the babe they'd rejected would repay them, unless they accepted the will of the Lords of Life, and reared you as parents should.

"They laughed in my face, bidding me rear the brat, myself, if I wanted her. So, seeing that through them spoke the voice of Destiny—which is above all gods, even the sun and moon—I bowed to them and left their palace. Two sons have come to them since that time, and young demons they are! And I say that when Granat and Ayara pass to their appointed places—which are *not* in the sun-mansions—those two princes will complete the work begun by their parents, and this race of Atlan will be wiped forever from the face of the earth, so thoroughly that naught remains but a tradition!"

The old *paha* lapsed into silence. I felt his eyes probing me, reading my soul. A strange look came on his beautiful old face and he whispered:

"Our Lord the Sun forfend! Let it not be by *her* hand... not hers... not hers!"

So low his tone I knew the words were not for my hearing...

𝕱rom the temple below us arose confused shoutings, thunderous crashes, and a chorus of ear-piercing screams and shrieks from the quarter where dwelt the priestesses. I nearly swooned! But old Ixtlil was a father indeed in that moment. He grasped my shoulder and shook me back to common sense.

"It has come," he said quietly. "The blow falls sooner than I expected, but 'tis ever thus! Now, Tekala, hasten after me, for this temple is no longer a safe place for you."

Down a narrow winding stair he led, and I followed, until I wondered if we would never cease descending. Finally we came into a great circular room, and across this he led into a small crypt.

"This is no time for false modesty," he said sternly. "Take off all your robes immediately."

Dazedly I obeyed. In the center of the little room was a big, flat, disk of copper let into the floor, and to that Ixtlil motioned me, and I stepped on it. What he did I know not, but from all directions at once came peculiarly tinted light-rays of a purplish hue, beating on my skin like a shower of needles. After a time Ixtlil did something which caused the purple rays to give place to a brilliant flood of light like that of the sun on a clear day.

He pointed to a wide, tall silver mirror against one wall, and I saw myself, and marveled at the magic which had changed the pale gold of my flesh to a brown tint so dark that I looked like any savage maid of the outlands. Even my light brown hair had become blue-black.

Truly the tale of Ixtlil's magic had not stated the half! Men said that he was past-master and sole custodian of all the magic lore and ancient wisdom brought from the stars by the Shining Ones, that he knew the secret of Life. In short, he was believed to be all-wise and all-powerful, but that could not have been true, or—but perhaps it *was* true, and in his mysterious way he worked through my hand, despite his aversion to using me, whom he loved, as an instrument.

He brought a robe fashioned from a beautiful pantherskin, a broad belt of silver bosses and links, a bow and a quiver of arrows, a long-bladed bronze knife, and bade me dress and equip myself. Then he handed me a leathern pouch attached to a beaded baldric so that it hung from my right shoulder to my left hip.

"In this pouch," he stated, "are a full year's supply of tiny food tablets. One will sustain you for an entire day. Also, there is a bottle of jade containing a wine so potent that one drop allays a day's thirst even in the hottest desert. Ten drops on the tongue of a dying man can renew his lease of life for a year, unless his wounds are hopeless. A small box of basanite contains a salve that heals wounds, sores, and bites of insects and reptiles, be they ever so poisonous. This ring"—and he slid an armlet of some dull, white metal lighter than chalk, above my elbow—"will become icy-cold whenever an enemy is nigh, but it will glow, warm and comforting, at the proximity of safety.

"Long ago I foresaw this catastrophe, and made all in readiness against the day of your need. Come now!" He pressed a stud against one wall and a section opened.

"Through that," he commanded. "Follow the passage. It is a long tunnel, and will take all day to traverse. Here is a bundle of torches to light your way. The passage slopes upward, finally, and emerges in the face of a cliff at the edge of the wild lands of Korgan. Wait till the stars proclaim midnight, then retire ten paces inside, sit on the floor, and look out of the opening. A star will apparently hang barely under the arch of the exit. Mark that star well.

"Stay in the tunnel until well after dawn, then survey carefully your surroundings ere you emerge, lest enemies see you, but if all seems clear, strike out across the desert holding to the direction whence the star arose. Keep that as your objective until the hand of Destiny leads, instead. And now, Tekala, princess as well as priestess of Atlantan, go! As for me, I must hasten back to the Great Shrine—"

"Let me return with you," I sobbed. "Send me not from you, O my spiritual father! I can handle bow and knife as well as any young man in Atlantan, thanks to the training we priestesses receive! Surely if danger threatens the Great Shrine of our Lord the Sun, my place is there! Why must *I* be thrust forth into the wild lands of Korgan, the Desert of Demons, while my sisters are privileged to defend the temple? Let me return, I say, and if need be, die—"

"Nay!" His voice was stern, implacable. "That, above all else, you cannot, must not do! In the wild lands, your hands may keep your head, but back in the temple, certain death is your lot! Child, in your veins is the old royal blood of the *Itans*, the ancient kings who founded Atlantan and the Atlan race! Granat and Ayara turned from the pure worship of Sun-God and Moon-Goddess and the simple offerings of fruits and flowers, to the dark mysteries of Mictla, god of Evil and lord of Darkness! And when King and Queen betook themselves to evil ways, courtiers and populace followed the prevailing fashion.

"And now, Mictla's wicked priest, Tizoq, has prevailed upon our rulers to allow him and his depraved followers to stamp out the worship of the ancient gods of our race! The old order is doomed, yet in time the destroyers may go too far, and arouse the wrath of the Eternal Ones, and then—remains Tekala, of the Blood-Royal, Queen of Atlantan and all her colonies! And in her hands will lie the power to bring a recalcitrant people back to the pure gods of the Elder Days, and a new and better era will dawn for our race. But for now—again I say: *Go!*"

I sank to my knees, and thence to the floor, prone at his feet, sobbing bitterly. He raised me, blessing me in solemn, holy words, laying his venerable hands on my head; kissed me on my brow, making the signs and symbols of Sun and Moon on my breast with his forefinger, and—abruptly turned and left! Weeping with despair, I turned and entered the tunnel, going straight away from all the life I'd known and loved.

Five days alone in the wild lands of Korgan!

I think most maids would have gone mad in that time, had they been bred as I, in the peace and seclusion of a temple. But now I know what then I did not comprehend—that when old Ixtlil placed his hands on my head and blessed me, he was transmitting a portion of his own spiritual strength and a generous share of his own magic powers to me—and I sorely needed them!

I'd got my direction from the star, and had carefully calculated so that I might hold the same course by night or day. And the white armlet helped in its mysterious way, for whenever I deviated, be it ever so slightly from the direct course, a chill ran up my arm, changing to a warm glow as soon as I rectified my course.

For the first two days I'd foolishly traveled during the hot, daylight hours, but then realized it was overtaxing my body. Wherefore, I rested all the third day in a little patch of shade cast by a clump of stunted bushes, and thereafter I traveled by night.

Idling there as I rested, my mind went back to the temple, and then I began to realize somewhat of Ixtlil's blessing. Gradually I commenced to see clearly. I saw the Ancient Shrine, and the great symbol of our Lord the Sun lying on the floor, battered, bent, its burnished golden surface defiled with dried blood. The entire place was a wreck. Dead bodies lay in all directions. A priestess I'd known and loved as an elder sister lay naked, slashed and torn. Priests who had died—surely the followers of Tizoq had done their work well in honor of their devil-god.

My soul went sick within me. But I prayed long and earnestly to Sun-god and Moon-goddess for the dead whom I'd known since earliest childhood—that they might dwell in his golden mansions by day, and rest in her silver chambers by night, and presently I felt better. But then a dreadful thought arose in my mind, and would not drown: What of Ixtlil?

The heat haze of the desert grew dark as I looked. Surely it was not yet night? Then I knew that I was gazing into a crypt beneath Mictla's temple. Dim, gigantic figures, half human, half owl, wholly demon, were sculptured on the walls. Their great round eyes, made of some luminous yellow stone, gave off enough light to see the venerable *paha* with heavy bronze fetters about wrists and ankles, and around his waist a heavy chain.

A prisoner! That kindly old man! And then, more clearly, I saw his face. A prisoner? Nay! A servant of the high gods whom not even fetters nor chains could bind. He did but wait whatever was destined, serenely assured that, come what might, at the last he would enter into his reward.

I like, even now, to think that across those drear distances of demon-infested desert he sensed me, knew that I was near him in spirit, for his lips moved, and I am sure that his words were: "Tekala, little sister, you do not forget."

While resting next day a tiny breeze came up, and as I enjoyed its caress—suddenly I heard it! And held my breath in sudden fright, although the armlet gave off no warning chill. It was a strange, wild, sobbing moan rising to a dolorous wail like a lost soul in search of the unattainable. Toward evening the keening died out, but I was shaken by fears and knew not whether to go onward or—

The armlet went cold! I rose to my knees and peered about, but naught could I descry. So I decided it was an intimation I'd best leave that place. Promptly I started, and well for me that I did! Just before darkness fell I glanced back, I knew not why, save that the armlet had not warmed up since its warning chill. I had just topped a rise and stood on the crest of the long sloping ridge of sand, and I could still see the place where I'd spent the long, hot day.

I saw far more than I expected! A dozen figures moved about the spot where I'd lain and slept. Although I could not hear their voices I knew they had correctly interpreted the signs I'd left. And when a bit later they grouped a moment and then started on my trail, I knew my peril. My sole hope lay in the possibility that they could not follow in the night. Which would give me a good ten hours advantage. But I merely deceived myself when I entertained that idea. The ridge whereon I stood ran in a long slant down into a great basin which, in some far-distant era, must have been the bed of some inland sea.

Reaching the floor of the huge bowl I lay flat and stared up at the crest of the ridge standing sharply against the stars. And over the comb of the ridge poured my pursuers. Down there I was invisible to them, but once they reached the floor of the basin, my chances were poor indeed of escaping their keen eyes. I betook myself to precipitate flight, running like a scared cat for at least two hours ere I constrained my racing feet to a slower gait.

Even so, I think they would have overtaken me ere dawn, save that once again that eery ululation came throbbing and wailing through the night. It bore a distinctly forbidding, angry, menacing tone—yet the armlet on my arm grew warm again, which cheered me immensely.

Deciding that the source of the sound—whatever it might be—was friendly to me, and quite otherwise to my pursuers, I hastened toward it as directly as possible. But it was well after midnight when I first saw, looming dimly against the stars, a tall, indistinct bulk, yet oddly suggestive of the human form. But a human form—so enormous? Never was a statue, even of a god, that big, but ere another hour had passed, I knew it surely for a robed and seated image, female in shape.

Was it a goddess of some forgotten race, pre-human perhaps? or was it an effigy of some demon holding suzerainty over this desolate land? Speculation availing me nothing, as usual, I pressed forward as if it were a well-known and welcome goal—a sanctuary against those savages who sought to capture me, for what purpose I could surmise only too well!

Dawn revealed that my pursuers were closer than I liked. To my relief I saw that none carried bows, although each carried a long spear and several throwing-knives. But their faces and their bodies! The apes in the royal gardens of Kalkan the Golden were actual beauties by comparison, both in features and figures; the chief difference being that the savages were hairless as to their bodies and of an ashen-gray hue. They were without exception, hunchbacked, their necks so short they seemed sunken into the wide shoulders; heavy, squat bodies with long powerfully muscled arms, and short, thick legs with great splay feet.

Finally they drew within bowshot, and I felt that I was done for. Yet still the armlet remained warm, unless I looked back, but in that case it instantly changed. Spread out, crescent-wise, the humped men raced forward, running two bow-lengths to my one. Two I slew with a couple of hard-driven shafts from my bow—and then the horns of the crescent passed me and began closing in. But my amulet stayed warm, and the great figure, which I now could see plainly was hewn from one enormous rough boulder, was but a short distance away. And I felt if I could gain its feet, I'd be safe. But I knew, too, that never could I make it. At the apex of desperation, I halted, arrow nocked, bow half raised, fairly aflame with fury. The humped men hesitated, one or another shifting a foot gradually, sneaking a little nearer—it became evident I was to be taken alive.

Then I cursed them. By Sun and Moon, by earth and air and fire. I cursed them by day and by night, sleeping or waking. By famine and pestilence, flood and tempest, by thunder and lightning and wind—

And as that last word fell from my lips a moaning screeching howl ensued! The sands of the desert came alive, rising in dense, dun-hued clouds that swept forward, roaring at terrific velocity. And in the space of a single breath—my pursuers were not! Only a low, crescent-shaped ridge showed where they had stood. Yet not one particle of grit from that hard-driving sandstorm had touched me!

I was all alone, staring dazedly at my work—aye, my work! Over me stole the assurance that old Ixtlil had indeed endowed me with more of his magic power than I was as yet capable of comprehending.

With neither let nor hindrance I walked, albeit somewhat shakily, the remaining distance to the feet of the huge figure of the Old Stone Woman who brooded ever, staring out across the desert, waiting for the world to attain to its supreme wickedness.

That immense figure was, in reality, a vast rock-hewn temple, shapen to the symbolic semblance it bore by the hands of a people so long passed into oblivion that no legend of them remained. The main entrance was between the two feet. The temple proper was wholly under the skirt of the robe and below the waistline. From there up it rose into the air as a high tower, hollow, within which ran a winding stair leading to a chamber occupying the entire head.

It was when I gained that lofty chamber that I learned the source of the mysterious noises; for the winds that blew free up there, even when the desert below lay gasping for lack of a current of moving air—the winds, I repeat, entering through the nostrils and eyeholes and escaping through the parted lips, caused the sounds which had at first terrified me, and after, guided me.

Times there were, as I learned ere all was done, when those winds uttered chants of warning, of prophecy, and once, a soul-shaking shout of triumph. Also, nightly, voices sighed and whispered, and I, listening, learned from them the secrets of the olden days—of magic, of gods and demons, and of the dreams of the ancient dead.

There was no one with whom to associate.

So far as I could ascertain by short trips of exploration in the near vicinity, there never had been a city or village built around the temple. And surely there should have been some traces remaining, for whoever they were who had used that temple, they were giants, judging by the heights of the lifts of the stairs. I was of average height, but while I could with ease tread the steps of the great Sun-temple in Kalkan, there in the Old Stone Woman temple I was obliged to raise my foot as if treading two steps at a time!

One room I found in that temple wherein were thin slabs of stone, graven with writings in small characters, bearing no slightest resemblance to our heavy, ornate Atlantan hieroglyphs; yet here again the spiritual gifts of Ixtlil became manifest, for I found that after poring over a slab the better part of a day I was able to read much of it. And after a few more days of study, I read the writings quite freely, much wisdom thus being revealed!

Nearly a year had come and gone since Ixtlil sent me forth through the underground passage from Kalkan the Golden to the wild lands of Korgan. Again and again I had sought out old Ixtlil, throwing myself into that state wherein the sight of the soul views clearly the events taking place at a distance. And always I found him still the captive of Tizoq, still chained in the crypt below the foul temple of Mictla. With practice I'd grown able to comprehend the purport and meanings of conversations without necessity of catching the spoken words. It appeared that Tizoq ever sought to gain, by coaxing and threats, some mighty secret from Ixtlil, and ever Ixtlil withstood the desire of Tizoq.

Time and again I contacted my mind with the mind of Ixtlil, beseeching him to unleash his fullest powers and compel Tizoq to release him, that he might fly into the desert and come to where I dwelt in safety and seclusions; but ever Ixtlil made the same reply: "Nay, Tekela, little sister; It may not be!"

Nor would he ever vouchsafe any explanation, but I knew I was beholding a servitor of that mightiest power in the universe, that power which Ixtlil had once spoken of as "Destiny," and that the eon-old struggle between Good and Evil was in full swing in that darksome crypt. And I bowed my head and wept, for my heart misgave me. I knew that Tizoq was totally mad with hatred and jealousy, for never had he possessed powers such as Ixtlil wielded. That I could sense as clearly as if I were in the damnable temple of Mictla, in the city of Kalkan the Golden, where stood the flat-topped altar beneath the looming effigy of the hybrid devil-god, half man, half owl.

Now, with a disembodied consciousness, I could see that a vast concourse of people filled the fane of Evil to overflowing, keeping the temple guards busy maintaining an open aisle all the way from the narrow entrance to the foot of the three steps leading to the broad dais whereon stood the altar itself.

It was a most important ceremonial impending, for I saw my parents, King Granat and Queen Ayara, and with them my two bad brothers, Dokar and Quamac. Then came the blare of trumpets and roll of drums announcing a processional. Tizoq, leading, was followed by his devilish acolytes, in the midst of whom walked Ixtlil.

Despite his bonds he walked with head held high, on his finely molded lips a calm smile, in his brilliant eyes a light of pity — not for himself, but for all the world — and surely no great

Emperor ever strode to his throne with truer majesty than walked the aged *paha* toward the altar of his adored Sun-God's demon enemy, Mictla.

Even the acolytes of the God of Evil betrayed by their attitudes—which sentiment seemed general—that they held this gentle old man in actual dread. For all that he was fettered and surrounded by his enemies who hated and feared him, yet the spell of his spirit dominated them, and they knew it, fearing that at any moment he might loose upon them the unguessable, even as they would have done had conditions been reversed.

The drums and horns increased their din as Ixtlil mounted the three steps, but then the clamor ceased. The great effigy of Mictla appeared to assume life and motion. Its wings unfurled, were outstretched as a canopy over the altar, and from the round, cruel, yellow-gleaming eyes a flood of light poured down, illuminating the scene as plainly as daylight. From the ugly mouth beneath the curved beak came thrice repeated the chilling, evil owl notes.

The *paha* was seized violently, and his naked form stretched on his back atop of Mictla's altar, where he lay staring up into the cruel eyes of the demon.

What humiliation had Tizoq in his malicious mind as he approached the recumbent Ixtlil? The owl-priest raised a hand. Again came three owl-notes from the demon-figure. Five acolytes seized the venerable *paha*—one at each wrist and ankle, and one with both hands clutched in his silvery-white hair. Tizoq raised his right arm on high; in his fist shone a knife whose blade was of ragged-edged volcanic glass. Tizoq's arm swooped down—I strove to shut my eyes by pressing both hands over them. And saw just as clearly! For a moment Tizoq bent above his victim, then turned facing the worshippers, crying:

"Thus deals the god Mictla with the high-priest of his archenemy, the Sun-God!"

Tizoq held up to view a dripping human heart!

"Behold, ye people! Bow ye before the power of Mictla! Lo, the heart of the first human sacrifice to the new god of Atlantan!"

He turned and flung the pitiful, quivering, sacred thing straight into the open beak of the devil-god.

I know not the words adequate to make plain to other understandings the awful anguish rending my very soul. Ixtlil, the holy one of Atlantan to die thus! My brain, stunned though it was by that sight of horror, was a volcano of hate and wrath, surcharged with desire for such vengeance as would make the devils in Mictlan cower in terror and seek to hide beneath the white-hot rocks of the great Sulphur Sea!

As moves a corpse animated by a life not its own, I rose from my place and started down the winding stair from my chamber in the head of the Old Stone Woman. On the landing level with the huge swell of her breasts, I stood vaguely wondering why I had halted.

Then a small spot of vivid crimson, like a drop of rich blood a-sparkle in the sunshine caught my eye and held my vacant gaze. Hesitant, as one knowing not what she does, I stretched forth a finger and touched that ensanguined spot—and from above, there pealed a thunderous shout of triumph from the lips of the Old Stone Woman. Dully I wondered why. Then a door, hitherto invisible, swung open, revealing a chamber in the left breast. I entered. Eyes still a-stare, I stood striving to understand. Suspended in the air, level with my face, yet upheld by nothing visible, hung a blood-red heart of enormous size which pulsated and beat like any organism, and yet was formed of a single crimson gem!

Directly beneath the beating heart stood a low stone table on which lay a tablet of polished black onyx, and atop of this a bronze mallet. I could have held back from that table as easily as I could have held back from breathing! And as I bent above the onyx tablet, in letters of living flame which faded as soon as noted, there formed the words:

"Tekala! In the day when your heart becomes harder than mine, lift this mallet, and if you dare, smite! Yet remember—vengeance is of the Gods!"

Vengeance?... Smite!...

The flame within my brain roared like the surges of a volcano's angry, molten sea!

Crash!

The pulsating heart of Atlantan burst into a scintillating shower of glittering red slivers at the impact of the mallet in my hand. And ere the tinkle of tiny falling fragments had ceased—

Roar upon roar of thunder, continuous, flash following upon flash of lightning, until the world was all a-glare with purple-white fire. The Old Stone Woman, ponderous as she was, swayed and lurched like a ship on a stormy sea as earthquake shocks added their destructive forces to the universal cataclysm! And *I*? I lay down on the cupped floor within that harsh stone breast, and slept! Aye, like a wearied babe cradled in its mother's comforting bosom! Nor did a single dream disturb me; and as for the tempest's turmoil, and the earthquakes, their din was but a lullaby wooing my sick spirit to deeper, most restful slumber.

How long that slumber lasted I never knew. Time had ceased when I awoke. Above, the skies were black as never midnight had been, and the very foundations of earth were trembling as each shock came with terrific violence.

My mind, inevitably, went out to Kalkan the Golden. Aye, Mictla's foul temple still stood, or at least, a part of it. The great fane was but a heap of tumbled ruins, yet the effigy of the Owl-Man Devil-God was unharmed. And on the ruined dais about the altar, some standing and some crouched, were assembled Tizoq, Granat, Ayara, Dokar, Quamac, and a few of Mictla's evil acolytes and dancing-women. Drawn up in solid ranks before them, facing outward, were the men of the Purple Cohort, the King's own bodyguard—and they were sorely pressed to defend their charges.

Down the streets converging upon the fane came people fleeing in terror before walls of water inexorably flowing inward. The sea had risen—or had the land subsided? The spears of the guards were dripping gouts of crimson, for the dais was the sole refuge, and many strove to reach it.

Even as I gazed, a levin-bolt sped straight from the black vault of heaven. Full on the round head of Mictla's effigy it smote with a vicious crackle—I sensed it, I say, in the distance! The great idol reeled, swayed, lurched far over, then with a dull roar it precipitated itself ponderously on the group occupying the dais. A cloud of dust arose, soon settled by the driving rain. I saw Tizoq, or, rather, his dead, ugly face, peering, hideously convulsed, from beneath a pile of debris. Then the waters reached the place, and naught remained save tossing, tumbling waves a-play with strange flotsam!

The terrific forces unleashed when I shattered the ancient heart of the Old Stone Woman were destroying an old land as well as an ancient people. The awful quakes were rending chasms wide and deep in the bosom of the solid ground, and long dormant earth-fires streamed upward. And ever the sea overcame the land. Shattering explosions took place as water and fire met. The entire continents of Atlantan became the picture of hell let loose. There was not a city left, and even the villages of savages in the wild lands were swallowed up in the vast cracks, or incinerated by leaping, roaring, whistling flames. Yet the Old Stone Woman still stared into space, waiting for a dying world to reach its end. And ever the inward rushing waters were victorious over earth and fire alike.

Atlantan was no more beneath the sun! The great continent with it millions of men, women and children, its temples and colleges and palaces, its gardens and glorious cities and fertile countrysides, its rivers and mountains and lakes and plains, its mines with eon-old hoarded treasures of precious metals and gorgeous gems, Atlantan rests at the bottom of the mighty ocean from which, ages agone, it arose!

And I, whose hand struck the fatal blow bringing all that to pass — because I usurped the prerogative of that awful power, "Destiny," I am still alive, nor can I ever die while earth endures; for in the hollow of the harsh breast of the Old Stone Woman, enclosed in a new red crystal heart, by Destiny's inexorable decree, I am compelled to take the place of the old shattered heart of Atlantan, there to remain ever young and undying until Atlantan shall again rise from the sea-slime!

* * *

The writing ceased. We three — Carman, Otilie, and I — sat staring at each other, in speechless amazement. Suddenly Otilie sighed softly and slumped to the floor in a dead faint.

"Good Lord!" Carmen ejaculated. "The strain was too prolonged for the poor creature! Help me, Henri, to lift her to the table-top."

But Tekala's "projection" raised a minatory hand. Gliding to where lay the prostrate form, she knelt, placed the palms of her hands on Otilie's temples for a second, and calmly arose, nodding confidently at us.

To our infinite surprise, Otilie awoke none the worse for her experience. Carman attempted to condole with her, but Otilie waved him aside scornfully.

"I'm all right," she stated. "For a minute I was out, no? But the Shining Lady" — as she designated our visitor — "gave me of her strength, and I feel stronger right now that ever in my life! And I would cheerfully go through a greater strain for her any time she needs me!"

Tekala started with surprise, as if she could hardly believe what she'd heard, but then an expression of absolute love for Otilie came upon her face as she signed her to take up her pencil again.

"It seems," Otilie's hand transcribed, "that I have found three friends, and I have searched the world over, inspired by such hope, but fearing that never should I succeed in my search.

"Tell me, you who are named Leonard, what would you do, were you Tekala?"

"Let me understand you more fully," Carman replied gravely. "Are *you* here, or in the heart of the Old Stone Woman?"

"My undying body is in the breast of the Old Stone Woman," Otilie wrote. "But all which is Tekala's self is *here!* Oh, I tell you that in all the long ages that have passed since the great cataclysm, I have had ample time to develop powers more than mortal! I could, with ease, materialize here and now for you, but to what avail? Ere long my will would grow wearied and I should again become but a luminous shadow. But, oh! To be free, in a proper, physical body—"

And right there, Carman interrupted:

"If I were you, I would search the wide world over for a suitable body, one young and fair, take possession thereof, and leave my old body right where it is till doomsday!"

"But my punishment—the will of the gods?" Tekala was visibly shocked.

"I'd not worry about the gods," Carman counseled. "The gods passed when Atlantan sank, nor can the lost gods ever return!"

"But where shall I find a body whose tenant is willing to be supplanted? I would not dispossess a soul in whom the love of life runs strongly. And I cannot, will not take a dead body—there are laws I dare not transgress—"

And at that point Otilie interrupted, somewhat diffidently, but decidedly, and in her melodious voice was a queer note of reverence and pleading.

"O Shining Lady! Can you use such an ugly body as mine? For if you can, I pray you, take it! I have nothing to live for! I am so ugly that little children run from me in the streets, and what man so low as to love poor, deformed Otilie? Perhaps with your powers you can make this twisted form straight and my hideous face fair. If so, tell me what to do, O most Beautiful, and I will gladly obey! But one thing do I ask—let there still be enough left of Otilie to remember how ugly she was, and know how beautiful she has become! Lady—Lady Tekala! Help poor Otilie! Set free her soul, and take her warped body and twist it to your own semblance! It would be the sole mercy I ever knew in all my dreary life, and it is mercy that I ask!"

Had Otilie struck Tekala the effect would have been the same! Tekala reeled and almost fell, but recovered her equilibrium and glided to Otilie. Long and earnestly the two looked at each other—the ugliest woman I have ever seen, and the loveliest woman the world has ever beheld—and what silent message passed between them I dare not surmise. But obviously both were satisfied, for Tekala bent her regal head and kissed Otilie full on her mouth. Carman and I, watching, saw a look of unearthly ecstasy transfigure Otilie's features, and then the unbelievable happened!

Otilie swayed and fell, lying on her back, and Tekala, standing there, turned about facing us, gradually leaning back and little by little merging herself with the other form lying so still on the floor, until the transformation was accomplished and the two had become one! And we two, staring spellbound, incredulous, saw the poor, twisted body of Otilie straighten, the bosom swell and heave, and the grotesque features slowly bloom into loveliness beyond all words!

Tekala arose from her recumbent position and faced us in triumph, and truly if she had been beautiful before, now she was Beauty's self! She held out her exquisite arms to me—*me, Henri d'Armond*—and her voice that still spoke with Otilie's deep, rich, bell-like resonance, uttered the words I'd hoped to hear, but had never believed possible:

"Henri, my beloved, I am yours, take me!"

In an instant my arms were about her, my lips claiming hers in insatiable hunger—my brain swaying, drunken with happiness, experiencing rapture unearthly—

There came a terrific *crash!* I saw a blaze of unbearable brilliance filled with figures not of earth, and in their midst yet dominant, a great Face, calm, majestic, awful in its inexorable justice. And I knew, even in my stunned and bewildered condition, that I looked full into the sublime countenance of Destiny itself, that power which is above all gods, and which I, a mere mortal, had, in my presumption, defied when I aided Tekala.

At the same moment I experienced an irresistible force snatch her from my arms despite the fervor of my embrace. I heard her voice, heart-broken, calling despairingly:

"Henri! Henri! Never again—"

My senses left me and I fell to the floor, unconscious.

How long I lay there I cannot say, but when my senses returned—I could see nothing but a blaze of light. Of Leonard Carman there was no trace, nor of Tekala.

Dimly I heard a voice saying in deep contralto tones:

"Mr d'Armond, are you alive?"

"Who speaks?" I demanded shakily, and heard the welcome reply:

"I, Otilie."

She helped me to my feet. My hand groped until I found hers. I heard her sobbing.

"Are you hurt?" I questioned, stupidly, for I was still dazed.

"Not hurt," she gasped. "But oh, that poor, dear, lovely lady, Tekala! Her gods were not dead, after all, even if Mr. Carman said they were—and they have taken their vengeance upon her—and me! For I am again Otilie, ugly as ever, and you—what have they done to you?"

"I—am blind," I repeated shakily. "Nor do I ever expect to see again! Help me to a chair."

Uttering little words of pity and sympathy, she complied, and as I felt her warm tenderness for me in my misfortune flow through me with the touch of her hand, I said, weakly:

"Otilie, I need you! Will you come and live with me and take care of a poor, blind fool?"

"I—I—am so ugly," she sobbed. "But if you need me—and can endure my presence—yes."

Otilie and I were married the next day. After all, I am rich as compared to her and can make life a little more bearable for her in her unfortunate condition. It is purely an arrangement of convenience, yet she takes excellent care of me, forestalling my slightest wish. She at least is happy. Yesterday I heard her singing as she went about the house.

As for myself—I am blind, as I said before. Ten years now I have dwelt in darkness—tortured by memory, and blessed by memory.

Three months ago I saw dimly a dull red light glowing in my everlasting gloom. Later it came again, growing stronger. At first I thought it was my sight returning, and found out that I was wrong. Ultimately it became a crimson glory like incandescent blood. And I knew it for what it really was!

Within the swelling breast of the Old Stone Woman, deep in the ocean's eternal gloom there beats still the great crimson crystal heart. And imprisoned, undying, facing each other yet unable to move, within the Heart of Atlantan are the two beings I loved, but who, in their arrogance, set at naught the awful fiat of Destiny—ancient priest and ancient priestess, whom Tekala recognized as Ixtlil of old, but yet the Carman I knew who counseled Tekala to her fall, and the priestess Tekala, whom, for so brief a moment I held in my arms, and whose lips I pressed but once ere she was torn from me! And there, undying and unchanging, they wait, wait, wait until Atlantan once more emerges from the depths.

Made in the USA
Middletown, DE
17 September 2018